Lost Daughters

MARY MONROE

Lost Daughters

Kensington Publishing Corp.
www.kensingtonbooks.com

Dedicated to Teresa, Anthony, and Monica

PROLOGUE

Silo, Florida, 1956

ELEVEN-YEAR-OLD VIRGIL MONTGOMERY WAS SO TERRIFIED OF HIS MOTHER that he would do almost anything to keep her happy.

Against his better judgment, Virgil made a pact with Mama Ruby on a sultry night in July that would have a profound effect on him for the rest of his life.

He promised her that he would never tell anyone she had just kidnapped her best friend's newborn baby girl and was going to raise her as her own. Virgil knew even back then that he would experience an enormous amount of guilt and shame and that it would probably destroy him someday, but *nobody* said no to Mama Ruby. . . .

"I'll kill *anybody* who tries to take this baby away from me," Mama Ruby vowed as she gazed at the beautiful baby in her arms that she had named Maureen, after her former beloved madam.

Virgil would never forget how Mama Ruby looked that night in that hideous, shapeless, black flannel duster that he had always hated so much. She sat at her kitchen table feeding the baby a concoction she had made with cornmeal and goat's milk.

Virgil had never seen his mother so nervous. Her hands were shaking, and sweat was streaming down her face like melting wax. No matter how fast he handed her a can of beer every few minutes like she demanded, she scolded him for being too slow. Even when he handed her a fresh can before she finished the previous one, he was still too slow for her. More than two-dozen empty beer cans had already been dumped into the trash barrel on the back porch of their shabby rural house—and that was what Mama Ruby had drunk in one day.

Mama Ruby couldn't keep her false teeth from slipping and sliding in her mouth, so she jiggled them out with her fingers and placed them on top of a pot holder on the table. Every few minutes she glanced toward the door. Each time she heard a movement outside, she held her breath. She had scratched her head and fussed with her hair so many times since she'd come home with the baby in a shoe box that it looked like she had combed it with an eggbeater.

It was a very long night for Virgil. After he got too tired to remain in his mother's company, he put on his long john pajamas and crawled into his tipsy rollaway bed in the tiny bedroom behind the kitchen. Before he could get to sleep, a bat squeezed through a crack in the wall and entered his room. Virgil flung some balled-up socks at the creature until it squeezed back out the crack. He was convinced that the bat's sudden appearance was a bad omen, and that frightened him. He lay there for hours gazing at the ceiling and out the window at the full moon, wondering what kind of mess his mother had gotten them into this time.

Virgil was not surprised when Mama Ruby entered his bedroom a couple hours later and ordered him to get back up. He had just dozed off, so it took him a few moments to realize what was going on. He sat up and rubbed his eyes, staring at Mama Ruby as she hovered over his bed. Her suitcase was on the floor in front of the doorway. The baby was still in her arms, rolled up in a towel like a cocoon. Even though she had already told Virgil that she was keeping Othella Johnson's baby, he had not believed her until now.

"Boy, drag your tail out of that bed and shake a leg. We fixin' to haul ass," Mama Ruby growled with her jaws twitching. She clamped her ill-fitting false teeth more securely onto her gums, hoping they wouldn't fall out of her mouth during the night like they often did. "Grab you a few sugar tits and some tea cakes out the ice box. Then go empty out your bladder and your bowels so we won't have to make too many stops."

Despite an assortment of crimes that Mama Ruby had committed over the years with Virgil as her accomplice, they had avoided jail so far. He didn't count the month that she had spent behind bars for leaving some white kids in her care unattended when she went to go shoot and kill her unfaithful husband, who was also Virgil's father. That had happened before Virgil was even born. But what Mama Ruby was about to do now scared him. He was well aware of the fact that kidnapping was a very serious offense, even if the victim was a black child in a racist, Southern town.

Virgil looked from the suitcase to Mama Ruby's face and opened his mouth to speak. But before he could get a word out, she gave him one of her grim "don't ask me no questions" looks, so he didn't. He scrambled out of bed and got dressed. After he had stuffed only what he could carry into a shopping bag, Mama Ruby made him creep around outside the house to make sure that the coast was clear.

"We ain't got nothin' to worry about. I even checked to make sure that everybody at Othella's house had gone to bed," Virgil reported, chewing on a sugar tit as he tiptoed back into the house.

"What about Othella's hound dog?" Mama Ruby's voice was hoarse. She had just raked a comb through her hair, braided it, and covered it with a plaid scarf. She had taken a birdbath in her kitchen sink, sprayed lemon-scented toilet water behind her ears and on her wrists, and changed into a fresh duster. She had even smeared on some lipstick and slapped rouge across her bloated cheeks. She had plain features, but she was still a very vain woman. Making herself look more attractive was one of her better habits, and it had always paid off. She had been a very popular prostitute back in New Orleans fifteen years ago, and she was still able to draw men in like a Venus flytrap.

"Oh, we ain't got to worry about that mangy creature. I gave him a hambone and tied him to Othella's pecan tree. Even if he was to see us leavin' and start barkin', he can't get loose." Virgil paused, swallowed the last piece of his snack, and gave Mama Ruby a curious look.

"What's wrong with you, boy? Why you lookin' at me like that?" she asked. She was still nervous and had begun to sweat even more.

"Um, I was just wonderin' . . ."

"Wonderin' what?"

"I was just wonderin' . . . uh, can you . . . uh . . . run real fast?" It was a question that Virgil didn't feel safe asking a woman who weighed almost four hundred pounds. There were times when Mama Ruby could barely stand up, let alone "run real fast."

Mama Ruby glared at Virgil and said hotly, "Yeah, I can run real fast if I have to! Why?"

"Well, things might get real serious," Virgil pointed out. "You ain't no spring chicken, you a little on the heavy side, and you kinda clumsy." There was an edge of sarcasm in his voice. He averted his eyes from Mama Ruby's and glanced down at his feet to make sure his shoelaces were tied—in case he had to suddenly run real fast from her.

"Look here. I got news for you, boy. Things is already real serious," Mama Ruby growled, ignoring Virgil's remark about her age and weight like she usually did.

"Mama Ruby, what I want to know is—and I ain't tryin' to be funny—do you think you can run fast enough for us to escape in case Othella's hound dog starts barkin' loud enough to wake her up?"

"Oh," Mama Ruby mouthed, scratching the side of her face with three fingers. "Well, tonight I bet I could outrun Tarzan," she whispered, looking toward the door again. "Make sure you pack my Bible and blow out all the lamps, and let's make tracks. Licketysplit!"

"Yes, ma'am," Virgil whispered back. By now he was almost as nervous as Mama Ruby. Other than a few pennies from her coin purse, a piece of candy, and some peanuts from the local grocery store, he had never stolen anything before in his life. Yet here he was now, involved in a conspiracy to steal another woman's baby!

*   *   *

Mama Ruby died suddenly in the first week of January 1983. Despite her unhealthy eating habits, her love of beer, and her dangerous weight, almost everybody believed that she had died of grief. She couldn't bear the thought of going on after Maureen had moved out on her own a few months earlier.

Two weeks before, the last time Virgil had seen his mother alive, she had reminded him of his promise to keep her crime a secret. "I'm so proud of you, boy. You been a good son, done almost everything I told you to do all your life. I knew you wouldn't blab to nobody about me stealin' Othella's baby," she said with a touch of sadness in her voice.

"No, I never told nobody. I ain't that crazy," Virgil said, and then he added, "My mama didn't raise no fool."

Ruby chuckled. "I sure didn't!" She chuckled again, and then she got serious. The sadness returned to her voice. "I swear to God, I would rather die than ever tell anybody what we done back in the summer of fifty-six."

"What do you mean, what we done? I didn't do nothin'. You was the one that stole Mo'reen and run off with her. If the law ever was to catch up to you, they ain't got nothin' on me. Besides, I was only eleven when it happened!" Virgil snorted, giving his mother a defiant look. He was the only man on the planet who could be so bold with her and live to tell about it.

"Well, you ain't no eleven-year-old boy no more. You pushin' forty now. I couldn't have avoided gettin' caught and gettin' locked up without your help all these years. That's what the law will look at." Mama Ruby paused. She glanced from side to side. Then she shaded her eyes and looked up the dirt road toward the pyramid-shaped hill that faced her house. The palm trees and thick bushes on both sides of the road were good places for busybodies to hide behind. The last thing she needed was for one of those busybodies to sneak up and overhear this conversation and report it to the one person in the world she wanted to keep it from. That person was not the sheriff. It was the "victim" herself: Maureen, who was now twenty-seven years old.

Mama Ruby occupied her front porch glider that Saturday afternoon, two weeks before Christmas. Virgil sat on the banister, facing her. They couldn't share the glider like they used to when he was a small boy and she was still a fairly normal size. Mama Ruby's four-hundred-plus-pound body, the weight that she had maintained for the past twenty years, lay slumped to the side, almost covering the entire glider. The same shabby Bible that she had been reading a few hours before she kidnapped Maureen now lay in her lap, splayed like a filet. A check mark, in red ink, highlighted a proverb that she had made Virgil memorize: He who guards his lips guards his life, but he who speaks rashly will come to ruin—Proverbs 13:3. A half-empty can of beer—her tenth one in the last four hours—was in her hand.

Mama Ruby was a wise woman. She even possessed supernatural abilities if you believed her and some of her associates. She had made a few lame predictions that had eventually come true, and she had laid her alleged healing hands on a few sick people and made them feel better. But even with her special powers, she couldn't predict how her precious Maureen would react if she knew that Mama Ruby had kidnapped her—and it was the one thing that Mama Ruby never wanted to find out. Kidnapping a baby was a secret that she was determined to take with her to the grave. She had told Virgil that on more than one occasion.

"Well, even if you told Mo'reen what you done now, you wouldn't have to worry about her real mama causin' no trouble and takin' Mo'reen away from you," Virgil eased in. "You took care of that when you killed that woman."

"That was self-defense, boy! I had to chastise Othella! She came at me with a blade in her hand—and in my own house at that! Even the cops sided with me!" Mama Ruby shot back with a nod and a grunt. She finished her beer and let out a mild belch. "Why you bringin' up this subject again anyway?"

"You the one that brought it up this time!" Virgil reminded.

"Oh. Well, anyway, we don't need to be talkin' about this incident no more, no how. What's done is done, and ain't nothin' goin' to change it."

Virgil dropped his head and rubbed the back of his neck. When he looked back up at Mama Ruby, he was surprised to see tears in her eyes. She was as rough and tough as a person could be. But she was also so sensitive that she would often burst into tears at the drop of a hat. She set her empty beer can on the floor and fished a large white handkerchief from inside her bra. She immediately began to weep like a baby.

"Now you stop all that bawlin'!" Virgil ordered. "I feel bad enough—and have for years—about you kidnappin' Mo'reen," he fumed.

"I can't help it!" Mama Ruby wailed, blowing her nose into her handkerchief. "I don't know why you won't lay this . . . this . . . situation to rest like I did." Mama Ruby stopped crying and gave Virgil a look that was so frightening it would scare a ghost. "The past is the past and we can't change it. I advise you not to mention this kidnappin' incident to me no more as long as I'm still breathin'. Do you hear me, boy?"

"Yes, ma'am. I . . . I . . . won't never bring this up again as long as you still breathin'," Virgil sputtered.

And he didn't.

CHAPTER 1

Goons, Florida, 1983

NOBODY WAS SURPRISED WHEN MAUREEN AND LORETTA, HER NINE-year-old daughter, returned to Goons, Florida, from San Francisco just two months after they'd left, three days after Mama Ruby's funeral.

Virgil had purchased their tickets to San Francisco, one way like Maureen had requested. She had assured him that she would never return to Florida. He had also given her a credit card and a little over two thousand dollars in cash, but he had also tried to talk her out of leaving.

"Runnin' away ain't goin' to help you get over losin' Mama Ruby," he had told Maureen.

"That ain't the only reason I'm leavin' Florida. This place has caused me too much misery. If I don't get up out of here now, I'm goin' to go stone crazy," Maureen replied in a bone-dry voice, already feeling like she had lost most of her mind.

"This is your home, Mo'reen. Everything you love, and everybody that loves you, is here," Virgil continued. He was worried about his baby sister moving so far away, but he knew that she had made up her mind.

"I know that. I just need to know more about life than Mama Ruby allowed me to learn. The way she kept me hemmed up in that upper room in that spooky old house of hers made me feel like a prisoner when I was growin' up. I need a fresh start, and I can't get that here."

Maureen got a fresh start all right, but not a very pleasant one. California was the land of dreams and hope for a lot of people, but it was more like a nightmare for her. Before she and Loretta could even claim their luggage and get out of the San Francisco airport, an earthquake hit. It lasted for only a few seconds, but it was strong enough to shake some common sense into Maureen's mind. Moving from one end of the country to the other, to a city where she didn't know a single soul, had made no sense at all, and now this. It had been a strong tremor. One that had people scrambling for cover and newspapers and books tumbling from racks.

"Baby, what did we get ourselves into?" Maureen asked, looking at Loretta, who had tumbled to the floor in front of the baggage carousel. "I heard about the earthquakes out here."

"Well, Mama, at least it didn't last as long as the hurricanes we have back in Florida," Loretta pointed out. She wobbled up off the floor, brushed off her jeans, and looked around. "These people up in here just keep walkin' around like zombies, like that earthquake wasn't nothin'. Maybe all of the folks out here do stay doped up on drugs, like everybody told us before we left Florida."

"Us bein' in a damn earthquake before we can even get out the airport ain't a good sign of things to come," Maureen said in a worried voice.

"Why did we come out here in the first place? Especially if you already knew about these earthquakes?" Loretta said.

"Huh? Oh, we just needed to get away, that's why. A change might do us a lot of good," Maureen insisted with a dismissive wave. "We'll get used to this place. We'll be all right."

But they wouldn't be all right.

They checked into a motel that rented rooms by the hour in San Francisco's seedy Tenderloin district. There was a massage parlor with tinted windows on one side of the motel and a porn video store on the other. Each day, Maureen and Loretta ate crackers, cheese, and bologna sandwiches for breakfast, lunch, and dinner. Their "neighbors" included hookers, marauding drug dealers, runaway teenagers sleeping under filthy blankets in doorways, and horny men beating a path to the nearby strip clubs.

Maureen enrolled Loretta in a school that was filled with gang members, some as young as seven. When she picked Loretta up after school one day during the first week, Loretta had a black eye because two mean girls had attacked her and taken her lunch money. That incident, and the fact that Maureen couldn't find a job or an affordable apartment by the end of the second month, was all she could stand. She used the credit card that Virgil had given her to purchase tickets back to Florida. It was more of a relief than an admission of defeat. She belonged in Florida where everything was familiar and, she prayed, where she would eventually find true happiness.

Maureen and Loretta returned to Florida on Loretta's ninth birthday, which was March 15. Loretta was still pouting about having to celebrate her special day with a Happy Meal at McDonald's near the San Francisco airport instead of a birthday cake. "This is the worst birthday I ever had!" she complained.

"I'll make it up to you once we get settled back home. I'm goin' to treat you like a princess from now on, girl!" Maureen promised, ignoring the simmering scowl on Loretta's face.

"You better do that, Mama," Loretta said in a voice that was disturbing coming from a child. "Or I'm goin' to make you real sorry." Loretta laughed and Maureen laughed along with her.

Many years later, Maureen would recall Loretta's ominous threat. . . .

Maureen's legs almost buckled as she ran toward Virgil in the baggage claim area in the Miami airport. He looked even more frazzled than Maureen. He had been worried about her and Loretta since the day they left.

"Let's get the suitcases and get the hell out of here and back home," Maureen told Virgil as she hugged him.

Loretta glanced from Virgil to Maureen. "Home? Back home to Mama Ruby's old house with the upper room where Uncle Virgil lives now?" she asked in an excited voice, picking at the dried snot beneath her nose. "Yippee!"

"No, sugar! I don't want to go anywhere near that place. I don't even want to be in the same house where Mama Ruby lived and died. Not for a while at least," Maureen said quickly, her eyes blinking like an owl as she looked from Virgil to Loretta. Maureen had loved Mama Ruby from the bottom of her heart. Mama Ruby was gone forever, though, at least from the physical angle. Maureen knew that if she wanted a chance at a normal future, she would have to let go of Mama Ruby from the emotional angle too. "Uh, we'll be stayin' with Catty until I find us a place." Maureen looked at Virgil again. "I have to move forward without bein' haunted by anything that'll remind me of Mama Ruby too much. She controlled every move I made. I can't let her control me from beyond the grave. I hope you understand."

Virgil nodded. "I do. Once Mama Ruby got her hooks in you, you either had to sink or swim. If I hadn't run off and joined the army when I did, there is just no tellin' what kind of man she would have turned me into." Virgil rubbed his nose and sniffed. "If I was you, I wouldn't step back into that house no time soon either. Ain't nothin' but bad memories there for you. Mama Ruby gave you a lot of protection and spiritual guidance. She raised you to be strong, too, so you'll do just fine on your own."

Maureen had no idea how far she would get without Mama Ruby's "protection and spiritual guidance." Mama Ruby had controlled Maureen's life from the day she was born, and she knew that Mama Ruby's influence would remain with her for a long time to come. Jesus was Maureen's main source of spiritual guidance now, and she prayed to Him every day of her life, but Mama Ruby's crude words still rang in her ears: *"Listen, girl, ain't nobody in this world, other than Jesus, can make you happy except me. You ain't goin' to do nothin' unless I approve it. Otherwise, you will suffer like a mad dog."* It had been a while since Maureen had heard those chilling words. They continued to haunt her on a regular basis.

Virgil's chest tightened as his hands gripped the steering wheel during the ride back from the airport. He had promised himself that if and when Maureen returned to Florida, he would tell her that Mama Ruby had kidnapped her. She deserved that much from him. He knew that with Mama Ruby out of the picture now, he had a moral obligation to come clean. He decided that it was just as important for Maureen's peace of mind as it was for his.

"Uncle Virgil, did you forget that today is my birthday?" Loretta asked as she bounced up and down in the backseat.

"Oh, that's right! I been so busy lately it had skipped my mind!" he yelled, glancing over his shoulder and giving Loretta a huge smile. "Happy birthday!"

Loretta waited a few moments for Virgil to reveal what he planned to do to honor her birthday. But he didn't mention taking her to Disney World or even to a pizza parlor like he had done last year. That made Loretta angry. What was wrong with her family these days? Didn't they realize how special she was? Well, one day they would. . . .

"I wish Mama Ruby was still alive. She would never let me down," Loretta said with a whiny sniff. "She never let nobody down."

Virgil had more important things on his mind than celebrating Loretta's birthday. But she was right about Mama Ruby. She had never let anybody down. For the first time in his life, Virgil knew that he was going to let Mama Ruby down in the worst way. He *had* to tell Maureen that she was not who she thought she was and that he was not her brother, or even related to her. The guilt was eating him alive. He had to tell her soon. Until then, his conscience would continue to torment him until he could no longer stand it.

Unlike Mama Ruby, he was determined to *not* take the secret to the grave.

CHAPTER 2

Five years later

*V*IRGIL COULDN'T BELIEVE THAT SO MUCH TIME HAD PASSED AND HE *still* had not told Maureen that she was the victim of a bizarre kidnapping. Every time he had thought the time was right to tell her, he found an excuse not to.

Some days and nights the facts of the case were all he could think about. Maureen's biological mother, Othella Mae Johnson, was dead. She had been Mama Ruby's last victim. She had experienced Mama Ruby's wrath when she'd tracked her down and attempted to reclaim Maureen when Maureen was twenty-five. Othella had a lot of relatives back in Louisiana, though. Virgil admitted to himself that it was not fair to Maureen to keep her cut off from that family.

However, he knew how important it had been to Mama Ruby for Maureen not to know the truth about her background. Would he be betraying Mama Ruby if he told Maureen now—especially since she was no longer around to "chastise" him for doing so?

"I don't know what to do about this mess now," Virgil said out loud to himself one evening while driving the two miles home to Goons from his job in Miami. He didn't need to work. Injuries that he had sustained while a prisoner of war in Vietnam had made him eligible to collect disability payments from Uncle Sam for the rest of his life. He worked anyway because it made his life seem more balanced, and he enjoyed being the chauffer for one of Miami's most powerful lawyers. "Besides, Maureen is happy now and I don't want to mess up her mind," he reasoned. "Let me shet my mouth," he snickered, looking around. "Somebody was to see me talkin' to myself they'll swear I done lost my mind." He stopped talking, but he couldn't stop thinking about his sister.

Maureen was happy in many ways. She had returned to her old job as a file clerk at a lobster factory in Miami, and she and Loretta lived in a nice little apartment about a mile away from Virgil. They visited each other several times a week and talked on the telephone almost every day.

Maureen didn't have much of a social life, even though she had resumed her relationships with her hard-partying old friends Catherine "Catty" Flatt and Emmogene "Fast Black" Harris. Every once in a while, Maureen accompanied them to the clubs and the neighborhood parties. She even went on an occasional date.

Unfortunately, romance was still as elusive as it had always been for Maureen. She was thirty-two years old now and had never been married or even involved in a serious relationship. She was lonely, but she didn't complain about it that often. As long as she had her daughter to keep her company, she was fairly happy.

Loretta had always been an attractive child, but by the time she was fourteen, she was so beautiful that people stared at her and complimented her on her looks everywhere she went. It was no wonder. She was five foot ten and had the body of a goddess, slim but curvy in all the right places. She had Maureen's beautiful brown eyes, high cheekbones, full lips, and long thick black hair. She had long legs and fair skin that she had inherited from the father whose true identity she would never know—a father whose true identity nobody else would ever know either, Maureen had decided.

Everybody, including Mama Ruby and Virgil, had believed Maureen's lie when she told them that she'd been seduced by an albino drug addict called Snowball. He had conveniently died of a drug overdose right after Maureen realized she was pregnant. The truth of the matter was Loretta's father was John French, the deceased son of Mama Ruby's Caucasian landlord. As toddlers, Maureen and John had played in the sand together and frolicked naked in the Blue Lake, near Ruby's house. They had ridden together on John's old mule and played marbles and hide-and-go-seek. They had romped in the blackberry patch behind Ruby's house. That was where John had overpowered Maureen one afternoon and raped her when they were seventeen. She didn't see or hear from him again until a few weeks later. She had tracked him down to let him know that she was pregnant and he was the one responsible for her condition.

She had asked John for the five hundred dollars she needed to get an abortion, so he'd attempted to rob a gas station. The attendant shot and killed him for his trouble. When Loretta and her identical twin, Loraine, had come into the world with very light skin, everybody believed Maureen's story about her tryst with the albino.

Mama Ruby had always wanted a baby girl to replace the one she'd given up when she was fifteen. Suddenly she had *three*, and it didn't matter to her that they didn't share her bloodline or that the twins' father was the dead albino. Mama Ruby told several people that if that "all-white devil" had not already died, she would have killed him herself for taking advantage of her baby girl.

Shortly after the twins turned eight, Loraine fell into the Blue Lake and drowned. Mama Ruby was devastated. She whooped and hollered for days. It had taken some powerful tranquilizers from her doctor to calm her down. "I don't know why Satan keeps messin' up my life!" Mama Ruby complained from bed where she remained for three days after Loraine's death. Once she was able to get up, she crawled to the upper room. She made Maureen and Loretta join her in prayer. The three of them got down on their knees and thanked Jesus that they still had each other.

Now that Mama Ruby was gone, Maureen was more attached to Loretta than ever. She knew that if she lost her, too, she couldn't go on. She promised herself that she would do *twice* as much for Loretta to make up for the loss of Loraine. She felt it was her responsibility to make every sacrifice she could to keep Loretta happy.

No matter what Maureen did for Loretta, though, it was never enough. When Maureen gave Loretta twenty dollars for her birthday one year, Loretta was horrified. She glared with contempt at the twenty-dollar bill in her hand and asked, "Is this all I get?" Maureen immediately gave her twenty more dollars. Loretta had more than a dozen Barbie dolls, a TV in her bedroom, and more toys than several of her friends combined. When Maureen treated Loretta to a weekend trip to Disney World to celebrate her tenth birthday, Loretta demanded a trip to Epcot the following weekend to make up for her disastrous ninth birthday during the San Francisco fiasco.

When Maureen bought Loretta her first bicycle, Loretta decided that it was too plain. Loretta sold it to a friend the same day. Then she begged and whined until Maureen purchased her the one she really wanted, even though Maureen had to borrow money to do so.

Maureen purchased her own clothes from discount stores, Goodwill, and the Salvation Army. Everything that Loretta wore had to come from places like the high-end stores on Worth Avenue in Palm Beach where a lot of the A-list celebrities shopped. Once when Maureen didn't have enough money to buy Loretta the designer jeans she wanted, Maureen found the same pair in a consignment shop. Even though the jeans looked brand-new, once Loretta found out they were "secondhand," she exploded. "You have to do better than that, Mama!" The next day Maureen used her rent money to purchase Loretta the jeans she wanted.

Virgil was concerned about the way Maureen was raising her daughter. "If you keep treatin' that girl so special, she'll end up believin' she's better than everybody . . . includin' you," he predicted.

Maureen didn't want to remind Virgil that Mama Ruby had raised him and her the same way and that they had turned out all right. "Lo'retta's so *beautiful* and that means she is special. Let's let her enjoy it," Maureen said instead. "I'm so proud of my beautiful daughter."

"Beauty is a double-edge sword. It cuts both ways. I'm tellin' you, if you let that girl get too stuck on herself, sooner or later that sword's goin' to swing in *your* direction," Virgil warned.

Maureen knew that Virgil meant well, but she laughed at his comments anyway. "Only a man would say somethin' that silly," she scoffed. He had never raised a daughter, so what did he know? Besides, Maureen enjoyed spoiling Loretta. She had to give her the love that she could no longer give to Loretta's deceased twin, so that meant doing double of everything. She would triple everything if she had to, if that was what it took to keep Loretta happy. Besides, she loved seeing the huge smile on Loretta's face when she was happy.

Loretta looked much older than fourteen, so grown men were among her many admirers. She thought that beauty was the ultimate reward. However, she had no use for other beautiful girls. She didn't want to share the spotlight. That was why she surrounded herself with plain-looking, frumpy girlfriends, and they had to be docile enough to suit Loretta's needs. Her best friend since fifth grade was Mona Flack, the ultimate flunky. Mona looked like Olive Oyl—Popeye's long-legged girlfriend—even down to her thumb-like nose, polka-dot eyes, and beaver-tail hairdo.

One of the few things that Mona had going for her was the fact that she was tall. Unfortunately, that didn't do her much good because she had wide hips and such an enormous butt that her body resembled a long pear. She usually wore loose-fitting dresses and skirts to hide this flaw, and she rarely wore jeans or shorts like Loretta. For some reason being close to a girl as beautiful as Loretta made Mona feel attractive. It was an illusion that Loretta milked like a cow. Mona was her own personal servant, her fool, and Mona was glad to be in such an important position.

Maureen was glad that Mona was so loyal to Loretta, but she had no idea just how loyal Mona really was. All Maureen knew was that Mona, the daughter of a nurse and the manager of a black-owned car wash, idolized Loretta. Like Maureen, Mona's goal was to keep Loretta happy. No favor or chore was too inconvenient, difficult, or nasty for Mona to perform when Loretta asked.

Each day, Mona sank lower and lower. She had become such a wuss that she even sacrificed her virginity for Loretta. When an older boy offered to take Loretta to a beach party if she had sex with him, she persuaded Mona to do it for her. Loretta had other plans for her virginity. It was a prize that she was saving for the right man. . . .

CHAPTER 3

LORETTA HAD A FEW QUIRKS THAT SEEMED HARMLESS TO MAUREEN AT the time. One was that Loretta was so impressed with her looks that it was almost scary. She couldn't walk past a mirror without stopping to check her makeup and her hair.

One day Maureen passed by Loretta's bedroom doorway and saw her sitting at her dresser staring at herself in the mirror. Twenty minutes later when Maureen passed by again, Loretta was still sitting in the same spot, still staring at herself in the mirror. Maureen thought that was strange, even for Loretta. She was pleased to know that her child had so much confidence and pride in her looks, but she was worried that Loretta might lose her perspective and think that looks were all it took for a girl to be happy. Maureen knew first-hand that that was not true. Even though people had always told her that she was as beautiful as a film star, Maureen had never felt like one. Especially now that she was in her thirties, working a dead-end job, and still unmarried. That was all the proof she needed to know that looks didn't mean everything. She prayed to Jesus that Loretta would do more with her life than she had done. With the Lord's help, Maureen would make sure that Loretta got everything she desired.

"You look beautiful already," Maureen told Loretta as she watched her apply a fresh coat of lip gloss one morning as she got herself ready for school.

"I know," Loretta replied with a smug look on her face. "I can see what I look like."

"Then don't keep puttin' on more lip gloss or anything else," Maureen advised.

"Mama, you wouldn't understand. *I* have to be the one to decide when I look beautiful *enough*," Loretta replied with a casual shrug. She applied another coat of lip gloss.

Maureen rolled her eyes and shook her head. Loretta continued to work on her face.

Loretta always looked like she'd just stepped off the cover of a fashion magazine. She didn't wear ripped jeans or oversized T-shirts like a lot of the other kids. On this particular day, she wore a white silk blouse with ruffles at the end of the sleeves, a plaid skirt, and white tights with black pumps that she had wiped and waxed so thoroughly she could see her reflection in them. She *never* wore sneakers or flip-flops, not even to the beach. She wore her long black hair with bangs almost touching her eyes, like Cher used to wear hers back in the sixties.

When Loretta joined Maureen in the kitchen a few minutes later, she had changed into a pink silk blouse and black leather skirt with a split up the side. A white silk scarf was around her neck.

"Lo'retta, why did you change clothes? You looked so cute in your plaid skirt."

"I know I did, Mama, but I just remembered that I wore that out-fit last month. It wouldn't be cool if everybody saw me in the same clothes again so soon," Loretta explained. She smoothed down the sides of her skirt and brushed off the sleeves of her blouse.

Even though Maureen showered Loretta with compliments on a regular basis, she always countered them by telling her that looks were not everything. That only made Loretta suck on her teeth, roll her eyes, and shake her head.

"A beautiful girl is special and has to act special. If she behaves like regular girls, that's what she'll be—regular!" Loretta insisted a few days after the lip gloss and plaid skirt episode.

"A lot of beautiful women lead regular lives," Maureen told her.

"Mama, you need to get with the program. The whole point of bein' beautiful is so you don't have to be regular. I bet if Liz Taylor hadn't acted special on account of her beauty when she was my age, she would have ended up bein' just a housewife sittin' on a porch with a cat," Loretta insisted. "Endin' up like that is my worst nightmare," she added with a grimace.

The following week, a man who was one of the sponsors of the annual "Miss Black Teenage Citrus Princess" pageant called up Loretta and invited her to be a contestant. Loretta was already in a good mood that Saturday afternoon. A few hours earlier, she had been among a huge crowd of spectators watching the filming of a *Miami Vice* episode, her favorite TV program after *The Cosby Show*. She had attracted the attention of one of the film crew members. He had made such a fuss over her beauty that her head felt like it had doubled in size.

As far as Loretta was concerned, no other teenage girl could compete with her. When it came to beauty and style, she was as good as it got. She eagerly accepted the invitation to be a contestant. She planned to put together an acceptance speech before the event because she was convinced she was going to win. It was an annual event, but last year when Loretta had expected to be invited to participate, no one had contacted her.

When she took it upon herself to fill out the application to be a participant, attaching to it the most glamorous picture she had ever posed for, those blind idiots ignored her! Loretta decided that the sponsors were a bunch of fools and that the whole event was probably nothing more than a dog-and-pony show anyway. Now that she'd been invited to compete, it was a completely different story.

Ben Porter, the elderly man who lived in the apartment next door to Maureen, was going to be one of the judges. When that information reached Loretta, she immediately began to visit Mr. Ben. She volunteered to perform a variety of chores for him. She was so relentless and determined to impress the old man that she didn't even utilize Mona's services. This was too important, and she had to be the one to get the credit. She ran to the store for Mr. Ben, mopped his kitchen floor, took his trash to the Dumpster, did his laundry, and one day she even baked him a pecan pie.

"Oh, Mama, this is just the kind of showcase I need to show people what a real black princess is all about. I've already memorized what I want to say when they put the crown on my head! Do you think I should sing somethin' or dance for the talent part?" Loretta gushed.

"I'm sure that whatever you do, you'll be the best, baby," Maureen told Loretta, praying that she would do well. Maureen was afraid to even think about how severe Loretta's meltdown would be if she didn't win *first* place.

Loretta was on cloud nine. For the next few days, she pranced around the house singing and dancing like she had already won first place. She was convinced that her beauty contest victory would be a potent tool for her to use when she approached the *Miami Vice* people. The least they could do was use her as an extra until she was old enough to play some fictional big shot's wife or girlfriend, or something. It would make up for the fact that Maureen had told Loretta that she was too young to try out for a part in *Scarface* (her favorite movie)—which had been filmed practically in their own backyard—a few years ago.

Unfortunately, things came crashing down a few days later when Loretta received a list in the mail with the names of the other contestants. She stormed the kitchen, where Maureen was cutting up the chicken they were going to have for dinner.

"Mama! Mama! You won't *believe* this! Just take a look at the names of the girls I'll be competin' against!" Loretta shrieked with a strangled gasp. Words could not describe how horrified she was. "I can't believe my own eyes!" She waved the list in front of Maureen's face, frowning at it like it was a soiled diaper.

Maureen quickly snatched the sheet of paper out of Loretta's hand, squinting her eyes as she scanned it. "Hmmm. I see your best friend Mona Flack is one of the contestants," she said with an incredulous grunt, giving Loretta a puzzled look.

"Can you believe this?" Loretta growled.

"Mona's a nice girl, but . . . I don't mean to sound mean, but I think she's kind of plain to be in a *beauty* contest. What's goin' on, Lo'retta? Is this supposed to be a joke?"

"No!" Loretta roared. "This ain't no joke!"

Maureen's eyes got big as she stood there with her mouth hanging open. She glared at the list of names as if she couldn't believe what she was seeing with her own eyes either. "Do you mean to tell me that this is a *real* beauty contest?"

Loretta's face looked hot, but her voice was like ice. "*Beauty* contest? This is goin' to be more like a 'who's who at the zoo.' Just look at the rest of these other names!" Loretta was so upset her finger was shaking as she pointed from one name to another. "There's enough *apes* on this list to make a Tarzan movie! And the name of every *dog* except Lassie is on this list!"

Maureen scratched her chin. "Maybe they don't want to focus too much on looks," she threw in.

Loretta's face was so hot by now she had to fan herself. "What's wrong with you, Mama? Since when do people have pageants that don't focus on looks?" She paused and stomped her foot on the floor so hard, some glasses on the counter rattled. "I can't believe those people asked *me* to be in this contest. What kind of funky mess are these people tryin' to pull?" Loretta hollered, looking at Maureen like she was the one behind the funky mess.

Ten minutes after receiving the list, Loretta called one of the sponsors and withdrew from the contest. She told him that she had a family event on the same day as the pageant that she had overlooked. When the sponsor told her that he would definitely want her to compete in the pageant next year, she promptly decided that she would have another "family event" to attend on that day too. She would come up with a lie each year until she got too old to compete, or until they stopped asking her.

When Mona won first place, Loretta was stunned, horrified, angry, and depressed. "That's the last time I get involved with one of these chitlin-circuit events," she vowed.

"What do you mean by 'chitlin circuit'?" Maureen asked, giving her daughter a puzzled look.

"Because the sponsors were black, all the girls were black, and only the black newspapers and black radio stations covered the pageant. Just like in the olden days when black entertainers got caught up in everything that was for black folks only. I should have known better. I am not goin' to settle for no chitlin-circuit lifestyle like you did."

Maureen's jaw dropped and she flinched as if Loretta had slapped her face. "Huh? What—For your information, *Miss Ann*, I have a good life! If it's what you call chitlin circuit, that's fine with me," Maureen retorted in a tight voice. She was tempted to remind Loretta how she always gobbled up at least two bowls of chitlins every time Maureen cooked some, but she didn't. She decided that there was already enough tension in her residence.

Maureen didn't like to think about what Virgil had told her about how Loretta might turn out because of the way she was being raised and because of the high opinion she had of herself. However, Maureen couldn't stop herself from thinking about Virgil's comments. Especially after the way Loretta had reacted when Mona won the contest. Maureen finally admitted to herself that Loretta had begun to believe that she was *too* special and even better than other people. Now she understood what Virgil had meant about beauty being a double-edged sword. Because the sword had begun to swing in Maureen's direction, and it was not a pleasant feeling. It wouldn't hurt to nip this problem in the bud while she still could—not too aggressively, though, Maureen told herself. Just aggressive enough to keep Loretta's attitude on a level she could tolerate.

"It would do you a lot of good to get down off that high horse you keep ridin'. You ain't no better than nobody else. Even though you *are* the prettiest girl around here," Maureen allowed, using a tone of voice that she didn't like to use. "It wouldn't hurt for you to be a little more humble."

"Humble? Do you think Diana Ross got to be where she is by bein' humble?"

"You ain't Diana Ross. Bein' humble is a virtue that can be just as beneficial as beauty." Maureen cleared her throat. She was angry with herself for letting things get to this point. "You can be beautiful and humble at the same time. That's how people succeed. Even Diana Ross."

"I'm sorry, Mama," Loretta fumbled. As weak as her apology was, it still made Maureen feel better. "I want people to see that I'm just as humble as I am beautiful." She wrapped her arms around Maureen and hugged her so hard that Maureen had to push her away so she could catch her breath.

"That's better," she told Loretta. It took only a few minutes for her to forget just how sharp and painful Loretta's chitlin-circuit comment in reference to her had felt.

CHAPTER 4

MONA CAME TO VISIT THE DAY AFTER THE PAGEANT TO SHOW OFF THE crown she'd won and to invite Loretta to spend that Sunday afternoon at the mall with her to help her spend the two-hundred-dollar first prize.

Even in makeup, a hairpiece, and a cute blue denim dress, Mona was still an absolute plain-Jane. Loretta gave her best friend a hug and congratulated her, and eagerly accepted her invitation to go shopping. That made Maureen feel better, but Loretta was still angry.

Mona treated Loretta to a steak and lobster lunch and bought her the latest Prince CD, but even those generous gestures didn't make Loretta feel much better. She couldn't stand the thought of another female, no matter *who* that other female was, getting what she wanted. When Loretta returned from the mall with a scowl on her face and went straight to her room to sulk in private, Maureen assumed she was still upset.

Maureen waited a few minutes and then she went to Loretta's room and cracked open the door. Loretta was lying on her bed with her face buried in her pillow. Maureen couldn't stand to see her baby hurting, so she racked her brain for something to say that might help ease her pain. "This is probably the only time any of those girls will ever be in a pageant. Someday you'll be so rich and famous everybody will be fightin' over you. You'll be on top of the world, but those other girls will just be housewives sittin' on a porch with a cat," Maureen offered. "Mona will never win another beauty contest, so she deserved to win this one. At least she was nice enough to let you help her enjoy her prize money. Don't forget, you thought that this pageant was just a creep-show anyway."

A few moments passed before Loretta sat up and faced Maureen. She had been crying. She sniffed and wiped a trail of tears off her face with the tail of her pillowcase. "You really think I'll be rich and famous someday, Mama?" Her voice sounded like it was coming from beyond the grave.

"I know so!" Maureen said firmly. "You'll be all over the place. Even on TV with Johnny Carson and Phil Donahue."

Despite the fact that Loretta was extremely self-centered, she was still a good daughter as far as Maureen was concerned. Therefore, she deserved only the best, and Maureen planned to do everything in her power to help Loretta reach her goals. Since Loretta might be the only child Maureen ever had, she couldn't bear to lose her or see her unhappy. Because of the loss of Loraine, Loretta had become two children rolled into one. How could Maureen *not* do twice as much to please her?

A few weeks after the beauty competition, Loretta told Maureen that she wanted to be a model. After that beauty contest fiasco, Loretta needed to find a way to restore her self-esteem.

"The girls in the big-time magazines make more money in a day than a lot of people make in a month," Loretta told Maureen, waving the latest edition of *Seventeen* magazine in Maureen's face.

"You'd have to go to New York to work for the big time magazines," Maureen pointed out.

"I can get started down here," Loretta argued, a pout already forming on her lips.

Maureen shook her head. "Modelin' would take up too much of your time right now. I don't want your grades to suffer. School is goin' to be out in a few months and you need to study real hard now."

"If I wait until school is out, I'll have to compete with a thousand other girls for work. Mama, let me try it now for just a little while. If my grades slip, I'll give it up. Just think of all the extra money we'll have comin' into the house. You won't have to be dodgin' all those bill collectors you've been dodgin' all these years."

Maureen gasped. "Well, the only reason I have to dodge bill collectors in the first place is because I buy you everything you ask for," she reminded her, offering a smile so Loretta wouldn't get too upset. "I'll think about it. You have some real expensive tastes, so I guess it wouldn't hurt if you did start makin' your own money." Then Maureen gave Loretta a weary-eyed look. It was the look of surrender that Loretta had come to recognize as another one of her mother's numerous weaknesses. Loretta decided that Maureen had already given her consent to let her pursue a modeling career.

Loretta ran up to Maureen and wrapped her arms around her waist. "Sometimes you can be the best mama in the world!"

"Not so fast now. I said I'll think about it," Maureen sighed, knowing that she was already going to give in to Loretta's latest demand.

The next day Loretta ran up to Maureen again. This time she didn't just hug her; she grabbed Maureen's hand and covered it with hungry little kisses. "You goin' to let me be a model or what?"

"I told you I would think about it," Maureen responded with a weary sigh.

Each day for the next week, Loretta gently badgered Maureen until she gave in.

"All right, Lo'retta. You can try it out for a little while, but only on weekends and after school as long as it's not too late in the evenin' and only on the days that you don't have a lot of homework. If your grades slip, you have to give it up."

The following Saturday, Maureen began to drive Loretta around Miami in her three-year-old Taurus from one photographer to another, hoping to find one who would put together the kind of photo portfolio Loretta deserved. Loretta was hard to please, though. She decided that one photographer was too old. Even though he seemed like a nice man and he was very professional, he kept calling her "LuAnne," which meant his memory was on the blink. A geezer like him would probably cancel appointments due to one age-related ailment after another, Loretta predicted. Another one was too fat and slovenly. Loretta didn't think that it would be good for her image to be associated with a slob, and there was not a chance in hell that she was going to work with the one female photographer they had encountered. Had Loretta known that L. B. Spencer was a woman, she never would have made an appointment with her in the first place. A woman! A woman with so many tattoos on both arms they looked like sleeves!

"Mama, did you notice how long and hard that lady photographer stared me up and down? She's a straight-up dyke," Loretta complained with a frightened look on her face as soon as she and Maureen made it back to their car.

"She didn't look at you any longer and harder than the other photographers did," Maureen countered. "If you feel like that about a woman in this business, there is no tellin' what a male photographer might try to do."

"That's why I need to be careful which one I decide to work with. Some of these photographers are up to no good from the get-go. They think models are stupid, so they take advantage of as many of them as they can. I read about a dumb blonde in Hollywood who was so stupid, a couple of photographers passed her back and forth until she got pregnant."

"I bet that blonde won't let somethin' like that happen to her again," Maureen commented.

"She sure won't because she's dead. One of those photographers strangled her when she tried to blackmail him."

Maureen looked at Loretta and shook her head. "That's a horrible story! Maybe we need to think this modelin' thing through some more. I didn't know they had photographers runnin' around loose, takin' advantage of young girls and then killin' them."

"Mama, you know me. You know that when somebody gets out of line with me, I tell you about it right away. Remember that college boy who squeezed my butt? And what about that church deacon who shook his pecker at me and Helen Barton? Didn't I tell on them right away?" Loretta yipped.

"Let's stay on the subject of photographers, okay?" Maureen suggested.

"Okay, Mama."

"Maybe you need to think about lookin' at another career," Maureen sighed. "As picky as you seem to be, by the time we find a photographer that you like enough to want to work with, you'll be too old to be a model."

"Mama, don't be so countrified. Don't say stuff like that! We will find the right photographer!" Loretta protested. "Somethin' tells me that the next one we talk to will be the one."

Loretta was right for once. Melvin Ross, the very next photographer they met with, was everything that Loretta wanted in a photographer.

And everything she wanted in a man . . .

CHAPTER 5

*I*T WAS LOVE AT FIRST SIGHT.

Loretta knew from the first time she laid eyes on Melvin "Mel" Ross the Saturday before Lincoln's birthday in February that she had to have him, body and soul. In the first few moments of their meeting, her imagination ran wild and the lusty grin on her face couldn't be removed with acid.

Mel was the man she had been saving herself for. Just based on his looks, he was everything she wanted in a lover. He was the same shade of pecan brown as Maureen, and he had the brightest brown eyes she'd ever seen on a man. Loretta couldn't determine his age. There were no wrinkles on his face, but there were a few faint lines around his eyes and the corners of his mouth. His thick, curly hair was jet black (probably dyed but she didn't care!). His face had that slightly "hard" look that comes with age, so Loretta estimated that he was in his mid- or late thirties. She didn't particularly care for hair on a man's face, but Mel's mustache was so neat and sexy that in his case it didn't matter. He could have been as hairy as an ape for all Loretta cared.

Loretta's mind went into orbit. Thoughts were zooming through her head like a jet. She liked the fact that Mel was tall, at least six foot two. She wouldn't have to lean down to kiss him like she did with most of the boys she'd been with (that was the only thing she hated about being five foot ten). He had long legs and long thick fingers, which, according to Mona Flack, usually meant a long thick piece of meat between his legs. He wore a thin T-shirt and skintight jeans so Loretta could see all of his important muscles. His thighs looked like they were trying to bust out of his jeans. She even glanced at his crotch, impressed to see such a large bulge. She could tell that this man was screaming for a blow job!

Mel was *the* man, and she was going to be *his* woman. So what if she was only fourteen? She was not as innocent as her mother thought she was. She had been fooling around with boys since she was thirteen and had participated in a variety of sexual activities. Technically she was still a virgin. She had picked up a lot of useful information just by eavesdropping on the cafeteria and locker-room conversations of the fast girls in her school. One thing she learned was that there were alternative ways to have a good time without getting pregnant or catching some nasty disease. She was amazed at how much impact a good blow job had on the average boy. Mel was probably no different. In fact, a man his age would probably appreciate a good blow job more than the boys her age, she told herself.

There was just one thing wrong with Mel. Apparently he didn't know a good thing when he saw it. Incredibly, he was paying more attention to Maureen than he was to her! Was he as blind as those beauty pageant fools? Getting her hands on this fine specimen of a man was going to be a real challenge.

When Loretta and Maureen had entered Mel's small apartment, which was also his studio next door to a private mailbox service, he had assumed they were sisters. Maureen had called him up a few days earlier and set up an appointment. She was surprised to see that he was black. On the telephone he had sounded more like some stuffy white dude from a Midwestern state.

Within ten minutes after meeting Mel, Maureen and Loretta knew the short version of his life story. He was originally from Chicago. After he had gotten tired of the brutal winters and his bossy mother and two older sisters (he didn't mention his pregnant ex . . .), he decided to relocate as soon as he could scrape up enough money. He moved to Tampa when he was in his senior year of high school to live with a widowed, childless elderly uncle. Mel had been married for a brief period of time, but he was divorced now and had no children.

That was all he wanted to reveal.

"Uh, when you called me up, I guess I misunderstood you," Mel told Maureen, giving her an apologetic look.

Maureen took a deep breath and gave Mel a stern look. "What do you mean by that?"

"You gave me the impression that your daughter was eighteen," he answered.

"Oh. Well, I told you that she was still in her teens, but I don't remember tellin' you she was eighteen." Maureen paused and then said quickly, "She looks eighteen, sure enough. See, she takes after the women in her daddy's family."

"Hmmm. How does the rest of your family feel about your daughter pursuing a modeling career?" Mel asked, looking at Loretta.

Before Maureen could respond, Loretta piped in, "It's my life and I can do whatever I want to do." She glanced at Maureen and when she saw that Maureen was not looking at her, she gave Mel a suggestive wink.

CHAPTER 6

LORETTA'S WORDS HAD STARTLED MEL, BUT HE REMAINED COMPOSED. Her wink had aroused him in more ways than one. Was she coming on to him? Or was she just aggressive and interested only in working with him? Either way, he liked feisty females. Especially ones who were easy on the eyes like Loretta and her mother. He looked at Maureen again.

"Your daughter seems very mature," Mel remarked. From the corner of his eye, he saw Loretta's eyes roll.

"She is. She's always been, uh, kind of grown," Maureen said with a giggle. "You know how it is with us black folks. When I was her age, people used to tell me all the time that I was too 'grown' for my age."

"How does the rest of your family feel about Loretta getting into modeling?" Mel asked again.

Maureen cleared her throat. "Her daddy's deceased, and I don't have any other kids," she answered. "Look, my daughter is a real good girl, and I want her to learn early what life is all about. She's got everything it takes to model—just look at her!" Maureen placed her hand on Loretta's shoulder and slowly turned her around so Mel could get a look at her from the front and the back. He was glad to do that too. This young girl looked good enough to eat, and he would certainly like to taste her. "You can't tell me that she's not as pretty as that Christie Brinkley or that Iman that everybody is makin' such a fuss over!"

"Your daughter is definitely model material," Mel agreed with a nod, wondering what it would feel like to play with a fresh pair of fourteen-year-old titties. Her appearance from behind was just as impressive as her appearance in the front. Maybe even better. She had a butt that wouldn't quit. Mel could see himself riding her doggie style, spanking her perky young ass with each thrust.

"I hope you won't let her age stop you from workin' with her. I read somewhere that some of the top models got started around thirteen or fourteen. That girl from England that called herself Twiggy back in the sixties, I read in the *Enquirer* that she reached the top of her game when she was just seventeen."

"That's true, but the teenage models on that level are with big agencies, and a lot of them attended modeling school. In many cases, they already know the ropes before they even approach a photographer," Mel said, looking directly into Loretta's eyes. He noticed the pout on her face. "I'm real sorry," he added, patting her on the shoulder and hoping she wouldn't cry like the last young girl had done when he turned her down.

"We don't have money for modelin' school," Maureen stated with a pout on her face just as big as the one on Loretta's. She looked like she was about to cry too. Mel could tell that this woman was devoted to her daughter. She was probably willing to do whatever it took to please her. "Can't you make an exception and give us a chance?" Maureen asked with a pleading look on her face.

Mel scratched his chin and gave her a thoughtful look. The fact that Maureen didn't have a husband or a few husky teenage sons who might come after him if he got out of line with Loretta made him reconsider. "Do you work?" he asked Maureen, hoping she wasn't another welfare recipient expecting credit. "I only accept cash or credit card payments."

"I have a job," Maureen said quickly. "I've been workin' since *I* was a teenager."

"Right now she's just a file clerk at that lobster factory near the docks," Loretta offered.

Just a file clerk in a lobster factory. Panhandlers probably made more money than Maureen did, Mel thought. It was a damn shame for such a pretty woman to be wasting her good looks on a lobster factory. Mel suddenly felt sorry for Maureen and her daughter, but he didn't do charity work. He had to make that clear.

"For the deluxe order, which is what I would recommend for your daughter, I would need a twenty percent deposit, cash, check, or credit card. Then the balance would have to be paid in full before I release the photos. No exceptions," Mel asserted.

"How much would that cost and what all would we get?" Maureen wanted to know.

"Oh, we'd negotiate a price and quantity based on what you can afford. In addition to glossy eight-by-tens, head and full body shots, the package includes a waterproof leather case, as many wallet-size copies as you'd like, and a thirty percent discount if you use my services again." Mel gave Maureen a serious look. "A lot of my long-time clients let me choose my own models when I do ads or local TV and department store catalog work. I can tell you right now that I would use Loretta on a regular basis." From the look of delight on Maureen's face, Mel could tell that he had her hooked. For a moment he thought she was going to kiss his ring.

"Hmmm. I have part of the money now, and I am sure I can borrow the rest," Maureen said, sounding hopeful. "As long as it's somethin' that I can afford."

"Like I said, we can negotiate a price based on what you can afford. I'm sure that we can work something out that you'd feel comfortable with."

Maureen nodded and slid her tongue across her bottom lip, which was so dry she couldn't wait to be on her way so she could stop somewhere and get a Slurpee. "Uh-huh. So, uh, can you take my daughter's pictures today?"

Mel shook his head. "I'm sorry. I have a very busy schedule for the next few days. In the meantime, maybe you should give this a lot more consideration before we make a commitment," he suggested. "I don't want to waste your time, and I can't afford to let you waste mine." He knew that the more "professionalism" he displayed, the better. He also knew that it was not too smart for him to seem too eager. "Uh, I am very demanding and I don't hesitate to drop a model if I don't like the way things are going."

"Mr. Mel, I won't disappoint you! I want to work with *you!*" Loretta hollered, shifting her weight from one foot to the other. "I mean, I looked at the pictures in your front window and they look real good."

Maureen jabbed Loretta's side with her elbow. "Maybe you ain't photogenic enough for Mr. Ross." Maureen sniffed. "We can go back to that guy out at the mall. That *white* guy . . ."

"Your daughter is very photogenic, Mrs. Montgomery, but this is a serious business. I work hard and I expect the models I work with to work hard. See, I don't just photograph a lot of them. I do a little managing too," Mel volunteered, knowing that if he got the chance, he would manage more than Loretta's career. His breath caught in his throat. He looked at Loretta. She winked again, and this time she slid her tongue across her juicy bottom lip. Oh yes. She was ripe and his hands were itching to pluck her. What was even better was the bait-and-hook method. It was the best way to catch a big fish.

"Let me think about it for a few days," Mel compromised, handing Maureen his business card. "I still have your telephone number, so I might call you in the next week or so. Thank you for coming by." He held his breath, hoping that he didn't sound too discouraging, but that was exactly how he sounded to Loretta. Especially when he added, "Now I hope that you ladies will enjoy the rest of your day."

Loretta was absolutely horrified. She decided to do what she had to do: beg. "Oh, please, Mr. Mel. Pretty please with sugar on it. Give me a chance. Do my portfolio and help me get some modelin' jobs! You won't regret it!"

Mel laughed and that only made Loretta angry.

"So, you don't want to work with me?" Loretta barked, giving Mel a harsh look. "What's the problem? You don't like my looks?"

"You're a very beautiful girl, Loretta," Mel replied with a toothy grin. "You are going to do well." Playing cat and mouse was one of his favorite games when it came to women. Give them just enough hope to keep them interested. Snatch it back and do it all over again until they were easy to manipulate.

"Then will you tell us what the problem is?" Loretta demanded. "You can't make up your mind right now?"

"I told you that I'd think about it. Whether or not I decide to work with you, I will call you in a few days to let you know."

"If we have to pay for you to do her portfolio anyway, what's the big deal? That's all we really need from you. We didn't come here lookin' for a manager to get my daughter some work. You don't need to do that if you don't want to. We can do that on our own," Maureen said firmly. "We just need somethin' to show the people with the modelin' jobs. I *know* my daughter can be a good model."

"Uh, yes. If that's all you want, I can do a portfolio only," Mel admitted. He could tell by the way Maureen blinked and smiled that she was still dangling on the hook. "I'll call you. One way or the other, I'll call you," he said again. It had been a while since Mel had encountered a level of desperation this high. Now he wasn't so sure Loretta would be worth the aggravation that it might cause him down the road. He moved toward the door and opened it. "You ladies have a blessed day," he said.

Maureen wanted to slap him. Who did this uppity punk think he was? She dropped Mel's business card into a receptacle on the sidewalk on the way back to her car. Had she known it was going to be this hard just to get a qualified photographer to help Loretta put together a decent portfolio, she would not have agreed to do it. However, from the look of disappointment on Loretta's face, Maureen knew that if she backed out now, she would never hear the end of it.

"None of those other photographers said anything about you goin' to modelin' school, and they didn't care about you bein' just fourteen. They were all anxious to take some pictures of you *and* hook you up with some of the local businesses," Maureen told Loretta as soon as they got into her car and had eased out into traffic.

"I don't want to work with any of those other people!" Loretta snapped. "Mr. Ross is the right photographer for me. I just know he is, Mama!"

"Lo'retta, you don't even know that man. What makes you think he's the right one?"

"For one thing, he's a brother and you and every other black person I know is always yip-yappin' about how we black folks need to support more black businesses. I don't think a white photographer would work as hard to get work for me as a black one would."

"I'll call this Mel man up again next week," Maureen said with a heavy sigh. "But if he gives me the runaround again, I'm through with him. If you don't want to work with one of the other photographers that already said they would like to work with you, you can forget it. Is that clear, Lo'retta?"

"Yes, ma'am."

CHAPTER 7

*T*HAT MONDAY MORNING AFTER MAUREEN LEFT FOR WORK, LORETTA leaped out of bed, got dressed, applied her makeup, and fixed her hair the way she did every morning before she went to school. She wasn't going to school today, though. She was going to visit her future lover. She didn't give a damn about the lack of interest that Mel had shown in her. She *knew* he was the one for her and she was determined to prove that to him.

Loretta hated riding on buses. The one she was on now was full of frumpy women, most of them in maid attire, and filthy-looking men. It seemed that no matter what bus she rode, it had a smell that reminded her of the grease Maureen used to deep-fry catfish and chicken wings. Loretta howled when she stepped on a soiled Pamper on her way to a seat in the back next to a middle-aged Cuban man whose face was covered in sores. She couldn't wait until she got her own car so she wouldn't have to stoop this low. Well, at least she was starting at the top as far as men were concerned.

Mel was surprised but pleased to see Loretta at his door. "What the—why little Loretta Montgomery! What in the world are you doing here? Is today a school holiday?"

"It is for me," she cooed. She had splattered so much lip gloss on her lips it looked like she had been drooling for days.

"Well, this is a pleasant surprise!" Mel exclaimed, looking over her shoulder, expecting to see Maureen. He was glad he didn't. "Uh, is your mother with you? Is she parking the car?"

"My mama's at work. Filin' lobster orders," Loretta replied with a smirk and a wink. "She's goin' to be there until late this evenin'."

"Um, does she know you're here?"

"Uh-uh," Loretta responded, shaking her head. "What she don't know won't hurt her. . . ."

Mel didn't invite Loretta in. She didn't give him time. She gently pushed him to the side and sauntered in, turning so she could keep her eyes on his face.

"Look, this is the deal. I want you to know that I'll do whatever it takes to jump-start my career," she announced as soon as she got inside. "And I do mean *whatever* it takes. . . ." Her last sentence gave Mel an instant hard-on.

"Well . . . ," he began, scratching the side of his face, hoping she wouldn't stay long so he could go stretch out on his bed and masturbate. He shrugged and closed the door. Then he folded his arms and cleared his throat a couple of times. Loretta assumed he was doing all of that because he was nervous. The truth was, he was so aroused that if this juicy young thing didn't leave in time, he was not going to be responsible for his actions.

"Why, look at you! You are hella nervous! Now I know a big strappin' grown man like you ain't scared of a dainty little girl like me," Loretta said with her head tilted to the side.

"I didn't expect you, that's all." Mel had met some bold young things before, but Loretta took the cake. "You didn't make an appointment with me."

"Do you want me to leave and come back when I have an appointment?" she teased.

"No, you don't have to leave," he managed. He put his hands in his pockets.

Loretta glanced with disgust at some of the pictures of the other models on his walls. Then she looked at Mel with contempt and shook her head. "I think it's time for you to have a model who looks like me. One with some color," she sneered, almost spitting out the last word.

"I . . . I told you I'd think about working with you," Mel stammered, his hands up in the air. Despite Loretta's bold proposition, Mel knew that he couldn't commit to anything without Maureen's knowledge and approval.

"What do you need to think about? I know you want me. That's cool because I want you too. You wanted me the minute I walked up in here the other day. I could see that even with my eyes closed."

"Are we on the same page? Are we talking about a working relationship, or do you have something else in mind?"

Loretta was glad she had on one of her sexiest ensembles—a pair of her tightest and shortest white shorts and a white V-neck T-shirt. She didn't need a bra. Her breasts were so firm and high she would be a damn fool not to show them off. Mel gulped when he noticed how erect her nipples were. She saw him but pretended not to.

"Don't play dumb with me," Loretta chortled. "You know damn well *why* I came back here." She opened her mouth and rapidly stuck her tongue in and out several times, and then she slid it across her bottom lip. She smacked her lips so loudly it sounded like she had snapped her fingers. "Any more questions?" she asked with a straight face.

Mel laughed and clapped his hands. "You seem like a real smart little girl, sweetheart, but that's just it. You are just a little girl." He was doing all he could to "discourage" Loretta, but that was part of his scheme. He wanted her to think that she was the aggressor. That meant less work for him. That maneuver had worked with a lot of other young girls over the years, but the bottom line was, he wanted this one as much as she wanted him, maybe even more. Her mother seemed reasonably naïve, so he could work around her. He had had enough experience, so he knew that *if* he played his cards right, he would never have to worry about Maureen causing trouble if he fucked her daughter. He would be taking a risk, but it was a risk that he could not resist. He was a dog and he knew it. What else could he do? Especially when girls as luscious as Loretta threw themselves at him like they were dog meat. "I am flattered—What are you doing?" he hollered.

"I want to see if you still think I'm just a little girl after I finish nibbling on your *third leg*, the one in the middle of your thighs," Loretta purred as she slid the zipper down on her shorts and began to wiggle out of them. Mel was not surprised to see that she didn't have on any panties. However, he was surprised to see that she had shaved her crotch.

Before Mel could stop Loretta, she stepped out of her shorts and kicked them all the way across the room. They landed on a goose-necked lamp on a table where he had been looking over some prints when she knocked. He stood stock-still as he watched her pull her T-shirt over her head and drop it to the floor.

"Do you want me to leave?" Loretta asked, flexing her well-defined shoulders.

"No, you can stay. Uh, would you like a bottle of soda pop?" Mel asked, moving toward the kitchen area in his small apartment. "I have orange juice too."

"Fuck a bottle of soda pop," Loretta snickered. "The only juice you need to be thinkin' about right now is this juice between my legs. Any more questions?"

Mel's eyes got as wide as saucers, but he managed to remain somewhat calm. "I can't think of any more right now," he admitted, his eyes watering with lust. He looked Loretta over some more. Under the circumstances, there was only one thing to do. He took a deep breath and then he locked his door. He smiled at Loretta as he placed the CLOSED sign in his front window.

"That's more like it. I know you ain't stupid enough to turn this down," Loretta insisted, speaking in the most mature and throaty-sounding voice she could manage. Mel's mouth dropped open, and he began to salivate as he watched her gently pat her crotch. Loretta thought of herself as a real woman now, and it was time for her to start acting like one. The only way for her to do that was to be with a real man.

Mel was no match for this vixen, and that was exactly what she was. He realized that in spite of how she looked and behaved, she was technically, and according to the law, still a young girl. He could go to jail because of her! He reminded himself that the possibility of going to jail had never stopped a man from doing what the average man would probably do even in the eye of a hurricane.

At least he wasn't "raping" Loretta like some men probably would have done by now. If anybody was about to get raped, it was him, and when it happened, he enjoyed every minute of it. When he realized it was her first time, he thought he'd died and gone to heaven. He had not been with a teenage virgin since he was a teenage virgin, more than twenty-five years ago!

Afterward, he held her trembling hand as he wiped her blood from her thighs and his sheet. She looked away when he pulled the bloody condom off his penis and tossed it into the trashcan next to his bed.

"It won't be as painful the next time," Mel told Loretta, giving her a quick peck on the lips.

"It was worth it," she whispered in his ear.

Loretta was the youngest female Mel had ever been with. She was also the best. She was so young, firm, and eager to please him that after just one session in bed with her, she had him feeling like a teenager.

She was like a drug, and he had become addicted to her already.

CHAPTER 8

*M*AUREEN WAS PUZZLED AS TO WHY LORETTA DIDN'T BADGER HER TO
call Mel. Not one single time. "Do you still want to look for a photographer?" she asked her during dinner, a week after their initial
visit to his studio.

"Uh-huh," Loretta mumbled. She didn't know what she would
do if Maureen found out what she'd been up to with Mel. She was
afraid to even let her mother look at her face for too long because
she didn't want her to notice that there was something different
about her. Love made her feel like a different person. Her mind
wandered and she got goose bumps just thinking about Mel and
that *third leg* in the middle of his thighs. . . . She couldn't even sit in
the same spot for too long. He had used a lubricant, and he'd been
gentle the first time, because it had been her first time. During
their last rendezvous two days ago, though, he had been so rough it
felt like he was still inside her body!

"I will— Sugar, why can't you sit still?" Maureen asked, alarmed.
"You wigglin' around in that chair like you sittin' on a tack. You got
your period?"

"Yep, that's it. I must have put my tampon in too deep," Loretta
lied.

"Well, since you insist on wearin' tampons instead of pads like I
do, you need to learn how to use them right so you won't be so uncomfortable," Maureen said as she passed the black-eyed peas to
Loretta.

"I will, Mama."

"Now like I was sayin'—do you still want to look for a photographer? Or do you want me to call up that Mel person?" Maureen said with a snort.

"Uh, yeah. He seemed like a nice man."

"Well, we'll find out soon enough. Now, unless you want to be modelin' full-figured outfits, you need to ease up on that buttered corn bread. I'll give Mr. Mel a call."

Since Maureen had tossed Mel's business card into the trash, she had to look up his telephone number again in the phone book. All kinds of thoughts danced around in her head as she waited for him to answer his telephone. Like, what kind of photographer would not want to work with a girl as beautiful as Loretta? Maybe she was too beautiful and he was afraid that he would not live up to her expectations. Or maybe he only wanted to work with white girls. That was probably what it really was. Maureen had not seen a single photograph of a black model displayed on his wall. He didn't want to deal with his own kind, and poor Loretta had been anxious to work with him because he was black.

The only reason Maureen was calling Mel now was because Loretta was still interested in working with him. Maureen prayed that she could make a deal with him somehow. She had no idea that Loretta had already made a deal.

When Mel answered his telephone on the fourth ring, he couldn't tell Maureen quick enough to bring Loretta to his studio the following Saturday around noon, with her face fully made up and with several different outfits, at least two swimsuits, and a cocktail dress.

"Hmm. I'll have to buy her a cocktail dress," Maureen mumbled, wondering how much a brand-new cocktail dress was going to set her back. She was already going to be in the hole after she paid for Mel to do the portfolio. "Do we really need a cocktail dress? My daughter is very high maintenance, so she will only settle for somethin' real expensive."

Mel laughed. "That's not a problem. I think I can handle that."

"Oh no! I can't let you get a cocktail dress for my daughter!" Maureen protested.

"Let me explain. I have a lot of prop clothing here that some of my former models left behind and never retrieved. I can let Loretta borrow anything she likes."

"Oh." For some strange reason, Maureen suddenly wondered if Mel had a woman. If he did, that woman was very lucky. Not only was he good-looking, but he was also generous. "I don't want to put you through a lot of extra work on our account. I can borrow the money to get my daughter everything you think she needs for her pictures."

"No problem! No problem at all," Mel sang. "To tell you the truth, I've been thinking about your daughter a lot since you brought her to my studio. I'd be happy to do her portfolio and provide my management services as well. I've helped a lot of beginners jump-start their careers. Quite frankly, your daughter's got a lot more potential than most of the girls I've worked with lately. I know I can get her a lot of work."

"I'm glad you think that. Because that's the same thing two of those other photographers said. But it sounds better comin' from a brother like you," Maureen volunteered, hoping that her last sentence stroked Mel's ego. She was pleased that he had come to his senses in time. She had thought that she was going to have to write him off. "We'll see you on Saturday at noon. How long will the session take? I'm meetin' some friends for dinner Saturday evenin'."

"Oh! Well, a good session could go on for hours. I've done some that stretched over a period of several days," Mel told Maureen.

"Several days? Can't you snap all the pictures on the same day? We might go to church on Sunday, and come Monday, I have to go back to work and Lo'retta has school."

"Not a problem. We could probably wrap things up within five or six hours. If that doesn't happen, we could finish up on the following Saturday."

"Well, do I need to be there all that time? I could drop Lo'retta off and pick her up later. If you finish up before it gets real late, she can take the bus home. I'll make sure she brings her bus pass with her."

"I wouldn't hear of her taking a bus home!" Mel exclaimed. "I'd be more than happy to drive her home after the session."

Maureen's silence made Mel nervous.

"Of course, I can understand if you don't feel comfortable with your daughter being alone with a man she just met. I can assure you that you have nothing to worry about. I work with a lot of young girls, and I haven't bitten one yet," Mel jabbered, with his fingers crossed.

"Well, you don't look like the type to bite. I would feel more comfortable with her comin' home in a cab, or on the bus if it came to that, but I think I should be there for the whole session. Lo'retta can be shy at times and she might not feel comfortable on her own. . . ."

"I understand." Mel paused and pressed his lips together. "Listen, when your daughter does the *Oprah Winfrey Show*, make sure she mentions my name." Mel laughed. "Seriously, I will do whatever I can to make this easy for you and Loretta. I can juggle a few things around on my schedule so that I can complete her session all in the same day and in time for you to meet your friends for dinner."

"You can? Well, I don't want you slappin' together a few pictures and rushin' us off. I want my daughter to have a portfolio that she can be proud to show around. Especially since I have to pay you—"

"Listen. I like to make a buck as much as the next guy, but I don't want you to think that all I care about is the money. It touches my heart to see black youngsters doing something with their lives other than having a houseful of babies, waiting on the mailman to deliver a welfare check every month, or joining a street gang. Now, like I told you, I can rearrange my schedule so that I can devote the whole day to Loretta. Believe me, I would never 'slap together' something—even for a model I didn't like. I have a reputation to consider."

Maureen regretted making the comment about Mel slapping together a few pictures. "I'll bring my checkbook when I come back on Saturday. I'd like to pay you the deposit right away. My brother said he'd be happy to lend me the rest of the money."

"That's fine, Mrs. Montgomery—"

"It's Miss," Maureen interrupted. "I don't have a husband."

Mel took this innocent clarification the wrong way. He honestly thought that she was being flirtatious. He couldn't count the number of times the mothers of other young models had "solicited" him. Well, he was never one to look a gift horse in the mouth. What better way to keep his hands in Loretta's panties than by getting close to her mother? Talk about killing two birds with one stone!

"Well, in that case, maybe I can invite you to have dinner and drinks with me in the near future," he suggested.

Maureen held her breath to keep from giggling like a schoolgirl. Mel seemed like a nice guy and he was good-looking, but he didn't appeal to her at all. However, she wouldn't mind having dinner with him. If he was going to be photographing and managing her daughter's career, she needed to get to know him better anyway.

CHAPTER 9

*M*AUREEN CAME UP WITH A LOT OF EXCUSES NOT TO GO OUT WITH Mel when he asked, which he did almost every time she saw him. A few examples of her excuses were she had a date with somebody else, she didn't feel well, or she had company coming over. Even when she used the same excuses more than one time, he kept asking.

"You work with beautiful models, and I know a man like you must mingle with all kinds of other women along the way," Maureen pointed out. "Don't you already have a girlfriend or somethin'?" she finally asked.

"Not at the moment," Mel told her, which was the truth. He had recently broken up with the woman he had been seeing for over a year when she told him she wanted to have his baby and was not going to take no for an answer. Well, he was not about to be bouncing a wailing baby on his knee and making child-support payments, so that was the end of that relationship.

"I'm glad I have thick skin," Mel joked when Maureen told him that she had to stay home every night that week to shampoo her carpets. He added with an exaggerated whine, "Otherwise, I'm liable to think that you really don't like me."

Maureen laughed. "I do like you, Mel." She didn't have the nerve to tell him that she didn't like him enough to start a relationship. She told him the next best thing. "But since you work with my daughter, maybe we should just keep things on a business level."

"Do I stink? Is my breath bad? Do I look funny?" Mel wanted to know, actually looking hurt.

Maureen laughed again. "The answer to all of your questions is no."

"Well, if the only reason you don't want to socialize with me is because I work with your daughter, that's not much of a reason. I have dated other women associated with my work. What if you go out with me for a business reason?"

"What business reason would that be? I don't want to be a supermodel."

"But your daughter does. Since she's still a minor, there will be things coming up in the future that you will have to approve for her. We could discuss things like that over a few drinks. Your daughter tells me you love to eat out. What's wrong with two business associates having dinner together?"

"Nothin' is . . . is wrong with . . . with that," Maureen stuttered.

"For your information, I have several female friends that I take out from time to time. Some are even married. Maybe in the near future, when you don't have to wash your hair or shampoo your carpet, you can join me for dinner or a drink. We can talk more about your daughter's future."

Maureen knew when she was trapped. She had a feeling that Mel was probably not going to stop badgering her for a "date" unless she did something drastic. Getting ghetto and cussing a pest out usually got that pest off your back. If she borrowed a huge sum of money from him and took her time paying him back (or not at all), that would probably do the trick too. Things like that were not Maureen's style, though. Maybe if Mel saw how much she ate and drank in expensive restaurants, that would scare him off. Or maybe if she did something to embarrass him in public, he'd lose interest in her. It didn't take Maureen long to decide that she couldn't do any of that. The last thing she wanted to do was ruin Loretta's chance for success before she even got her feet wet.

Another thought, this one quite frightening, suddenly popped into Maureen's mind: If she didn't keep Mel happy, he just might retaliate by severing his relationship with Loretta! If that happened, living with Loretta would be like living with a human pit bull with a thorn stuck in its paw. Maureen decided that the most reasonable thing for her to do was go out with Mel. Besides, he was handsome and he had a lot going for him. . . .

"Discuss my daughter's future? Uh-huh, we can at least do that over dinner and drinks," she told Mel.

Had he known that all it would take for Maureen to fall into his plan to have more access to Loretta was for him to mention Loretta's future, he would have brought that up long before now.

It started with just dinner and drinks, and they always "discussed Loretta's future." By the sixth date, though, their agenda included a two-hour romp in a motel near Miami Beach. To Maureen's surprise, Mel had made it worth her while. He was one of the best lovers she had ever had.

When Mel reared back in his seat and told Maureen that he was in love with her over dinner at Beanie's, the popular soul-food restaurant where they'd had their first date, she looked at him like he was crazy. A few seconds later when he sucked in his breath and asked her to marry him, she choked on her wine.

"We don't even know one another that well!" she told him, blinking so hard an eyelash fell into her eye. "We just met a few months ago."

"It doesn't matter. I've known you long enough to know that I like everything about you, Maureen." Mel poured more wine into her glass.

"Get married? I don't remember the last time I was even in a serious relationship. It's been *years*," she confessed, dabbing at her eye with a damp napkin.

"I find that hard to believe. What's wrong with these men around here?" Mel said as he passed Maureen some more pinto beans.

Maureen shrugged. "Nothin' is wrong with the men around here."

"You just haven't met the right one," Mel said with a level of smugness on his face that Maureen had only seen displayed by Mama Ruby.

"I've met the right ones, but they all had the wrong ideas." Maureen laughed as Mel stared at her. Then she gave him a wounded look. "It's my fault, I guess. People say I'm too picky, and that's kind of true. I don't want just any man for a husband. He has to be special. But the real reason is that I've devoted my life to my daughter, so I haven't really had the time to find a man who wanted to marry me."

"Well, you have now. We found each other." Mel reached under the table and squeezed Maureen's knee. "Will you stay with me tonight?"

Maureen gasped and gave Mel an incredulous look. "Oh goodness gracious no! I can't stay out all night and leave my daughter at home by herself. She has school tomorrow, so I have to go home to make sure she gets to bed on time. I can't let you spend the night at my place this soon. I don't want to set a bad example for her. See, she's a good girl. She's so innocent and unworldly. I know how hard it must be for her to stay that way with all these loose-bootied young girls runnin' around here bein' such a bad influence on girls like Lo'retta. I want her to stay the way she is for as long as she can," Maureen insisted. "A virtuous woman is a godly woman. The man that gets Lo'retta will be gettin' a grand prize."

That's for sure, Mel said to himself. *One of the best pieces of ass I ever had.*

Loretta didn't have a lot of girlfriends because she didn't trust too many females. She considered them to be too treacherous. The fact that she was ready, willing, and able to betray her own mother was proof of that. But Mona Flack was still the best flunky in the world for a girl like Loretta to be best friends with. Mona was happy to lie to Maureen and say that Loretta was with her when she wasn't.

Mona was two years older than Loretta, but they were in the same grade. Mona was somewhat slow, so she had flunked the third and the fifth grades. She already had her driver's license and had access to her daddy's station wagon. Loretta had called her up a couple of hours ago and told her that she needed a ride over to Mel's place.

"I know there is a shortage of men, but of all the men in this world, why do you want the same one that your mama is involved with?" Mona asked Loretta as soon as she picked her up. "What if you get caught? Your mama would have a fit and you'd get a whuppin'."

"My mama is a Kentucky-fried country bumpkin! She's so clueless!" Loretta snapped. "She wouldn't know what to do with a luscious, sophisticated man like Mel. Besides, they are *just* friends anyway."

"Just friends, my foot! I've seen Mel's SUV parked in front of your buildin' late at night and early in the mornin' plenty of times. Is he sleepin' with your mama or what?"

"Well, yeah, but only to keep her from gettin' suspicious about him and me." Loretta got quiet and screwed up her face like she had just sucked on a lemon. "My mama thinks I'm stupid. She gets busy with Mel when she thinks I'm asleep, but him sockin' it to her don't mean nothin'. He's only doin' her to keep her in the dark and under control. I hate to admit it, but my mama is still kinda pretty, so it's more fun for him to do her than to masturbate or go after some skank if he gets horny and can't get to me in time," Loretta said, patting the side of her hair as she glanced in the rearview mirror. "But Mel is *my* lover. He's kinda old, but he's got a young man's body. I'm goin' to get a lot of mileage out of him."

"Well, since he's your photographer *and* manager, you better get as much mileage as you can out of that too," Mona advised. "I hope he don't cheat you out none of the money you make modelin'. Or do somethin' else crooked like some managers do . . ."

"Mel only takes ten percent of what I make. A lot of managers take fifteen percent from their models. One of the girls he used to work with, she was just on the cover of *a trendy local* magazine. He got her the job, and he did all the pictures for that shoot. He will be hookin' me up like that too."

Mona was thoroughly impressed. "Dang! Did that girl have to fuck him to get that job?"

Loretta gasped and gave Mona a disgusted look. "What's wrong with you, girl? Who said anything about a model havin' to fuck to get work—especially one like me? I'm sleepin' with Mel because I want to!" Loretta was talking so fast she choked on some air. As soon as she cleared her throat, she added, "I don't have to sleep my way to the top."

"I'm sorry. You mad at me?" Mona bleated, bowing her head submissively. If she had a tail, she would have tucked it between her legs.

"No, I'm not mad at you. I just wish your questions made more sense to me." Loretta clucked, not even trying to hide her impatience. "What's your point anyway?" she added, snapping her fingers.

"What I mean is, ain't you worried that you fuckin' Mel might mess up things? What if he gets tired of you? Do you think he'll still want to work with you then? If you and him so in love, how can y'all work together and keep your hands off one another?"

"We know how to keep things under control. There are always other people around when we go out on shoots. We get it on in hotels every now and then, but we *never* show our true feelin's to one another when we are out in public workin'," Loretta said. "Right now the best way he can be alone with me is in my mama's house or at his place."

"Hmmm. You're the only one of my friends that's foolin' around with a man Mel's age." Mona gave Loretta a concerned look.

Loretta looked at Mona like she was speaking in tongues. "You make him sound like some kind of geezer from *Jurassic Park*! He's not old. He's just mature!" Loretta insisted. "Keep your eyes on the road. There's joggers comin' out of nowhere."

"Does that grown man know what a huge crush you got on him?" Mona asked, her eyes directly on the road.

"*Crush*?" Loretta erupted, almost choking on the word. "Have you not heard anything I just said? I don't have no crush on Mel! I don't go around screwin' people I have crushes on! How many times do I have to tell you that I'm in love with him, and he's in love with me? We're goin' to get married as soon as I'm old enough."

CHAPTER 10

"GIRL, YOU MET MEL A YEAR AGO AND YOU'RE ALREADY TALKING about marrying him? For reals?" Mona yelled. Her eyes looked like they were about to pop out of their sockets.

"Yes, for reals!" Loretta yelled back.

"Nuh-uh! You just turned fifteen back in March." There was a touch of envy in Mona's voice.

"Mona, don't be so ignorant! We will wait until I turn eighteen and graduate. In the meantime, Mel and I will really get to know one another."

For Mona to be so slow, she often made some smart remarks. "Humph! If you ask me, I say you and Mel need to get to know one another real good before you even think about gettin' married. You are goin' to meet a lot of hot men workin' as a model. What if you meet one you like more than you like Mel?"

"I won't. He won't meet a girl he likes better than me, neither. I know it," Loretta insisted.

"I don't know, girl. I have a hard time believin' that your mama's man is goin' to marry *you*."

"Yes! He said so himself. Why are you actin' like that's such a big deal? Men marry the women they love all the time."

"Well, for one thing, you and Mel gettin' married is goin' to surprise the hell out of everybody. Especially when they find out y'all been together all this time—wooo!" Mona slapped the side of the steering wheel, and even though she had her eyes on the road, she almost hit a jogger anyway.

"Watch it!" Loretta hollered, grabbing the steering wheel. "I knew I should have taken the bus or a cab to Mel's place!"

"You know I don't mind drivin' you over there. I just wish you would let me drive you all the way instead of you gettin' out at the corner and makin' me wait for you in some spooky parkin' lot, or the movies, or the mall."

"I don't want Mel to see you. He's already worried about somebody seein' me over there when I'm supposed to be somewhere else with you." Loretta softened her voice. "Uh, I hope you don't mess things up for me."

"You know I would never blab on you. I mean, I don't mind coverin' for you and Mel . . . as long as there's somethin' in it for me." Mona sniffed and began to tap the steering wheel with her finger, anxious for Loretta to respond to the last part of her sentence.

"Oh yeah! You can pick up those black pumps you wanted to borrow when I get home this evenin'," Loretta said.

"One more thing. I need to borrow your brand-new Gucci purse too," Mona added.

"My Gucci purse?" Loretta hollered.

"Yes, your Gucci purse. When you sent me into that adult store behind that strip club to get that slimy lubricant for you and Mel— and that humongous, disgustin' dildo—because you were too embarrassed to go in and buy that shit yourself, you promised me that I could borrow your Gucci purse. Don't you remember?"

Loretta scratched her head and gave Mona a thoughtful look. "I remember sendin' you into that adult store, but I don't remember tellin' you that you could use my only Gucci purse."

"Well, you did and I want to use it!" Mona snapped. "And another thing, don't forget to bring me some gas money. I don't want my daddy askin' me how come I used up so much gas when I'm only supposed to be goin' to your house."

"Oh! The things that I have to go through just to be with my man!" Loretta lamented. Then she giggled. "I'm almost sorry that I found out sex was so damn good. Girl, if you could just see Mel naked! And the way he kisses! Ooh wee! I can't get enough."

"Tsk, tsk, tsk." Mona sucked on her teeth so loudly it made Loretta flinch. "Lo'retta, I hope your mama never hears you sayin' crazy shit like that. She would whup your ass if she thought you were screwin' already."

"Don't you worry about my mama. I got her in the palm of my hand. She thinks I'm into Jesus as much as she is. She would never think that I was screwin' already." Loretta lowered her voice to a conspiratorial whisper and leaned her head closer to Mona's. "Let me borrow a few condoms in case Mel runs out again."

Maureen found out that Loretta was "screwing already" in the worst way possible. One Friday night while Loretta was "at the movies" with Mona, Maureen went into her room to put away her laundry. Just as she was about to leave the room, she looked down and saw a condom wrapper on the floor by the side of Loretta's bed.

Maureen was so crushed she wanted to cry. She couldn't believe that her baby had crossed such a serious line so soon. When she called up Virgil a few minutes later and told him, he only made her feel worse.

"Well, the girl is fifteen goin' on twenty-five and almost looks it. These boys around here ain't goin' to ignore a cupcake like Lo'retta. She's been up for grabs for a while now, so this was bound to happen sooner or later," Virgil told Maureen with a snicker. "If I was you, I'd keep a real close eye on her, though. It ain't like it was when me and you was her age. Gettin' pregnant used to be the worst mess that a young girl could get herself into. Them days is over, though. It's a whole new ballgame now. Nowadays, they got diseases goin' around that a witch doctor can't cure." Virgil let out a loud, deep breath. "One of the guys I used to play cards with just found out he got AIDS. . . ."

"Now why did you have to go *there*. I feel bad enough. You don't have to make me feel no worse by talkin' about AIDS and all the other mess goin' around!" Maureen blasted.

"Look on the bright side. At least Lo'retta's got *some* common sense. Enough to make sure she protects herself. Don't let no condom wrapper upset you too much. Be glad you found a condom wrapper and not one of them pregnancy testin' doodads."

"I'm not glad I found a condom wrapper in her room. I'm not glad to know that my child is havin' sex already! Loretta is my baby."

"Your *baby*? Honey, I got news for you. You ain't got no baby no more," Virgil said, putting a lot of emphasis on his words.

"She's still a baby to me! She's still—"

"A baby that's trapped in a woman's body," Virgil broke in.

"I know that already. I just wish she could have waited a couple more years," Maureen wailed. "All this time, I thought I was raisin' Lo'retta up right."

"You can raise a child up 'right' and they'll still turn out to be a fool! I know raisin' one by yourself is hard," Virgil declared. "All you can do is the best you can and pray that you don't end up with a Charles Manson on your hands. Shit. I hear all kinds of complaints from my ex all the time about my son actin' up, but she chose to run off and be on her own—and I know she's a good mama. If you ask me, kids need two parents to turn out like they got some sense. Me and Corrine have been tryin' to make a baby for years now. When and if we ever do, I guarantee you that I'm goin' to be in that child's life no matter what. If Corrine was to take that child and up and move to another state the way my ex done, I'm goin' to follow behind her like a bloodhound. I don't care if I have to haul garbage or rob banks—I am goin' to be around my child. I didn't have no daddy when I was growin' up. You didn't have no daddy, neither. I think that's why me and you had so much unhappiness in our lives. Loretta needs a daddy and you need a husband."

"I would love to be married, Virgil. I would have been married a long time ago if I could have found a decent man who wanted to marry me."

"Maybe you shouldn't be so picky."

"Picky? Virgil, I ain't a spring chicken no more. Men my age want young girls, and I don't want no old man that I'll wind up bathin' and spoon-feedin' when he can no longer do it for himself."

"What about that photographer Loretta's been posin' for? Mel.

You oughta know him real good by now. And you must like him a whole lot to be goin' out with him so much."

"Mel is a nice guy and Loretta loves him to death. He even quit workin' with all of the other models he used to work just with so he could devote more time to Lo'retta. He just hooked her up with some more ads for some of the top department stores in Miami. Some that almost never use black girls!"

"Hmmm. That's good to hear. I'm real impressed with the dude. He must really know his business, then."

"Virgil, Mel is a real good photographer, and he's so thoughtful and generous. Every time he comes over to my place, he brings us something—wine, a bucket of chicken, flowers. That's the kind of man he is."

"You must be impressed with the dude, too, huh?" Virgil asked.

Maureen laughed. "I do like him, I guess. I even let him make a dark room out of my pantry. That way he can develop prints at my place. I gave him a key to my apartment in case he needs to get into his dark room when me and Lo'retta go out shoppin' or someplace else. He even offered to pay me to use the room, but I told him that wasn't necessary. You know, I never knew takin' pictures and developin' them was so interestin'. Poor Mel. He has so much patience with me and Lo'retta askin' him questions about this and that."

"Maybe you can get him to snap some pictures of me and Corrine so we can frame 'em and put 'em on the wall. I keep tryin' to get over to your place so I can meet him, but it seems like every time I got time, he ain't got time."

"I'm goin' to make sure you get to meet him soon." Maureen took a deep breath. "Mel is the first man I've dated that Lo'retta took a shine to so fast. He's become real important to her."

Virgil gave Maureen's words some thought. "Important how?" he asked.

"You ought to see how her face lights up when I tell her he's comin' over. She loves Mel to death. Poor Lo'retta. If I had known how bad she wanted a daddy, I would have spent more time with some of my use-to-be boyfriends."

"Uh-huh. All I got to say is, I hope Lo'retta don't get too attached to that man if you ain't goin' to let him stay around too long."

"I don't know what I'm goin' to do about Mel. I . . . I just don't love him," Maureen reluctantly admitted.

"What's wrong with him?"

"Nothin' is wrong with him. I just don't love him enough to want to marry him and spend the rest of my life with him. This is one thing I really have to think hard about."

"Well, sometimes you can't get everything you want. I know quite a few couples that didn't love one another, but they got married anyway and they seem real happy together. Now that you know Loretta done . . . uh . . . got her feet wet in the sex pool, she'll need supervision now more than ever."

"Tell me about it," Maureen quipped. "But I don't know if I want to burden Mel with another man's child—even though I know he's just as crazy about Lo'retta as she is about him."

"Baby sister, give the man a chance. I don't want you to grow old alone," Virgil said gently. "Think about it."

"I will think about it," Maureen muttered.

CHAPTER 11

*I*T HAD BEEN A YEAR SINCE MEL STARTED PROPOSING TO MAUREEN. SHE still needed more time to "think about it." What if she married him and then met a man she really did love? That was one of the things she had to think about.

Another reason she was reluctant to marry Mel was because she didn't like the idea of divorce, and having an affair while she was married was out of the question. Despite her devotion to Jesus, she participated in enough worldly things already.

Mel was convenient to have around for sex and companionship. Maureen admitted that. But there was an even more practical reason for her to hang on to him: Loretta. Because of him, she was doing so well as a model that Maureen knew that someday her child would share the spotlight with Beverly Johnson, Christie Brinkley, and Brooke Shields. Maureen looked forward to the day that she could kick back in a house in the exclusive Coconut Grove area that Loretta had promised she would buy her someday. She wanted Maureen to "live like a queen."

If Maureen would eventually "live like a queen" because of the way Mel was guiding Loretta to success, would she feel obligated to marry him then? However, she knew she couldn't "think about" Mel's proposal forever. Her friends made that clear to her.

"Girl, you better go ahead and marry that man. You ain't got too many chances left. Matter of fact, other than Mel, you ain't got no chance left at all, if you ask me. You ain't Cinderella." One thing about Catherine "Catty" Flatt, Maureen's off-and-on best friend since childhood, was that she didn't bite her tongue. Catty said whatever was on her mind and she didn't care how it sounded.

"Listen to the pot callin' the kettle black," snickered Emmogene "Fast Black" Harris, Catty's former mother-in-law and a woman who was just as oafish and crude as Catty. Fast Black had never been married herself, but she had lived with a Chinese man in San Francisco who had fathered her only child, her son Jack "Yellow Jack" Harris. Yellow Jack, once Maureen's closest male friend, had moved to Brooklyn three years ago to be with a woman he'd met through a dating service.

"You do need a husband, Mo'reen," Fast Black said. Fast Black was the one who had bragged about the "glamorous" life she had enjoyed in San Francisco and had encouraged Maureen to go there. Well, since that didn't work out for Maureen, she was not that anxious to take any more advice from Fast Black.

"I don't love Mel, y'all," Maureen protested.

"Bah! Love ain't nothin' but a four-letter word!" Catty griped. "If a man has a decent job, is easy on the eyes, and gets along with your child, you better take him and run before some other woman snatches him up."

"Catty's right, Mo'reen. You ain't got to be in love with nobody to have a good life with them," Fast Black added. "Look at me. I ain't never been married, but I done had more than my share of men. As strange as it sounds, the one I cared about the most was Yellow Jack's daddy."

"So why didn't you marry him?" Maureen wanted to know. "Did you have a good reason not to?"

Catty and Fast Black guffawed at the same time.

"That Chinaman didn't want to marry my black ass," Fast Black admitted. "He was with me for the same reason I was with him—I was lonely and curious."

"I'm lonely, but I am not curious," Maureen offered.

"You horny as hell, though. I can tell by the way you keep crossin' and uncrossin' your legs every time we talk about Mel," Catty accused with a smirk on her round face. Unlike Maureen, whose looks had improved with age, Catty looked hard and tired. The wrinkles that she referred to as "laugh lines" crisscrossed her face from side to side and top to bottom. Her wavy black hair had only a few strands of gray, but she had lost the petite girlish figure that she had once been so proud of. Now she hid her flab and lumps in baggy dresses and oversized smocks.

Fast Black was approaching fifty, but she was just as wild and feisty as ever. The flat face that she'd been born with was even flatter now, and her once-smooth chocolate-brown skin looked like leather that somebody had left out in the sun for too long. She went to the gym a couple of times a week, and she engaged in a lot of strenuous physical activity, such as one or two barroom brawls a month, but it didn't do her much good. Everything on her frame still sagged and drooped like deflated balloons. She didn't care one way or the other about all the gray hair on her head because she hid it underneath wigs and scarves. In spite of her dowdy appearance, she was still very popular with men. She was currently involved with three different men, and since they treated her like a queen, she decided she was an authority on affairs of the heart.

"Catty's right, Mo'reen. You do act horny. If you don't keep that affliction under control, you'll go crazy and start humpin' trees," Fast Black warned with a snicker. "You need to come clean and tell us everything. We ain't blind. Everybody in Goons and Miami knows that Mel's been munchin' on your pleasure pie."

"So what?" Maureen snarled, rotating her neck. "Yes, I have been to bed with Mel, and I'm goin' to keep doin' it."

Right after Catty and Fast Black departed, Maureen called up Mel and invited him to have dinner with her and Loretta that evening. Not only did he accept her invitation without hesitation, but he also offered to pick up a bucket of chicken so she wouldn't have to cook.

It was a very enjoyable evening. Maureen didn't even notice the looks of scorn that Loretta kept aiming in her direction every time she got affectionate with Mel. After dinner the three of them went into the living room to watch an episode of *Miami Vice* that Loretta had recorded.

"I got hired to work as an extra in a crowd scene on an episode last year," Mel reported. "I'll bring the tape with me the next time I come over, and the pictures that I took of Don Johnson and some of the other stars on the show."

Hearing this impressed Loretta. "For reals! I watched them shoot some scenes one time, and one of their crew told me I was the prettiest thing he ever saw," she squealed.

"He wasn't lying," Mel mused, giving Loretta a conspiratorial wink.

"Honest to God, Mel. A man like you should have your own TV show," Loretta swooned, giving Mel a dreamy look. "Huh, Mama? Don't you think Mel is sexy enough to be a TV star?"

"Uh-huh," Maureen mumbled, gnawing on her second chicken wing.

Loretta's comment about Mel being sexy enough to be a TV star made a lump form in Maureen's throat. That (and the condom wrapper she'd found on Loretta's bedroom floor) was another indication that her baby was growing up.

After Loretta excused herself to go to her room, Maureen waited half an hour before she checked to make sure she was asleep. Then she came back into the living room and grabbed Mel's hand. No, she didn't love him, but she loved the way he made her feel in bed. At least for the time being. Maureen quietly led Mel to her bedroom.

After they had thrashed around for a good twenty minutes, Mel rolled to his side of the bed, with Maureen still in his arms. He stopped huffing and puffing long enough to ask her, "Did you think about what I asked you last week?"

"About us gettin' married?" Mel had been more aggressive in bed than usual this time. Toward the end of the session, he had almost humped Maureen clean off the bed. She was still gasping for breath.

"Uh-huh," he replied, huffing and puffing some more.

"I think about that a lot," Maureen told him in a shy voice. It was hard not to think about Mel's frequent marriage proposals.

"Well, will you marry me?" he asked again.

CHAPTER 12

"MEL," MAUREEN SAID IN A HEAVY VOICE, SITTING UP IN BED AS she gently rubbed his shoulder. "Didn't I tell you that I don't love you that way? Why would you want to be in a loveless marriage?" She had repeated these same lines so many times, she sounded like a broken record. Mel was beginning to get on her nerves. However, she had to admit that she was flattered to know that a man like Mel wanted to marry her so badly.

"Maureen, sweetheart, there is a lot more to marriage than love. If you ask me, I say that love is the least important part of the bargain. We need to be more concerned about the financial security and other benefits of marriage."

Maureen gave Mel a puzzled look. "You make marriage sound more like a business venture."

Business venture was right. Marriage to the right woman was a smart career move as far as Mel was concerned. Once he had realized what a prize package Maureen and Loretta represented, he decided to take them. Maureen and Loretta had the potential to provide the security he deserved. If he played his cards (and "played" Maureen and Loretta) right, he could be set for life. He'd marry Maureen first, which is what Loretta had begun to strongly advise him to do. She wanted him to live under the same roof with her so they'd have easy access to one another until she became of age. Like with his first wife, Loretta was in love but he was in business. He was willing to please her so she would be willing to please him, and if that included marrying her mother, that was all right with him. That thought had crossed his mind the first time he'd made love to Loretta anyway. The more he got to know Loretta and saw how easy it was to line up modeling jobs for her, the more he was convinced that she would hit it really big someday.

Mel didn't want to waste too much time. He wanted to get his plan under way as soon as possible, so he had to work hard and fast on Maureen. Yes, he'd marry her and stay with her for as long as it took him to get everything he wanted. He'd married for the same reason once before and saw no reason not to do it as many times as necessary. His second marriage would be much more enjoyable than his first. He wouldn't have to get drunk to sleep with Maureen like he'd had to do with his first wife, a fat, hairy, old meal ticket. Making love to her had been like sticking his dick into a dried-out pothole. Maureen was a beautiful, luscious woman with a decent body, but Loretta was so young and tender it brought tears to his eyes when he thought about her. He wanted to control her in every way now and when she made it to the top. Using her body along the way was icing on the cake. She was the perfect fool! Therefore, he would eventually have to marry her too. She'd be rich, and as her husband, so would he.

However, had Mel known that Maureen was going to be so reluctant, he probably would have thought things through a little more carefully before plunging in so hard and fast. Every businessman had to take a few risks and expect a few setbacks, though. Facilitating a "project" as unique as this one was a first for him. Not only was it a challenge but it did wonders for his ego too. Having a beautiful young girl like Loretta practically kissing his feet so aggressively had altered his thinking. Maybe, just maybe, after Maureen had outlived her usefulness and he'd disposed of her and married Loretta, he would remain with her permanently (or until he found a bigger fish to fry or she left him). However, if his relationship with Loretta fizzled out before he'd reached his goal, he would simply kick them both to the curb and follow the same agenda again with someone else.

Until then, he would follow his plan accordingly.

"In real life, marriage is more of a partnership, Maureen. Security and companionship are a lot more important than romance. Shit. Love is for teenagers and soap opera stars. Even if you're in love with a person when you marry him or her, it usually doesn't last for the duration of the marriage anyhow. It's a law of nature. Most of the married people I know can't stand their partners, but they stay in the marriage because it's the smart thing to do."

Maureen wondered if Virgil had been coaching Mel. What he had just said sounded a lot like what Virgil had told her!

"I'm sure they were in love at one time. I know love fades over the years, but I'd like to experience it at least once in a marriage," Maureen said.

Mel sat up and looked at Maureen with a pleading look in his eyes. Then he cupped her face in his hands. He was surprised at how cold her skin felt against his flesh. He wondered if her heart was just as cold. In spite of what she had just said, he knew that she had to have *some* feelings for him. Beautiful women didn't go around screwing men they had no feelings for unless they had just been released from prison or were desperate as hell. There was nothing desperate about Maureen. She was honest about her feelings, and he admired her for that. However, he could never be honest enough to tell her that he didn't really love her either—and never could. Loving her or any other female was still an impossibility for him. Even if he eventually got over the pain of his past, he could never really love a woman as independent as Maureen.

Without giving it much thought, Mel altered his plea. "Then why don't we just live together?"

"Uh-uh. I don't want to live with a man I'm not married to. My mama would turn over in her grave!"

What in the world was wrong with Maureen? Mel wondered. He had made a lot of progress with her, but he was not going to pursue her forever. His clock was ticking. Had he not truly believed that Loretta would be the cash cow he had been looking for his whole life, he would have given up and moved on by now.

He almost wished that the sex with Loretta was not so damn good. That would make it a lot easier for him to throw in the towel.

He decided that he would give this project just a few more months. Maybe he would continue to fuck Loretta and work with her on a limited basis, but he would drop Maureen like a bad habit.

"All right, Maureen, but think about it from a practical point of view. If we get married, we'll both be able to save more money. We both need newer cars, and don't you want to own your own house someday?"

"Yes, I do want my own house someday, and I will get me one eventually," she vowed.

"Not with what you make filing lobster orders!"

Maureen gave Mel an incredulous look. "I plan to get a better job someday, Mel," she said sharply. "Things are fine the way they are with us. Why do you want to get married so bad?"

"I loved being married. I'd still be with my ex if she hadn't run off with *her* ex. Neither one of us is gettin' any younger. When and if you do decide you want to get married, in love or not, there might not be anybody interested in you. You need to give that some serious thought."

"I already have," she confessed. She had begun to weaken, but she had other issues she wanted to address and resolve before seriously considering Mel's proposal.

The main thing she wanted to sort out was Loretta.

She was more than a little concerned about her daughter being sexually active.

It had been a year since Maureen had discovered the condom wrapper on Loretta's bedroom floor and she still had not confronted her about it. She planned to do so eventually, but in the meantime, she was more interested in keeping the peace. "That Harris boy asked about you when I was at the market the other day," Maureen said to Loretta over dinner the next day as she reached for her second deep-fried pork chop. "That boy has been eyeballin' you since y'all was in first grade."

Without even looking up from her plate, Loretta replied, "The boy has a cone-shaped head, pimples, a flat nose, and bad breath. His kids will be born with hooves. Besides, I wouldn't waste my time with a boy who bags groceries for a livin',” Loretta insisted. When she looked up, Maureen noticed a gleam in her eyes that she had never seen before. “I want me a man who is goin' to go places and take me with him. A man like Mel.”

“Well, when you get old enough, you can look for a man like Mel,” Maureen told her. “Until then, I think you need to focus on school.”

“And my modelin'. I just lined up a couple of new jobs to do later this month.”

“Oh? Didn't I tell you to let me know about new job offers before you accept them? You are still a minor, and I need to be involved in everything you do. I don't want anybody takin' advantage of you.”

“You don't have to worry about anybody takin' advantage of me. Mel's got my back. He . . . uh . . . he really looks out for me.” Loretta returned her attention to her plate, pushing the peas around with her spoon like marbles.

“I'm glad to hear that you feel that way, but Mel's not your daddy. He can only ‘have your back’ up to a certain point. He can't make legal decisions for you. He can't sign contracts or photo releases for you or anything else unless I know about it and approve it. That's been our agreement from the get-go.”

Loretta gave Maureen a blank look. “I'm glad you brought that up, Mama.”

Maureen held her spoon up in midair. Peas fell back onto her plate like pebbles. “Glad I brought up what? Contracts?”

“Uh-uh. About Mel not bein' my daddy . . .”

“Well, Mel is not your daddy.”

“He told me yesterday that he asked you to marry him again.”

“And I told him that I had to think about it.”

“Why? *What* do you need to think about? You ain't Zsa Zsa Gabor. Men ain't linin' up to marry you. Besides, you like Mel and he likes you. He's makin' decent money, and he spends more time here than in his own place anyway. What's the problem with you marryin' him?”

“I don't love him,” Maureen said with a gasp. “I want to be in love with the man I marry.”

"Oh, Lord! Mama, do you know how you sound? You sound like the women from the olden days! I . . . I can't believe my ears!"

"Lo'retta, what's so bad about a woman wantin' to be in love with the man she marries?"

"Nothin' if your name is Farrah Fawcett or Tina Turner. Celebrities are the only ones who can afford to be that silly. Love! Bah! That's such a pipe dream!" Loretta's logic only made sense to her, as usual. She wouldn't even consider the fact that her being in love with Mel was a "pipe dream."

"Well, I don't care what you or anybody else says or thinks. I am not interested in marryin' a man I don't love. The man I fall in love with has to have certain qualifications."

"Like what?"

"Well, he has to be sensitive, good-lookin', ambitious, employed, and the right age."

Loretta gave Maureen a pitiful look and shook her head. "Mama, you just described Mel Ross!"

"I just described a lot of men, but I don't love them either," Maureen insisted.

"That's why you walkin' around here at your age and ain't never been married! Other than a few jokers that fly by night with you every now and then, and that bald-headed dude that takes you to Disney World once a year and to a rib shack a couple of times a month, you don't have any other man in your life—except for Mel."

"It wouldn't be fair to Mel or me if I marry him feelin' the way I do."

"Look, Mama, life is not fair to everybody. You told me that yourself. At least if you marry Mel, it would be fair to me, because I'd finally have a daddy. If Mel knows you don't love him and he still wants to marry you, I don't think he's worryin' about what's fair and what's not."

CHAPTER 13

MAUREEN WAS NOT COMFORTABLE SLEEPING WITH MEL IN HER apartment when Loretta was home. After the first time in the motel, she had made love with him in his cramped place, which was not very romantic. Mel had all kinds of miscellaneous photography materials cluttering up his tiny apartment. His bedroom was the worst of all. Magazines and circulars that included some of his work were all over the floor, the top of his dresser, and on half of his bed.

Making love on Mel's hard, lumpy couch was like making love on a bed of rocks. And like so many single men, his housekeeping skills were not up to Maureen's standards. Dirty dishes, empty food containers, and other debris dominated his kitchen. Dust, crumbs, and even a chicken bone or two were always on his living room coffee table.

So most of the time when Mel wanted to be intimate with Maureen, it was in her apartment at her request. She only made love with him after she made sure Loretta was asleep. She still only allowed him to spend the whole night when Loretta was sleeping over with her uncle Virgil and aunt Corrine or with one of her friends.

Since Mel had entered Maureen's life, she had stopped seeing other men—except a bald-headed dude named Billy Jim Martin. She finally told him that she didn't want to see him anymore.

"Why don't you want to see me no more?" Billy Jim asked nastily while they sat munching on some barbecue at one of Maureen's favorite rib joints. Since Maureen had had nothing better to do that Friday night when Billy Jim had dropped by her apartment, she had jumped into his Jetta like a carjacker. "What did I do wrong?"

"Nothin', Billy Jim." Maureen paused and held her breath. She didn't like to hurt anybody's feelings, but there were times when that couldn't be avoided. "Uh, I'm seein' another man, and I think it's goin' to get real serious between me and him. He's even talkin' about marriage."

"Is it that picture-takin' sucker I seen you with at the club last week?" Billy Jim asked, a scowl forming on his face. "Melvin Ross?"

Maureen nodded. "Yes, Mel is the man who wants to marry me," she said, her voice cracking. "He's asked me several times already, but I keep puttin' him off."

"Harrumph!" Billy Jim boomed, giving Maureen a disgusted and disappointed look. "If he keeps askin' and you keep puttin' him off, he needs to move on. If he's a real man, that's just what he's goin' to do eventually," Billy Jim laughed. "You know how we do."

"Thanks a lot for tellin' me that. That's somethin' I didn't know!" Maureen snapped.

"Aw, Mo, don't be gettin' all hot and bothered with me. We've been friends for a long time, but let me give you some advice— don't overplay your hand. If you don't make up your mind with Mel Ross and stop draggin' him along, you goin' to end up by yourself. Black women can't afford to be too picky no more. Not with all the white girls, Latinas, and Asian cuties y'all got to compete with for us brothers now. Now let me tell you one more thing you probably don't know—one woman's trash is another woman's treasure. I bet the next woman Mel asks to marry him will take him and run. Girl, you better shit or get off the toilet. Marry Mel while you can." Billy Jim gave Maureen a stern look. Then he looked at his watch and started tapping his fingers on the table.

"I just might do that. My brother and everybody else feels the same way you do. Even my daughter."

"Your girl. Holy moly! That's another thing I need to run by you," Billy Jim volunteered, sounding even more disappointed now. The puzzled look on Maureen's face prompted him to be more specific. "Most men don't want to raise another man's child. Especially a teenage girl."

"My daughter gets along real good with Mel," Maureen insisted. "He's managin' her modelin' career and doin' a real good job. Because of him and his contacts, she's gettin' so much work she can't handle it all. If Mel didn't like teenage girls, he wouldn't be workin' so hard for Lo'retta."

"That don't mean nothin'. Kids is crazy as hell these days. Most stepdaddies and stepchildren don't mix too good. They never did and probably never will. Workin' with 'em and raisin' 'em is two different things. Especially gals! Your girl bein' so cute and doin' all that modelin' and whatnot, she probably thinks her booty don't stink. She will draw boys to your apartment like flies to pig shit—if she ain't already doin' that. It's goin' to take a hell of a man to get along with her and keep her in check. I picked up on that the first time I came to visit your place. Loretta gave me some serious attitude."

Maureen was anxious for this date to end. Even if she stopped seeing Mel, she would never date Billy Jim again. He had struck Maureen's last nerve when he brought up Loretta's name. "Like I said, my daughter and Mel get along just fine. I think it'll be good for her to have him livin' with us full-time. She's goin' through that moody stage now. With all of these horny boys around here, it might be good to have Mel in the picture to help me keep them in line."

"Okay, you got a point there," Billy Jim said with a nod and a mysterious look on his face. "Who's goin' to keep Mel in line? I went to high school with him, and I can tell you one thing—his eyes like to roam," he sniped.

"What's that supposed to mean?"

"Nothin' . . ." Billy Jim glanced at his watch again and signaled for the waiter to bring the check.

Maureen could see that Billy Jim was anxious to leave now. This was the first time he had not encouraged her to order another drink and some dessert. It was also the shortest date she had ever been on with him in their two-year relationship. She was just as anx-

ious as he was to call it a night, and she let him know that by looking at her watch too. As usual, the waiter took his time bringing the
check. To keep from feeling even more awkward and uncomfortable, Maureen kept the conversation going.

"If you are hintin' that Mel might cheat on me, don't waste your
time. If and when he cheats on me, I know how to deal with him.
That's one of the best things I learned from Mama Ruby."

*"Mo'reen, when it comes to men, if a woman don't take no mess, won't be
no mess,"* Mama Ruby had advised her. Maureen was eleven when
Mama Ruby told her that. That same day, Mama Ruby had chased
one of her unfaithful suitors from her house after she had almost
flattened the back of his head with a cast-iron skillet.

"How come you got that big grin on your face, Mo'reen?" Billy
Jim asked, grimacing so hard it looked like somebody had squirted
vinegar in his eyes. "Did I say somethin' funny?"

"Oh. Nothin' like that. I was just thinkin' about somethin' my
mama told me when I was a little girl."

They finished their meal and left the restaurant a few minutes
later and got into Billy Jim's car. Except for a few comments about
the weather and other mundane subjects, they rode in silence.

When Billy Jim parked in front of Maureen's apartment, he
shook her hand, told her to have a nice life, and then he sped off.

Maureen was in the kitchen pouring a glass of wine when Loretta
sauntered in with her bathrobe on inside out. There was sweat on
her face, and she looked like she had just run five miles.

"Why did you come back home so soon, Mama?" Loretta asked,
blinking rapidly and nervously glancing toward the door.

"Billy Jim didn't want to continue the date after I told him that
Mel wanted to marry me," Maureen replied, heading toward the
living room with Loretta close behind. "Did you do your homework
and put away the laundry like I told you before I left?"

"Uh-huh."

"Did Mel call or stop by?"

"Uh, yeah. He called. He said to tell you that he would call again
later. "

"What's wrong with your face, girl?" Maureen narrowed her eyes and gave Loretta a critical look. "How come you breathin' so hard, Lo'retta?"

"What do you mean?" Loretta asked. She rubbed the side of her cheek and held her breath as long as she could.

"You look as red as a strawberry." Maureen laughed as she plopped down onto the couch, kicking off her shoes.

"I was on the phone with Mona and she was tellin' me somethin' so funny I laughed for five minutes. It made the blood rise in my face. . . ."

Maureen shrugged. "That's the downside to bein' high yellow. I'm glad I never had to worry about that." She sipped from her wineglass and then gave Loretta another critical look. "Is that why you breathin' so hard and funny?"

"Oh! Well, just before Mona called, I jogged a few laps around the block faster and longer than I usually do. With all the fattenin' food you like to cook, I have to do somethin' to keep my weight down."

"Well, you better slow down. You don't need to lose any weight. Listen, baby. I guess I'm goin' to go ahead and marry Mel. He's gettin' real pushy about it. If I don't keep him happy, he could take it out on you and stop helpin' you get work and all." Maureen gave Loretta a pensive look. "You work so hard, and I want to see you make it to the top." Maureen took another sip of her wine. "I know that with your good looks and ambition, you could probably do all right without Mel's help, but I don't want to take that chance. I don't want us to lose Mel."

Loretta sat down in the seat facing Maureen, looking relieved. "I am so glad to hear you say that, Mama! It's about time. I'm glad Mel hasn't given up! He's a good man, and I don't want us to lose him either."

"After he moves in, I hope you'll continue to behave yourself," Maureen said, giving Loretta a stern look. "Mel's takin' on a lot of responsibilities by marryin' me and havin' to be a daddy to you."

"I know, Mama. And you don't have to worry. I'll be real good. Mel won't regret marryin' you. . . ."

Loretta was glad that her hair was long enough to cover the sucker bites that Mel had left on the side of her neck an hour ago.

This was one night that she wanted to forget as soon as possible. Minutes after Maureen had left to go on her date, Loretta had called Mel and told him that if he came over to "keep her company," she would make him very happy.

After they had drunk a couple of beers, they had gotten busy in Loretta's bedroom and lost track of the time. If Maureen had not coughed when she entered the apartment, they would not have known she had returned until it was too late.

Mel had grabbed his clothes and shoes and crawled out of Loretta's bedroom window and slid to the ground like a seasoned thief. He was hiding behind the Dumpster in the backyard, waiting for Loretta to let him know when the coast was clear.

Ten minutes later, Maureen finally got up off the couch and went into the bathroom. One minute later, Loretta sprinted to the back door. Mel had put on his clothes and was sitting on the ground wiping sweat off his face. He had parked two blocks away, but he had to pass by the front of Maureen's building to get to his vehicle. Since the owner of Maureen's apartment building had recently installed a tall gate around the backyard, the exit door to it led to the front of the building. If she happened to look out the bathroom window, she would probably see him. Mel had no choice but to leave the same way he had come—through the front door of Maureen's apartment.

"Mel, Mama's in the bathroom! You better make a run for it now!" Loretta told him, speaking in a low voice. "Come on, honey!"

"Shit!" Mel cursed, stumbling up the porch steps. "I thought you said she wouldn't be back home until around ten!" he snarled. He walked behind Loretta as they crept in through the back door and down the hall toward the living room.

"That's what she told me. Then that fool she went out with got crazy jealous when she told him about you, so he brought her home early." Loretta glanced down the hallway. They had almost made it to the front door.

"This was a little too close for comfort, you know," Mel whispered as he eased open the front door. "I don't like playing Russian roulette with my dick."

"Don't worry. You'll be movin' in with us soon."

Mel gave Loretta a curious look. "What?" he asked, turning his head so that he was looking at her from the corner of his eye.

"She told me a little while ago that she's goin' to marry you." Loretta poked Mel's crotch. "It was a long time comin', but it was worth it."

Mel was just about to speak again when they heard the toilet flush. He gasped and stumbled over the threshold onto the porch. He tiptoed down the steps and ran the two blocks to where he had parked.

Loretta went back into the living room where Maureen had already returned to the couch and poured another glass of wine.

CHAPTER 14

*T*HE NEWS THAT MAUREEN HAD DECIDED TO MARRY MEL MADE LORETTA'S day, but there was a worried look on Maureen's face that Loretta couldn't ignore.

"You don't look that happy, Mama." Loretta joined Maureen on the couch. "If I was you, I'd be turning somersaults all over this room if I was about to marry a man like Mel. You look more like you about to bury him instead of marry him."

"I am happy. It's just that I was thinkin' about Mama Ruby. I know she had some strange notions, but do you think she would have accepted Mel?" Maureen said in a sad voice.

"Shoot no! Even though Mel is the kind of man that no woman could deny."

Both of Maureen's eyebrows shot up. "What do you mean by that?"

"Huh? Oh! I mean, no *normal* woman can deny how wonderful he is. He's cute, he makes good money, and he's funny and generous. What more could a woman ask for? Everybody knew that Mama Ruby was no normal woman, so she could have never appreciated a man with all that Mel got goin' for him."

Maureen shrugged. "Yeah, that's right, I guess." She gave Loretta an affectionate pat on her arm. "Don't worry, baby. Someday you'll marry a man with all that goin' for him."

"I know I will," Loretta said with a sniff.

Loretta didn't feel the least bit guilty about betraying her mother.

If anything, she felt that Maureen was betraying her and Mel! The most potent part of Loretta's logic, and the most ridiculous, was the fact that Maureen didn't love Mel—and she made no secret of it. There had to be hundreds or thousands of women in America who would have fallen in love with Mel the moment they laid eyes on him like Loretta had. But this was almost like a catch-22 situation. Loretta didn't want Maureen to have Mel on a permanent basis because she wanted to marry him someday. For now, she wanted access to him seven days a week, and the only way she could do that was for Maureen to marry him so he could move in. In a way, that would make it seem like she was already his wife, Loretta decided. She knew that once Mel moved in, they would be in each other's arms every time Maureen turned her back. It was an underhanded way to land a husband, but Loretta had a feeling that whoever said "all's fair in love and war" had probably been in a similar situation.

"I can't wait to see what it's like to actually live with a man," Maureen said, sounding almost like a giddy teenager herself.

"It'll be nice to have a man around to take care of us." Loretta giggled with a glazed look on her face.

Maureen gave her a surprised look. "We don't need a man to take care of us. I can take care of myself and you. I've been doin' it for years," she said in a stiff voice.

"Mama, I know that, but you know what I mean. Me and you never lived with a man before. It'll be nice to have him on the premises at all times in case we need a leaky faucet or somethin' else fixed."

Maureen didn't bother to remind Loretta that whenever they needed something fixed, she had always taken care of that herself too. "Yeah, it'll be nice to have a man around in case we need somethin' fixed." Maureen sucked in some air and gave Loretta a look that made her tense up. "Sugar, I need to ask you somethin' and I need for you to be honest with me. Do you love Mel?"

Loretta gasped so hard she almost swallowed her tongue. "What?"

"What I mean is, do you think you will ever love Mel the way you probably would have loved your real daddy if he hadn't died?"

"Oh." Loretta was so relieved she almost peed on herself. "I think I could . . . uh . . . love Mel."

"I was hopin' you'd say somethin' like that. The thing is, I'm doin' this more for you than for myself. You started pesterin' me for a daddy as soon as you learned how to talk. Catty, Fast Black, and even your uncle Virgil seem to think that it would be a good thing for me to marry somebody."

"You won't be just marryin' *somebody*, Mama. You will be marryin' *Mel*. A woman like you couldn't do no better unless you had a fairy godmother helpin' you." Loretta laughed.

Maureen nodded and laughed, too, even though she didn't like Loretta's last remark. "I hope you'll still feel that way about Mel once he moves in with us and gets settled. Him livin' with us will be a whole lot different from him just visitin'. He can't tell me or you what to do now, but once he becomes the man of the house, he might set up a few rules."

"I don't have no problem followin' rules," Loretta scoffed. "Ever since I was in first grade, I've been gettin' nothin' but straight As in citizenship."

"Followin' rules in school is different. A stepdaddy might have different expectations that you probably won't like."

"Mama, me and Mel have been workin' together for a long time now. Everything he tells me to do is for my own benefit. He works real hard to get modelin' jobs for me. He and I have been gettin' along just fine so far, so I think I can handle him livin' with us."

"Workin' with him is one thing. Livin' with him is a different story. I know you are growin' up, and pretty soon you are goin' to get more involved with boys. Right?" Maureen dipped her head and stared at Loretta with a knowing look on her face.

Loretta blinked. "Uh-huh."

"With a strong male presence in here, those little funky-tail boys you know will think twice about makin' a fool out of you, I hope."

Loretta blinked some more.

"I hope that you will mind Mel and continue to treat him as good as you have been doin' ever since we met him. I want you and him to be even closer than you already are. Most of the men in my life over the years didn't want to get too serious with me because they didn't want a ready-made family, but that's exactly what Mel wants. He wants to be a daddy." Maureen laughed. "I'm sure he won't mind you callin' him that. It's got a nice ring to it, huh?"

"Uh-huh." Loretta looked away and took a deep breath.

"I'm goin' to call him up and ask him to come over here so I can tell him to his face that I'll marry him," Maureen said with a sigh and rose from the couch. She finished her wine. Then she reached for the telephone on the end table and dialed Mel's number. He answered right away. "I need to talk to you about somethin'," she told him.

"Oh? Wh-what about?"

Maureen laughed. "I would rather say it to you in person."

Well, if she's laughing, it can't be anything for me to be too concerned about, Mel thought. "It's kind of late. Is it somethin' that can wait until tomorrow?"

"I guess it can wait. I've already discussed it with Lo'retta," Maureen said.

"Oh?" Maureen's response made Mel's chest tighten. It made Loretta's chest tighten too. "Maybe I should come over there right away, huh?" he said.

Loretta held her breath.

"Mel, it can wait until tomorrow," Maureen said, laughing some more. Loretta was happy that Maureen was in such a jovial mood. "I'll call you tomorrow and you can decide when you can come over."

"No, it can't wait," Mel said quickly. "I want to know what's going on. I'll come over there as soon as I can."

Maureen took a deep breath and exhaled so slowly tears pooled in her eyes. "All right. I won't keep you in suspense. I didn't want to say it over the phone, but I'll marry you if you still want me to," she said in a shy voice.

"Oh, baby, that's wonderful!" Mel hollered. "I'm so glad to hear that!" He wiped bullets of sweat off his face and rubbed his chest. He was so relieved he felt light-headed. His dirty little secret was still intact.

Loretta was even more ecstatic than Mel. The last thing she

wanted was for her mother to find out that she had had a man in her bed tonight.

Maureen found out anyway. A few minutes before Mel arrived, she decided to take out the trash. On her way to the Dumpster in the backyard, she stumbled and fell against the porch banister, dropping the large garbage bag. Along with empty milk cartons, dried bones, and other debris, a used condom rolled out and landed at her feet.

CHAPTER 15

*L*ORETTA HAD RETURNED TO HER ROOM AND SHUT HER DOOR BY THE time Maureen finished emptying the trash and got back inside.

Maureen didn't bother to knock like she usually did. She opened the door to Loretta's room and entered, with the nasty condom dangling on the end of a twig. "What the hell is this?" she yelled, waving the twig in Loretta's stunned face.

Loretta gasped and almost rolled off her bed. She couldn't believe that she'd been busted.

"I asked you what the hell this is!" Maureen hollered.

"I . . . I . . ." Loretta stood up by the side of her bed, trembling so hard her teeth rattled. "Mama, I . . . I—"

"You had . . . you had . . ." Maureen stopped talking because it was difficult for her to continue. The words felt like poison sliding off her tongue. "You had *sex* tonight in this apartment, didn't you?"

Loretta's eyes almost popped out of her head. "Who, me?"

"Yes, you!"

"Mama, let me explain!"

"Explain what? You don't need to do that! I know about you messin' around with boys in here when I'm gone, and I know it's been goin' on for a while. I found a condom wrapper on your bedroom floor last year! You'll stop your shenanigans after Mel moves in here. I don't expect you to be perfect when it comes to boys—I wasn't. I did my share of foolin' around when I was a teenager, but I had a lot more respect for my mama than you have for me, girl."

A suspicious look crossed Loretta's face. "Do you mean to tell me that you never got busy with a boy in Mama Ruby's house?"

Maureen froze. She didn't have the nerve to tell Loretta that she had not only given her virginity to Bobby Boatwright in Mama Ruby's house, but also it had happened *in the upper room*—the only place outside of heaven that Mama Ruby had held as much regard for. Had Mama Ruby found out that Bobby Boatwright had even poked his head into the upper room, let alone entered it and had sex with Maureen, he would have been "residing" in the cemetery right now instead of Seattle with his third wife and their four kids.

"I did have sex in Mama Ruby's house, but I didn't disrespect her by leavin' condom wrappers and used condoms where she could find them!" Maureen was so hurt and disappointed she wanted to scream.

"Mama, I'm sorry. It won't happen again, honest to God!" Loretta swore. From the wounded look on her face, you would have thought that she was the injured party in this case.

"I had always hoped . . . I didn't want you to do . . . what you did . . . this soon. A child your age should not be havin' sex!"

"A child? I am not like other girls my age, Mama. You should know that by now. You tell me all the time that I'm 'goin' on twenty-five.'" Loretta let out a very nervous laugh.

"You ain't twenty-five yet. Don't start actin' old before your time. You'll be old soon enough and you'll be wishin' you could be young and innocent again." Maureen shook the twig with the condom on it in Loretta's face again. "I am so disappointed in you, Lo'retta. Real disappointed."

"I said I was sorry, Mama." Loretta bowed her head. Then she looked back up with a pleading look on her face. "Don't be mad at me."

"All I want to know is, was it worth it?" Maureen asked, her voice cracking.

Loretta bowed her head again and shook it. "No, ma'am. It wasn't worth it."

Maureen held her breath and shook her head too. Then she

closed her eyes for a moment and shook her head again. "Was it the Warren boy or the Harris boy?"

"Uh, neither," Loretta said in a broken voice. "It's a boy you don't know. His family moved here last year from . . . uh, Memphis. His whole family is real snobby, so they keep to themselves. That's why you don't know them."

"Well, this boy can't be too snobby if he's over here makin' a fool out of you!" Maureen shouted.

Maureen was too tired to give Loretta the whupping she deserved. Maybe if she had done that last year when she found that condom wrapper, they wouldn't be having this conversation now. Loretta stood in the middle of the floor with a pitiful look on her face. "Look, I know you will do things that I don't want you to do. I know I can't stop you, but don't let some funky-tail boy make a fool out of you. Be better than that."

"I will, Mama. Anyway, that funky-tail boy already kicked me to the curb for some bowlegged Cuban girl. Before he left here tonight, he told me he was through with me."

"See there! That's what boys do! You got a lot goin' for you, Lo'retta. If you really want to be a supermodel, you have to put your hormones on hold. Don't let some boy ruin your future. You work too hard, and I don't want it all to be for nothin' at the end of the day."

"I know. I will take your advice. Honest to God, I will," Loretta said, even crossing her heart with her fingers.

"Uh, now this is between you and me and whoever that boy is. If you plan to be sneakin' around with him in the future, or any other boy, the least y'all can do is get a cheap motel room. I'm not goin' to have you doin' your business under my roof—not at your age— and please make sure your boyfriends *always* use protection!"

"Mama, can we drop this subject? I get the message," Loretta snapped, flopping back down onto her bed.

"You better get the message! I still know how to swing a switch, girl!"

"You finished?" Loretta rolled her eyes. "Anything else you got to say about this?" She snatched a *Glamour* magazine off the side of her bed and started to flip the pages.

"I don't want Mel to know what you've been up to tonight. He'd be so disappointed. I know it won't be official until I marry him, but he already treats you like his own daughter."

Loretta shrugged. "I know, I know," she sighed, not even looking up from her magazine.

"Or your uncle Virgil. He'd be so hurt. I already told him about that condom wrapper I found. He's the only family we have out here in Florida now, and he's had enough misery in his life." Maureen blew out a tortured breath and glanced at her watch. "Well, I guess I need to go call Virgil and tell him I'm goin' to marry Mel." Maureen paused and shook her finger at Loretta. "You can't have no company or go to the mall with Mona for two weeks! Do you understand me, girl?" Maureen shouted. "Now you put that magazine away and get some rest."

"Yes, ma'am," Loretta mumbled, rolling her eyes as soon as Maureen looked away.

After Maureen had disposed of the condom, she went back into the kitchen and picked up the telephone to call Virgil. He was happy to hear that she was going to marry Mel.

"I don't want you to spend the rest of your life alone," Virgil said. "I just hope Mel is the right one."

"Well, from the way my love life has been goin', Mel is the *only* one. If I don't marry him, this might be my last chance. But . . ."

"But what?"

"But maybe I should just be engaged to him for a while first. Like Mama Ruby was with Slim, that old man that died a month after she did."

"Why?"

"Just to be sure," Maureen answered.

Virgil choked on some air. "Mama Ruby and Slim stayed engaged for over twenty years, and they was no closer to gettin' married when she died. You ain't Mama Ruby, so don't do none of the crazy shit she did. Besides, Mel might not want no long engagement. From what you keep tellin' me, he is anxious to move in with you and Loretta. You done already made it clear to everybody that you won't live with a man unless y'all married."

"Yeah. I just don't want to make a mistake."

"Mo'reen, you won't be the first person to make a mistake. Makin' a mistake is a good way to learn what to do and what not to do. Marry the man and if it don't work out, get a divorce, girl. I married the wrong woman the first time, or she married the wrong man, whatever way you want to look at it. We got a divorce and moved on and I'm with a better woman now. If Mel turns out to be the wrong one for you, you will find out soon enough. You will eventually find the right man, if you lucky."

A few minutes after Maureen's conversation with Virgil, Mel arrived with a bottle of red wine. He gave her a very wet kiss before he said a word. "Baby, you've made me the happiest man in Florida!" He caressed Maureen's chin.

"I'm happy, too, Mel. I think marryin' you is what I need to do, and I'm glad you didn't give up."

"Oh, I love hearin' you say that!" Mel kissed Maureen again and then he glanced around the room. "Where's Loretta?"

"In bed, but I don't think she's asleep yet. Go say hello to her while I get the wineglasses," Maureen said over her shoulder as she headed toward the kitchen.

Mel set the bottle of wine on the coffee table and headed toward Loretta's room. She had been listening at her door, so when he entered her room, she was already standing in the middle of the floor with a huge smile on her face.

"Hello, sweet thing," Mel whispered, glancing over his shoulder, then back to Loretta. "I'm sorry I had to rush off this evenin'."

"She found the condom wrapper on my floor last year from the first time you and me did it here, and she found the used condom in the trash this evenin'! I told her that I was with some boy that already dumped me," Loretta hissed, looking over Mel's shoulder. "I thought you had flushed that damn thing down the toilet tonight like you always do!"

"Dammit! I meant to, but you know how worked up you had me. We'll be more careful from now on," Mel replied, burying his nose in Loretta's hair. The scent of her green-apple shampoo made him dizzy with lust. He wanted to grab her and fuck her brains out again. He was just as excited now as he had been when he was on top of her a couple of hours earlier. He was not too worried about getting some release because he knew that Maureen would take care of him before the night was over. Now that she had agreed to marry him, there was just no telling how hard she would work to please him once they made it to her bedroom. He would go home with a smile on his face for the second time tonight.

"Kiss me." Loretta's arms were already wrapped around Mel's neck like a necktie. "I said kiss me, dammit!" she said again, pulling him closer.

"Now you behave yourself!" he ordered, pushing her away. "It's too risky! We can't be taking chances when she's in the house. Listen, I've got another shoot lined up for you in Miami Beach in a couple of days. It's the last part of the Jupiter dress store contract that we have to fulfill. My client is comping me a room at the hotel where we'll be shooting, so you and I can hook up for a little while there and celebrate." Mel paused and gave Loretta a triumphant look. "We did it, babe! Your mama and me are getting married. I'll be living here with you and we can be together a lot more than we are now. Just the way we planned it." Despite how much Mel hated women, he still loved what they could do for him. He would never get tired of that.

"Let's not talk about you gettin' married to my mama. I'd rather talk about us." Loretta paused and gave Mel a dreamy-eyed look. "That little romp we had this evenin' only made me hotter. I want to make love again so bad, I can barely stand still!" That was for sure. She kept shifting her weight from one foot to the other, almost hopping like a rabbit.

"So do I, baby! I just can't fuck any more tonight!"

"Not even my mama?"

"Huh?"

"Don't you think *she'll* want some dick tonight?"

"Uh, she most likely will," Mel said, nodding. "Baby, we've come a long way, but I have to continue to play my part, and I have to play it right. It won't be easy and I'd rather get my groove on tonight with you again, but what the heck. If your mama wants me tonight, I have to do what I have to do."

"Just don't enjoy it too much," Loretta advised.

"I won't," Mel grunted, rolling his eyes. "Now you get back to bed and let me go spend some time with your mama. The last thing we want is for her to change her mind about marrying me! Then we'll be right back where we started."

Mel gave Loretta such an extreme French kiss she almost choked on his tongue. Afterward, he wiped his lips with the back of his hand and returned to the living room. He plopped down next to Maureen on the couch and kissed her the same way he had just kissed Loretta.

CHAPTER 16

"*W*HAT TOOK YOU SO LONG? IS LORETTA STILL UP?" MAUREEN ASKED Mel as soon as his lips left hers. She draped her arm around his neck, pleased to see such a sparkle in his eye.

"Uh, I had to take a leak. My bladder was about to explode. And, yeah, Loretta was still up, but she was so tired she wanted to get to sleep real fast. She's real happy that I'm going to be her daddy," Mel said, pouring himself a glass of wine. He crossed his legs, hoping to hide his massive erection.

"I . . . Your hands are shakin' like leaves," Maureen noticed. "I know you must be real nervous about us gettin' married. Especially after I put you off for so long. That's all right because I'm nervous too," she chortled, patting his knee. She didn't notice that his knee was shaking too. "I know we've been together for a while, but marriage is such a big step, so I guess it's normal for us to be nervous."

"Now don't you worry your pretty self about anything. Everything's going to be just fine," Mel said. He sniffed and took a long drink from his wineglass. "So when do you want to do it? As soon as possible I hope."

"Yeah. We'll work on a date later. Listen, us gettin' married is not the only thing I wanted to talk to you about tonight."

"Oh? What else did you want to talk about?" Mel asked, his chest tightening, his blood pressure rising. It was stressful being who he was. At the rate he was going, he was bound to have a heart attack or a stroke, so he told himself to slow down.

"What about your family?" Maureen asked, giving him the kind of goo-goo-eyed look that made him want to laugh out loud.

Mel's jaw dropped. "My family? What about my family?"

"I know you said you don't have much to do with them, but don't you want your mama and your sisters to know you decided to get married again? They might want to come down here for the weddin'. Even though you put them on the top of your shit list, I'd still like to meet them someday."

"I really don't want to discuss my family right now. Like I already told you, I am not that close to my folks." That was putting it mildly. Mel hadn't spoken to any members of his family in over a year. He had not responded to the few messages that his mother and sisters had left on his answering machine. He had sent his mother a card on her birthday and last Christmas. He didn't think she deserved one for Mother's Day, so that was one card he would never send. As far as those bitch sisters of his were concerned, he would never send them any kind of card, period. "Some families will never be close. Didn't you tell me that you had folks somewhere in Louisiana that you haven't spoken to since you were a child?"

"That's true," Maureen admitted with a mild groan. "And that's only on my mama's side. I don't know a thing about my daddy's folks. After he took off, he never even tried to contact me or my mama. Oh, well. Like you said, some families will never be close."

"To be honest—and I hate to admit this—I don't care if I ever see my folks again. They caused me a lot of misery that I would rather not discuss right now. It's too . . . painful," Mel barely managed to say. He had to force himself not to break down and cry.

Maureen shook her head in pity. "In that case, I won't mention your family again unless you do. I guess we just need to keep our minds on ourselves, and especially on Lo'retta. I have a feelin' she's goin' to need more supervision than ever these next few years."

Even though Maureen had told Loretta she didn't want Mel to know that she had had sex with some knuckleheaded boy in her bedroom, Maureen now felt this was something she shouldn't keep from him. He would have to know about it sooner or later. Especially since he was going to be in such an important position in her and Loretta's life now. Mel had a right to know what he was getting into. It might even make him change his mind about marrying Maureen and becoming the father of a teenager.

"Baby, what's wrong?" Mel asked. "Is Loretta in trouble?"

"I really hate to start dumpin' loads of shit on you already, but it's important for you to know what all you are gettin' yourself into. You don't have any kids, so you don't really know what raisin' one is all about."

"I had two older sisters. I saw what we all put my mama through. I decided a long time ago that I didn't want any kids," Mel informed Maureen. "I don't want to be tied down with that responsibility."

Maureen's jaw dropped and she gave Mel a sharp look. "That's what I'm talkin' about! If you don't want to be bothered raisin' kids, especially one that ain't even yours, why do you want to marry me? My daughter will be livin' with me at least until she finishes high school, and that's two more years from now."

"I realize that," Mel replied. He held up his hand. "You've pretty much raised your daughter already, so there won't be much for me to do. Like you just said, she'll be on her own when she finishes school."

"Until then, though, she's a big responsibility," Maureen croaked. "Two years is a long time."

"Maureen, I am the one who brought up marriage in the first place. Don't you know me well enough by now to see that I know what I'm doing? If I thought for one minute that Loretta was going to be a problem, I would have been out of your life by now."

Maureen rose up off the couch high enough to look behind her toward the hallway that led to Loretta's bedroom. "I'll be right back," she said in a low voice as she stood up. She darted across the floor and tiptoed down the hall. She stood in front of Loretta's door and listened for a couple of minutes. Then she tiptoed back to the living room and sat down next to Mel.

"Is everything all right?" he asked, puzzled and curious.

Maureen leaned her head toward his. "I found out that my daughter is, uh, havin' sex," she blurted. She took a long drink from her wineglass. "For at least a year now."

"Oh me, oh my," Mel muttered, sounding reasonably alarmed and disappointed. "Well, I'm surprised that she held out this long. I mean, she is a teenager. A lot of young girls today start doing it at twelve and thirteen." Mel gave Maureen a sympathetic look and patted her shoulder. He drank some more wine. He was glad that it was potent enough to give him a nice buzz so quickly. He needed one to get through this night. "Face it, Maureen. Kids nowadays are fucking the hell out of each other. With people like Madonna and Prince rubbing sex in their faces all the time, it's no wonder."

"Tell me about it, but I always told Loretta that when she got ready to have sex to let me know. I wanted to make sure she was protectin' herself properly."

"Loretta is a very mature and responsible child. She wants to go places. She's not going to give that up to raise a baby. How do you know she's not protecting herself?"

"Oh, she's protectin' herself all right. I found a condom wrapper on her bedroom floor last year. I don't know when it got there or if that was the first one."

"How do you know she was the one who used it? She's got a couple of wild girlfriends. One of them could have been in her room with a boy. I see that Mona girl out at all times of the night. I wouldn't be the least bit surprised if she talked Loretta into letting her bring one of her horny boyfriends over here. You know how kids are these days. They cover for each other all the time."

Maureen shook her head. "It wasn't Mona or any of the few other girls that Lo'retta associates with. I asked her about it a little while ago and she admitted it. Whoever the boy is, he must have been here this evenin' too. I found a used condom in the trash tonight."

"Well, I'm sure she's just curious. It's normal. Let her grow up and learn from her mistakes. Don't hold on to her too tight the way you told me your mama did with you."

"My mama was not normal. She didn't want me to even *think* about boys, let alone screw one."

"Well, you didn't get pregnant by yourself—"

"True. But that was different. That boy ra— Uh, that boy . . ." Maureen couldn't finish the sentence. She wanted to forget about John French and how he had raped her in the blackberry patch behind Mama Ruby's house. She could never forget it if she told the wrong person, or any person for that matter. "My mama had a fit when I got pregnant."

"I don't think we have to worry about Loretta getting pregnant." Mel was so emphatic it startled Maureen.

"What makes you think that, Mel?"

"Like I just said, Loretta wants to go places."

Maureen felt better knowing that Mel was so optimistic. "You got a point right there, I guess." She sighed. "One good thing is that she and her boyfriend use condoms. There may come a time when they don't. I know how easy it is to forget to make a trip to the drugstore, and I know how easy it is for some boy to talk a girl into lettin' him make love to her without protection."

"Honey, don't get too worked up over this," Mel advised, patting Maureen on the back. "If it'll make you feel better, sit the girl down and have a long talk with her on a regular basis. Let her know that you are not being judgmental, just concerned. That way she'll know how much you care about what she's up to. See, the problem with most parents these days is they don't communicate with their children."

For someone who wasn't a parent, Mel sure had some reasonable theories when it came to raising kids. Maureen was so impressed that tears pooled in her eyes. She blinked hard and took a series of deep breaths.

After she felt more composed, she continued. "Most teenage girls don't want to discuss their sex lives with their mother. I know I didn't and neither did any of my girlfriends. I just don't want my child to grow up too fast. Too many emotions are involved when it comes to sex, and I don't want her to get hurt."

"Maureen, like I said, Loretta is a responsible young lady." Mel was getting tired of repeating himself, but he was prepared to say or do whatever was necessary. He had come too far and invested too much time and sex in Loretta and Maureen to give up now.

"Lo'retta admitted to me that havin' sex with that boy wasn't worth it, so maybe she won't do it again until she's older," Maureen said with a hopeful look on her face.

Mel nodded. "Uh-huh. I'm sure she won't. It's something you have to get used to. For girls Loretta's age and their lack of experience, the first few times can be a real letdown. Especially with some inexperienced, frisky boy that only cares about his own needs. I was like a jack-in-the-box with my first girl," Mel laughed. He didn't laugh long when he saw the sad look on Maureen's face. He cleared his throat and continued. "Loretta probably found her first few times just as painful and disgusting as most teenage girls, so you shouldn't worry about her becoming some kind of sexpot anytime soon. You can bet your bottom dollar that I will do my part to make sure she stays on the straight and narrow."

Mel's support was a blessing to Maureen. It pleased her to know that she was not going to have to deal with this situation alone. She didn't feel as agitated or as let down now. As a matter of fact, Mel's attitude made Maureen feel a little more empowered. He was just as concerned about Loretta's behavior as she was. He was going to be a good father.

"Thanks, Mel. I'm so glad to hear you say that. If you don't mind, I'd like to wait a little while before we get married."

Mel's breath caught in his throat. "Oh?" he croaked. "You got cold feet already?"

"No, not that. Now that we have this situation with Lo'retta, I'd rather wait until I feel a little more relaxed about that. What she did is a lot for me to take in. I don't want to get married feelin' the way I feel right now."

Mel kissed Maureen again and hugged her so hard he almost cut off her circulation. "Baby, whenever you're ready to get married, just let me know."

"I promise I won't make you wait too long." Maureen hauled off and kissed Mel so long he had to push her away so he could get some air.

No, Maureen didn't love Mel, but she loved that he was in her life at such a crucial time. Maybe he was right. Maybe it didn't take love to make a successful marriage—just two people with common sense and similar goals. Once they took that step, she was going to do everything she could to make him glad he married her, and she was going to do everything she could to make herself glad that she had married him.

CHAPTER 17

MEL FELT SORRY FOR OTHER MEN. HE HAD TWO BEAUTIFUL WOMEN in his life—one in the palm of his hand and her daughter in his bed whenever he wanted her. Some days they pampered him like he was a new puppy. He had never experienced so much adoration.

What was so ironic about this tragic comedy was the fact that even though he hated women, they gave him so much pleasure. That balance was the reason he was able to continue his charade so well. What more could a man ask for?

Unfortunately, despite the importance of the two women in his life and all of the fun he was having, each one got on his nerves in her own way. Loretta was a sexual pest. He enjoyed sex as much as the next man, but even he had some limitations. After all, he was not as young as he used to be. That Loretta was so frisky she pounced on him every chance she got. Like last Wednesday evening after that Parker Department Store shoot. She couldn't wait to get home or even to a motel so he could cool her off. He drove his SUV into an alley behind the mall where they humped each other like rabbits for half an hour. When they got back to Maureen's apartment, there was a message on the answering machine from her. She had informed them that she was going out for drinks with some coworkers and wouldn't be home until after around 8:00 or 9:00 p.m. Loretta wasted no time. After she'd made sure the doors were locked, she grabbed Mel by the hand and led him to her bedroom. The juice from their earlier tryst was still wet in the crotch of his boxers.

"You are going to kill me, girl," Mel had playfully complained as Loretta straddled him.

"Can you think of a better way to die?" she had huffed, tongue hanging out of her mouth like a dog.

"Not really. If I have to die before my time, getting fucked to death is the way to go, baby girl." Mel paused and pinched Loretta on the side of her butt. "Now roll over so I can hit it from behind."

Maureen was a totally different kind of "pest." She *claimed* she didn't love him, but the way she pampered him, she made him feel like he was the last man on earth. She liked to cook special meals for him, iron his boxer shorts, shave him, and do other silly shit on the spur of the moment. Last Sunday, she had surprised him with a platter of chicken that she had dipped in buttermilk batter and deep-fried. She liked to give him foot massages and back rubs when he least expected it. She took him around her brother and his wife, two miserable busybodies Mel didn't have any use for, but he never complained—at least not to her.

He didn't even complain when those two disgusting, ignorant, gossiping black crows Catty and Fast Black dropped in with their di-arrhea of nasty remarks. What a pair! He couldn't stand the sight of either of them; he wondered how they managed to keep men in their lives. And the way they meddled! One recent afternoon while Catty and Maureen were in the kitchen picking some collard greens and didn't know that Mel had entered the apartment, he had over-heard something that enraged him almost to the point of no re-turn.

"Girl, you and Lo'retta need to stop kissin' Mel's funky black ass all the time. *He ain't nobody!* The first time I laid eyes on him, I could tell he thought his shit didn't stink. If y'all don't stop spoilin' that sucker, you're goin' to have a fine mess on your hands—espe-cially after you marry him," Catty snarled. "Me, I wouldn't let him fuck me with Prince's dick."

That bitch! Mel could not believe his ears. He wouldn't fuck that dollar-store Jezebel with a dead man's dick.

Instead of making his presence known, Mel had tiptoed back out of the apartment, seething with anger. He wanted to cuss out the world for letting a woman like Catty roam around like a loose wheel. He had to hold his breath to keep from screaming like a banshee. He wanted to slap Catty's hag face off so he could dance in the street with joy. Since he couldn't do that, he had to get back at her another way. While she was in the kitchen with Maureen, probably still trashing him, he shoved a nail into one of the back tires on that rusty jalopy of hers. As bald and threadbare as the tire was, it wouldn't go flat right away, but it would be as flat as a pancake by the time she got halfway home. Hopefully she'd be on the freeway.

A few minutes after his mischief, Mel went back into the apartment. This time he whistled so the women would know he was present. Like the two-faced crone she was, Catty gave him a big hug, lying through her liver lips about how good it was to see him again.

"It's always nice to see you, Catty. You're looking as lovely as ever. Is that a new dress? It looks nice on you," Mel said, almost choking on his words.

"Yeah, it's new, but you should have seen me yesterday. I wore a frock that was even cuter than this one," Catty hollered with a cheesy grin. "I'm glad to see that all your taste ain't in your mouth like I thought it was," she added.

That did it. Mel had another treat for that bitch. When she and Maureen moved to the living room, he offered to get them some wine. Maureen declined, but being the alcoholic pig that she was, Catty jumped at the chance. Mel didn't think she deserved any of the good wine that Maureen kept in the cabinet—especially the bottles that he had paid for. He poured her a glass of the buy-one-get-one-free shit that Virgil had given to him and Maureen. Then he hawked the biggest wad of spit he could manage into the wineglass and stirred it with the same finger that he had just used to pick his nose. Catty gulped down the wine so fast he offered her some more. It was a good thing she declined and left a few minutes later because he had some more boogers and spit he wanted to get rid of.

Despite Maureen's meddlesome and obnoxious family and

friends, Mel managed to enjoy his life with her anyway. He had a good thing going, and he planned to keep it going for as long as possible. He was forty, so he didn't have a whole lot of time left to hit it really big and enjoy it. He had to keep Maureen and Loretta happy, especially since he still believed Loretta was going to be his ticket to ride. She was in such big demand now that he was more convinced of that than ever. There was no way he was going to let a bunch of countrified peasants ruin his plans! He couldn't wait for the right time to spirit Loretta off somewhere so he could have complete control of his future. Two more years to go . . .

Maureen didn't mention her concerns about Loretta's sexual habits to Mel that often, and she eventually stopped altogether. There had been no more evidence of her having sex in the apartment.

It had been a year since Maureen had agreed to marry Mel. He had been patient and not badgered her to set a date, but she didn't want to push her luck. She didn't want to risk losing out on what was probably going to be her last chance to be a married woman. However, during the year that she had put off the wedding date, she had almost secretly wished that Mel would change his mind. She was nervous about making such an important commitment. However, every time she even thought about backing out of the engagement, she thought about how disappointed Loretta would be. Maureen would never admit to her friends or her brother, but she felt like she had slipped and fallen into a spiderweb and couldn't get out. Therefore, she would make the best of the situation.

"Mel, I think we can go ahead and get married now. Lo'retta's been behavin' herself, so I don't have to worry myself about that anymore."

"I'm glad to hear that, baby. I was gettin' a little worried," Mel admitted.

"I figured you would be, but I had to get my mind right about Lo'retta first," Maureen reminded him.

"I'm sure that she'll continue to behave herself. She's seventeen now and more mature than ever. You've raised a fine daughter."

"Thanks for bein' patient enough to wait on me this long to get married. I think we'll be a happy family. I hope you don't mind if Lo'retta starts callin' you Daddy. That would make me very happy."

"I would like for her to do so if she wants to. I feel blessed knowing you feel this way, Maureen."

"If things continue to go well between you and her, maybe you can adopt her someday so we can all have the same last name. I'm sure Lo'retta would like that. As long as we keep an eye on her and make her realize how much we love her and don't want some horny boy to make a fool out of her, I bet she won't have time to be thinkin' about sex. Me and you gettin' married could be the best thing that ever happened to her, huh?"

"Could be," Mel agreed. "Could be . . ."

Loretta thought about sex every day and every night. Her most recent tryst with Mel occurred on Maureen's wedding night. Maureen and Mel had exchanged vows that evening at the courthouse. It was a day they would remember for a long time to come, and not just because it was the day they got married. While they were enjoying a celebratory drink in a downtown sports bar with a large-screen TV on each of its four walls, a news bulletin interrupted the regular program. A disturbing video came on showing several white police officers beating a black man named Rodney King in L.A.

"Holy shit," Mel said, looking around the bar. Other patrons, black and white, sat looking at the screens in slack-jawed amazement. "If that brother lives, he'd better take some Italian lessons."

"What for?" Maureen asked, her eyes glued to the screen directly in front of them.

"For when he moves to Rome and buys a villa with all the money he's going to win in a lawsuit," Mel said with confidence.

The black bartender slapped Mel's palm in agreement.

"I guess this'll be all we hear about for a while," Maureen predicted, shaking her head.

"This is one way we won't forget our wedding anniversary," Mel laughed. Maureen laughed, too, but it was a hollow laugh. The last thing she wanted as a reminder of the day she got married was the image of a black man being brutalized by the police.

After they left the bar, Mel took Maureen to a French restaurant they both loved, and they had a light dinner and more drinks. Then they went to Mel's place to collect the rest of his belongings.

After about fifteen minutes of vigorous sexual activity in Maureen's bedroom (with Loretta listening at Maureen's bedroom door with disgust), Maureen was so exhausted all she wanted to do was sleep. What she didn't know was that Mel had slipped a couple of sleeping pills into her wine at the restaurant so that she wouldn't be a problem later that night.

From around 2:00 a.m. until almost dawn, Mel and Loretta wallowed around in her bed like *they* had just got married.

This is the life, Mel told himself as he eased back into bed with Maureen. She was sound asleep. He gave her a quick peck on the cheek and then he dozed off too.

CHAPTER 18

A YEAR LATER, THINGS WERE BETTER THAN EVER. EVERYBODY WAS happy—at least that was what Maureen thought until Virgil brought up a subject that had never entered her mind.

"Don't you think Lo'retta and Mel spend too much time alone together?" Virgil asked Maureen during one of her visits to his house, which had become less frequent since she'd married Mel. Virgil didn't visit her as often as he used to, either. The more he got to know Mel, the less he liked him. Virgil had Mel's number, and he didn't care much for it. For one thing, his new brother-in-law was secretive and sneaky. The stupid grin that was plastered on his face every time Virgil saw him was as fake as an aluminum Christmas tree. No man could be so happy that every time a person saw him he was grinning like a country preacher.

"What? What in the world do you mean by that? Mel's her daddy now," Maureen said with an amused look on her face.

"Stepdaddy," Virgil clarified, folding his arms. He stood in the doorway of his living room, facing Maureen and his wife, Corrine, who were seated on opposite ends of the couch. A pitcher of iced tea and a plate of tea cakes sat on the coffee table.

"Whatever. Mel treats Lo'retta as good as a real daddy would, and she loves him the way she would a real daddy. I hear all kinds of stories from other women about how their kids don't get along with their stepdaddies." Maureen paused and looked around the room, then back at Virgil. She didn't like the concerned look on his face, and she couldn't understand why he was so worried about Loretta and Mel in the first place. Especially since he was one of the people who had encouraged her to marry Mel!

"Besides, Lo'retta and Mel work so well together. He's preparin' her so she will know how to deal with other people in the industry when she hits the big time," Maureen added with a broad smile. "On top of that, she's makin' more money from her catalog work in one day than I make at the lobster factory in a week. Now Mel is talkin' about takin' her to the next level. He's talkin' to the folks who run the boat shows and fashion shows for the A-list celebrities and those swimsuit people."

"That ain't what I meant. I'm glad Lo'retta's gettin' a lot of work, and I know you appreciate the beaucoup money she makes—not to mention the extra money Mel brings into the house."

"Well, what did you mean, then?" Maureen lifted her chin and gave Virgil a guarded look as she waited for him to respond. She didn't like this conversation and she was anxious for it to end.

"Mo'reen, I know it ain't my business, but I'm goin' to have to make it so," Corrine interjected. Her light brown face looked tired and thin. Hairy black moles dotted her chin and neck like bird droppings. It was hard to believe she had once been one of the prettiest women Maureen knew. "Lo'retta is a young teenage girl. She ought to be out spendin' more time with kids her own age."

"She does that," Maureen protested. "Just last Sunday after she came home from church, she went to the movies and the beach with Mona, that Ramsey boy who had a crush on her all through junior high school, and some girl named Toni Jean. She also sees her other teenage friends so much already that sometimes I have to remind her to keep her modelin' appointments. Thank God Mel stays on top of that."

Virgil and Corrine looked at each other, wondering the same thing: *What else is Mel staying on top of?*

"I don't know what y'all are gettin' at, but I know my child and I know that she is very responsible. As long as she is safe and happy, that's all I care about," Maureen stated.

"Don't you think *you* should spend more time with your daughter than you do now? That's all me and Corrine care about," Virgil said gently.

"If you kept closer tabs on her, you'd know for sure she's bein' responsible," Corrine added. "With all that extra money comin' in now, you don't even have to work if you don't want to."

Maureen shot a look at Corrine that was so hostile it frightened Corrine. "So what am I supposed to do? Quit my job at the lobster factory after I practically begged them to take me back, and then sit around the house watchin' talk shows and gettin' fat?" Maureen's eyes gazed critically up and down Corrine's thirty-pounds-overweight body.

Corrine sucked in her gut and folded her arms across the protruding belly she couldn't hide. "No, you don't have to quit your job if you don't want to," she replied. "You told us yourself that some days when you get home from work, Loretta and Mel don't come home until several hours later. They are also gone practically most of the weekend, every weekend. You don't have a problem with that?"

"Not really." The only problem Maureen had was Virgil and Corrine meddling in affairs that didn't concern them. It amazed her how people who had never raised a teenager liked to dole out unwanted advice to people in her position.

"Mel is a man, honey child," Corrine said with a sour look on her face.

"So?" Maureen refused to even consider what Corrine was insinuating. The idea of Mel and Loretta *together* was ludicrous. "For one thing, if Mel ever said or did anything inappropriate to Lo'retta, that girl would come up to me and tell me in a heartbeat. I know y'all still remember how she told on that college boy and that church deacon when they got out of line with her?"

Virgil and Corrine nodded, but Corrine still had that sour look on her face. The look on Virgil's face was not too sweet-looking either.

"I know y'all can find somethin' else to be worried about—somethin' that needs to be worried about," Maureen quipped.

"That's just what me and Virgil is doin'," Corrine said sharply, rotating her neck and puckering her lips like she was about to flood the room with a tidal wave of more ridiculous remarks.

But Maureen was not about to give Corrine the chance to do that. She checked the time. "Goodness gracious! I didn't realize how late it was," she said. She rose with her eyes still on her watch. "I need to haul ass!" She didn't really want to leave just yet, but she knew that if she stayed around longer, Corrine or Virgil would say something about Mel that would really upset her.

"You just got here a little while ago," Virgil reminded her, his hand in the air.

"You ain't goin' to stay for no fish?" Corrine asked, nodding toward the kitchen. "The only reason I thawed out them catfish in the first place was on account of you asked me to." Corrine didn't even bother to try hiding her disappointment. There was a pout on her face that belonged on a toddler.

Even though Maureen's mouth had been watering for some deep-fried catfish for days, she was too agitated to eat any now. She couldn't wait to leave. "Fast Black told me she was goin' to slide through here later on tonight. She can have my part of the catfish," Maureen mumbled, moving toward the door with her car keys already in her hand. "If y'all have any left over, maybe me and Mel can come over tomorrow and finish it off."

"Mo'reen, I know it sounds like we tryin' to get all up in your business—"

"*Sounds* like?" Maureen hollered, cutting Virgil off. "If you think it just sounds like y'all tryin' to get all up in my business, I would hate to see what it feels like if y'all really did get up in my business. I wish both of y'all would get your minds out of the gutter and cut poor Mel some slack. He had a real unhappy life in Chicago, and he don't need to go through the same thing here. He is my husband and I . . . I . . . uh, he is my husband." Even though she was defending Mel, Maureen could not bring herself to say she loved him. She knew she probably never would, but Mel had given up his freedom to be with her and help her raise Loretta. For that reason alone, he deserved some respect and credit. If he couldn't get it from her loved ones, he would definitely get it from her. Her hand was on the door and she was about to open it when Virgil padded over to her and wrapped his arms around her waist.

"I don't like to see you this upset, baby sister," Virgil told Maureen, rubbing her back. "We just tryin' to look out for you and Lo'retta, that's all. We want to make sure you stay on top of things."

Stay on top of things? Maureen had a great relationship with her daughter and her husband. Neither one of them had said or done anything for her to be concerned about. What things was she supposed to stay on top of?

Maureen didn't want to antagonize Virgil and Corrine any further, and she didn't want them to antagonize her any more. She had reached her limit of tolerance, but to keep the peace, she offered them a huge smile and said what she thought they wanted to hear. "I will stay on top of things from now on," she said, her voice cracking. She glanced at her watch again. "I better skedaddle. I don't like to be out drivin' too much after dark."

It was a long, slow, and difficult drive home for Maureen.

Instead of going directly to her apartment, she drove around until it got dark. She even cruised all the way into the heart of downtown Miami, shaking her head at all of the luxury cars lined up along the streets and the garishly dressed women strutting around like peacocks.

Maureen meandered down one unfamiliar street after another, trying to organize and make sense of the numerous thoughts occupying her tortured mind. Whenever her thoughts got as jumbled as they were now, they always included Mama Ruby.

"What will you do when I get married and leave home?" Maureen, seventeen at the time, had asked Mama Ruby that question one Sunday afternoon after they had come home from church.

Mama Ruby had rushed into the kitchen and started humming her favorite spiritual, "I Been in the Storm Too Long," as she stirred a pot of Chinese mustard greens on the stove. She didn't even bother to turn around as Maureen fidgeted in a chair at the table, wondering how she was going to tell Mama Ruby that she was pregnant.

"You ain't goin' no place," Mama Ruby casually told her. "As long as you got me, you don't need no husband. Marriage is too much trouble. How many times do I have to tell you that, girl?" It was hot and they were in the house alone, so all Mama Ruby wore was a half-slip that looked more like a white tent and a matching bra. She had draped the crisp white usher's uniform that she had worn to church around her shoulders like a cape.

When Mama Ruby turned around to face Maureen, Maureen could see the handle of the switchblade she always carried—even when she was in bed asleep or making love to one of her men friends or in church—sticking out of her bra.

"Don't you want grandchildren?" Maureen asked, swallowing hard. She touched her belly and pressed her lips together to keep from moaning, knowing that what lay in her belly, getting bigger each day, could mean certain death for John French. It didn't matter that Mama Ruby adored John. As a matter of fact, she used to look after him when he was a baby, so she regarded herself as a "mammy" of sorts in his case. Had she known that John had raped Maureen, she would have chastised him severely. It made no difference that John was white. Mama Ruby jokingly referred to herself as an equal-opportunity enforcer, and she had proven that on more than one occasion.

"What's wrong with you, girl?" Mama Ruby asked. "You know how much I love kids! I want me a bunch of grandbabies. You don't need no husband for that!"

"So how do I make those babies for you, then?"

"The same way I made . . . uh . . . you. Now, I know you human and bound to make mistakes. I sure did. You might get drunk and forget your religion and end up in some man's bed and get pregnant a few times. I won't have no problem with that. That could happen to anybody, and if you ask me, that's the best way to get a family. You don't need no husband to be cookin' and cleanin' for just so he can pester another woman after you done trained and groomed him!"

"You had a husband when you got pregnant with Virgil and another one when you got pregnant with me," Maureen reminded. "Two different men." Ruby had been married only once—to Virgil's father. The story that she and Virgil had concocted about Maureen's father had become so vague and inconsistent over the years that Maureen rarely asked about him. All Maureen and everybody else knew was that the "low-down, funky black dog" had deserted Mama Ruby before she gave birth to Maureen. The latest version of the story had him living in a foreign country with a Jewish woman.

"You see what that got me! Neither man was *man* enough to stay with me. Both of them mangy dogs left me while I was still pregnant, and even after I had y'all, neither one of them came to see his child."

"I know my daddy just up and left with that Jewish woman, but you shot and killed Virgil's daddy," Maureen piped in.

"That's another thing! It's on account of a *husband* that I got a police record. Me—a child of God! I bet Jesus wept when they threw me into jail that time." Mama Ruby snorted and began to speak more gently, even though she was still fired up and ready to condemn every man on the planet if she had to just to make Maureen see things her way. "See, marriage is like havin' your bowels blocked. Once you get that mess out of you, you'd be a fool to let it happen again. That's why I ain't in no hurry to marry Slim after all these years that me and him been engaged. I just let him think that we gettin' married so he'll keep bein' generous to us. Come taste these greens and tell me if they need more seasonin'."

That was the day that Maureen knew for sure she could never tell anybody the truth about how she got pregnant. Not even Virgil. He had enough problems of his own, so she couldn't understand why he was so worried about Loretta and Mel. She wasn't! Mel was a good man and Loretta was a good girl.

The biggest problem that Virgil had these days was trying to decide when he should tell Maureen that Mama Ruby had kidnapped her. With the way things were going in her life, he had gradually changed the "when" to an "if," and that made him feel better about the situation.

Despite his concerns about Mel's relationship with Loretta, Virgil was still pleased that Maureen was married. She seemed happy. She had everything she needed. Therefore, Virgil asked himself again, *What good would it really do if I tell her?*

Virgil had no idea that approximately two months later, he would revise his intentions again, and for the last time.

He would have no choice but to tell Maureen everything. . . .

CHAPTER 19

*T*O MAKE UP FOR THE HONEYMOON THAT THEY DIDN'T GO ON WHEN they got married last year, Mel offered to take Maureen on a Caribbean cruise. However, since they had recently spent an entire weekend with Loretta at Disney World celebrating her eighteenth birthday, Maureen promptly declined. She told Mel that she would rather spend the money on some new kitchen appliances.

Maureen did not need any new kitchen appliances. The stove and refrigerator she had now were less than three years old. There was another reason why she didn't want to go away with Mel on a romantic cruise and be holed up in a cabin with him for seven days. That reason made all the sense in the world to her. She felt that since she was going to spend the rest of her life with him now, she wanted to spend as little intimate time with him as possible. Now that she was married to Mel, she didn't enjoy having sex with him as much as she did before. Now she only did it when he initiated it, and even then, there were times when she "had a headache" or pretended to be asleep when he approached her in bed. It was bad enough that she had settled for a man she didn't love. Just dating him was one thing; marrying him was so final. In spite of all her reservations, Maureen promised herself that she would be a good wife and make the best out of the situation. She told herself that since they were both fairly young, she still had a lot of time ahead of her to enjoy sex with him again.

Maureen was so glad that Loretta was still in the home. With her barging into her bedroom whenever she felt like it, and often sitting between Maureen and Mel on the living room couch when they watched a TV program, Maureen didn't have to worry about getting too affectionate with Mel that often. And she was glad about that. No matter how much she tried, she couldn't bring herself to love him. She liked him, but she liked a lot of men. Since she had never been truly in love, she didn't know exactly how love felt.

The fact that Mel's touch sometimes made her skin crawl told her all she needed to know.

Not only did she feel guilty about her feelings, but also she had already begun to regret getting married. She told herself that as long as Loretta lived under the same roof with her, she would do her best to set a good example. What would her daughter think if she decided she didn't want to live with Mel after all and divorced him? Especially since Loretta had become even more attached to him since the wedding.

Each morning when Maureen opened her eyes and looked at Mel sleeping next to her with his mouth hanging open like a goldfish, she asked herself, *What in the world did I get myself into?*

"How come you been workin' fewer hours since you got married?" Catty asked Maureen one evening as they shared a bucket of hot wings in Maureen's living room.

Maureen let out a long, heavy sigh. "Virgil keeps tellin' me that I need to spend more time with Lo'retta. She sees more of Mel than she sees of me and Virgil thinks that's unhealthy."

"I'm glad you brought that up. I been meanin' to tell you that same thing myself. I ain't got no kids, so I don't know firsthand, but young girls these days ain't got no shame."

"What's that supposed to mean? My girl's got good sense," Maureen said defensively, reaching for her third hot wing.

"That's true. And that's the problem. Your girl is too smart and too pretty. But remember that time when Mama Ruby told you that a sword cuts both ways?"

Maureen stopped chewing and asked, "How did we get from you talkin' about my work hours to double-edged swords?" She wondered where Catty was going with this conversation. "Now that you mention it, Virgil told me that, too, a few years ago."

"See, a girl with good looks and brains can make a man do some strange shit. She can have him actin' like a fool," Catty stated. "You ought to know 'cause you seen *me* do it to Yellow Jack. Remember how I bamboozled him, wooing him into marryin' me just so I could get me some weddin' gifts and then I left him the day after we got married?"

"Woman, will you please stay on the subject of Lo'retta," Maureen complained. "I already know your whole life history."

"Anyway, Lo'retta is a gal with a lot of ambition. She wants to go places, hobnob with celebrities. Cruise around in limos and wear only the top designers' frocks. She told me her goal is to be on the covers of *all* the top women's magazines, especially the snooty white ones like *Cosmopolitan* and *Vogue*. She wants to strut her tail on them catwalks in Europe and shit. Every time she comes to my house, she goes through my *Ebony* magazines with the Fashion Fair pictures, talkin' about how much prettier she is than most of the models they use. Ridin' a high horse don't even come close to describin' Loretta. That girl is ridin' on a giraffe's neck."

"What's wrong with her wantin' to make it big? At least she ain't out in the streets runnin' around with a gang or doin' drugs."

"Look, until you got married, you worked them long hours at that lobster factory, leavin' Lo'retta on her own for hours on end. Too much time on a teenage girl's hands is a recipe for trouble. Do you remember how much mess we used to get into when we had a lot of time to ourselves durin' our teenage years?"

"Yeah, you and I used to sneak around and drink alcohol every chance we got. I even let Bobby Boatwright talk me out of my panties," Maureen recalled with misty eyes. "Every generation is goin' to do what they want to do no matter what people say or do. In my case, I had a mama the devil would run from, so I was very bold back then to do what I did, but I turned out all right."

"Mo'reen, Mel is your husband, but I suspect that Loretta looks at him as just a convenience for her benefit. You told me yourself that when you told her you didn't love him, it didn't even faze her. All she cared about was havin' a daddy, or so she claimed."

"Yes, I did tell her that and I told him the same thing. I wanted to be honest with them both about the way I felt. I did want to get married at least once in my lifetime, and from the way my life was goin', Mel was probably my last chance."

"Harrumph! Lord knows that ain't sayin' much. Anyway, you missin' my point about Lo'retta. My point is, I got a feelin' she is cookin' up a master plan. She's goin' to break Mel down. She is goin' to milk him like a pregnant Guernsey cow. Once he helps her get rich and famous, she won't have no more use for him. She'll drop him like a bad habit—real quick."

Maureen didn't even try to hide her exasperation. "Now, you look here, Catty. Not only is Mel a good man, but he's a smart man too. Do you think he'd let a teenager take advantage of him? The man is from Chicago. If the mean streets of Chicago didn't break him down, nothin' will."

"Harrumph! You can think whatever you want, girl. If you ask me, I say Lo'retta is goin' to pull somethin' out of a trick bag and then all hell will break loose. I can already smell the brimstone."

CHAPTER 20

"So what if Lo'retta is usin' Mel?" Maureen had never asked a guest to leave her residence before, but right now she was close to doing just that. However, she knew that it would do no good. Because whenever she saw Catty again, they would resume this conversation or one just as disturbing. Catty had arrived twenty minutes ago unannounced, but since she had come with a bucket of hot wings, Maureen had been happy to see her. "Everybody uses somebody in some way! People have used me and you, and we've used people from time to time. I could even say that Mel is usin' me. By movin' in with me, he'll be gettin' home-cooked meals every day and . . . and even sex whenever he wants it."

"He didn't have to marry you for that! He was already gettin' all of that!" Catty yelled. "Put a little more rum in the drink you should have made for me by now."

Maureen fixed two rum and Cokes and gave Catty the larger of the two glasses, which Catty snatched and immediately began to guzzle.

"Can we talk about somethin' other than Mel?" Maureen asked, returning to the other end of the couch and facing Catty.

Catty shook her head. "Uh-uh. Let me finish." She set her glass on the coffee table and gave Maureen a hot look. "I bet you wouldn't have married Mel if Mama Ruby was still alive."

Maureen took a drink from her glass and gave Catty a thoughtful look. "Him or anybody else," she responded in a calmer voice.

Catty cocked her head to the side and smirked. "Truth be told, if Mama Ruby was still alive, she probably would have chastised Mel by now and buried him in her backyard like she done with that—"

Maureen held up her hand. "Please don't go there right now. I know about all the people my mama chastised."

"I hope you never forget. Nobody loved you the way your mama did. All she wanted was for you to be happy."

"That is exactly what I want for my daughter," Maureen said with a sniff. "What I want you to tell me is why you think my child is goin' to start usin' my husband?"

Catty reared back in her seat and gasped. "What do you mean 'goin' to start'? She done already crossed that bridge. I can see that with my eyes closed!" Catty hollered, giving Maureen an incredulous look. "Mel is a good photographer and he's makin' some good connections. That brother has been workin' hard for years and pretty soon it's goin' to pay off. He knows how to bullshit the folks with all the modelin' work so they'll kiss his ass to work with him. He fits right in with that uppity crowd. He got everything it takes for that, even a nonthreatenin' appearance."

"What's his appearance got to do with anything? He's smart and he does good work."

"Do you think them uppity Miami department stores and modelin' folks—even the black ones—would have a damn thing to do with Mel if he was some ignorant-actin' porch monkey with gold teeth and his hair in cornrows?"

Maureen gave Catty a disgusted look, but she couldn't stop herself from laughing. "I am glad that not everybody thinks the way you do. Ugly people wouldn't have a chance gettin' jobs."

"Speakin' of jobs. There is a spot open at my work," Catty announced. "I think you need a change."

"I don't want to work in nobody's kitchen," Maureen replied, shaking her head. "Especially not at that nursin' home you work for. Fast Black told me all those old people eat is mush, grits, and baby food."

"That's a damn lie," Catty snarled, tossing a chicken bone back into the bucket. "We cook steaks and bacon and eggs and everything else regular folks eat. Even chicken wings," she added, reaching for another wing. "Yeah, we do have to mash up certain things for certain patients, but it ain't that bad. Anyway, the openin' I'm talkin' about ain't in the kitchen. It's a nurse's aide spot. You'd be assistin' the nurses. It's part-time, just three days a week, but a lot more money than what you make now at that dead-end-ass job at the lobster factory. They got a bunch of cute single orderlies and cooks workin' there. I got me a hot date with this real sweet brother from Haiti this weekend. They hired him to be the head cook on the day shift." Catty paused and a glazed look appeared on her face.

"Oh?" Maureen didn't exactly love her current job and never had. Not only was it a 'dead-end-ass job' like Catty said, but it was also boring. It paid her bills, though, and would have to do until she decided to look for something else. Maybe now was a good time for her to do that. "Can you put in a good word for me, please?"

"They keep askin' me and everybody else that works there if we know of anybody who would want the job. The last three women that came in to apply, they got hired on the spot."

"Oh? If they can't keep people in this position and are willin' to hire somebody on the spot, there must be somethin' real wrong with the job," Maureen pointed out, giving Catty a concerned look.

"There ain't nothin' wrong with it." Catty waved her hand dismissively. "The only thing wrong is they keep hirin' the wrong people. You just might be the right person."

Maureen blinked. "You could be right, but I was hopin' to eventually do somethin' glamorous, like bein' a hostess in a fancy restaurant or a cocktail waitress in one of the upscale nightclubs where all the famous people and good-looking single men our age party at. The way things look right now, I'll never meet Mr. Right."

"Bah! Listen to you talk. You done gave up your chance of meetin' a Mr. Right—or did you already forget about Mel?"

Maureen giggled. "Well, if I take this nursin' home job and me and Mel don't make it—like if he leaves me—maybe I can hook up with a cook like you did, huh?"

"I don't see why not." Catty nodded but then a troubled look slid across her face. "You know, it's a damn shame when women like us have to look for our soul mates in a nursin' home, ain't it?"

"As long as that soul mate ain't one of the patients." Maureen sighed.

"You want me to talk to the folks tomorrow about you applyin' for that job?"

"Yeah. Why not?" Maureen replied. "What do I have to lose?"

"Don't get your hopes up too high about meetin' no man there. There is too much competition. Half of the women on staff, married ones included, be eyeballin' the few men that's left."

"Oh, I wasn't serious about meetin' another man. I'm goin' to make my marriage work. Besides, for years I prayed to Jesus for Him to send me my soul mate, but because of my bad luck, even He couldn't perform that miracle," Maureen moaned.

"That's still true today," Catty agreed.

"Mel's as close to a soul mate as I'm goin' to get, I guess."

Maureen had no idea just how wrong she was, but she would soon find out.

CHAPTER 21

CATTY GAVE MAUREEN THE NURSING HOME DIRECTOR'S NAME AND A telephone number to call her up to set up an interview.

Two days later, while on her lunch break at the lobster factory, Maureen went to the pay phone in the employee break room and called up the nursing home director. It was the strangest telephone conversation she had ever experienced in her life.

"When can you start?" Mrs. Larsen asked immediately after Maureen had identified herself and the reason for the call. "Catty has already told me so much about you and what a hard-working, dedicated, and capable girl you are! I can't wait to put you on the payroll."

"Huh? You mean I got the job?" Maureen asked with an amused look on her face. Either the woman was kidding or she had Maureen confused with somebody else. "Don't I have to do an interview first?"

"An interview? This is the interview, sugar," the woman said quickly. "Didn't I already say that?"

"Uh, no, ma'am, you didn't."

"Well, it is."

"Okay, but what about the application, ma'am? Shouldn't I fill that out first?"

"You can do that when you get here. We are so shorthanded, we need somebody in here right away. This place is like a madhouse. Now, Catty has told me all I need to know about you, and Catty is a straight-up Christian girl, so I know I can go by anything she tells me. When can you start? Today? Tomorrow?"

"Uh, I'm still employed and I can't just up and walk off this job today and start workin' for you tomorrow, ma'am," Maureen said. For one thing, Maureen didn't want this prospective new employer, or any new employer for that matter, to think she was the kind of woman who would leave one job for another at the drop of a hat. Dependable workers didn't do that.

"Oh. I was under the impression that you really needed this job and were already available," Mrs. Larsen said, obviously disappointed. "I can hold the position open until week after next. If you can't start before then, when can you start?"

Maureen could hear the desperation in the woman's voice, but she wasn't going to let that bother her. She had worked with white women before, so she knew how melodramatic and hysterical they could be sometimes. "I don't know right now," Maureen said.

"I need to know for sure by close of business tomorrow. The other girl left without notice, and now Rhonda Sue, she's the girl who works the other four days in the week, has had to do double duty, and that's not easy for a girl in her sixties. So if we don't get her some help soon, she might end up a patient here herself."

"All right. I am pretty sure I can start on Monday." Maureen paused and tried to gather her thoughts. This was happening too fast for her. She didn't feel comfortable committing to a new job without even knowing what she would be required to do. "First I need to know exactly what it is that will I be doin'? I don't know much about what goes on in a nursin' home. Workwise, I mean. Would I be kept busy enough so I won't get bored?"

"Bored? Honey, the only people who have time to get bored around here are the dead ones—the patients, I mean. Speaking of dead folks, you wouldn't have a problem dealing with the dearly departed, I hope. This is a nursing home, so the death rate around here is pretty high." Mrs. Larsen paused but not long enough for Maureen to respond. "You'll be performing all kinds of interesting duties, honey child!"

"Like what?" Maureen hoped she didn't sound like she really wasn't that interested. She was interested. But she was more interested in knowing why this woman was willing to hire her so quickly and without checking references, work history, attendance record, or anything else. For all this woman knew, Maureen could have a lengthy criminal record or even be some kind of maniac on the loose.

"Listen up, now. You'll need a pair of white shoes, like the ones nurses and women who work in school cafeterias wear. We'll supply two sets of scrubs, but you'll have to pay for additional sets. Once you get here and we get you settled and on the payroll, we will have you go through the required CPR training. Then we'll bring you up to speed on a few light nursing procedures, like dressing a minor wound or monitoring a scab or a bedsore. You don't have any serious allergies, do you? Do you catch things easily?"

"Not that I know of. Why?"

"Uh, accidents happen around here from time to time. One of the patients might accidentally sneeze in your face or dribble something on your hand and you might forget to wash it. If you have even an itty-bitty cut or scab, something getting in it might be a problem for you. You will help the patients with their grooming, and you will serve meals to the ones who are too fussy or unable to eat in the dining room. Now, let me think what else. Oh! You'll keep them occupied and entertained by reading to them or taking them for walks, and you'll help the less ambulatory ones in and out of bed or to the commode. You will be asked to assist with baths and bedpan procedures, and you'll have to help spoon-feed the ones who can no longer do it on their own. You'll do any and everything else that the nurses you assist don't do."

Maureen gulped in some air and swallowed so hard she had to rub her neck to keep it from throbbing. "Well, if you don't mind me askin', if the nurses' aides do all of that, what do the nurses do all day?" It was a reasonable question, Maureen thought.

"Oh, they have more to do than you can imagine. They administer shots and any other serious medication. They maintain the charts. If a patient falls and breaks a bone, only the nurses or doctors on call are authorized to assist. My nurses are so overworked that when quitting time rolls around, they leave this place running every single day. Now tell me, my dear, do you have any more questions?"

Despite the fact that Mrs. Larsen sounded even more impatient now, Maureen didn't want to make a firm commitment until she had all of the necessary information she needed. "What about salary and benefits?" she asked.

"You'll start at the bottom, sugar. Then you'll have to work your way up. Our starting salary is commensurate with all the other homes in the South Florida area."

"Well, I don't know what that is, ma'am."

"I'll tell you what. When you get here Monday morning, we can negotiate your salary. Then we can discuss all of the other benefits that go with the job, plus a few that we don't show on the books, such as a fifty-dollar cash bonus for whoever makes employee of the month and a Christmas-gift exchange. . . . Oh! You're not Jewish, Muslim, or into one of those mysterious Eastern religions, are you?"

"No, ma'am. I'm a straight-up Baptist. I was raised in the church, and my late mama was a devout Christian woman," Maureen said proudly. "So is my daughter and my husband."

"You're a Baptist! So am I. Good! We had a Muslim woman working here last month. I declare, Jesus must have wept every time she showed up wearing that burnoose—or whatever they call those things—on her head. Everybody was glad she only lasted a week, but right after that unholy episode, we had a Buddhist woman working here." Mrs. Larsen paused, sucking on her teeth and letting out a couple of loud sighs. "That woman just about scared the daylights out of everybody! She would chant all kinds of gibberish in the break room. It was a blessing when she left after just four days. Anyway, another bonus is that you can take home any leftover food at the end of your shift. Now, I hate to rush off, but I need to be in a meeting in five minutes. You need to be here no later than 6:00 a.m. on Monday morning. I normally work from nine to five, but until we get back on track, I'll be coming in at 6:00 a.m. If you get here before I do, go up to the girl at the front desk. As soon as I get in, I'll give you a brief orientation, go over salary and everything else, and then put you to work. It was nice talking with you, Maureen. Bye!"

Maureen listened to the dial tone and stared at the telephone for a few seconds before she returned to her workstation. She didn't know what to think now. She couldn't help but wonder what kind of place this nursing home really was for the director to be so anxious to hire somebody sight unseen. Her job at the lobster factory was about as loosey-goosey as a job could be, but even for that job she had been required to fill out an application, suffer through two interviews, and have her background checked!

Thanks to Mama Ruby cracking such a mean whip every day of Maureen's life, she was a responsible person. She didn't want to make Catty look bad for recommending her, and making her sound like some kind of superwoman at that. Mrs. Larsen sounded so desperate that Maureen didn't want to disappoint her. The least she could do was try the job out on a trial basis, but she didn't plan on telling Catty and Mrs. Larsen that part. Or Loretta and Mel, for that matter. When she had mentioned changing jobs to them the night before, they seemed very supportive and had already begun to plan their schedules around her new one.

"Baby, it's time for a change," Mel had told her, giving her an affectionate pat on the butt.

"I'm happy for you, Mama," Loretta said with a smile. "Workin' in a nursin' home ain't a job I'd want, but somebody's got to do it," she added with a grimace on her face.

"I'll be able to spend more time with you both," Maureen was happy to announce.

Mel and Loretta gave each other a sly look.

It was not easy for Maureen to leave the security of the lobster factory. It had been one of her security blankets for more than ten years now.

It was a sad departure. One of Maureen's coworkers rushed out and bought a farewell card and had everybody sign it. Two of the older women actually shed a few tears during the farewell cake and coffee break that they held for Maureen that Friday morning. Steve Faulk, Maureen's sad sack of a supervisor, insisted on taking her to lunch, and he gave her the rest of the day off with pay. With the card and a bouquet of assorted flowers, and a box that contained her personal items, Maureen left the lobster factory almost in tears.

So far, Mel seemed supportive about Maureen changing jobs, but he also made comments that made her wonder just how supportive he really was. "If this nursing home thing is what you really want to do, I wish you all the luck in the world," he told her, glancing at Loretta across the table as they ate dinner the following evening. He seemed to be more interested in the wineglass in his hand than he was in Maureen's new job. "I just hope you don't regret it."

"I feel the same way," Loretta volunteered.

"I will only have to work three days a week—Monday, Tuesday, and Wednesday. Now you and I don't have to wait to go to the mall in the evenin' or on weekends. We can do it on a Thursday or a Friday," Maureen told Loretta, squeezing her hand.

"You would rather be emptyin' smelly bedpans and wipin' old people's butts just so we can spend more time at the mall?" Loretta asked, wiggling her nose. "I liked visitin' you at the lobster factory after school, but I don't think I'll be visitin' you at that old folks' home. What were you thinkin'?"

The sudden shift in Mel's and Loretta's attitude and their comments worried Maureen, but she still managed to keep a smile on her face. "Lo'retta, I'm really doin' this more for you and Mel than me," she replied. Then she turned to Mel. "I'm a married woman now, and I want to spend more time in my home takin' care of my family."

Loretta stole a glance at Mel. He couldn't have looked more indifferent had he been attending a funeral for somebody he didn't like. However, when Maureen spoke again, he almost fell out of his chair.

"Virgil got on me about spendin' more time with you, Lo'retta," she said, smiling and rubbing Loretta's hand. Then she turned back to Mel. "Him and Corrine keep worryin' about you and Loretta spendin' so much time together alone."

The wine that Mel had just sipped almost spurted out of his mouth. He couldn't have looked more frightened if he had just been placed in front of a firing squad.

CHAPTER 22

*L*ORETTA'S BREATH CAUGHT IN HER THROAT, AND SHE ALMOST CHOKED on the chunk of biscuit she had just chewed. She swallowed so hard, her neck felt like somebody had wrapped a noose around it. "Uncle Virgil and Aunt Corrine are so nosy!" she snapped, with biscuit crumbs on her lips. "Always up in my business."

"They care about you," Maureen said in a gentle voice, pouring herself some of the Merlot that Mel had brought home that evening.

"Well, I wish they didn't care so much about me that they keep sayin' all kinds of stupid stuff! Especially that frog-face Aunt Corrine—she ain't even a blood relative, and Uncle Virgil ain't my daddy. Mel is!"

Maureen gave Loretta a harsh look and then she turned to Mel. His lips were already moving. Loretta felt triumphant because she knew that no matter what she said, Mel would agree with her.

"Well, you can ask that meddlesome brother of yours and his wife how they expect Loretta and me to do the work we do if we don't spend a lot of time together? One ad could take half a day to shoot and then the client might decide that they want to reshoot it. That's another half a day! I thought they liked running around here bragging to everybody about how their niece was a model and all." Mel didn't try to hide his disgust. Was there no end to those damn fools and their meddling? he wondered. He couldn't decide who irritated him more: Virgil and that battle-ax he was married to or that damn Catty and Fast Black.

"Uncle Virgil needs to stop drinkin' that cheap wine. It's startin' to pickle his brain," Loretta decided.

"He just means that you're at the age where it's real important for you and me to have a good relationship," Maureen said. "He wants you to start actin' more normal."

"You and me already have a good relationship!" Loretta exploded. "I'm just as normal as he is! What in the world is he talkin' about? Besides, I am almost out of school and then I'll be on my own."

"*Almost* out of school and on your own is right. Until you get to that point, you need to listen to people who care about you," Maureen said sharply.

"Oh, is Uncle Virgil tryin' to say that Mel don't care about me?" Loretta asked.

"No, that's not what Uncle Virgil is tryin' to say. His concern is for you to be a teenager. You don't spend enough of your time with other kids your age. The more I think about it, and the more I hear about it from your uncle and your play aunties, Catty and Fast Black, I have to agree with them." Maureen sniffed. She didn't like the look of disgust on Mel's face.

Mel was more than just disgusted now. He had been expecting Catty's and Fast Black's trifling names to come up in the conversation. Virgil and his wife took the cake, but Catty and Fast Black were the bitter black bile icing!

"Maureen, you need to tell those people that you can handle your own business," Mel advised. His jaws were twitching so hard his molars ached.

"Those people love me. They love Lo'retta, too, so they want her to do the right thing. They want to see her happy, and I really think she'd act more like a teenager if she spent more time with other teenagers," Maureen declared.

Loretta's mouth flew open so wide Maureen could see her tongue flapping like a fish out of water before she even said a word. When the words did come out, they sounded like the croaking of a frog. "What? I got a lot of friends my age. I spent the night with Mona just last Friday. I was plannin' to ask Warren to take me to the movies this weekend—since you always tellin' me about all the times he asks you about me."

"I'm glad to hear that. I also understand where Virgil and Corrine are comin' from." Maureen looked at Mel and blinked. "Baby, I appreciate you helpin' my daughter with her modelin' career, but since she's still in school and her grades are slippin', maybe you should turn down a few jobs from time to time. When she finishes school, she can model full-time."

"That's fine with me, but she might miss out on the jobs that will help get her to the top," Mel said with a shrug. "At this stage in her career, exposure is essential. She needs to be in the right place at the right time. The fewer jobs she accepts, the fewer chances she'll be able to do that." Mel snatched his second biscuit out of the bowl on the table next to the platter of deep-fried prawns. "The thing is, I've been turning down new girls so I could keep my focus on Loretta." Mel let out a deep breath and looked at Loretta, shaking his head. "I guess you should forget about that BMW auto show next Saturday, sweet pea."

Loretta gasped. She reared back in her chair and glared at Maureen. "Mama, don't you dare do this to me. I've been waitin' all month for those BMW people to pick the girls for that auto show!"

"I didn't say you couldn't do *any* modelin'. Since you have other responsibilities, though, I think you should reorganize your priorities. I am proud of the fact that you can get work so easy. I want you to be just as successful and famous a model as that Brooke Shields. Like I said, though, you'll have plenty of time to do that when you finish school in a few months. The way it is now, you spend more time around adults than you do other teenagers. You don't want to be old before your time. That's the point your uncle and aunties keep tryin' to get across."

Loretta's face was burning with anger.

Maureen gave Loretta a serious look. "Look, baby. You and me will be spendin' more time together and that's final. You used to love doin' things with me." There was a hint of anger in Maureen's voice. She rose from the table clutching her wineglass. She took a long swallow and then stomped into the living room.

"Do you think she's gettin' suspicious?" Loretta whispered to Mel as soon as she heard Maureen turn on the TV.

"If she even thought there was something going on between you and me, she would have said something by now. Don't worry about her. She's still clueless."

"Well, I hope she stays that way. We've come too far to let her ruin things for us." Loretta glanced toward the living room and back to Mel with a puppy dog expression on her face. "Mel, I love you to death and I am not goin' to give you up so soon or so easy. We had a deal. We agreed to act normal until I finish school. Then we'll tell her about us and then go to New York so we can work on my modelin' career and get married."

"That's still the plan, but we have to be careful. We can't do anything that might make her suspicious. This new job of hers is going to work in our favor, baby. She'll be going into that nursing home two hours earlier than she went to that lobster factory. You don't have to leave for school until seven-thirty, so we can spend all that time together now."

Loretta's eyes got big. "Oh, *Daddy*! You're right. I hadn't thought about that," she squealed. She was so excited she forgot to whisper.

"You hadn't thought about what, Loretta?" Maureen asked, walking back into the kitchen. This was the first time she'd heard Loretta refer to Mel as "Daddy" and it warmed her heart.

CHAPTER 23

*L*ORETTA'S FACE HAD BEEN BURNING QUITE A BIT IN THE LAST FEW MIN-
utes. Now it was sizzling like a bonfire. She thought she was going
to melt as she sat there looking at Maureen with her lips quivering.

"Did I miss somethin'?" Maureen asked, looking from Loretta to
Mel as she padded across the floor to the refrigerator, talking with
her back to them. "Y'all didn't have to stop talkin' on my account."

"Uh, Mel was just tellin' me that everything you just said makes a
lot of sense," Loretta lied, looking to Mel for confirmation. "I'm
glad you feel that way, Mel," she added, gently kicking his bare foot
under the table. She turned her head so that Maureen couldn't see
her wink at Mel.

"See there. I was right all along and I'm glad you realize that
now." Maureen closed the refrigerator door without removing anything. "I guess I need to run to the store and get some milk. I also
need to go out to the mall and pick up some of those funny-looking
white shoes that nurses wear. That's what I'll be wearin' with the
scrubs the nursin' home will provide for me to work in. I would invite y'all to go shoppin' with me, but I told Catty and Fast Black that
I'd meet them later on for a drink," Maureen announced.

"Oh, you go right ahead. I have to finish my homework," Loretta
said. "Finals are comin' up."

Maureen looked at Mel and tilted her head to the side. "You
want to come with me, baby? I know you don't care much for Catty
or Fast Black, but they like you and keep tellin' me they want to get
to know you better. I'm sure they won't mind if you tag along."

Mel's stomach turned as if he had just stepped into a pile of shit. He would rather shovel that pile of shit than spend time in a bar drinking with Catty and Fast Black. He shook his head so hard his ears rang. "Oh, no, I have some paperwork to go over and some prints to develop. I have that cruise ship assignment coming up next week, too, so I need to move a lot of other things off my plate. Maybe I'll join you and your homegirls the next time."

Maureen gave Mel a wistful look. "Don't you work too hard, Mel. You startin' to look and act real tired lately. I know you love your work, but I don't like that your job is wearin' you down to a frazzle."

Mel had been looking and acting more tired than usual, but it had nothing to do with his work. Loretta was the only "job" that was wearing him down to a frazzle. It was getting harder and harder for him to keep up with her enormous sexual appetite. She was like a junkie and he was her drug of choice. Besides, in addition to him having the time of his life (especially after all of the trouble that those other bitches in his past had put him through), he chose to look on the bright side of his current situation. His vigorous workouts with Loretta kept him in such good shape that he no longer had to go to the gym. Another thing about Loretta was that as long as she fulfilled his needs, he would do whatever it took to keep her satisfied. If that meant fucking her eight or nine times a week like he'd been doing lately, that was fine with him.

As soon as they heard Maureen's car pull out of the driveway, Loretta sprinted across the floor toward Mel. She leaped into his arms like a jackrabbit. She threw her head back and began to moan and groan and kick her legs back and forth like somebody having a fit. In a way she was having a fit—a fit of ecstasy.

Cradling Loretta like a big baby, Mel darted into her bedroom huffing and puffing.

The following Sunday around six in the evening, Maureen drove to Virgil's house. Mel and Loretta had left right after breakfast to do a shoot in Tampa. Loretta was going to be the lead model in an ad for a boutique that specialized in trendy clothing for young girls.

Virgil was glad that Maureen was making a career move so that she would have more time to spend with Loretta. He was glad that things were going so well in her life and he prayed that things would get even better. Shortly after she'd arrived, he got nosy. "By the way, how is married life treatin' you, Mo'reen?"

"Everything is as sweet as pie. It's so nice to have Mel livin' in the house. Just to let you know, him and Loretta told me they plan to cut back on her modelin' jobs so she and I can spend more time together. This nursin' home job came right on time. It's goin' to be hard, but I don't really care. I'll do whatever I have to do to make a good life for my child and my husband."

"I'm so glad to hear that," Virgil said, relieved. It looked like everything was going to work out just fine. The way things were going for Maureen, there was a chance that he would *never* tell her about her background. His feelings about having a moral obligation to do so had changed over the years. Some days he didn't think telling her was that important, and some days he did. Especially on the days when he told himself that if he had been the baby that Mama Ruby had kidnapped, he would certainly want to know.

Spending time with Virgil and Corrine turned out to be one of the most pleasant evenings that Maureen had experienced in a long time. They watched a couple of TV programs, drank two pitchers of lemonade, and caught each other up on the latest gossip.

She returned home to an empty apartment. Loretta had left a message on the answering machine telling her not to bother cooking because she and Mel were going to have dinner at the Cracker Barrel before they left Tampa.

It had been a long day for Maureen and she didn't realize how tired she was. She fell asleep on the couch watching an *I Love Lucy* rerun.

When Maureen opened her eyes several hours later, she was pleased to see that Mel and Loretta had come home. Mel was in bed snoring like a moose. Before Maureen removed her clothes and joined him, she checked on Loretta. She was curled up in a fetal position and was sleeping like a baby.

Maureen felt like making love. She thought that a good workout would be a nice way to relieve some of the tension she had been experiencing the past few days. She tried to shake Mel awake. This was the first time she had ever made such a bold move regarding sex with him. When shaking him didn't work, she grabbed his limp penis and gave it a good squeeze. That aroused him.

"Girl, you stop that! You know a man my age can't always get it up—" Mel caught himself. He and Loretta had made love before and after their visit to the Cracker Barrel. As a matter of fact, they had ordered their food to go. The rip-roaring sex and the drive to and from Tampa had Mel feeling every one of his forty-one years. He almost rolled out of the bed when he realized where he was and that it was his wife in bed with him.

"*Girl?* Thank you, baby. It's been years since I was a girl," Maureen giggled. "I don't count how often the old white folks around here like to refer to all black females as *girl*," she said, rubbing Mel's thigh. "I'm your girl now." She was trying so hard to love this man, and she was glad that she did have more feelings of affection toward him now than she did before she married him.

"Hi, baby," Mel mumbled, lifting his head just high enough to give her a quick peck on her cheek. "You looked so tired and peaceful on that couch I didn't wake you up, plus you have to get up so early in the morning to get to that nursing home for your first day." He sat up and placed his arm around Maureen's naked shoulder.

"I'm not that tired," she insisted, rubbing his thigh even harder. She glanced at the clock on the nightstand and then at Mel's crotch. She was doing everything she could think of to show him how hard she was trying to make their marriage seem like a normal one. They were still newlyweds. The least they could do was make love as often as most newlyweds did.

"Oh," he said, forcing a smile as he reached for her. He made love to her like he was jacking off—no tenderness, no foreplay, and no passion. It made Maureen feel like she was a piece of wood. His clumsy performance helped relieve her tension, but she was glad when it was over. Knowing what a long day he had endured, she managed to give him the benefit of the doubt.

Afterward, Maureen went to the bathroom, and when she returned to her bed just a few minutes later, Mel was once again snoring like a moose.

She got very little sleep that night. Despite her odd "interview" with Mrs. Larsen and a few other apprehensions, she was looking forward to her new job.

However, her first day was almost her last.

CHAPTER 24

CATTY HAD TOLD MAUREEN THAT A FEW AIDES HAD QUIT AFTER ONLY A few hours on the job. One had quit after only fifteen minutes. Could the job be that bad? Maureen wondered.

All kinds of crazy thoughts had already begun to run through her mind. Like, maybe the boss was too hard to get along with, or maybe the work was just too hard. The thought that the place was haunted even crossed her mind. After all, Catty had told her that patients died there on a regular basis, sometimes two or three on the same day. Maureen decided she had to find out for herself just why the director had practically begged her to take the job.

From the outside, the York Nursing Home looked like an upscale motel. The sixty-bed facility was a warm shade of blue with a circular driveway, a neatly trimmed front lawn, palm trees with benches on either side of the driveway, and a wishing well in the center of the lawn. It was located near a strip mall that contained several fast-food restaurants, a nail shop, a dress shop for full-figured women, and a gas station. It was also just a few minutes away from downtown Miami. Some of the nursing home staff, as well as some of the people who worked in the strip mall businesses, often walked into Miami when they wanted to eat at the more upscale restaurants or shop at the trendy boutiques.

Maureen's heart skipped a beat when she saw *two* hearses parked in front of the building. She gulped and stopped in her tracks and was tempted to run back to her car as fast as she could. However, she had come too far to turn back now, so she continued walking until she made it to the front door. She was met by a birdlike white woman with red cheeks, dark circles around her eyes, and limp hair hanging to her shoulders like a gray spiderweb.

"Maureen?" the woman asked in a high-pitched voice. There was a hopeful look on her face.

"Yes, ma'am," Maureen replied.

"Oh, I'm so glad you made it!" the woman gushed, looking at her watch. "Twenty minutes early too." A name tag, hanging lopsided on the left breast pocket of her light blue scrubs, identified her as JANICE LARSEN, DIRECTOR.

"Hello, Mrs. Larsen," Maureen said, offering her most sincere smile. "I'm happy to be here," she added, and she meant it too. But she didn't feel that way for long.

After a ten-minute orientation, some paperwork, and discussing her benefits and salary, Maureen was put to work. She would be "trained" on the job, learn as you go, she realized. Well, if these people were so desperate that they were willing to hire her and put her to work right away, even though she had no experience or training in this area, Maureen wasn't going to argue with them.

The first thing the director did was introduce Maureen to the staff, and then she took her around to introduce her to the patients she would be assisting.

The very first patient, a hairy old beast with bulging eyes, spat on Maureen's foot when they entered the room he shared with another patient. "Now, Mr. Bailey, you behave yourself," Mrs. Larsen scolded, giving the grumpy old man a slight tap on the top of his head. "He's kind of fussy this early in the morning, but by the time your day ends, he'll be as cuddly as a kitty cat," she whispered to Maureen. "Be thankful that he can still feed himself, so you won't have to worry about that. He's got a real bad case of dementia. He thinks he's a baby again, so he likes to bite."

Mr. Bailey's roommate had been in a coma for the past five years and had to be fed through a tube. He wasn't going to be much trouble. Half of the other patients couldn't even get out of bed, but they were still lucid enough to feed themselves.

"I hope you're not too squeamish," Mrs. Larsen said to Maureen as they entered another room. Maureen was thrilled to see that the two patients in this room were both still asleep.

"I'm not squeamish at all." Maureen had gutted fish, skinned squirrels, and even helped Mama Ruby slaughter a few hogs. She had never been squeamish . . . until she heard what Mrs. Larsen said next.

"Then it shouldn't bother you to change diapers."

Diapers! "Um, I don't think that'll bother me." Maureen had not changed a diaper since Loretta was a baby—and that had been unpleasant enough. To change a diaper on an adult had to be pretty gruesome.

"I have to let you know that some of these people can be downright hostile. Some even tend to get . . . uh . . . violent." Mrs. Larsen let out a nervous laugh, but that didn't stop Maureen's thoughts from running wild.

"Just how violent?" she asked.

"Oh, you might get poked with a cane or have a walker thrown at you now and then. Or pinched, or bitten, or deliberately run over by a wheelchair. Nothing really serious, so don't worry about it. You are kind of petite and fragile-looking, though. Oh well, if something serious happens to you, we have three doctors and several nurses on the premises at all times."

Maureen glanced toward a window that faced the parking lot. The hearses were still present. "Ma'am, I noticed the two hearses in the parkin' lot when I got here," she mentioned, nodding toward the window. "They kinda scared me."

"Oh, they kinda scare me too. Always did and always will," Mrs. Larsen said with a dismissive wave. "You'll get used to seeing them, though. You'll see ambulances here all the time too. The paramedics spend so much time out here, some days they come before we even call them. After all, this is the end of the line for most of our residents. That's a crying shame because so few of them have families that still care about them. Once they tuck their loved ones in at a place like this, they think their job is done. Death visits this place more than relatives." Mrs. Larsen gave Maureen a pitiful look and then touched her arm. "Most of these poor souls just go to sleep one night and never wake up." Maureen's new boss took a deep breath and added with a quick smile, "I hope to go that way myself when the time comes."

"That's how I want to go, too, I guess," Maureen responded, hoping that she would be able to take care of herself to the very end so Loretta wouldn't dump her off at a nursing home. Like Mrs. Larsen, Maureen wanted to go to sleep one night and not wake up when her time came. That was the way Mama Ruby had passed over. Just thinking about the day Mama Ruby died made her sad. She blinked back a tear and gave Mrs. Larsen a big smile. "I hope to spend my last days in my own home," she said, "but it's good to know that there are homes like this for the folks that need them."

Mrs. Larsen gave Maureen a peculiar look. "You said you have a daughter and a husband?"

Maureen nodded and offered an even bigger smile. "We're all very close. If me or my husband ever get disabled and can't take care of ourselves, I am sure my daughter will make the right decision about our care. I'm so blessed that I can count on her for anything."

When the tour resumed, Maureen witnessed several incidents of violence. One old man eased out of his bed as soon as they entered his room, grabbed his three-legged cane, and started swinging it at them. Two burly male orderlies rushed in and subdued him. In the next room, a large blind woman rose from her bed to hug Maureen and involuntarily vomited on her new shoes.

These unpleasant incidents didn't seem to faze Mrs. Larsen that much. However, each time, she rolled her eyes, mumbled something under her breath, gritted her teeth, and sighed with exasperation.

"The employee restroom is just across the hall. Go get your shoes cleaned off and we'll take a coffee break," Mrs. Larsen told Maureen, clasping her hand like she was afraid she was going to bolt.

CHAPTER 25

*A*FTER MAUREEN HAD MOISTENED A PAPER TOWEL AND WIPED OFF HER shoe, she looked at herself in the restroom mirror. "I don't know if I can handle this job," she admitted to herself out loud. "Lord Jesus, please show me the way," she prayed.

One of the many things that Maureen gave Mama Ruby credit for was instilling a strong Christian ethic in her. Despite Mama Ruby's violent nature and laundry list of crimes, she had been a very religious woman. At least by Mama Ruby's standards. *"You be good to the Lord, and the Lord will be good to you,"* Mama Ruby used to say.

If Maureen ever needed spiritual assistance, it was now. She entered a stall and got on her knees and prayed in a low voice. "Lord Jesus, only You can keep me from goin' crazy up in this place. I know you got somethin' good in store for me, so there must be a reason I'm here. . . ."

After a ten-minute coffee break in the employee break room with Mrs. Larsen, Maureen met more of her patients. By then, though, she was ready to leave the place running, jump back into her car, and make a beeline back to the lobster factory. Based on what she had seen and experienced so far, she was convinced this was not a job she could handle after all. As a matter of fact, she had already decided to use the pay phone in the break room and call Mr. Faulk to see how soon she could return to the lobster factory.

Catty worked different hours than Maureen, so she couldn't talk to her until later in the afternoon. In a way Maureen was glad. She knew that if she told her what she was planning to do, Catty would go out of her way to talk her out of it. But Maureen didn't care one way or the other how her leaving would make Catty look now. This position seemed more like a punishment than a job.

The last straw for Maureen was when one of the most combative patients, a former professional wrestler who was still quite strong, grabbed Maureen by her hair and pulled it so hard she fell into bed with him. She screamed and struggled to untangle herself from his grip. As soon as she was free, she ran from his room in tears. She sprinted to her locker and grabbed her purse and would have kept running until she reached her car if Mrs. Larsen had not intercepted her in the lobby.

"My dear! You look like you've seen a ghost!" Mrs. Larsen hollered. She ran up to Maureen with her arms outstretched. "Please tell me what's the matter."

"I'm sorry, but I can't do this job," Maureen whimpered, shaking and pointing back down the hallway she had just run down. "If I stay here, I'm goin' to get hurt." Maureen was almost hyperventilating as she rubbed her arm and shifted her weight from one foot to the other. "The man in the room across from the supply room, he just attacked me. I can't do this. I am sorry, but I can . . . not . . . do . . . this . . . job." Maureen swallowed hard and rubbed her scalp. The man had pulled her hair so hard, she was surprised that he had not yanked out a clump.

"I didn't think so," Mrs. Larsen said wearily, her face a mask of disappointment and despair. "You can leave now if you want to. I'll make sure Bobby Jean cuts you a check for the whole day."

"I am so sorry, Mrs. Larsen. This . . . this is not what I expected," Maureen stammered. "I had no idea it would be this hard, and I haven't even met the last of my patients. Because of the ones I have met, I can tell that this job is not for me."

Maureen agreed to finish the day, but she spent as much time hiding out in the ladies' room as she could. Around 3:00 p.m. she walked past the receptionist desk. She was on her way to the pay phone to call her old supervisor at the lobster factory and beg him to let her return.

The pretty young Asian woman at the desk waved to Maureen. "Excuse me, your name's Maureen, right?" she asked with a slight Chinese accent that contained the hint of a Southern drawl.

Maureen nodded and walked over to the desk. She had used a rubber band to hold her ponytail in place before she left her apartment that morning. The rubber band had popped off during the melee with the ex-wrestler, so Maureen's hair was now hanging around her shoulders and face like limp vines. After all she had endured so far today, she felt like she'd been wrestling with a bear.

"By the way, I'm Peggy Wong. I moved down here from Cleveland last year to be with my fiancé, and he took off a week after I got here. I couldn't go back home and this was the only job I could get," the receptionist revealed with a smile, but Maureen could tell that it was forced. "I hope your first day is going well. This place is so depressing and stressful," Peggy added, slowly shaking her head.

"I figured that much out real quick," Maureen said with a shudder, brushing hair off her sweaty face.

"The two girls that started last Monday went to lunch at noon and never came back. I'm surprised you're still here."

"I'm surprised I'm still here too," Maureen said flatly. "I don't think I'm goin' to stay either," she admitted. "I told Mrs. Larsen that a little while ago."

"That's too bad. I used to do your job and I felt the same way until I learned the ropes. It's not so bad once you get used to it."

"Well, I don't think I can get used to what goes on around here." Maureen heard a commotion behind her. She turned to see two orderlies dressed in white wheeling a gurney toward the front door. Whoever was on that gurney was not coming back, because they had covered his or her face with a sheet.

"That's poor Mr. Blake." Peggy sniffed, shaking her head. "I knew he was on his way to meet his maker. Just yesterday he started hallucinating, seeing and talking to his dead wife. She was a patient here until last month when she died. Poor thing."

Maureen and Peggy watched through the glass doors as the orderlies loaded Mr. Blake into the back of one of the hearses.

"Oh well," Peggy said with a heavy sigh and a weak shrug. "We all gotta go sometime." She sighed again. "Could you do me a favor and deliver a message to Mrs. Freeman? She's the nice little lady in the last room on the left down the hall. She didn't answer her phone, so it rolled over to my line."

"Yeah, I guess. I didn't get to meet her or any of the people down there yet," Maureen said, reaching for the pink telephone message slip.

Maureen looked at her watch and was happy to see that she had less than an hour to go. As she walked down the hall, dragging her feet like there was a gurney waiting for her to be loaded onto, she glanced at the telephone message in her hand and gasped at what it said:

M
I will visit you soon
Jesus

Maureen stopped in her tracks. She blinked hard a few times and shook her head.

She had always been superstitious. After all, Mama Ruby had been the seventh daughter of a seventh daughter and had bragged about her "special powers" from time to time. What those alleged special powers entailed was still a mystery to Maureen. She had never witnessed Mama Ruby perform anything that she considered divine, but she recalled the time that one of Mama Ruby's friends had read Mama Ruby's fortune with a deck of cards and told her that one of Maureen's twins wasn't going to be around for long. Not long after that day, during a picture-taking session with a cheap camera, Maureen noticed a thumb-size shadow in every picture that contained her twins. The shadow had only covered Loraine's image. When she fell into the Blue Lake near Mama Ruby's house and drowned, Maureen was not surprised. After that, each new incident made her even more superstitious.

And now: *A message to M from . . . Jesus?*

"Uh, does Mrs. Freeman's first name begin with an *M?*" Maureen asked Peggy.

"Uh-uh. Her first name is Leona. I just put *M* for 'mother' instead of writing it out. The message is from her son."

"Oh." The telephone message in Maureen's hand intrigued her. Even though it was for Mrs. Freeman in room 108, she had a feeling that this message was also for her.

And it was.

CHAPTER 26

*T*HE DOOR TO MRS. FREEMAN'S ROOM WAS AJAR, BUT MAUREEN knocked and entered before the old woman had time to respond. She was pleased to see that Mrs. Freeman was black. Other than a hostile, ninety-six-year-old man named Mr. Sands who used to manage a restaurant, and Mrs. Darby, a retired high school principal, Mrs. Freeman was the only other black patient on the premises that Maureen had seen so far.

She walked with caution toward Mrs. Freeman's bed. This old woman didn't look like a threat, but Maureen didn't want to take any chances. She left the door open and stood a safe distance away from the bed.

It was easy to see that Mrs. Freeman had once been a very attractive woman. She had bronze-colored skin, slightly slanted eyes, and very high cheekbones. Her long hair, which was parted down the middle and in two braids, was completely white. "You look like my niece," she remarked, sitting up with a smile on her face. "Except you're prettier."

"Thank you. I'm sure your niece is a nice person." Maureen moved a little closer to the side of the bed.

"She was, but she passed a long time ago," Mrs. Freeman stated, her voice cracking. "My son is all I got left in the world. You the new aide?"

"Yes and no, ma'am," Maureen replied, breathing deeply.

The old woman sat up straighter, squinting and looking Maureen over from head to toe. Then she looked Maureen in the face and asked in an angry voice that had an ominous rattle to it, "What do you mean by that? Yes, you're the new aide who is going to help take care of me or no, you're not. I've been after them to get a colored gal in here so I can get my hair braided properly."

"Yes, I'm the new aide, but no, I won't be helpin' take care of you. I'm not comin' back after today," Maureen clarified, handing the telephone message to Mrs. Freeman.

The old woman snatched the piece of paper out of Maureen's hand so hard the corner of it remained between Maureen's fingers. Mrs. Freeman snorted and shook her head as she looked at the message. "Hmm." A sudden smile appeared on her heavily lined face. "It's from my son. Bless his heart. He says he's coming to see me soon. I hope it's to take me back home! I done told him over and over that I want to die in my own bed!"

"Oh. If you don't mind me sayin' so, seein' who your message was from gave me a chill when I first saw it. Then I realized that Jesus is a pretty common name in Florida, especially in families with a Latin background. I went to school with a boy from Honduras who was also named Jesus, but it was pronounced *Hay-soos*."

Mrs. Freeman nodded. "My son don't like for folks to call him Jesus, even when they pronounced it *Hay-soos*. That's what some people call him anyway. I guess it makes them feel good to talk to a person with the same name as the Lord. Especially the folks in this place. I call him Jay. I wish you could meet him."

"I wish I could, too, but like I said, I don't think I'm goin' to come back after today."

Maureen enjoyed listening to Mrs. Freeman brag about her son and his job installing cable television. The old woman also talked extensively about her plants, her original recipes, her favorite TV shows, and the poodle that she had once owned. Maureen knew that she was spending more time with this patient than she should have, but since she had decided to leave at the end of the day, she couldn't get fired, so she had nothing to lose.

It was one of the most enjoyable afternoons that Maureen had experienced in a long time. The elderly woman was very charming and easy to talk to. Maureen sincerely regretted that she would not be around to get to know her better. After talking with Mrs. Freeman for a few minutes more, it didn't take long for Maureen to change her mind about leaving. She told Mrs. Larsen that she had decided to stay, but only until she could find someone to replace her.

Just before 3:00 p.m., after helping one of the other aides lift the lower portion of a large paralyzed man in his bed to change his diaper, Maureen prepared to go home—and it was not soon enough for her. It had been a long and difficult day. However, even after everything she had endured earlier, she was glad that she had remained around long enough to meet Mrs. Freeman.

Peggy was on the telephone when Maureen walked by the front desk on her way to the parking lot, but she abruptly ended her call and waved to Maureen. "I heard you decided to stay until they find somebody to replace you. I'm glad. I hope the rest of your days here are more pleasant than today was."

"I hope so too," Maureen said in a tired voice as she exited the building. She was glad to see that both of the hearses had left the parking lot. When she reached her car, she glanced to her side and caught a glimpse of a tall, nicely built black man getting out of a green Thunderbird. He had just parked a couple of rows over from her. He wore a uniform, so Maureen assumed he was some kind of maintenance or utility worker.

The man was walking with his head down, dragging his feet like he was on his way to the gallows. Just as Maureen was about to open her car door, he looked up. He smiled and gave her a nod. She smiled back. Maureen didn't know why, but there was something about the man that made her feel warm all over. She suddenly felt more relaxed.

After she had entered her car and started the motor, she turned and looked toward the nursing home entrance. The man had stopped walking. He stood in front of the building entrance with his hand on the door, looking in Maureen's direction. He smiled at her again and this time he saluted her. She did the same thing and then she quickly drove off.

Maureen was a careful driver. She had never even come close to having an accident, but today she drove like she was in a daze. She ran two red lights and one stop sign. She was lucky she didn't cause an accident or run into a cop. She couldn't stop thinking about the man in the parking lot.

He stayed on Maureen's mind until she got home.

She was glad that the apartment was empty. It had been a stressful day and she needed to unwind. Loretta had left a note taped to the microwave oven that she had gone to Mona's house so they could work on a science project. Maureen assumed Mel was still on the assignment he had told her about the night before.

"How was your first day on the new job?" Mel asked Maureen when he got home around 7:00 p.m. He dropped a tripod and some other equipment onto the living room floor.

Maureen was glad that Mel had asked about her day, but from the indifferent look on his face, she knew he was just trying to be nice.

"It was very interestin'," she told him. As tired as she was, she was still able to leap up off the couch and give him a big hug. "But I was glad when my shift ended."

"That bad, huh?" Mel chuckled as he tickled Maureen's chin. Then he hugged her and gave her a long passionate kiss. "As soon as we both get rested, I'll make you feel better." He pinched her left breast and kissed her again.

"I saw two hearses in the parkin' lot when I got there this mornin'," Maureen reported with a shiver. "One of the patients had died. They didn't take him away until the afternoon. If I had known there was a dead body lyin' around all that time, I don't know what I would have done."

"Is that why you have such a glazed look on your face?"

"Huh? Oh . . . yeah," Maureen stammered, shaking her head to get the image of the nicely built man in the parking lot off her mind. "Any more of that wine you brought home last week?"

After she had drunk a glass of wine, Maureen felt more relaxed. Twenty minutes after Mel had come home, Loretta returned from

Mona's house. She slunk into the living room and flopped down onto the couch close to Mel. Maureen occupied one of the two easy chairs facing the couch.

"Hi, Mama. Hi, Mel. Y'all wouldn't believe the prom dress that Mona had the nerve to buy. Whew! She looked like a sack of potatoes in that thing! I told her that I was takin' her to the mall this weekend so we can find somethin' more appropriate for her bell-shaped body." Loretta paused and gave Maureen an amused look. "You look tired, Mama. How was the first day on your new job?"

"It was okay, I guess. It's a job," Maureen said with a casual shrug, determined to divert Loretta's and Mel's attention so she wouldn't have to reveal too many details. "I hope y'all don't mind fried chicken for dinner again."

Mel and Loretta grunted at the same time.

"Why do you have teeth prints on your arm?" Loretta asked, staring with wide eyes at one of the wounds Maureen had sustained. "Have you got a boyfriend at that new place already?" Loretta snickered. "Mel, you'd better keep your eyes on Mama! She might run off with one of those old geezers down at that nursin' home."

Maureen gave Loretta a dismissive wave. "You stop that, Lo'retta. Mel knows he has nothin' to worry about. Every single male patient in that place is at least old enough to be my grandfather."

Mel didn't even bother to look at Maureen. Instead he looked at Loretta and shook his head, but Loretta continued to tease Maureen.

"Nuh-uh! I've passed by that place on my way to the mall. I saw a couple of male workers in white scrubs goin' up in there, and they didn't look like grandfathers to me," Loretta pointed out.

"Like I said, Mel has nothin' to worry about," Maureen said again, her voice faltering. *At least not yet*, she thought as she recalled again how the man in the parking lot had stared and smiled at her.

Maureen had already decided not to tell Mel and Loretta, Catty, or anybody else just how bad her first day as a nurse's aide had actually been. She had also decided not to tell them that she probably wasn't going to work at the nursing home for too long.

The next day when she went back to work, though, she learned from the receptionist that the nicely built man that she had seen in the parking lot the day before was Mrs. Freeman's son, Jay, or *Haysoos* (she refused to think of him as Jesus).

"I know you saw Mrs. Freeman's son as you were leaving yesterday. If you had waited one minute longer to leave, you could have seen him up real close," Peggy said with a dreamy look on her face.

"I got a glimpse of him just before I left the parkin' lot," Maureen told Peggy.

"Do you think he's sexy?"

"Huh? Oh! I couldn't tell," Maureen fumbled.

"Well, he is." Peggy pretended to swoon, batting her eyelashes in a way that embarrassed Maureen. "He could park his shoes under my bed and hang his bathrobe next to mine any old time."

"I . . . I barely noticed him," Maureen lied.

"It's just as well. He won't give me, or any of the other women here, the time of day. He's one of the most aloof men I've ever come across. All this time he's been coming here, he has never even smiled at me." Peggy frowned and added, "He must be gay."

"Maybe he is," Maureen replied. *But he smiled at* me, she said to herself.

She wasn't so sure about leaving the job at all now.

CHAPTER 27

MAUREEN HAD BEGUN TO FEEL LIKE SHE WAS LOSING HER MIND. SHE was in the process of cooking her own goose. That was the only explanation she could come up with as to why she felt so attracted to Mrs. Freeman's mysterious son. She had not even met him and had seen him only once, but he'd been on her mind ever since. She was having the kind of erotic thoughts about him that she should only have been having about Mel!

If that wasn't proof that her goose had been in the oven for too long, nothing was. Therefore, just like Mama Ruby had predicted years ago, Maureen was losing her mind. "If you get too hung up on a man, you'll go crazy just like Satan planned," Mama Ruby had told sixteen-year-old Maureen when she confessed that she had a crush on Al Pacino. Had Mama Ruby been right? *Is this the beginning of the end for me?* Maureen wondered. Despite how she felt, she was determined to keep things in perspective. She had a daughter and a husband who needed her. She didn't want them to have to visit her in the state mental institution.

On her second day at the nursing home, Maureen endured just as many unpleasant mishaps as the day before. Some were quite violent. Roy Fitzgibbon, a toothless eighty-year-old who refused to keep his false teeth in his mouth, grabbed her arm and gnawed on it with his gums until two orderlies ran into his room and rescued her. A few minutes after that, seventy-five-year-old Lois Borden deliberately ran over Maureen's foot with her wheelchair.

Maureen and two other fairly new aides spent most of the morning in the ladies' room wiping vomit and snot off their shoes and clothes and dressing an assortment of scratches and bite marks that each of them had sustained.

"This is it for me," one of the aides said, inspecting a bite mark on her cheek in the mirror. "Part of my parole agreement is that I have to keep a job, but I'd rather go back to prison than put up with this kind of madness. I'm out of here."

"I'm right behind you," the other aide said, applying a Band-Aid to a minor wound on her arm where a patient had stabbed her with a fork. "Maureen, girl, you are insane if you stay around this madhouse."

Yes, I am insane, Maureen thought to herself. At least temporarily. She had already decided that. But her mental condition had been caused by a different reason, and if she didn't see the source of her insanity again, to try and determine what it was about Mrs. Freeman's son that had her feeling like a fool, she would stay crazy.

Maureen continued making her rounds, humming Luther Vandross tunes and smiling as she went along. Her cheerful attitude annoyed some of the other frustrated aides, but that didn't bother Maureen. She arrived at Mrs. Freeman's room a few minutes before noon. She was stunned and surprised to see the same well-built man she had seen in the parking lot the day before sitting in a chair by the side of Mrs. Freeman's bed. Not only did he look stunned and surprised to see her again, too, but this time he looked downright happy. She didn't want to stare at him too long, but she looked at him long enough to see that he had nice, average-looking features and a smile that seemed to light up the room.

"Oh, Maureen! I want you to meet my boy Jay," Mrs. Freeman said, bursting with pride. Then she said to Jay, "After that baboon you married, don't you wish you had a woman this pretty on your arm?"

"Uh, yes," Jay managed, looking embarrassed. As soon as Maureen got close enough, he extended his hand. "I noticed you yesterday," he told her. "My mother has been talking about you ever since I got here."

Maureen blushed. She was glad her skin was not light enough for Jay to see the blood rising in her face. "Sayin' good stuff about me, I hope," she responded with a nervous chuckle, looking at Mrs. Freeman. "I can come back later to read the Bible to you like you asked me to."

"I'd rather you give me a bath—and it better be real soon. I'm feeling real ripe right about now," Mrs. Freeman said, wiggling her nose.

"Um, that's one of the other aide's responsibilities right now. That's part of the trainin' I still have to go through," Maureen explained.

"Say what? Why do you need to be trained to wash my booty?" Mrs. Freeman hollered, slapping the side of her hip. "What do they need to *train* you to do that a woman your age don't already know?"

"Well, they have rules here and I have to follow them. I'm still new on this job," Maureen explained. She glanced at Jay. She could see that he was clearly embarrassed. "I think that by next week I will be up and runnin' and anything you need done, I can do."

Mrs. Freeman stared at Maureen. "Horse feathers!" she shrieked. Then she turned to Jay and calmly asked, "You paid my bill for this month?"

Jay nodded. "Mother, you behave yourself. This young lady is only doing her job the way she's been told to do it." He gave Maureen a wan look.

He had eyes like an angel, she thought.

"Horse feathers!" Mrs. Freeman shrieked again, kicking her covers.

"Mother, you promised me that you'd behave," Jay reminded in a weary voice.

"Oh yeah." Mrs. Freeman looked puzzled, looking at Jay. "I did tell you that, didn't I?"

"After the other girl gives you your bath, I'll come back to read to you," Maureen told Mrs. Freeman.

"All right, then. Lynda is coming to give me another damn enema after I have my bath," Mrs. Freeman snapped. Then she shot a hot look at Jay. "I told you that doctor didn't know what he was talking about. My bowels are still obstructed. I haven't had any success in six days. If ever there was somebody full of shit, it's me!"

"Um, I'll let y'all have some privacy," Maureen fumbled, looking at her watch.

"Honey, nothing is private around here," Mrs. Freeman laughed. "You don't have to leave. I want my boy to get to know you better."

"That would be nice, but it's almost time for me to go to lunch anyway," Maureen said nervously, forcing herself not to look at Jay.

"Don't you move, girl!" Mrs. Freeman ordered, shaking a gnarled finger in Maureen's direction.

Before Maureen could respond, Jay shook a finger and his head at his mother like she was a surly child. She flicked her tongue out at him before she bowed her head and poked out her bottom lip.

Jay turned to Maureen and rose from his seat. "I was about to go out and get some lunch myself. I would like it very much if you'd join me," he said with a hopeful look on his face.

"Oh, uh, I was only goin' to get some fries and a burger at that place next to the big woman's dress shop," Maureen mumbled.

"Good. That's where I was going too," Jay lied, already ushering Maureen out of the room with his hand on her shoulder.

Maureen gasped and almost tripped over her own feet. Somehow she managed to look normal as they strolled down the hall.

By the time they reached the lobby, Jay's arm was around Maureen's waist and he was holding her so tightly, it felt like the inside of her stomach had turned upside down. Peggy was playing games on her computer at the front desk. When she saw Maureen with Jay, she gasped and stood up. She folded her arms and stared at Maureen in slack-jawed amazement until Maureen and Jay left the building.

"I would sure hate to get you in any kind of trouble, so I hope it's all right for employees to go to lunch with visitors," Jay said as he and Maureen walked across the parking lot toward the burger joint. He had a strong, deep voice but no identifiable accent. There was not even a hint of a drawl, so Maureen knew that he had not been raised in the South. As a matter of fact, his accent was a lot like Mel's. Just thinking about Mel made Maureen feel guilty. She was not exactly sure what she was guilty of, but she knew that the way Jay made her feel was wrong.

"I don't know if they have a rule against it, but I doubt very seriously if they'll fire me," Maureen said with confidence.

She was glad that it was a short walk. They remained silent the rest of the way.

"My mother has already grown attached to you, you know," Jay told Maureen after they had been seated in a booth in the back of the burger joint and ordered. "You remind her of someone she cared so much about."

Maureen nodded. "Her late niece. She told me a little about her." Maureen couldn't remember the last time a man had made her feel nervous. She had to cross her legs to keep from tapping her toe on the linoleum floor. Then she began to tap her fingers on the tabletop. When she realized she was doing that, she folded her arms.

"I can see that I'm making you nervous," Jay said with one eyebrow raised. He reached across the table and cupped Maureen's clammy hand in his and squeezed it. "If I'm being too forward, I apologize and I won't bother you again after today."

"Oh, no, you don't make me nervous!" Maureen blurted, her free hand in the air. "I just have a few things on my mind, that's all."

Jay nodded.

"I'm glad you invited me to have lunch with you," she told him. "I don't like that dinin' room or the vending machines in the break room. Those ready-made sandwiches look right deadly." Maureen smiled, and that made Jay feel more at ease. "I . . . I really like your mother. She's the only one of my patients so far who has not bitten, kicked, or vomited on me."

Jay made a face and shuddered. "I don't know what all you said to Mother, but she's been here a little over three months and yesterday was the first time I saw a smile on her face." Jay paused and looked Maureen in the eye and gave her the most sincere look of gratitude that he could manage. "That was because of you." For a moment, she thought he was going to shed a few tears. That told her he was sensitive, a quality she admired in a man. Something she didn't see enough of in Mel . . .

A tear formed in Maureen's eye. She had to blink hard to hold it back. "This job is not for me, so I won't be around here that long, but I will try to keep a smile on your mama's face until I leave."

"Well, Mother won't be around too much longer either. I hope you stay until she goes. I sure would appreciate that."

"Oh? You goin' to take her home and hire a home-care nurse or put her into a different facility?"

Jay shook his head. "She's got a rare form of bowel cancer. She could go any day now."

"Oh my goodness! I'm so sorry. I didn't know she was that sick. She doesn't look it and nobody told me."

"She is that sick. She won't be leaving this place alive." Jay paused and looked away for a few moments. "Hey. Let's talk about something more pleasant." He let out a loud breath and gave Maureen a look that made her heart flutter. "When can you have dinner with me? I'd love to see you again."

Maureen was so taken aback she almost fell out of her seat. "I wish I could," she replied with a bashful smile, meaning it from the bottom of her heart. "But I can't. My husband wouldn't like that."

CHAPTER 28

*J*AY'S BROWN EYES DARKENED. HIS BREATH CAUGHT IN HIS throat. HE was so disappointed now he could barely talk. "I should have known," he managed. "Well, you can tell your husband that I said he's a very lucky man. Do you have any kids?"

"I have a daughter. She's eighteen and her name is Lo'retta. Other than my older brother and his wife, and my husband, she is the only close relative I have in Florida."

"If she's half as pretty as you, she is a lucky girl." Jay paused. "Other than my mother, I don't have any close relatives, period. At least none that I know of. It's just been Mother and me since I can remember. You must be really close to your daughter. Like I said, if she's half as pretty as you are, she's very lucky."

"Oh, she's much better-lookin' than I am. She's one of the most successful models in Miami. She's been workin' since she was four-teen. She started out doin' department stores and local magazine ads for various products. Now she does catalog work and TV com-mercials, and she's on billboards. Eventually she's goin' to do run-way and the major fashion magazines, and I hope she'll be doin' things even bigger than that. Maybe even movies."

Jay gave Maureen an incredulous look. He was thoroughly im-pressed. He knew of so many black youngsters who were either in jail or dead. "Oh my! You and her daddy must be very proud of her!"

"We are—and he's her stepdaddy."

Jay nodded. "Maureen, I don't care about you being married. I respect that, but I would still like to get to know you a little better. Just knowing how much you mean to my mother and how it's lifted her spirits suddenly makes my job easier. I promised her that I would make her last years as comfortable as possible."

"What about the rest of your family? Are they helpin' you out in any way?"

"Like I said, it's just my mother and me. I don't have any siblings or children. My wife couldn't deal with how committed I am to my mother, so she divorced me a couple of years after we got married."

"I'm sorry to hear that—about your wife, I mean. I'm still a newlywed. I've only been married for about a year."

"I see. Well," Jay said with a heavy sigh. "As usual, my luck is still in the toilet. I have a lot of friends at the cable company I work for, so I keep myself busy. Once Mother is gone, it's going to be hard. We've always been very close. She had me late in life after several miscarriages," Jay said with a wistful look on his face.

The more Maureen looked at Jay, the better looking he got. She couldn't understand why she was sitting here thinking about this man's looks when she had a husband at home.

"We've lived in a lot of different places—Boston, Cleveland, and Milwaukee to name a few. My dad left when I was still in diapers, so I don't even remember him at all. Mother got restless and had to keep moving from one place to another. She cleaned houses for wealthy families for all those years." A puzzled look slid across Jay's face. "She had other skills, but that was the only kind of work she would look for and she would never tell me why." Jay shook his head. "Who can figure out older people and some of the strange things they do? Most of them have skeletons in their closets that we'll never know about."

"Tell me about it. Before my mother passed, she did a lot of mysterious stuff too. She never had a real job. She did a lot of domestic and field work. But she had a whole lot of men friends helping her out so I'm sure she had a few skeletons lurkin' in her closet too."

"I just wish my mother had told me more about herself. She's completely estranged from her family, so it's been a real lonely life."

"Have you ever tried to find any other family, Jay?"

"I wouldn't know where to begin looking. Like I told you, my daddy left when I was a baby and Mother refuses to talk about him. I didn't even know his name until I saw my birth certificate when I was eighteen. Mother told me she had some kind of falling out with her siblings over money, and that divided her family in a way that couldn't be fixed. One thing led to another and by the time I arrived on the scene, she had stopped associating with everybody in her family, except the niece she mentioned to you. When the niece died, Mother packed up our things and we started roaming around like gypsies." Jay cocked his head to the side. "I was glad when she decided to settle down in Florida."

Maureen felt sorry for Jay. He seemed like such a nice man. She wished that she could get to know him better, but she couldn't. Mel was too good to her and she would never do anything to risk losing him—especially because of another man.

At the same moment that Maureen was telling herself she would never cheat on Mel, Loretta was tumbling into the front passenger seat of Mel's SUV. She had left school during lunch and met Mel in a grocery store parking lot a couple of blocks away.

"I don't know why you can't pick me up in front of the school. We are family now, you know, so we don't have to be sneakin' around to hook up the way we do," Loretta complained, twisting her itchy behind from left to right in her seat as she struggled to make herself more comfortable.

"If somebody sees me picking you up during school hours, they might start asking questions," Mel explained. "It might get back to Maureen and we'd have some explaining to do."

"So? Like I just said, we are family now. What's suspicious about you pickin' me up from school and us bein' seen together durin' school hours? We live in the same apartment. We *work* together. What's the big deal, Daddy?"

"We have to be careful, sweetie. All we need is for the wrong person to see us checking in or out of a motel and mentioning it to your mother. She might check up on my appointment schedule, and if she doesn't see that we had a job on the books, there is no telling what she'll think. Now, we agreed that if we have to get together during school hours, we don't want anybody to know about it. The good thing is, it'll all be over soon. Just a couple more months and we can take off and never look back."

"That's good to hear," Loretta cooed. "Because I'm sick and tired of sneakin' around like some lowlife criminal!" she complained. "I'm just a woman in love and that is no crime!"

Mel silenced Loretta by leaning over and kissing her firmly on the lips. "I'm a man in love. Just be patient a little longer. Soon we can shout our love from the rooftop," he whispered. "You are the best thing that's ever happened to me."

"I know," Loretta whispered back. She looked around and then she looked at Mel like he was the sexiest man alive. As far as she was concerned, he was. "Mel, I love you to death."

"I know you do, baby, but you need to stop cutting class to be with me. I can't keep interrupting shoots to come spend a few hours with you. We can't afford to keep pushing our luck."

Loretta leaned back and gave Mel a petulant look. "I thought you wanted to be with me as much as I wanted to be with you. You even tried to get me to stay home from school today so we could spend the day enjoying ourselves. What's up with that?"

Mel shook his head. "Shit, baby. I wasn't thinking straight this morning. I mean, oh, baby—you really laid some good loving on me before you left for school this morning. I couldn't stop thinking about it. I couldn't help myself when you called and told me to pick you up."

"So then why are you complainin'?" Loretta ran her finger along the side of Mel's face.

"I'm not complaining, honey," Mel replied, grabbing her hand and sucking on her finger. "It's just that we need to keep this thing we got going under control."

"This thing?" Loretta snapped, snatching her finger out of Mel's mouth. "So now our love is 'this thing' to you?" You didn't say stupid shit like this before you married my mama! Maybe we should have left 'this thing' the way it was. Maybe you shouldn't have married her after all."

"You practically *forced* me to marry your mother so she would let me move in!" Mel reminded her. "And that's so I can have some legal rights when it comes to some of the jobs you do. There may be contracts that'll come up that she might not want to sign. She's refused to sign too many already, and that was a bunch of money we lost out on. As your legal guardian now, I can sign them and she wouldn't even have to know about it. We don't have to sneak around and forge her signature on releases and contracts like we sometimes used to when she wouldn't."

"Well, I realize all of that, but I'm startin' to feel a little guilty about fuckin' you in my mama's apartment. I hope you're right about us bein' able to go public soon. I wouldn't want her to find out any other way. That nosy-ass Mr. Ben next door keeps lookin' at me like he knows somethin'. Maybe he heard us makin' love in my room or somethin'. His bedroom is on the other side of my bedroom wall."

"That's why we should continue to rent motel or hotel rooms when he's home. Or do our business on the living room couch or your mama's bed." Mel paused and started the car. "Now that we got that all out of the way, give me some sugar."

Loretta kissed Mel long and hard, and they remained silent until they made it back to the apartment. They were disappointed to see Mr. Ben's car parked out front. That old goat was usually out and about this time of day.

"Shit! Mr. Ben's home. You want to go to a motel?" Loretta hissed, marching alongside Mel as they made their way up onto the front porch.

"No," Mel answered, looking up and down the street, glad he didn't see anybody he knew nosing about. "Your mama won't be home for a few hours, and her bed is much more comfortable than yours anyway. We just have to remember to change the sheets before she gets home."

Loretta started to undress as soon as they got in the front door.

"Baby, don't do that!" Mel hollered, shaking a finger at her and giving her a stern look.

"Why not?" she giggled, kicking off her shoes. "I do this all the time."

"Your mama or that nosy oaf of an uncle of yours could come here unannounced. If we just had enough time to get out of the bed, and they see your panties and clothes on the floor by the door, what would they think?"

"Oh," Loretta said with a pout. She snatched up her clothes and shoes and followed Mel to the bedroom he shared with Maureen.

They spent the next hour making love in Maureen's bed. Afterward, they got dressed and moved to the living room. Loretta brought Mel a beer and they piled onto the couch to watch a couple of TV game shows with Loretta sitting on Mel's lap.

"I can't get enough of you," Loretta whispered in Mel's ear during a commercial. "I can't stand the thought of my mama gettin' what's mine. I think we should tell her today—or tomorrow. I can't wait another couple of months for my graduation."

"Are you crazy?" Mel yelled, almost choking on some beer.

"I'm tired of sneakin' around with you," Loretta whined. "Why don't we run away to Costa Rica or Mexico so we can be together out in the open *now*? I want the whole world to know about the man I love, Daddy!"

Oh, how Mel loved it when she called him Daddy. It was music to his ears. A symphony! He had this little gold mine hook, line, and sinker, but there were times when she tested his patience. Like now. "You don't want to graduate? You didn't get this far in school to drop out when you have only two more months to go. That would be insane! What about your career? What about my career? I'm a lot older than you, and if I don't make it big soon, I probably won't. Stop talking crazy. Things are going just the way we planned."

"Mel, you are the only man I will ever love," Loretta vowed. "You're the best thing that ever happened to me."

Mel had heard words to that effect so many times before from so many different young girls, it didn't even impress him anymore.

"I know, sweetie. I appreciate hearing you say that. I am a lucky man." Mel kissed Loretta on the tip of her nose and slapped her butt. "Now get up and get dressed and let's take a ride to the beach. We're going to be shooting down there this weekend for the Gardner swimsuit ads. We can pick up some ribs on the way home so your mama won't have to come home and cook today. That's the least we can do."

CHAPTER 29

*M*AUREEN WAS IN LOVE. FOR THE FIRST TIME IN HER LIFE, SHE WAS hopelessly in love. She was in love with Jay Freeman. Thinking back, she realized that she had fallen for him the first time she laid eyes on him.

"There ain't no such a thing as love at first sight! It's *umpossible*. You got to get to know a person real good before you can fall in love with 'em." Mama Ruby's words taunted Maureen as she drove home from work that evening. Mama Ruby had been wrong, though.

There *was* such a thing as love at first sight, Maureen told herself. It was not "umpossible" like Mama Ruby had told her. Maureen was in love, but under the current circumstances, she couldn't do a goddamn thing about it.

Despite what Mama Ruby had tried to teach Maureen about love (even though Mama Ruby had confessed to her that it had been love at first sight when *she* met her first husband), Maureen knew what was in her heart. She didn't know much about Jay, but she knew all she needed to know. He was charming and sensitive and she loved a man with a sense of humor. During their lunch, he had said cute, funny things that had made her laugh out loud, something Mel rarely managed to do. The fact that Jay was so devoted to his mother was another point in his favor. He had his share of flaws, but nothing she couldn't live with. He was not classically handsome, but she liked his looks anyway. His eyes were too small, his nose was slightly crooked, and there was a small bump on the ridge. Father Time had already claimed a noticeable portion of his wavy brown hair, but she could overlook his receding hairline and the bald spot on the back of his head. He was well groomed and so polite that he made her feel socially clumsy.

Maureen's attraction to Jay seemed almost supernatural. She felt like she had known him all of her life. Her emotions had already spun out of control. She didn't know what to do with herself. And Mel. Poor Mel. He was so good to her and Loretta. Maureen could never hurt him. If only she had waited just a little longer to marry Mel, she would probably be with Jay. But she was married to Mel and she would stay married to him.

Unless he left her on his own, or died . . .

Maureen scolded herself for even allowing such a ghoulish thought to enter her mind, but she couldn't help herself. The more she thought about Jay, the more she wanted to get to know him better—and the more she wanted to be with him than she wanted to be with Mel.

When Maureen got home, Mel was in the living room, slumped in one of the easy chairs, sipping from a beer can. She didn't like what she saw. She fantasized about him packing up and leaving, but she knew he wasn't going anywhere anytime soon—if ever—and she had no intention of making him pack up and leave. She had too much of an investment in Mel: her daughter's future. If she dumped him, Loretta would be devastated and their relationship would never be the same. That alone was reason enough for Maureen to put Jay out of her mind.

But she couldn't.

"How was work today?" Mel asked.

"Oh, it was all right, I guess," Maureen muttered, kicking off her shoes. "I met this one old lady's son today, and he was really nice and friendly. He even took me to lunch," Maureen added, curious as to how Mel would react to her socializing with another man.

"That's nice, dear," Mel said, more interested in his beer than in Maureen. He took a long drink and let out a burp that sounded like a growl.

"His name's Jay. His mother is kind of fussy, so I felt real sorry for him today. I really enjoyed talkin' to him. . . ."

"That's nice, dear," was all Mel said again.

Maureen was disappointed. She expected Mel to be curious about her new male friend, but she was also glad to know that he was not the jealous type. "Is Loretta home?"

"Uh, she's at the mall with a couple of other kids," Mel answered.

"I'm glad she's spendin' more time with her young friends," Maureen said with a thoughtful look on her face. "I'll thaw out some pork chops and get dinner started."

"Oh, you don't have to worry about cooking dinner. I picked up some ribs on my way home," Mel said quickly.

"That was real thoughtful of you, honey!" Maureen said. "You are goin' to spoil me rotten."

"I hope so, baby," Mel crooned.

I don't deserve this man, Maureen told herself. The man had married her knowing that she didn't love him, just so he could help her provide a real home for her daughter. How many other men would be willing to do something that noble? The fact that Mel didn't have a problem with her having male friends was another bonus. Maureen enjoyed a lot of other bonuses, too. Since Mel moved in, he had purchased new living room furniture, he'd paid off Maureen's two credit cards, and he paid most of the monthly household expenses.

Loretta was also very generous. Last week she bought Maureen new clothes from some of the most expensive boutiques in Miami, and she'd sent Maureen to a spa where she'd been pampered for four hours straight. She'd even purchased a new bed mattress for Maureen (Loretta and Mel had practically worn the old one down to the floor). Maureen had so much going on in her life now, and she didn't want to lose it. She *had* to keep her increasing obsession with Jay Freeman under control.

Later in the month, Maureen went into the kitchen at the nursing home as soon as Catty started her shift and told her about Jay. She had not mentioned him before because she had been trying to put him out of her mind, but she couldn't, so she had to share her feelings with her best friend. Catty listened with great interest as Maureen regaled her with the details of her fascination with Jay. "Girl, there is somethin' about that man. Maybe I'm goin' through my midlife crisis a few years early, huh?"

"Midlife crisis my ass!" Catty guffawed, shaking a spatula in Maureen's face. "You been bit by the love bug, honey. You just need some strange dick, that's all."

Maureen rolled her eyes and gave her friend an exasperated look. "I'm a married woman, Catty."

"Uh-huh! I knew somethin' like this was goin' to happen after you married Mel. You should have waited," Catty teased.

"Hush your mouth! You kept tellin' me I'd better marry Mel while I had a chance!" Maureen wailed.

"Well, you don't have to stay with Mel," Catty said with a shrug. "I hate to keep remindin' you, but I left my husband within hours after we got married."

"I couldn't do that to Lo'retta."

"You ain't doin' nothin' to Lo'retta."

"If I dumped Mel, he wouldn't want to keep workin' with my daughter."

"So what? She don't really need him no more! Her name is well known now. I see three different billboards with her face on 'em on my way to work every day, and I can't crack open a newspaper that don't have at least one ad with her in it. That girl is doin' so well now, I know she could hook up with some other photographer and manager real quick," Catty declared.

"You got a point there. She could probably do all right now without Mel's help," Maureen agreed.

"Then what's the problem?" Catty paused, shook her head, and mumbled profanities under her breath. The spatula was still in her hand and she waved it some more as soon as she spoke again. "I mean besides that damn Mel!" Catty snarled, spitting out Mel's name like it was a wad of stale chewing gum. As far as she was concerned, that was exactly what his name was. She knew from the hostile stares he gave her when she visited Maureen and the sarcastic remarks he made when she tried to talk to him that he still didn't like her. It was no wonder she resented Mel more than ever now. Because on top of everything else, he was blocking Maureen from being with a man she did have feelings for.

Maureen blew out some air. "I don't know what to do. I'm just gettin' used to bein' married."

"Then do the next best thing—do a little somethin' on the side with Jay," Catty suggested.

"Me? You want me to cheat on my husband?" Maureen gasped. She lowered her voice when she noticed a couple of other kitchen workers looking and listening. "You of all people ought to know that I would never do somethin' like that," she muttered.

"Why not? I do it all the time!"

"You don't have a husband anymore."

"After I divorced Yellow Jack, I was a common law wife to several other men, and I had affairs on all of 'em," Catty boasted. "If I ever be another man's common law wife, I'd probably cheat on him too. Cheatin' is human nature. It keeps folks from gettin' bored."

Maureen shook her head and laughed. "I need to get back to work."

"You need to start actin' more like the rest of us, girl," Catty hollered at Maureen as she scurried out of the kitchen, still laughing and shaking her head.

When she entered Mrs. Freeman's room, Jay was there.

"Hello, Maureen. I haven't seen you in a while," he said.

"I guess you've been coming by while I was tendin' to one of my other patients or on one of my off days," she told him.

"Well, I'm happy to see you again," Jay said. "Very happy."

"Me too," Maureen replied with a huge smile on her happy face.

CHAPTER 30

*T*HAT THURSDAY AND FRIDAY, WHEN MAUREEN DIDN'T HAVE TO GO TO work, she didn't know what to do with herself. Loretta had plans to hang out with some friends after school on Thursday. On Friday evening, she was scheduled to do her second auto show assignment in less than a month. With prom coming up, Loretta was giddy about that. She had already purchased two different dresses, but she still made trips to the mall every other day to search for another one.

Though Loretta was fairly careful with her money, she did like to splurge now and then, and not just on herself. She had purchased a brand-new Mustang for Maureen the day before, and that had made Maureen so happy she cried. What puzzled Maureen was that Loretta had not purchased a car for herself yet. "I'm goin' to wait until this summer," was all Loretta had said when Maureen asked her about that.

Since Loretta couldn't take Mel to the prom and she didn't want to miss out on such an important night in a high school student's life, she had settled for Tyrone Hardy, one of Mona's cousins. Since Tyrone was gay, he wouldn't be any trouble. Besides, the boy could dance like Michael Jackson.

It seemed like Maureen's plan to spend more time with her daughter had backfired. Now instead of Loretta spending so much time with Mel, she was running from here to there with Mona and a few other teenagers. At least that was what Maureen had been led to believe. Loretta was spending more time with Mona and her other friends but not that much. She still had Mona at her beck and call. She thought nothing of calling her up at a moment's notice. Like she did that Thursday evening. "I need you to give me a ride. Mel has a shoot in Lauderdale this Saturday that don't include me, but I want to go with him. If my mama asks, I spent the night with you."

"I don't like lyin' for you. Especially when I know you still fuckin' your mama's husband," Mona protested.

"I'll give you a hundred bucks," Loretta offered.

"Cool!" Mona yelled. "What time do you want me to pick you up and where do I have to drop you off to meet Mel?"

Loretta had become even more attached to Mel. She could barely stand for him to be out of her sight or share the same bed with her mother. Waiting until June, when she'd be out of school and free to leave home with him and let the rest of the world know how she felt about him, was almost unbearable. But she had no choice.

Maureen had no choice either, but she was beginning to weaken. The more she saw Jay, the more she wanted to be with him, not Mel. The people who knew her best noticed a change in her demeanor.

"Mel must really be tunin' up your body in the bedroom on a regular basis," Fast Black commented to Maureen during one of her unannounced visits to Maureen's apartment. "I bet he got the right tool to do it with too. Them tight pants he wears protects the property, but they don't hide the view, if you know what I mean. I don't remember the last time I rode on a train as big as his."

"Keep your voice down, you nasty thing you!" Maureen ordered, looking toward the hallway. "Get your mind out of the gutter! I don't want my daughter to hear you talkin' that trash." Maureen lowered her voice even more. "And yes, Mel is takin' care of business in the bedroom on a regular basis."

Maureen's last sentence was a lie. Well, almost. Mel was taking care of business in the bedroom on a regular basis but not with Maureen. The last time Mel tried to make love to her, she told him she had cramps, but she was not about to reveal that information to a big mouth like Fast Black. Fast Black and Virgil had once been lovers and were still very close. She would blab Maureen's business to him in a heartbeat. Besides, Maureen told Virgil what she wanted him to know herself. She wanted him to know how she felt about Jay.

"I don't know exactly what it is about Jay, but I feel a real strong connection to him and it's about to drive me crazy," she confessed to her brother over the telephone after Fast Black had left.

"What do you plan to do about it?" Virgil asked, holding his breath. The last thing he wanted to hear was that his sister was going to cheat on her husband.

"Nothin', I guess. If Mel ever leaves me, maybe me and Jay can get together." *Or if he dies,* she thought, shuddering so hard her whole body ached.

Maureen knew that Virgil had initially had some concerns about Mel's relationship with Loretta, but now that Loretta was spending more time with kids her own age, her spending too much time alone with Mel was a subject that Virgil rarely brought up anymore. Now he had something else to worry about: Maureen's attraction to another man.

That Monday morning when Maureen went back to work, she went to Mrs. Freeman's room around ten to grease her scalp and braid her hair. Mrs. Freeman was sitting up in bed with tears rolling down her face.

"What's the matter?" Maureen asked. She set the tray that contained a wide-toothed comb and a jar of Royal Crown hair grease on the nightstand and rushed to the side of Mrs. Freeman's bed.

"My son is on his way over here," Mrs. Freeman sobbed.

Maureen was confused. She couldn't imagine why Mrs. Freeman would be crying about Jay coming to visit her. "Shouldn't you be happy about that?"

Mrs. Freeman shook her head. "Not this time. There is something real important that I have to tell him while I still can."

"All right, then," Maureen replied, still confused. She waited for Mrs. Freeman to say more on the subject. When she didn't, Maureen added, "I can come back after he leaves."

*   *   *

Maureen was tending to other patients, so she didn't see Jay when he arrived. When she passed by the receptionist's desk a few minutes later, though, Peggy promptly reported that he'd already entered the premises.

Whatever Jay's mother had to tell him had to be very private because the door to her room remained closed for hours. It was still closed when Maureen prepared to go home. Jay's car was not in the parking lot, but another hearse was. Maureen didn't know until one of her coworkers called her at home around 7:00 p.m. to tell her that Mrs. Freeman had passed away during Jay's visit. That was only the beginning of an unimaginable turn of events.

For one thing, the verdict in the Rodney King case a few days ago had angered a lot of people. The cops who had been caught on tape beating Rodney King had gotten off with a slap on the wrist. People had been rioting and looting in L.A. and several other cities, even parts of Miami, since the verdict had been announced. Two young men who lived across the street from Maureen had been arrested for looting a beauty supply store, and the Puerto Rican family that lived on Maureen's block, the parents and their four grown sons, had all been arrested for breaking into the corner grocery store. They had loaded up the back of their truck with everything from video games to cartons of beer.

The next day when Maureen left for work, she saw numerous police cars and a few TV news vans along the way. Several streets had been closed, the windows in a lot of stores had been broken, and there were angry-looking people on almost every corner. A great sadness came over her when she saw that several of the businesses in the strip mall near her work had been looted. When she pulled into the nursing home parking lot, she saw a news van from one of the local TV stations parked near the entrance. Several reporters and cameramen were in the lobby scurrying around like squirrels, speaking into walkie-talkies and scribbling on notepads. Her first thought was that this all had something to do with the riots.

"Peggy, what in the world is goin' on around here with all these newspeople?" Maureen asked as she approached the receptionist.

Peggy's eyes got so big and wide she no longer looked Asian. "You didn't hear?" she choked, wiping her nose with a Kleenex.

"Hear what?"

"Mrs. Freeman passed yesterday after you left," Peggy reported.

"I know that. Darla called me at home last night and told me. Is that what all of this fuss is all about? Was Mrs. Freeman somebody important?" Maureen was so confused she could barely stand still as her mind raced with one thought after another. Why would the newspeople be interested in Mrs. Freeman? If that little old lady was somebody important, how come Jay hadn't mentioned that when Maureen had lunch with him?

"Was Mrs. Freeman connected to that Rodney King in some way?" Maureen asked.

Peggy shook her head and gave Maureen a long, sad look. Then she handed her the morning newspaper. The headline made Maureen's head spin almost off her shoulders.

WOMAN CONFESSES ON DEATHBED TO THIRTY-SEVEN-YEAR-OLD KIDNAPPING

"What's this . . . I . . . ," Maureen stammered as she read. As soon as she saw that the woman on the deathbed was Mrs. Freeman and that Jay was the victim of the kidnapping she had confessed to, Maureen ran to the restroom and threw up.

CHAPTER 31

*V*IRGIL HAD JUST SAT DOWN TO EAT HIS BREAKFAST WHEN THE TELE-phone rang. It was Maureen and she was hysterical. "Virgil, you won't believe what's goin' on!" she wailed. "I just can't believe it! I just can't believe it!"

Even though a lot of innocent people had been hurt by the riot-ers, Virgil hoped that that was not the case with Maureen. He also hoped that Mel had not hit his baby sister or run off with another woman. With his sneaky eyes and curly hair, he seemed like the type of man who would hit his wife and run off with another woman. Being that he had such a sissified job that had him associ-ating with beautiful models all the time, it would be just like him to get involved with one.

Virgil's thoughts began to run from one extreme to another. The unbearable thought that maybe Mel had done something to Loretta sent chills up and down his spine. With the kind of money she was making, and allowing that sucker to help manage it to boot, it wasn't much of a stretch of Virgil's imagination for him to think that Mel had run off with Loretta's money. Virgil's very next thought was how hard he was going to bash in Mel's head if he had done anything to hurt his baby sister or his niece.

"What's the matter, sugar? Is it Lo'retta? Did Mel do somethin' to one of y'all?" Virgil asked.

Corrine stood over him holding a pot of coffee. There was a wild-eyed look on her face. She adored her sister-in-law and niece, and if Mel had done something to them, he had a head whupping coming from her too. "I knew there was somethin' about that man," she snarled.

"Virgil, did you read today's newspaper?" Maureen croaked, dismissing the comments about Mel. Right now he was the least of her worries.

"No, why? Hold on a minute," Virgil said to Maureen. Then he looked at Corrine. "Baby, see if the paperboy delivered the newspaper yet." Virgil returned his attention to Maureen. "You in some kind of trouble, sugar?"

"Jay's mama passed yesterday. Before she died, she told him . . . she told him that he wasn't her real son and that she kidnapped him when he was a baby!" Maureen paused to catch her breath. Then she shrieked, "JAY IS A KIDNAP VICTIM!"

Virgil yelped and dropped the telephone. When Corrine returned to the kitchen with the newspaper, he looked like a zombie sitting at the kitchen table.

Corrine waved her hand in front of Virgil's face, but he didn't even blink. She picked up the telephone. "Mo'reen, what did you say to your brother? I think he just had a stroke or somethin'. You need to get over here lickety-split!"

There was so much chaos going on at the nursing home, reporters running around like headless chickens and such, that nobody noticed when Maureen ran out the front door like somebody was chasing her with a stick.

When she got to Virgil's house, he was stretched out on his living room couch looking up at the ceiling with a blank expression on his face. If he hadn't blinked, Maureen would have thought he was dead.

"What's the matter with him?" Maureen asked Corrine as they both hovered over Virgil. "Did you call the doctor?"

"I'm all right," Virgil wheezed, looking at Maureen with tears in his eyes. "I think it was somethin' I ate." He slowly sat up and then swung his legs to the side of the couch. Maureen flopped down beside him, her arm around his shoulder.

"I can't believe what they're saying about Jay. That nursin' home must be a madhouse by now," Corrine said.

"That's where I called y'all from. That place was crawlin' with re-porters! It was crazy there, so I had to leave," Maureen explained. "I can't go back to work today. First this story about Jay bein' kid-napped when he was a baby, and my favorite patient bein' the kid-napper, and now Virgil actin' and lookin' so strange."

Corrine checked her watch; then she looked at Virgil. "Speakin' of work, I should call my boss at the cannery and tell her that I might come in late today."

"No, you go on to work, baby," Virgil told Corrine in a weak voice, waving his hand. "I'll be all right."

"You don't look all right. You look like you seen a ghost," Mau-reen told Virgil.

"I'm fine, y'all!" Virgil hollered, rising. "I think I'll take the day off, though."

Maureen suddenly looked toward the coffee table where Cor-rine had dropped the newspaper. "Did y'all read the whole news-paper story?" she asked, looking at Virgil.

"I did. I can't believe what I read. Lord Almighty! Jay was kid-napped?" Corrine said, lifting the newspaper. "What kind of woman would take another woman's baby and keep him all these years? I don't like to speak ill of the dead, but if that old woman hadn't died, the law should have her put up *under* the jailhouse!" Corrine turned to Virgil. "Am I right, baby?"

Virgil swallowed hard and gave a weak nod. "Um . . . sure enough," he mumbled. "But how do they know this old woman is tellin' the truth?"

Corrine and Virgil looked at Maureen at the same time. "Yeah, how do they know? The paper didn't say," Corrine pointed out.

"On my way over here, the radio news said some investigators flew down from St. Louis late last night with Jay's real birth certifi-cate that had his footprints on it. They matched Jay's," Maureen said. "Not only that, but the news also said Jay has a purple birth-mark on the back of his neck and so did the kidnapped baby. Plus, Mrs. Freeman still had the jumper, the cap with his name stitched on it, the same socks, and the shoes that Jay had on when she kid-napped him—every item that the mother had described to the cops. Mrs. Freeman had kept everything in a plastic bag in her freezer."

Corrine, with her mouth hanging open, turned back to Virgil. "Like I just said, if that old woman hadn't died, they should have put her up under the jailhouse."

Virgil just blinked. For now, he had to act as normal as possible. He wanted to "enjoy" his life while he still could because his instincts told him that Jay's kidnapping was just the tip of an iceberg. One that could potentially crack the case of Maureen's kidnapping wide open. Virgil had no idea what was in store for him: a stress-related fatal heart attack or prison for being an accomplice in Maureen's kidnapping. He couldn't decide which would be worse. Just from Maureen's initial reaction to Jay's situation, Virgil knew that he had to unburden his guilt before he died.

"Thank you. Mrs. Freeman was a nice old lady and I liked her a lot, but what she did was unforgivable!" Maureen yelled, turning back to Virgil.

"I'll read the paper later on," he muttered with a series of nervous, prolonged coughs. "I guess I need to get my tail on to work after all, y'all."

"You ain't goin' no place," Maureen told Virgil. "Either you come home with me so I can look after you, or I'm goin' to stay here with you today until Corrine gets home from work."

Maureen only agreed to go home because Corrine decided to take the whole day off so she could stay home and look after Virgil. Virgil was anxious for Maureen to leave. The bombshell that had just been dropped on him made it hard for him to look at her. Just knowing how she felt about what Jay's "mother" had done to him, Virgil didn't even want to think about how Maureen would feel if he told her that Mama Ruby had done the same thing to her.

Virgil felt even worse after Maureen had left, but his pain became almost unbearable after he read the entire newspaper story. It was a lengthy report, taking up three columns. It included pictures of Mrs. Freeman as a young woman and a more recent picture of her, and several pictures of Jay as a teenager and as an adult. The details of Mrs. Freeman's confession were chilling. The grim

story had begun in St. Louis, Missouri, in June 1955 when Jay was
eighteen months old. Mrs. Freeman's teenage niece had snatched
him from his stroller while his mother was in a neighborhood grocery store. It was supposed to be a prank. The girl didn't like Jay's
mother and had wanted to "teach her a lesson." But after just a few
hours, the young girl panicked. She was too afraid to return Jay to
his mother in person, so she left him with Mrs. Freeman, her late
father's widowed, childless younger sister, until they could figure
out what to do next. Mrs. Freeman didn't want her niece to go to
prison. She put her on a bus and sent her to live with relatives in
rural Mississippi that same day. Then she called up her employer
and told him that she had shingles and wouldn't be able to come
back to work for at least a week, maybe two. She needed more time
to figure out her next move.

A few days later, Mrs. Freeman received word from her relatives
in Mississippi that her niece had committed suicide. She had not
left a note, so the relatives had no idea why the girl had taken her
own life. Mrs. Freeman panicked. She really didn't know what to do
next! With the niece no longer around to tell the authorities what
really happened, Mrs. Freeman was afraid that *she'd* have to take
the blame for the kidnapping if she returned the baby to his
mother. She was in her late forties at the time, and she certainly
didn't want to spend her golden years in prison. After a few high-
balls, she came up with a plan and it was obvious what she had to
do next: She would keep the baby and raise him as her own. His
real name was Lawrence Dwayne Foster but Mrs. Freeman re-
named him Jesus Christopher Freeman.

A week after the kidnapping, Mrs. Freeman left St. Louis on a
Greyhound bus. She left no forwarding address or any other way
for her relatives or friends to communicate with her. For years she
roamed from one state to another working as a domestic. She had
homeschooled Jay until he reached his teens. She moved to Miami
in 1973 and had lived there ever since.

The report included additional details that were just as chilling
as Mrs. Freeman's confession. A year after Jay's abduction, his alcoholic father strangled Jay's pregnant mother to death and received

a life sentence in prison with no chance of parole. Jay's only sibling, an older brother, had to be shuffled around from one relative to another. He had dropped out of high school and become one of the most vicious pimps in St. Louis until one of the prostitutes in his stable shot and killed him. Then ten years ago, Jay's father had a massive heart attack and died in prison. Jay's biological grandparents on both sides were deceased, but he had a lot of other relatives still living in St. Louis. He was in the process of being reunited with them all.

Virgil and Corrine agreed that this was the kind of story that Lifetime TV had cut its teeth on. As far as Virgil was concerned, Jay's kidnapping was even more sensational than Maureen's.

After Virgil had read the newspaper article twice and watched a TV report on the six o'clock news, he called Maureen's apartment. His stomach turned when Mel answered the phone. "Dude! I'm so glad you called," Mel hollered. "Your sister is damn near delirious. What I want to know is why she is so worked up over this Jay character—or whatever the hell his name is now. She just met him . . . or so she claims!"

"Well, if you think Mo'reen is foolin' around with Jay, you don't have nothin' to worry about. I know my sister and I know she would never go outside of her marriage," Virgil said stiffly. He had to bite his tongue to keep from saying what he really wanted to say. He knew that if he ever lost his temper with Mel, he would say some pretty hellish things to him. The last thing in the world Virgil ever wanted to do was hurt Maureen. Especially now . . .

"I know she wouldn't, and neither would I, but I hope you can talk some sense into her," Mel said. "I'm really worried about her."

"How come you so worried about my sister, my man? Jay is her friend, so naturally she'd be upset about what he's goin' through."

"I know that, but I don't want her to get all caught up in this mess. I don't want a bunch of nosy reporters or anybody else coming to my place trying to interview Maureen. She's not the sharpest knife in the drawer, so she might say something real stupid and make *me* look like a fool. That could cost me a few jobs."

"Excuse me, brother, but that apartment is Mo'reen's place too.

If she wants a reporter or anybody else to come over there to talk to her, that's up to her." Virgil had to hold his breath and press his lips together because it was almost impossible for him to remain civil to Mel. "Would you please put her on the telephone?" Virgil requested with his fist balled, itching to slam it against the side of Mel's head.

"Hold on. She's in the bedroom lying down. I just made her take a pill, so she might be too groggy to talk."

About a minute later, Maureen came on the line. "I'm fine," she told Virgil. "But I don't feel like talkin' right now. Can I call you back?"

Virgil had to wait three agonizing days for Maureen to call him back.

"Did you hear from your friend Jay yet?" Virgil asked immediately, putting a lot of emphasis on the word *friend*. He hoped that that was all Jay still was to Maureen.

"Uh-huh. I looked up his number in the phone book and I just got off the phone with him a few minutes ago," Maureen answered in a hoarse voice.

"He must be goin' out of his mind."

"That's puttin' it mildly. He's in a state of shock. Other than that, he's doin' about as well as you can expect somebody in his position to be doin'," Maureen choked. "He can't sleep or eat much, though. He had to go to the emergency room last night to get some medication because he thought he was havin' a nervous breakdown."

"Oh my Lord," Virgil moaned. "I'm so sorry to hear that Jay's takin' this so hard. Sounds like that brother is fallin' apart."

"Wouldn't you be fallin' apart if you just found out somebody kidnapped you when you was a baby and kept it a secret from you for more than thirty-five years? I know that if somethin' like that had happened to me, I would be fallin' apart too," Maureen said.

CHAPTER 32

VIRGIL FELT LIKE HE WAS ABOUT TO HAVE A NERVOUS BREAKDOWN himself. He was having heart palpitations and chest pains, and his stomach felt like it was on fire. He knew that he couldn't let that happen right now, though. He had to be strong for Maureen.

"Uh, Mo'reen, so far everything about Jay on the TV and in the newspaper is doom and gloom. I'm surprised he ain't been carted off to a mental hospital by now. But from what you told me about him, he seems like a strong, levelheaded brother. He turned out all right. Much better than he would have if he *hadn't* been kidnapped and raised by such a good woman. He had a blessed life because of her. I hope he ain't goin' to let this news destroy his life now. I'm sure he got a lot of things to live for."

"Jay is blessed. He has a lot to be thankful for, praise the Lord. And, yes, that woman did raise him right. I just hope that some-thin' else good comes out of this," Maureen replied.

"I hope so too," Virgil said hopefully.

"Two big-time therapists already contacted Jay, offerin' him their free services, but he wouldn't be needin' a therapist in the first place if he hadn't been kidnapped! Talk show people and book publishers keep callin' him, and reporters keep comin' to his house, even buggin' his coworkers and his neighbors. And he told me that one of his so-called cousins is tryin' to figure out who *he* can sue."

"The cousin wants to sue somebody? Is that what Jay is plannin' to do? Who would they sue? That old woman and the girl that snatched him are both dead."

"The cousin claims the St. Louis cops didn't do a good enough job of lookin' for Jay, so he thinks they ought to be sued. But Jay's a simple man. Money and all of this outrageous publicity don't even faze him. All it's doin' is gettin' on his nerves. He just wants to be left alone now. People keep comin' out of the woodwork tryin' to cash in on Jay's story in some way. His own preacher went on a talk show to tell how he 'guided' Jay and his mother to the Lord. Other than his boss and a few of his friends from work, I'm the only person he wants to talk to right now."

"Well, this is a big story, Mo'reen. A lot more folks are goin' to want to talk to Jay. Is Jay what he will keep callin' hisself? I like it better than Lawrence."

"As far as I know, he's goin' to continue goin' by Jay. I know what you mean about more people goin' to want to talk to him, though. While I was on the phone with him, a pushy woman from some New York magazine had the operator cut in on our call. She's doin' a piece on a bunch of other kidnapped kids and wants to add Jay. He is the only black victim so far, and that magazine woman thinks it's a big deal because kidnappin' is not that common among black folks." Maureen paused and sucked in some air. "I know we black folks got just as many problems as the rest of the races. Other than Jay, I don't think I ever heard of a black baby gettin' kidnapped. Not for ransom or by somebody that wants a child to claim as their own so they can raise it—which is more cruel than demandin' ransom. At least with a ransom situation, the family would probably get their baby back if they paid the kidnappers. I can't imagine all the pain Jay's real mama must have gone through before her husband killed her. It's awful! It's a sin and a shame. Don't you think so?"

"Yeah." Virgil cleared his throat and rubbed his chest. He had to keep shaking his head to make sure he was awake, because so far, this seemed like a nightmare.

"I couldn't imagine doin' somethin' so unholy," Maureen said angrily. "I love kids more than I love life. I didn't think I'd ever get over losin' Loraine. Nothin' is more painful than losin' a child, but my child died and I eventually learned to live with it. If somebody had kidnapped one of my kids, *I couldn't live with that.* I would rather have my child die than get kidnapped and me never see him or her again."

"But Jay can see the folks he got left again. If he had died, that couldn't happen. Do you really think it would be better for a child to die than be kidnapped, Mo'reen?"

"I don't know, Virgil. I can't even think straight right now. All I know is what Mrs. Freeman did goes against God and nature."

"Maybe . . . ," Virgil continued hesitantly. "Maybe it would have been better if that old woman had died and never told Jay the truth. He wouldn't have ever found out."

"That would have been even worse!" Maureen yelled. "Only a real evil person would do somethin' that mean. I don't care how good a person Mrs. Freeman was and how good a mama she was to Jay. I don't think they would let her into heaven if she had not come clean on her deathbed."

Virgil remained silent for a few moments. He had to remain as composed as possible because he didn't know how he could go on with his life now knowing how Maureen felt.

"Um, don't you kind of feel a little bit sorry for that old lady? Maybe she couldn't have babies of her own. At least she was a better role model than anybody in Jay's real family."

"I don't care if his real family were demons. Nobody has the right to take somebody else's child. There ain't no reason good enough for them to do that. And yes, Mrs. Freeman raised Jay up to be a good man, but him knowin' what he knows now, can you imagine the kind of emotions he must be goin' through? Somethin' like this could make a person go crazy! He might never trust another person again. He might never feel comfortable with his real identity and might spend the rest of his life feelin' like a man with a split personality. This might have a bad effect on all of the relationships he got now—with his coworkers, his friends . . . and even *me*!"

"Well, the least you can do is continue to be there for him. If he decides he can't deal with the reality of his new life now and don't want to continue bein' your friend, you'll just have to live with that."

"I know that already. I can live with that. I still got my family and my life is goin' just fine. My biggest problem right now is makin' sure Loretta keeps up with her homework and continues to stay out of trouble." Somehow Maureen managed to laugh. "At least I know who I am and where I came from. My past ain't a *Twilight Zone* mystery like Jay's is."

Virgil's heart skipped a beat and his stomach churned. For a few seconds he thought he was going to have to duck into the bathroom and throw up. "Call me if you need me," he said before he hung up. He resumed his zombie-like state, sitting on his couch staring at the wall with a grimace frozen on his face. It looked like he had on a mask. He remained that way for the next two hours.

By the end of the next day, Virgil felt like he was ready to be embalmed. Maureen had called him up several times, each time revealing more details about Jay's case. "Jay is even worse than he was before," she reported. "I went to his house last night, and he couldn't even sit down for more than five minutes at a time. His telephone was ringin' off the hook and another reporter was knockin' on his front door. So far, *all* of Jay's kinfolks sound like straight-up thugs." Maureen paused and shook her head. She took a deep breath and continued. "Jay told me that he didn't know what he would do if he hadn't met me. Last night I sat for two hours listenin' to him talk about all the confusion and strange emotions he's feelin'. I'm goin' to talk to him on the phone as much as I can."

"Mo'reen, I know you like Jay, but you have to remember that you got a family and they need you too. You can't be neglectin' them and gettin' too caught up in Jay's situation. I think you did enough for him already. From this point on, this is somethin' that the brother needs to sort out on his own."

"Virgil, there is no way in the world I'm goin' to turn my back on Jay right now. Especially after he told me he didn't know what he would have done if he hadn't met me. As soon as I cook dinner for Loretta and Mel, I'm goin' back over to Jay's house."

Virgil had been feeling like hell ever since the news about Jay broke, but now he felt even worse. He had to abruptly conclude his conversation with Maureen and run to the bathroom to throw up again. The knowledge of what he knew about Maureen had been nipping at his heels for thirty-six years. He knew that it was just a matter of time before it consumed him completely.

"Lord, help me decide what to do now!" Virgil prayed as he leaned against the bathroom door and stared at the black bile he'd just deposited into the commode. He felt like he had been physically attacked and every wound that he had ever sustained in his life had been reopened.

Before Jay's story had been revealed, Virgil had almost convinced himself that it was no longer important for Maureen to know the truth about her past. He didn't see any reason to tell her as long as she was happy and enjoying her life. The last couple of years he had asked himself repeatedly, *What good would it really do for her to know now?* And he had told himself, *She wouldn't gain anything by knowing, and she might be so traumatized by the news that it might destroy my relationship with her.*

Virgil could no longer ignore the inevitable. He had to tell Maureen as soon as possible.

CHAPTER 33

THE LOCAL TV STATIONS HAD REPEATED PARTS OF JAY'S STORY SO MANY times, it had become old news by now and it had only been a week since Mrs. Freeman had made her confession.

The day before, Maureen had attempted to call Jay to let him know that she was still praying for him and to get the information for Mrs. Freeman's funeral. She had been unable to reach him and that had saddened her even more. She couldn't imagine the kind of pain he was experiencing.

Maureen, and a lot of other people, continued to be fascinated by Jay's story. There were some who were not, though. Mel was one of those people. He was sick and tired of hearing about Jay. "Baby, you don't need to go to that old woman's funeral. You had just met her and this Jay dude. Just send him some flowers and be done with it," he told Maureen. "He's not related to you, so I don't understand why this mess is causing you so much grief."

Loretta was another person who had heard enough about Jay. "Mel's right, Mama," she said, pausing long enough to pick her teeth with a toothpick at the dinner table. "You don't need to get any more involved with that man."

"That man is my friend!" Maureen snapped. She had ignored the plate of fried perch and fries in front of her so far, but Loretta and Mel were eating like they hadn't eaten in days.

"Somebody pass me the biscuits, please," Mel said with his mouth full of food.

Loretta handed him the basket that contained the half-dozen biscuits Maureen had picked up from Tiny's Seafood restaurant down the street. "Get a sympathy card to go with the flowers you send and let me and Mel sign it too," Loretta grunted before she stuffed a few more fries into her mouth. She stopped chewing long enough to add, "This story gets stranger by the day. In today's newspaper they talked about how that old woman had told all of the people she worked for while she was on the run that she was hidin' from a psycho husband! Like the image of black men ain't already bad enough. Huh, Mel?"

"Tell me about it," Mel growled. "Sometimes the shit comes down on me so hard, I ought to be wearing a hard hat."

An additional piece of information to the strange story was the fact that Jay was actually three weeks younger than he thought. None of the information on the fake birth certificate that Mrs. Freeman had concocted was true. It didn't bother Maureen that the local media was still all over Jay's story and that *some people* had lost interest in it; she continued to follow the news reports like a bloodhound.

"Jay must be so confused about his identity now," Maureen said as she finally began to nibble on a piece of fish. "With everything that has already come out, all he needs to hear now is that insanity or some deadly disease runs in his family."

Loretta heaved a mighty sigh and hauled herself up out of her seat, waving her arms like a windmill. "I am tired of hearin' about this kidnappin' story," she complained, her voice shrill with indignation. "It's been a whole week now. Every time I look up, and everywhere I go, that's all I hear. From the TV, the newspaper, and you, Mama. What is the big deal?" Loretta flopped back down into her seat still ranting and raving. "People get kidnapped all the time. Shoot, I could see if this was one of Bill Cosby's kids, or one of the Kennedy kids. Jay is just another run-of-the-mill John Doe!" Loretta bit into a piece of fish, brutally snapping it in two like a pit bull.

"You could be a little more sympathetic, girl," Maureen scolded. "Jay is not 'just another run-of-the-mill John Doe.' He's one of my closest friends."

Loretta stopped chewing and added, "Mama, I know he's your friend, but will you please get a grip? Let's talk about somethin' else." Crumbs and grease decorated her chin, as usual. Maureen couldn't understand how a girl who paid so much attention to her grooming and appearance could be such a sloppy eater. She wondered if Loretta was this uncouth when she and Mel ate meals with some of the sophisticated people they worked with. Loretta noticed Maureen staring at her chin, so she wiped herself with her napkin. "Can we talk about the dress I'm wearin' to prom?"

"Your prom dress? What, is that all you care about right now? You need to get it through your head that the world does not revolve around you, Lo'retta," Maureen retorted, turning to Mel for support.

Mel abruptly stopped chewing. From the deer-caught-in-the-headlights look on his face, Maureen didn't know what he was thinking. Finally he nodded. "Your mama's right, sweetie," he said, blinking at Loretta. She stared from him to Maureen and back, her anger bubbling like a pot of boiling water. Mel turned to look at Maureen again. "Baby, did you know this dude before you went to work at that old folks' home?"

"No, I didn't know Jay before I went to work at the home," Maureen stated emphatically. She had just swallowed a piece of fish and hadn't even tasted it. The fries on her plate looked like the fingers on a dead man's hand to her.

"Well, if you just met this man recently, how is it that he is already one of your 'closest friends'?" Mel wanted to know. "You haven't even had time to get to know him that well."

Maureen's jaw tightened. She rarely got angry, but when she did, she didn't try to hide it. It was one of the few characteristics that she was glad she had inherited from Mama Ruby. "So what god-dammit! Just a few minutes after I first met Jay, I felt like I already knew him better than I know you *now*!"

Loretta gasped and her jaw dropped.

Mel held up both of his hands. "Don't trip too hard," he said. "I didn't mean anything by that. I am glad to know that you've made a new friend. Even if it is a dude. I would rather have you running around with him than that slutty Catty."

"I bet he's gay anyway," Loretta quipped. Then she turned to Mel. "You shouldn't even be worried about him."

"Can we talk about somethin' else?" Maureen said with a groan. "It's been a rough day and I would like to have some peace in my own home."

Mel squeezed her hand. "I'm sorry, sugar. I didn't mean to upset you." Then his eyes got big and both of his eyebrows shot up, looking like horseshoes. "I've got an idea. Why don't we all go over to visit this Jay. I've been dying to meet him anyway."

Maureen's heart skipped a few beats. "Do you mean that?" she asked Mel.

"Of course I do. I wouldn't have said it if I didn't," he replied.

Maureen gave him a huge smile and then she leaned over and kissed him on the cheek. "I think Jay would like that a whole lot. Somethin' tells me he needs a break," Maureen said, patting Mel's hand. When she spoke again, her smile was gone and her voice was filled with contempt. "Three of Jay's cousins got in from St. Louis the night before last. From what he told me last time I talked to him, they look and act like a cross between the Munsters and the Addams Family. One cousin already drank up every drop of liquor that Jay had in the house and dropped a lit cigarette on his couch and burned a hole in it. Another one, who just got out of prison for robbin' a grocery store, went out the same night he arrived lookin' for a prostitute. The third one has already asked Jay for a loan."

"Damn! It sure sounds like your friend has a motley crew," Mel said with a horrified look on his face. "Maybe it would be safer for us if he came over here. I don't want to go around his folks and get knocked out and robbed."

"We could invite him to dinner or somethin'. I've never met a kidnap victim before. I want to see if he behaves like a normal person," Loretta said thoughtfully.

Maureen gave her an exasperated look. "You mean you want to see if you can figure out if he's crazy or not?"

"Yeah, I do. If findin' out you got kidnapped thirty-somethin' years ago don't drive a person crazy, nothin' will," Loretta replied.

"I'll check with Jay and see when he's available. Maybe I'll invite

Virgil and Corrine too. I'm sure Virgil would like to check out Jay and see how he's holdin' up." Maureen paused and rose from the table. "I'll call Jay right now," she said as she headed toward the telephone on the kitchen wall.

Jay eagerly accepted Maureen's invitation and told her to just let him know when. He declined her offer to send flowers and he told her that Mrs. Freeman had instructed him to have her cremated and not to have a funeral or a memorial service for her. She had also told Jay to spread her ashes in the ocean. The method of Mrs. Freeman's disposal horrified Maureen. Being cremated and then dumped into the ocean seemed barbaric and so *unholy*. Wasn't that what the folks in India did when somebody died? With no grave for Jay or any of Mrs. Freeman's friends to put flowers on, it would be like she never existed. Maureen couldn't fathom such a thing. She didn't know what she would do if she couldn't visit Mama Ruby's grave. She knew that Jay was going to need all the support he could get.

Maureen called up Virgil right after her brief conversation with Jay and invited him to have dinner with them that following Monday. Virgil told her that he had to drive his boss to Tampa that Monday evening. She asked him two more times that week, and each time he lied about having other plans. When she asked him the fourth time, she refused to take no for an answer. "We'll plan the dinner on a day when you don't have nothin' to do. So pull out a calendar and tell me what day that is," she insisted.

"Uh, how about this comin' Friday," Virgil suggested in a small voice. He had finally decided that the sooner he got this dinner over with the better. He couldn't avoid Jay too much longer. Maybe after meeting him face-to-face, he could decide exactly when and how he was going to confess to Maureen practically the same story that Mrs. Freeman had confessed to Jay.

CHAPTER 34

*F*RIDAY HAD ARRIVED TOO SOON FOR VIRGIL. AS SOON AS HE ENTERED Maureen's apartment for dinner and had been seated at the table right next to Jay, he wanted to melt and disappear into the floor.

It didn't matter that Loretta, Mel, and Corrine were also present; Virgil felt like a condemned man. He was glad that the dinner had started off well. Everybody was cordial and upbeat, even Jay.

The dinner turned out to be more pleasant than Maureen had thought it would. She received numerous kudos for the short ribs and garlic mashed potatoes that she had prepared. The conversation included the latest news on the Rodney King case, the economy, the state of the world, and even the latest hurricane that had ripped through the state. By dessert, nobody had mentioned Jay's kidnapping. Maureen hoped that they would get through the evening without discussing it, but she was still on pins and needles.

So were Loretta and Mel, for that matter. Virgil almost caught them kissing in the kitchen after everybody else had finished dinner and moved to the living room. As soon as Virgil had entered the kitchen, Loretta removed her arms from around Mel's neck and scurried into the living room, wiping her lips with the back of her hand. Mel remained in the kitchen with Virgil to do damage control, but it wasn't necessary. Virgil had so much on his mind that he hadn't even noticed Loretta and Mel's suspicious behavior.

Mel returned to the living room and went on about his business like he didn't have a care in the world. But Loretta was uncomfortable as she sat down on the couch. She couldn't even look Virgil in the eye when he sat in a chair across from her. She was afraid she was going to slide to the floor. To divert his attention, she began to brag about the new car she had bought for Maureen, her upcoming graduation, how she was going to start modeling full-time after she finished school, and the ton of money that she had in the bank.

"Do you plan on staying in Miami to work after you graduate?" Jay asked Loretta.

"Yep. For a while at least," Loretta chirped. Then she looked at Maureen. "I'll stay around just long enough to make sure Mama's goin' to be all right on her own."

"On my own? Mel will still be here," Maureen laughed. She was glad that Loretta was going to be out of school soon, but she was not glad to hear that she was anxious to move out on her own. Well, at least Mel would still be with her. Even if she quit working and became just a housewife sitting on a porch with a cat, Mel would be sitting on that porch too.

"Yeah. Well, I'll make sure you and Mel are all right before I move on," Loretta added, rolling her eyes upward. Then she yip-yapped nonstop for fifteen minutes about her latest modeling assignment.

Corrine had caught Mel off guard by asking him how long he planned to "manage" Loretta's career.

Mel wanted to bitch-slap that nosy bitch's face. "Oh, this is just the beginning. I am going to do everything I can to make sure Lo'retta goes all the way to the top. She's going to be a super-model!" he exclaimed with a gleam in his eyes that reminded Corrine of the big bad wolf.

"A model can only go so far in Miami. All the supermodels are in New York and Paris," Corrine said, shaking her head and giving Mel a skeptical look.

That heifer! Loretta wanted to slap Corrine too. What did a middle-aged frump like her know about modeling? she wanted to scream.

"See, that's a misconception that a lot of folks have about modeling. If you have the right look and the right people guiding you,

you can make it big in any city. Miami is not some hick town," Mel said, nodding. "I've got some very big plans for Loretta."

"I wouldn't be where I am right now if it wasn't for Mel," Loretta said in a whiny voice. "Uh, anybody want some iced tea? I made a pitcher."

After Loretta had poured everybody a glass of iced tea, she plopped back down onto the couch and looked across the room at Jay in the easy chair facing her. "So, Jay—oops, is it all right if I call you Jay?"

"Now, you know better, Lo'retta. I raised you to call grown folks either Mr., Mrs., or Miss, unless it's somebody you are related to," Maureen reminded. She occupied the hassock at the end of the couch.

"That's not what I meant." Loretta sniffed. "I didn't know if I should call him by the same name that that old woman gave him or the name his real mama gave him."

A pensive look crossed Jay's face as he cleared his throat. His heart rate accelerated. Maureen was the only one who noticed the tears pooling in his eyes. "For the record, as far as I am concerned, Leona Freeman was my real mother. All my life she was the only relative I knew, so she was very special to me—and still is." Jay paused and smiled at Loretta. His eyes were red and his lips were so dry that when he smiled, his lips looked like they had been molded out of clay. "Call me Jay."

"Cool. So, Mr. Jay, didn't you ever wonder how come she didn't have any relatives? How is it that old woman kept you all to herself all these years?" Loretta asked.

"Yes, I did wonder about that. From the time I was able to talk, I asked her about it. She told me that all of our folks were dead," Jay replied.

"Harrumph!" Loretta snorted. "Even I wouldn't swallow a story that flimsy. I mean, everybody has at least an uncle or an aunt or some cousins or somebody somewhere in the world. Even homeless people livin' on the street. Maybe the family members are not close, but there should at least be some pictures or some evidence of other family." Loretta paused long enough to take a long drink from her tea glass. "Mr. Jay, I'm surprised that you never got up in that old lady's face and scared the truth out of her. It's just not possible for a human bein' to be born into a family and then everybody on both sides of his family up and dies! Things like that only happen in the Bible. You should have known that old woman had done somethin' shady."

Jay looked like he was in a daze. Virgil looked like his mind was a thousand miles away. Maureen wanted to give Loretta a good whupping.

Corrine gave Loretta a tight-lipped, exasperated look and shook her head. "What about people who were deserted when they were babies, Lo'retta? There is no way in the world for them to know anything about family," she pointed out.

"Whatever, whatever." Loretta's lips snapped brutally over her words as she responded to Corrine's comments, adding a dismissive wave. She returned her attention to Jay. "Now, Mr. Jay, I think that if you had been on top of things, you could have straightened out this mess before now."

Maureen couldn't believe her ears. She was appalled to hear Loretta being so blunt and borderline disrespectful. Especially since she had already told her how traumatic this situation was for Jay. "Lo'retta, Jay would probably be more interested in hearin' more about how well you're doin' as a model," Maureen suggested, her face burning with embarrassment. The last thing she wanted to put Jay through in her own apartment, in front of her family, was a bunch of insensitive comments and questions. Loretta had done enough damage. "I know you'd rather talk about your modelin' some more anyway." Maureen gave Loretta one of her sternest looks and Loretta gave her one of her most defiant looks.

Jay spoke before Loretta had a chance to start up again. "That's all right, Maureen. I don't mind talking about it. I don't like to talk about it, but for some strange reason lately the more it's discussed in my presence, the easier it is to deal with. The day Mother told me, I didn't think I could survive the night. I'm all right now, though." Jay's smile went around the table.

Jay was not "all right now." He was still in a tremendous amount of pain. Maureen could see it in his eyes. She wanted to wrap her arms around him and hold on to him until his pain went away, but she knew she couldn't do that, especially with her husband sitting just a few inches away from her.

At the same time that Maureen was sitting there wanting to console Jay, Virgil wanted to do the same thing for her.

He knew he would do just that. Any day now.

CHAPTER 35

MAUREEN HAD NOTICED HOW QUIET AND AGITATED VIRGIL APPEARED to be toward the end of the evening. She knew he had been under the weather lately, but he'd been sick before and she'd never seen him look so pitiful. She also knew that he still had flashbacks related to his ordeal in Vietnam. He didn't like to talk about that experience, so it was rarely discussed. She assumed that that was the reason for his gloomy demeanor.

But Jay was a different story. Each time Maureen saw him now, he looked a little worse. The dark circles around his eyes made him look like a panda. The lines on his face, which had barely been noticeable before, now looked like they had been carved into his skin with a blade. A few times tonight he had spoken and moved like a robot. After he had nibbled on a short rib and swallowed a few sips of the tea that Loretta had made, he ignored everything else on the table—except the wine. It was the only thing that he and Virgil consumed more than anybody else.

Virgil was still not feeling well, so he wanted to get home and take a long bath, swallow some aspirin, and drink a huge hot toddy. He hugged Maureen and Loretta, nodded at Mel, and shook hands with Jay and wished him well. Then Virgil practically pushed Corrine out the front door.

After Jay had finished his fourth glass of wine, he was so tipsy it was a struggle for him to get up from the couch. He moved like a man twice his age. With an involuntary burp and a weak smile, he turned to Maureen and thanked her for inviting him to dinner, made a few comments to Mel and Loretta, and then prepared to leave.

Jay had come to Maureen's apartment in a cab. It was a good thing he had done that. He had been so distraught and distracted lately that he didn't feel safe driving his own car anyway. A look of relief had slid across his face when Maureen insisted on driving him home. She silently prayed that Mel would not offer to go with her, but a prayer wasn't even necessary for that. As soon as Mel heard her offer to drive Jay home, he announced that he had some last-minute prints to develop and promptly excused himself. By the time Maureen had collected her purse and car keys, Mel had already disappeared from the room as swiftly as a thief.

Loretta got up off the couch and walked Jay and Maureen to the door. "It was nice meetin' you, Mr. Jay. I hope you get over that kidnappin' thing real soon," she said, shaking her head and giving Jay a pitiful look. "I'm surprised you haven't had a complete nervous breakdown by now."

Jay chuckled. "I think I'll be just fine, Loretta. Good luck with your future modeling assignments. If I don't talk to you before your prom, have fun. I'll attend your graduation if I can."

It was a quiet ride to Jay's house. It seemed like he and Maureen went out of their way not to discuss his kidnapping, but it was on her mind as much as it was on his.

"Jay, I hope everything works out for you. No matter what, you can always count on me for anything you need," she told him as soon as she parked in front of his house.

"Not everything, Maureen," Jay replied. He didn't want to look at her because he didn't want to see the look on her face. But he did look at her when she touched his arm a few seconds later.

"I can't do anything about that and I'm sorry you feel the way you do," she said hoarsely.

"Sorry I have feelings for you?"

She shook her head. "No, not that. I'm just sorry about what's goin' on with you right now. I'm not sorry you have feelin's for me, Jay. I have feelin's for you too. But . . ."

"You don't have to keep reminding me that you're married. I just want to say one thing about that."

"Like what?"

"Listen to me, just from what I observed tonight, you deserve more than what you settled for, Maureen. You can do so much better than Mel." Jay quickly opened the door on his side and leaped out of Maureen's car before she could respond. She sat there until he got inside his house, shaking her head and thinking about what he had just told her. The more she thought about it, the more she agreed with him.

Confused and more concerned than ever now, Maureen couldn't imagine what other thoughts were going through Jay's head now that he had had a glimpse of her life with Mel. As if Jay didn't have enough to think about already! He had made it clear that he didn't want to dwell too much on his situation. He wanted to focus on her. Under the circumstances, though, Maureen could not figure out how he could even have "romance" on his mind with all of the chaos going on in his life right now.

However, it pleased her to know that Jay still had feelings for her.

"Alone at last! I thought that dinner would never end. It was torture!" Loretta remarked with a grimace on her face. She and Mel had returned to the kitchen table after Maureen and everybody else had left. "Jay reminds me of a puppy that nobody wanted."

"Having Jay in the picture could work in our favor. Babysitting him will give your mother something else to do with her spare time," Mel said. "That means more time that you and I can be alone together."

Loretta yawned and stretched her arms high above her head. Then she unbuttoned the two top buttons on her blouse and pointed to her bosom. "You still hungry?" she asked, massaging her right breast.

"I still want to *feed*, if that's what you mean," Mel replied, looking at Loretta with a hungry eye.

Mel stood up and waltzed to the other side of the table and stood next to Loretta, staring into her eyes. After squeezing and thumping her breast like he was inspecting a melon, he leaned down and kissed her so hard she gagged. He grabbed her hand

and pulled her out of her chair. They strolled arm in arm to her bedroom, glowing like they were Prince Charles and Lady Diana, but they were about as far from being "royal" as a couple of street bums. Mel threw Loretta down onto her bed and ripped off her clothes and underwear like a rapist. And she enjoyed every minute of it.

Loretta was soaking in rose-scented bubble bath up to her neck when Maureen returned home. Mel was in the kitchen organizing a stack of prints on the table. He didn't hear or see Maureen come in and she didn't disturb him. She was asleep when he came to bed about an hour later.

With her head propped up on two pillows, she looked so sad lying there. This was the first time since Mel had started sleeping with her daughter that he felt sorry for her. She had lost her mother and a child, and she had never experienced the love of a man. Not even now. She was too weak for her own good, but after all she had been through, a weakened spirit was to be expected. She was still attractive for a woman her age, and she was a kindhearted, sensitive, hard-working woman. However, she had other flaws that Mel could not accept in a woman. For one thing, she was too gullible and trusting. A more observant woman would have seen what he was up to with her eyes closed! The last time he'd involved himself with a sweet young thing, her busybody of a mother had figured it out by the end of the first week! There had been many others in the past and he had enjoyed each one. Loretta was different. She was ambitious and willing to do whatever she had to do to succeed. Unlike her mother, she didn't have a problem being deceitful and using other people to get what she wanted. Like him, Mel thought with smug pride, Loretta had no problem using her looks and body to get her way. He liked that. She was a lot like him, and at the same time, she was just stupid enough to let him control her life without her even knowing it.

For the first time in his life, Mel had *almost* everything he wanted. When Loretta finished school in June, he would take his plan to the next level. He would divorce Maureen and marry Loretta. If everything continued to go according to his plan, and he had every reason to believe that everything would, the girl would be so successful that she would be the ultimate meal ticket. He would be rich and probably as famous as she was going to be. He didn't expect a marriage to Loretta to last, but as long as it lasted long enough for him to get a toehold on the life he deserved, that was fine with him. The thought of all the benefits he would enjoy as Loretta's husband made him almost pass out from glee. What a coup he had pulled off this time!

Unfortunately, there was a potential roadblock, but Mel decided that it was not a big one by his standards. As a matter of fact, he thought of it as more of a detour. *Virgil.* That meddling bastard was the biggest thorn in Mel's side since his ex-wife. All through dinner, Virgil had given him dirty looks and each time he opened that hole in his face, nothing but shit came out as far as Mel was concerned. Mel was ten steps ahead of that naked ape. Now that he and Loretta had everybody thinking they didn't spend so much time together anymore, maybe that sucker would keep his two cents in his pocket and mind his own business.

At the same time that Mel was roasting Virgil in his thoughts, Virgil was basically doing the same thing to him. Except he wasn't keeping his thoughts to himself. He had an attentive audience. "I just don't trust that dude," Virgil told Corrine for about the tenth time after they got home. "Every time I said somethin' to him this evenin', he went out of his way not to look me in the face. I seen enough anyway. Dude's got what I call 'lyin' eyes' and lyin' eyes mean a lyin' soul. Somethin' about him ain't right. I suspect the dude is bad to the bone."

"I don't like him much myself, but if he's *that* bad, Mo'reen would have seen that by now," Corrine said, handing Virgil his second hot toddy. "Mel is from Chicago, a place known for breedin' savages, so he probably don't know the first thing about bein' a do-right man like you. Maybe some of Mo'reen's good nature will eventually rub off on him. We just need to give him a chance."

"Chance my tail! That man is up to somethin'. I can feel it," Virgil yelled, waving his glass so hard, hot toddy splashed onto the floor. He lay in bed with his throbbing head propped up on three goose-down pillows.

"The bottom line is, the man is Mo'reen's husband, so we have to tolerate him regardless," Corrine said, already on her knees wiping up the hot toddy with a sock. "You know what, after meeting Jay and seein' him and Maureen at the same time, I got a feelin' they would like to be more than just friends."

"I thought somethin' like that before I even met him, but it's goin' to be a while before his mind is straight again. He's goin' to need all kinds of help from a professional. He might end up losin' his mind behind what happened to him. Uh-uh, honey. With all the baggage Jay got on his hands, Mo'reen is probably better off with a scallywag like Mel after all."

CHAPTER 36

*I*T BEGAN TO RAIN LATER THAT NIGHT. THE LIGHTNING WAS SO SEVERE
it lit up Virgil's darkened house like a strobe light. The thunder
was even more frightening. Every few minutes it rolled across the
sky and boomed like dynamite being set off in his own front yard.
Large hailstones hammered his roof and the sides of his house,
and even cracked one of the two windows in the living room. For
most of his life, Virgil had endured the vicious storms that South
Florida was known for. He had experienced several monsoons during his stay in Vietnam, so he was used to violent weather. Tonight
was different, though. In addition to everything else that was on his
mind, the bad weather made it difficult for him to go to sleep. It
took another large hot toddy to help him relax enough to do that.

During the night, Virgil had a nightmare that was so disturbing
it woke him up. In it, Mama Ruby was holding the shoebox she'd
put Maureen in after she'd kidnapped her. He sat bolt upright in
bed, flailing his arms and kicking the sheets off his bed like they
had suddenly burst into flames. He was dripping with so much
sweat he had to get up and put on another pair of pajamas. He was
glad that Corrine was a hard sleeper. She was the kind of woman
who could sleep through a tsunami, so she didn't hear him moaning and hollering like a dying man.

He went through the same thing the following night, and the
two nights after that. He knew there was only one way to end his
nightmares.

The following Thursday when Virgil knew that Maureen didn't

have to work, he called her up around 3:00 p.m. from a pay phone. "I need to talk to you about somethin' real serious," he told her. "Me and you need to be alone somewhere. . . ."

Maureen couldn't imagine what it was that Virgil needed to talk to her about that was so serious they had to be alone. A few moments of ominous silence passed before she responded. "All right. Loretta's still at school and Mel is out on a shoot, so we can be by ourselves here. I just made some hog head cheese, and I'll make some tea and we can—"

"This ain't goin' to be no tea party," Virgil broke in gruffly. "This ain't goin' to be no social visit."

"Okay. Well, like I said, I'm here by myself, so we can have all the privacy you need."

Maureen's head immediately began to throb. One thought erupted in her mind like a volcano and it almost brought her to her knees. Virgil was *sick*. He was going to die. Oh, Lord! That had to be what he wanted to discuss with her! Just like Mama Ruby had once predicted, some odd, rare fatal disease that had taken root while he was imprisoned in that hellhole in Vietnam had finally reared its ugly head. What else could it be?

"I don't want to talk to you at your place. Can you meet me at Ronnie's?" Virgil said.

"That bar around the corner from the funeral parlor down the street?" Just the thought of Mason's Funeral Home, six blocks from Maureen's apartment, made her flesh crawl. It was the same place that had interred Mama Ruby's remains. It represented death in the worst way. Was this another one of her ominous premonitions? Was her beloved only sibling really going to die? "You want me to meet you in a bar? How come you have to talk to me in a bar?" Near that funeral parlor!

"Because I'll be needin' a real strong drink," Virgil replied, snorting dramatically.

Maureen's breath caught in her throat. First of all, whatever Virgil wanted to talk to her about had to be *bad* if he needed to have a drink to get through it. "Will *I* need a drink to hear what you have to say?" Somehow she managed to laugh, but there was nothing humorous about this conversation so far.

Virgil's silence frightened her even more. "I didn't hear you," Maureen said, swallowing hard. "Virgil, whatever it is, I want you to know that we can work through it. If you got a deadly disease or somethin', you don't have to worry. I will take care of you—"

"It ain't nothin' like that. But . . . I might be real sick afterward," he told her, his voice getting weaker by the second. "How soon can you meet me?"

"I'm in the middle of moppin' my kitchen floor. I was just about to finish up."

"I'm leavin' as soon as I hang up this phone," Virgil rasped.

"You can't even give me a little hint as to what this is about?" Maureen asked, her voice rising. "You know I don't like a lot of suspense."

"Mo'reen, trust me, this ain't somethin' I can talk about over the telephone. When you find out what it is, you'll feel the same way."

"All right. I'll get to Ronnie's as soon as I can," Maureen said. "Whatever it is, it better be good and it better be important."

"I can't promise you that it's good," Virgil muttered. "But it is important."

Maureen didn't even bother to finish mopping her kitchen floor. She wrung out the mop and propped it upside down in a darkened corner by the stove where it looked like a thin woman with one leg.

She grabbed her purse, slid her feet into her flip-flops, and trotted out the door. Mel had driven her car because he wanted to take it to the car wash on his way home. She didn't like to drive his clumsy SUV, it was either do that or call a cab or take the bus to Ronnie's. She drove the SUV. Even though it needed gas, she didn't bother to stop at the gas station on the corner. She was in too much of a hurry.

A detour and an accident forced Maureen to take a longer route to the bar. By the time she finally got there, fifteen minutes later, she was so nervous she fell getting out of the SUV.

She was on her second glass of wine by the time Virgil hobbled into the small dimly lit neighborhood bar twenty minutes later. He looked like he had not had a good night's sleep in days—and he hadn't.

Maureen watched as he greeted the bartender and ordered a double shot of bourbon before he slunk across the barroom floor toward her. Virgil was a beer and cheap wine drinker. He had not drunk liquor as potent as bourbon since the day Mama Ruby died.

"You look like hell," Maureen told him as soon as he slid into the booth, clutching his glass with both hands.

"I feel like hell too," he admitted, sighing convulsively.

Virgil took a long drink before he looked at Maureen. He had large dark circles around his eyes and stubble on his face. His hair looked like a patch of cockleburs, and his plaid shirt was so wrinkled it looked like he had slept in it. Maureen could smell the funk coming from his armpits. She couldn't understand how Corrine could let her man leave the house looking and smelling like a hobo.

Virgil took a deep breath before saying, "I was hopin' that this day would never come," he whispered.

"You got me real scared. Is what you got to tell me somethin' I *need* to know?" Maureen asked with her head tilted. "Is it about Corrine?" She adored her sister-in-law. She was a dependable and loving woman, and she clearly loved Virgil. However, Mary, Virgil's first wife, had been the same kind of woman and she had up and left him without warning on a Sunday morning right after they had returned home from church.

"No, it ain't," Virgil said.

"Oh, well, is this about my husband—"

Virgil held up his hand and vigorously shook his head. "This ain't about Mel, or Lo'retta, or none of your friends," he replied, his voice cracking. He drank some more and looked around. Then he scooted closer to Maureen and put his arm around her shoulder. "This is about you."

Maureen let out a mild gasp. She reared back in her seat and squinted her eyes and stared at Virgil. "What about me?" she asked in a low and hollow voice.

Virgil covered his mouth and coughed before clearing his throat. He kept his eyes on Maureen's face, which appeared to be frozen in place. "This thing about Jay really got you in a tizzy," he said. "I was surprised to hear how much it upset you. When I saw how you kept gazin' at Jay durin' dinner the other evenin', I realized then that you was hurtin' almost as much as he is. What happened to him . . . uh, really got to you."

"Yeah, it did," Maureen said with a nod and a sigh. "Is that what this is about? You want to talk to me about the kidnappin'?"

"Somethin' like that," Virgil squeaked. "I need to talk to you about a kidnappin'."

Maureen shook her head, blinked, and gave Virgil a confused look. "*A* kidnappin'?"

Virgil nodded. "That's right. *A* kidnappin'." He placed his head in his trembling hands and sobbed. For the next few moments, his mind was in another place, another time. He saw himself standing in the kitchen in Mama Ruby's house in Silo again, watching her feed the baby she had just delivered.

And stolen.

Maureen noticed the bartender watching her and Virgil. She gave the nosy man an annoyed look, so he went back to wiping off the counter. When she looked to her side, a male patron at the table a few feet away was looking at them too. "Virgil, get a grip. These people in here keep starin' at us." She shook Virgil's arm, forcing his mind to return to the present. "What is the matter?"

His reply, when it came a few seconds later, was a hoarse whisper. "I ain't who you think I am, Mo'reen."

Maureen gave Virgil an amused look. "Is that all?" she asked with a sigh of relief. "You had me come out here to tell me *that*? Look, I know you ain't the man you used to be."

"What do you mean by that?" Virgil's eyes looked so strange and hollow they reminded Maureen of bullet holes.

"I know you went through hell in the war in 'Nam. Bein' captured and put in a prison and all. You changed a lot because of that, but I still love you." Maureen gave Virgil a warm smile. "Did you do somethin' crazy while you was over there?" Then her eyebrows shot up. "I thought you said this was about a kidnappin'."

"That's just it . . . ," Virgil rasped.

"That's just what?" Maureen wanted to know, running out of patience.

Virgil looked Maureen straight in the eye and said in a very firm and clear voice, "I ain't your real brother, Mo'reen . . . and Mama Ruby wasn't your real mama."

Maureen looked at Virgil like he was speaking in tongues. "Huh?" was all she could say.

CHAPTER 37

*V*IRGIL'S WORDS HIT MAUREEN LIKE A BRICK, CONFUSING HER EVEN more. "What did you just say?" she asked. She suddenly felt captive, like a worm in a robin's beak. She wanted to bolt, but she couldn't. She had to hear everything that Virgil had to say.

Virgil blinked and repeated what he had just said.

Maureen's mouth was so numb she couldn't form another word until she gulped some air and some more wine and moistened her lips. "You ain't my real brother and Mama Ruby wasn't my real mama?"

"That's right."

"I . . . I . . . don't know what to say to that," she stammered. There was a look of absolute disbelief on her face.

"Say whatever you want to say," Virgil suggested. "I need to know how you feel about this."

"Well, it ain't the worst thing in the world. Is that what's got you so upset and actin' so strange lately?" Maureen asked with a sigh of relief. "So I was adopted, huh?" A weak smile appeared on her face. Her smile disappeared when she looked in Virgil's eyes.

He shook his head. "I wish that was the case."

"Look, Virgil. You ain't makin' much sense. If you need to tell me somethin' crazy, you need to tell me before I go nuts. With you cryin' and lookin' like a whupped puppy, these people in here must think one of us is already coo coo."

"Mo'reen." Virgil paused and looked at her long and hard. His lips kept moving, but it took a couple of seconds for the rest of the words to leave his mouth. "Mama Ruby kidnapped you from your real mama the night you was born."

Maureen kept her eyes on Virgil's face. Then she froze like a block of ice. She couldn't speak, move, or even blink her eyes. When she finally came out of her trancelike state, she shook her head and cocked it to the side, cupping her right ear.

"My ears must be playin' tricks on me because I don't think I heard you right," she said, her lips quivering.

"Ain't nothin' wrong with your ears," Virgil told her, grabbing her hands and squeezing so tightly, her fingers and his became temporarily numb. "You heard me right."

"Then I don't believe my ears," Maureen crowed, shaking her head. She looked toward the wall, then around the bar.

It was still fairly early in the day, but there was a modest crowd. There was a construction site nearby and several other businesses on the other side of the funeral parlor. Ronnie's bar had a loyal crowd of regular drinkers. Maureen was glad she didn't see anybody she knew today. She was also glad the bartender and the nosy man at the other table had stopped paying attention to her and Virgil.

"Virgil, you must be playin' a joke on me," Maureen accused. She looked directly into his eyes, wondering how he could spout such nonsense with a straight face. Especially with the news of Jay's kidnapping still so fresh!

"Now, why would I joke about somethin' like this?" he asked, looking frustrated and frightened at the same time.

They stared at each other for a few tense moments.

"Mo'reen, I wanted to tell you this all my life, but I couldn't do it as long as Mama Ruby was alive. You meant the world to her. It would have killed her if you ever found out she'd kidnapped you. She didn't want you to know she could commit such a serious crime."

"A *serious* crime? She didn't want me to know she could commit such a serious crime? What about all the people she killed? What could be more serious than that? She didn't have a problem with me knowin' about that."

"I know, I know."

Maureen looked away for a moment and then she gave Virgil a sharp look. They both blinked at the same time. "Virgil, whose child am I?" she asked in a voice that sounded like it was coming from the bottom of her soul. "Do you know?" She sounded so sad that Virgil wanted to cry some more.

He nodded, blinking hard to hold back his tears. "Uh, remember that woman that stabbed you? The woman that Mama Ruby chastised in Fast Black's cousin's house? She came at you out of nowhere, talkin' crazy and swingin' a knife."

"Yeah, I remember that woman. She was crazy. Mama Ruby was only defendin' me that day. To this day, I don't know what possessed that woman to attack me. A random crime, I suspect. She was talkin' all kinds of gobbledygook, like me and the twins goin' home with her and all." All of a sudden Maureen's jaw dropped. "Was that woman . . ." She couldn't finish her sentence.

Virgil nodded. "That crazy woman was your real mama. Othella Mae Johnson. She used to be Mama Ruby's best friend until . . . until Mama Ruby delivered you that night and decided to keep you. Me and her skipped town that same night, with you wrapped up in a towel."

"What about my daddy? Did you know him too?"

Virgil gasped. "Girl, Othella had so many men comin' and goin' I bet even she didn't know who your daddy was."

Maureen's head began to spin. Her lips were moving, but she couldn't get any words out for a few moments. "Now everything makes sense! No wonder that woman came up to me that day and wanted me to leave town with her. She knew I was her kidnapped daughter!"

Maureen was trembling so hard her bones felt like they were going to crack into little pieces. She moaned under her breath like a wounded animal. She was not drunk or even tipsy, but when she rose, she wobbled like somebody who had been on a binge for days. Some of the other patrons started to whisper about her. Virgil grabbed her arm and forced her back down into her seat.

"Mo'reen, take it easy," he pleaded, offering a fake smile to the people who were still staring at them.

"I think I'm goin' to fall out," Maureen whispered, fanning her face and gasping for air. This was the first time in her life that she had hyperventilated.

"Take some deep breaths," Virgil ordered, fanning her face with a napkin. "You'll be all right."

Maureen dropped her head and looked at the back of her hands, then the palms. Then she looked at Virgil, squinting her eyes. "Mama Ruby died ten years ago. How come you didn't tell me this sooner?" Her voice no longer sounded like the one Virgil knew. "I ain't who I thought I was all these years. Just like Jay."

"No, you ain't who you thought you was. I didn't tell you before now because . . . well, I just couldn't. I was scared to death of losin' you."

"What about my birth certificate?"

"Oh, it's a fake."

"Jay told me that when he saw his real birth certificate, he found out he was three weeks younger than he thought he was." Maureen's eyes got big. She leaned back in her seat as if preparing herself to hear another frightening piece to this bizarre puzzle. She held her breath and asked, "Am I even the age I think I am?"

"The date of birth on your birth certificate is true, but nothin' else is. All Mama Ruby had to do was go up to the county folks and tell them that she had you at home. She gave them some bogus midwife's name, and they didn't ask her no questions. They just filled out the birth certificate and sent her on her way. Back then in the fifties, white folks didn't care nothin' about rules when it came to black folks."

"I don't know what to say," Maureen rasped. She stared off into space, trying to process this incredible news.

Virgil looked in her eyes. "I just . . . I . . . well, you see, when the news broke about Jay and you kept goin' on and on about how you felt about it, that was when I *knew* I had to tell you real soon."

"If the news about Jay had never come out, would you ever have told me all of this?"

"I had planned to do it right after you got back from San Francisco, but every time I got close to doin' so, I changed my mind.

You was so unhappy as it was, I didn't want to make your life worse. I wanted to wait until things got better for you."

"You ain't makin' no sense," Maureen snapped.

"All I ever wanted was for you to be happy. That's why I wanted you to get married and all that. When you married Mel, I got to thinkin' that you didn't really *need* to know about your true past after all. I kept tellin' myself that what you didn't know wouldn't hurt you."

"I always felt like I was somebody else," Maureen said, more to herself than to Virgil.

"What do you mean by that?"

She blinked hard, but not hard enough. The tears finally came. "Jay told me that before he found out who he really was, he used to feel like he was a fraud. He didn't feel like he really belonged to Mrs. Freeman. The funny thing about him sayin' that was, I have felt the same way all my life. After Mama Ruby died, that feelin' got even stronger. I had no idea why I was feelin' that way. Until now." Maureen slapped the side of her head. "Now everything else makes sense too. Like why I don't look like you or Mama Ruby, and why she was so determined to keep me under her control."

"Guilt is a bitch, and I couldn't carry it no longer. It's been a beast on my back ever since the night you was born. I just hope you can forgive me someday. I apologize."

Maureen's eyebrows rose and her body stiffened. "You apologize for what? You didn't kidnap me, Virgil."

"I was part of the crime. My hands got just as much dirt and blood on them as Mama Ruby's did! And now . . ." Virgil paused and a wild-eyed look appeared on his face. "Oh Lord have mercy on me! The newspapers will have a field day with your story. Especially since the smoke ain't even cleared from Jay's!" Virgil placed his head back in his hands and sobbed some more.

CHAPTER 38

MAUREEN RUBBED VIRGIL'S BACK UNTIL HE STOPPED CRYING AND looked up. He blew his nose into a napkin and wiped tears off his face with another napkin. He looked like hell and felt even worse.

"I didn't know it was goin' to be this hard on me," he moaned. "I thought you'd take it a whole lot harder than me." Virgil put his head down on the table, moaning and groaning.

"Did you tell Corrine about this? Or anybody else?" Maureen asked in a gentle voice, her hand still on Virgil's back.

Virgil's head jerked up like a mole climbing out of its hole. He stopped moaning and groaning and cleared this throat. "Goodness gracious no! Until today, I ain't talked about this with nobody but Mama Ruby. There ain't no way in the world I want to share this with anybody else. Not even my wife."

"Then don't. It would do no good for her to know what you just told me."

"It was hard enough for me to tell you," Virgil added. "I knew it would hurt you real bad."

"I'll get over it." Maureen smiled. "Uh, that woman who was my real mama, did she have any other kids?"

Virgil wiped tears off his face with the sleeve of his shirt. "She did. Eight when we knew her. You was her ninth. She got around a lot, so she might have had a few more since she had you. Mama Ruby told me that somebody told her they all died in a house fire while Othella was out partyin' one night. Mama Ruby stole you and then Othella lost all her other kids too. I guess that's why she went crazy."

More tears rolled down Maureen's face as she processed what Virgil had just added to his incredible confession. "Do you mean to tell me that the only blood kin I got left in the world now is Lo'retta?"

"Your real mama had a bunch of folks back in Louisiana. I know her mama died and Othella never knew her daddy, but she had some sisters, brothers, aunts and uncles, and whatnot. The last time I talked to Mama Ruby's three livin' sisters, they told me that some of Othella's brothers and sisters still live there with their kids and grandkids."

"I have a *real* family . . . just like Jay." Virgil was surprised at how gentle Maureen's voice was. He had not expected her to sit and listen to this devastating news so peaceably. One of the reasons he had chosen to tell her in a bar was in case she got hysterical. He could have easily blamed her meltdown on the alcohol if the bartender or any of the other patrons got nosy. Maureen closed her eyes for a moment. She gently rubbed her temple with the balls of her fingers and then she gave Virgil a look that was so cold and hard it made him flinch.

"You . . . you all right?" he asked, scooting a few inches away.

"I don't want my real family to ever know what Mama Ruby did. I don't want nobody else to know, either. Mama Ruby must have had a real good reason for doin' what she did."

"She did. There was nothin' in the world she wanted more than a baby girl for years. She went to church and prayed to the Lord to bless her with one. One of the worst and most desperate things she done was she even tried to raise me as a girl."

"She what?"

"Honest to God. She tried to turn me into a girl. It's a wonder I didn't grow up to be a sissy."

"That is a wonder," Maureen agreed.

"When I was a little boy, Mama Ruby made me play with dolls and she let my hair grow real long. She usually braided it, but some days she made me wear curls and ponytails with ribbons and bows. She even made me wear dresses from time to time."

"That sounds like somethin' Mama Ruby would do," Maureen said with a nod and a chuckle. Then she let out a mighty sigh. There was a look of unbearable sadness on her face. "I'm goin' to need you more than ever now. You are the only person in the world who knows who I really am."

"Do you want me to be with you when you tell Mel and Lo'retta?"

Maureen gasped. "I don't know if I want them to know. What good would it do?"

"That's one thing you have to decide on your own. This is about you, Mo'reen. Me keepin' it a secret was one thing. What you do with this news is up to you. Now, if you change your mind about tellin' Lo'retta and Mel and want me to be with you when you do it, I will."

Maureen almost slid out of her seat. "Goodness gracious no! They are the last two people on the planet that I want to know. Mel might get crazy and leave me. And Lo'retta? You know how crazy teenagers already are anyway. What good would it do for Mel and Lo'retta to know?"

"I just thought that since everything is out in the open now, they ought to know."

"I don't agree with that. And don't ever tell Corrine, Catty, or Fast Black!"

"What about Jay? Maybe if he knew about your situation, it would help him deal with his a little easier. He looked so lost at the dinner table that night."

"I don't want Jay to know about me." Maureen's voice was stiff and detached, like it was coming from another direction and from another woman's mouth.

"Don't you think that you and Jay havin' such a strange thing in common is some kind of sign?"

Maureen gave Virgil a curious look. "A sign? A sign for what?"

"A sign that y'all was meant to be friends. Maybe y'all was brought together for a reason—to comfort each other. From what I keep hearin', his real family ain't givin' him much comfort."

Maureen dropped her head. "Now somethin' else makes sense too."

"What?"

"Like the connection I felt to Jay right after I met him. He told me that he felt a connection to me too. There was somethin' that we couldn't put our fingers on that seemed to draw us to each other. It made me feel a bond that I never felt with another person before in my life." Maureen smiled. "Now I know why. Poor Jay. He was born into a family of thugs. Mrs. Freeman saved him from God knows what kind of life."

"Yeah, that old woman did save Jay." Virgil paused and gave Maureen a guarded look. "Uh, and from what I know and heard about your real mama's folks, most of them walked on the wild side too. You and Jay got that in common as well."

"Mama Ruby saved me." Maureen smiled again, but not for long. A few seconds later, sadness filled her eyes once more. "Virgil, where is my other mama buried?"

"Huh?"

"Do you know where my other mama is buried?"

"Uh, yeah. Her grave ain't but a few feet away from where we buried Mama Ruby."

Maureen blinked back another tear.

"The next time we go to the cemetery to put flowers on Mama Ruby's grave, I want to put some on my real mama's grave too. I want to do that every time we go to the cemetery from now on. It's the least I can do for the woman that gave me life."

CHAPTER 39

"M O'REEN, I KNOW YOU SAID I DIDN'T HAVE NOTHIN' TO BE APOLO-gizin' for, but I'm doin' it anyway. I'm doin' it for Mama Ruby, may she rest in peace till we join her. She was my mama and I will always love her, so it's the least I can do for her."

"Mama Ruby must be spinnin' in her grave by now," Maureen croaked.

"Just try not to hate her too much. She was desperate. I mean, she honestly thought that you was born dead and that she brought you to life when she laid her healin' hands on you. To Mama Ruby, that was a sure sign that God had answered her prayers. She stole you out of love, not to get back at Othella or just to be playin' a prank like that young girl that took Jay out of his stroller."

Maureen stared off into space, trying to absorb everything she had heard so far. She almost accused Virgil of playing a joke on her again. Maybe this was his way of getting her to stop dwelling on Jay's case so much, but Virgil wasn't the kind of man to play jokes on people, especially her. Who in their right mind would tell a woman a story as bizarre as the one he'd just told her?

"Mo'reen, I hope you ain't too mad. Do you hate Mama Ruby now?" Virgil asked, with his face looking like he wanted to disappear.

Maureen smiled and vigorously shook her head. "I could never hate Mama Ruby, Virgil. I can't believe you would even think somethin' like that. There is just no tellin' how I would have turned out if my real mama had raised me! Why, I could even be dead. I could have burned up with the rest of her kids that night!"

"You still real upset, ain't you? You feelin' as lost and confused as Jay?"

Maureen started to shake her head but stopped and shrugged instead. "I don't know. I don't know what I'm feelin' right now," she admitted. "Mama Ruby was a strange woman, but who would have thought she'd run off with another woman's baby?"

"Nobody would have guessed that she'd do somethin' like that. Especially to her best friend. I hope this don't change things between me and you," Virgil said, looking like he had lost every friend he had in the world. "I'll get out of your life completely if you want me to."

Maureen's eyes got big. "What's that supposed to mean?"

Virgil shrugged tiredly. This conversation had taken a heavy toll on his rapidly weakening body. "If you don't want to have nothin' more to do with me, I understand. Every time you see me now, you will think about everything I just told you. Maybe I should haul ass so you can live in peace."

"Do you want *me* out of your life?" Maureen asked, choking on a sob. "You must be feelin' real strange about me now, too, Virgil. I don't even want to think about how hard it must have been for you to know what you know and look at me every day all these years. Where would you go if you do decide to leave Florida to get away from me?"

"Corrine keeps whinin' about movin' back to Georgia to be closer to her folks."

"Oh. Do you want to move to Georgia? If you want to move with your wife so y'all can be closer to her family, that's fine with me, but I don't want you to leave just so you won't have to be around me. Don't you even think like that!"

"Well, other than you and Lo'retta, I ain't got no reason to stay on in Florida nohow."

"What about your job? I know how crazy that lawyer you work for is about you. I know you like drivin' him around in that big limousine of his too."

Virgil waved his hand. "Aw, shoot. I could get a job anywhere. The thing is, I even thought about reconnectin' with some of Mama Ruby's kinfolks back in Louisiana anyway. I get a letter or a phone call every now and then from distant cousins and other kinfolks I hardly know."

"What about Othella's family back in Louisiana?"

"Huh?"

"You said she had folks back there."

"That's right. We can go out there and track 'em down if you want to. It would be nice for you to know them and for them to know you."

Maureen shook her head. "If we do go to Louisiana, I don't want them or anybody else there to know what Mama Ruby done."

"If they are your kinfolks, don't you think they have a right to know?"

"For all we know, they could be ten times worse than Jay's kinfolks," Maureen said in a distant voice. "You said my mama's folks walked on the wide side."

"You got a point there. Look how a bunch of crazy relatives disrupted Jay's life. I bet he wishes now that Mrs. Freeman had not told him . . . never mind."

Maureen gave Virgil a pleading look. "Please don't talk like that. Mrs. Freeman did the right thing by tellin' Jay, and you did the right thing by tellin' me." Maureen exhaled as she wiped some sweat off Virgil's face with her napkin. "I would like to meet somebody in my real family at least once. If they turn out to be gangsters, too, I don't have to deal with them again if I don't want to."

Virgil nodded. "Well, we'll go to Louisiana real soon. Now, if you ready to go home to finish moppin' your kitchen floor, that's fine with me. I didn't know if I was goin' to be able to walk out of here on my own or not, so I want to thank you for not coldcockin' me."

"Don't talk like that, Virgil. I would never hurt you." Maureen patted her brother's hand and gave him a mysterious look. "You know, I think Mrs. Freeman did the right thing by confessin', but in a way I wish she hadn't."

"Why not? The way you was walkin' around talkin' about what an evil thing she done! A minute ago, didn't you *just* say she done the right thing by tellin'? Why did you change your tune so quick?"

"Because if Jay's story hadn't come out, he would still be the happy-go-lucky guy he was when I met him. If his story hadn't come out, maybe mine wouldn't have either."

"You would still be the same happy-go-lucky woman you used to be?"

"I might and I might not," Maureen said with a faraway look in her eyes. Then she frowned and said, "Forget what I just said about Mrs. Freeman not tellin'! I don't know what I'm sayin'. It's just that I got to get used to all of this."

"I'll help you do that. I hope you can still act normal. The last thing I want is for you to start actin' so odd that people will notice that somethin' is wrong and badger you until you tell them."

Maureen gasped and her eyes got big again. "Virgil, you don't have to worry about me tellin' anybody. I know how to keep a secret."

"I thought I did too," Virgil said, "but I was wrong. I couldn't keep Mama Ruby's secret after all, and I'd promised her I would."

"Well, you kept the secret as long as you was supposed to," Maureen said with a yawn. "Such a promise was meant to be broken sooner or later."

Virgil nodded in agreement and then he yawned too. "You look tired. Go home and get some rest," he said. "I need to do the same thing. This conversation took a lot out of both of us. Call me if you need to talk about it some more, though."

The next morning, Maureen felt like she had been run over by a steamroller. She looked awful with her puffy face and red, swollen eyes. Loretta didn't hesitate to let her know that.

"You look like somethin' that a cat dragged in, Mama. Maybe I should stay home from school today and keep an eye on you," Loretta said as she followed Maureen from the living room into the kitchen.

"You have a math test today. You need to go to school," Maureen told her, stopping in front of the stove to pour herself a cup of the coffee that Mel had made. Maureen was glad that he was still in the shower. She didn't want him to hear what Loretta was babbling about this time.

"You pregnant?" Loretta asked with a frown, pressing her palm against Maureen's belly. "Please say no. I would never be able to show my face around here again if you got pregnant."

Maureen gasped. "What makes you think I'm pregnant, girl?" She slapped Loretta's hand away. Loretta followed Maureen back into her bedroom.

"I heard you throwin' up in the bathroom a little while ago. Ever since you came home yesterday evenin', you been lookin' and actin' strange. Mel said you was probably just drunk."

"I wasn't drunk, and you won't be gettin' a baby brother or sister." Maureen stopped in front of the mirror on her closet door. Loretta was still behind her.

"You look weird too. Your eyes are all glassy," Loretta pointed out.

Maureen turned around and faced Loretta, wrapping one arm around her shoulder and giving her a firm hug. "I'm fine, baby. You don't have to worry about me. I'm just a little tired from workin' so hard at the home."

Loretta moved a few feet back. "I know that thing about Jay is still on your mind. Maybe you should break off your friendship with him. That long face he walks around with might rub off on you sooner or later. The thing I'm really worried about, and Mel is, too, is Jay goin' off the deep end and takin' you with him."

"What's that supposed to mean?"

"Mama, Jay could snap at any time. I can't imagine a person who was kidnapped and findin' it out after so many years like he did not goin' crazy sooner or later. I know I would!"

Maureen tickled Loretta's chin. "You don't have to worry. I didn't kidnap you. Mama Ruby wouldn't even let me bring home a puppy, let alone some other woman's baby." Maureen caught herself when she realized what she was saying. A frightened look appeared on her face.

"What's wrong now?" Loretta hollered. "Your face looks like it's about to crack open."

"Nothin' is the matter," Maureen replied.

A couple hours later, Maureen felt profoundly sad. She knew that her life would never be the same again, and she couldn't even discuss it with her husband or her friends. Despite the fact that they would be supportive, the last thing Maureen wanted to have to deal with was Catty, Fast Black, and her coworkers treating her like some kind of alien. That was how some people were treating Jay now.

However, Maureen's biggest concern was that she had already noticed a difference in Virgil's behavior. He had not been to her apartment or called her up since they left the bar yesterday. She had called his house earlier in the day, knowing that he and Corrine had probably gone to work, but she'd left him a message to call her as soon as he could. He didn't call her back until after 9:00 p.m.

"I meant to call you back before now, but the lady Corrine carpools with got sick and couldn't bring her home from the cannery, so I had to go pick her up. Then we went to that steak house off the freeway," Virgil explained.

"I had called because I wanted to make sure that everything was all right with you," Maureen told Virgil. "You didn't look too good when we left that bar."

"I-I'm fine," he stuttered in a heavy voice, like he could barely stand the weight of his words. "You need anything?"

Maureen thought that was an odd question for him to ask.

"No, I don't need anything right now. I'm fine too," she replied.

"Yeah. Well, I'm kind of busy right now. I'll talk to you later," was all Virgil said next. Then he hung up.

CHAPTER 40

*V*IRGIL CALLED MAUREEN BACK A FEW MINUTES LATER. "CORRINE WAS close by so I couldn't say much," he explained, taking a long pause before continuing. "I been real worried about you ever since I told you what I . . . you know . . . about what Mama Ruby done."

"I was hopin' I'd wake up this mornin' and realize that everything you told me yesterday was just a bad dream," Maureen told Virgil with a dry laugh. "If you took it all back and told me that it was a joke, I'd believe you. We'd never mention it again."

"Everything I told you was the truth, Mo'reen. You know I don't play games. At least none this damn serious."

"I know you don't, and I'm sorry I even thought this was a joke at first."

"I wish to God it was," Virgil said firmly. "I . . . I just need to know one more thing, though."

"What?"

"Do you not want to talk about this again, or is this somethin' we need to talk about from time to time? Another thing I thought about was, maybe you should do what Jay done. If he ever takes one of them publishers up on a book deal, he'd be set for life. I'm talkin' about some real big money. Think about it."

Maureen gasped. "You mean I should think about goin' public? I thought we both agreed not to tell anybody else."

"I know we did, but if you change your mind ten years from now and want to do newspaper and radio interviews or talk shows, the media folks might not be interested. I wouldn't want you to hold that against me because I told you we shouldn't tell nobody. I know that a lot of people would love to hear about what happened to you. Look how they all over Jay. Maybe you should strike while the iron is hot."

"Oh HELL no!" Maureen said quickly, looking around to make sure Loretta and Mel were not close by. "I don't want a bunch of meddlesome reporters and other busybodies all up in my business like they are with Jay. Not after the way it's messin' with his mind."

"Well, I guess I can understand why you don't want this made public. Besides, your life *and mine* would never be the same again if you do that."

"That's already the case," Maureen pointed out. "Even with just you and me knowin', our lives won't ever be the same again, Virgil. We have both been livin' a lie all this time!"

"Yeah, I guess so. We can't change that. Anyway, it could cause problems between me and Corrine. Me not tellin' her before now wouldn't sit too well with her. What about you gettin' some counselin'?"

"I'm not crazy," Maureen quickly insisted, sounding offended. "I can handle my case on my own."

"I sure hope so, Mo'reen. I wouldn't know what to do if you lost your cookies and ended up in some asylum."

"Well, with the Lord's help I won't."

"I didn't want to bring this up, but we need to look at this from every angle."

Maureen hesitated for a few seconds. "What other angles do we need to look at this from?" she asked, her voice low and weak.

"Well, Mo'reen, I don't know much about the law in a situation like this, but the man could come down real hard on me, you know."

"*You* didn't kidnap me!"

"It don't matter. I knew about it from the get-go. Yeah, I was a child myself when it happened, but some sharp prosecutor might find some kind of loophole that'll cook my goose for good. After everthing I been through already, all I want is a peaceful life. So . . . I'm happy that you don't want to go public with this."

"Virgil, I'm goin' to be just fine. Please don't worry about me."

Maureen was glad that Virgil couldn't read her mind. Maybe it would have been better if he had not told her about her kidnapping after all, she thought. What if this situation eventually made her snap? Oh what a mess Mama Ruby had created and left for Virgil and her to sort out! Even from beyond the grave, Mama Ruby was wreaking havoc in Maureen's life. But, Maureen reminded herself, would she even be alive if Mama Ruby hadn't kidnapped her? She could have perished in that fire with Othella's other kids. No, she wasn't going to go crazy over this. She couldn't bear the thought of being put into an asylum and leaving Loretta and Mel to fend for themselves. How would they get along without her?

"Well, if you ever change your mind about gettin' some professional help, I'll be with you all the way. If you don't mind me sayin', it probably wouldn't hurt. If I had not talked to a couple of professionals about that mess I went through in 'Nam, I might be in a nuthouse by now."

"Well, if I ever do think that I need some help, I'll get it."

"You didn't answer my question regarding us not talkin' about this ever again. Do you want to talk about it every now and then?"

"Virgil, I can't answer that right now. That's somethin' I need to think about some more. But . . ."

"But what?"

"If somethin' happens to you or Corrine, or Mel, or Lo'retta, I won't have anybody else in the world. No family. I don't remember much about the kinfolks in Louisiana that Mama Ruby took me around when I was a little girl. But maybe . . ."

"Listen, I really think we should take a trip to Louisiana as soon as we can. You feelin' all right about things right now, but who knows how you'll be feelin' down the road. Gettin' more familiar with your real mama's kinfolks might do you a world of good," Virgil suggested.

"Yeah. I need to do that for my own peace of mind, I guess."

"You remember Cousin Lee? You met him when Mama Ruby took you to Louisiana that one time when I was in prison in 'Nam. The last time I talked to him, he told me that one of his friends is married to one of Othella's nieces. Guess what? Her name is Mo'reen too."

"I remember Lee all right. If I don't meet any of the other folks, I'd like to meet his friend's wife. Us havin' the same name must mean somethin', huh?"

"It must," Virgil agreed. "I'll make our travel arrangements as soon as I can."

The following morning, shortly after Virgil got out of bed, he called the airline. He wanted to keep things moving rapidly so he wouldn't change his mind. He made reservations for himself and Maureen on the first available flight from Miami to Shreveport, which was the following Friday evening.

"How long will you and your brother be in Louisiana?" Mel asked. He stood by the bedroom window drinking from a can of beer as he watched Maureen pack her suitcase.

It was a few minutes past 8:00 p.m. the night before her trip. Maureen had eaten dinner with Mel and Loretta at a nearby Italian restaurant. She had not felt like cooking since Virgil had dropped that bombshell on her a few days ago.

"This trip is kind of sudden," Loretta commented, sitting on the side of Maureen's bed with her freshly waxed legs crossed. "I thought all of our folks back there died a long time ago."

"No, we still have a few that are livin'," Maureen said to Loretta. Then she turned to Mel. "I'll just be gone for a few days. I don't even have vacation or sick leave accrued at the nursin' home yet, so I won't get paid for the days I'm gone."

"Baby, we are not hurting for money. Your salary is pocket change compared to what Loretta and I are bringing in," Mel said with a smirk.

Maureen was proud of the fact that her daughter was making so much money, even more than Mel. Loretta was not only generous to her, but also she put most of her earnings in the bank in a joint savings account that she shared with Maureen. What Maureen didn't like was that Mel often rubbed it in her face that her daughter was the main breadwinner in the house. Because she had too much on her mind right now, she didn't respond to the tacky remark he'd just made about her salary, but she did give him a look that was stern enough to make him flinch.

"I didn't mean anything by that," Mel said, laughing nervously.

"I know you didn't," Maureen said in a python's whisper that made Mel's spine tingle.

Loretta didn't even notice the tension in the room. "So what's wrong with this sick cousin in Louisiana?" she asked Maureen, curling a lock of hair around her finger. "Is he goin' to die and leave us a bunch of money or somethin'?"

"Cousin Lee is not dyin'. And he's only forty-one but he thinks he's a old man so he wants to see me and Virgil before it's too late." Maureen looked at the floor before continuing. "Even after he passes, I don't think he has anything to leave anybody anyhow. Like you need it!" Maureen teased, tossing a pillow at Loretta. Then she gave Mel a serious look. "You can send Lo'retta over to Catty's house if she gets on your nerves or if you need to go out of town or somethin'. Fast Black said you can send Lo'retta to her house, too, if you need to."

Mel was amused by what Maureen had just said, but Loretta was absolutely horrified at the thought of spending one minute alone with either Catty or Fast Black. "I wouldn't be found dead in Catty's house or Fast Black's!" Loretta said through clenched teeth. "Now, Mama, you ought to know better. You know I can't stand either one of those two heifers. All they do is gossip and stir up mess in other peoples' lives. I wish you would find some better friends and get rid of those bad news bears anyway."

"Lo'retta, I was friends with those 'bad news bears' before I gave birth to you," Maureen declared. "I love them like family. I love all of my friends, and if you don't have friends worth lovin', *you* need to find some new friends."

"I guess that means you love Jay, too, huh?" Loretta teased.

"What's that supposed to mean?" Maureen asked. She didn't want to look at Mel to see his reaction, but she heard the exasperated groan he let out.

"Jay's your friend too," Loretta quipped.

"Yes, Jay is my friend and I care about him a lot," Maureen said, slamming her suitcase shut. She left the bedroom in a huff, but Loretta and Mel stayed behind. They didn't speak until they heard Maureen turn on the TV in the living room.

"You didn't have to say that about Jay," Mel told Loretta, shaking his finger in her face. "That's so not cool!"

Loretta dismissed his comment by placing one hand on her hip, rotating her neck, and snapping her fingers ghetto-style. "You're her husband. You need to be a little more concerned about her relationship with another man. Or do you *still* not care that Mama is not in love with you?" There was a devilish gleam in her eyes.

"I don't care what she says or does. She does care about me . . . in her own way," Mel grumbled.

"So do I. I will show you just how much I care about you as soon as she leaves tomorrow," Loretta said, grinding her groin against Mel's.

CHAPTER 41

MAUREEN HAD SPOKEN TO JAY ONLY ONCE SINCE HER MEETING WITH Virgil in Ronnie's bar. Jay had told her that another one of his "long lost relatives" had contacted him and had already booked a flight to pay him a visit, which he was not looking forward to.

Jay also told Maureen that he planned to visit his hometown within the next few days. He wanted to know more about his roots and what effect his true identity might have on his future. She was glad that their trips were happening around the same time, but she was not happy they were happening for basically the same reason. She couldn't tell that to Jay, though.

Maureen had told Jay the same story she and Virgil had concocted to tell everybody else: They were visiting a sick cousin in Shreveport. That was all they needed to know. Her moving forward with her life was going to be difficult enough. Even though she was happy to hear that she had a real family, she was concerned about what else she might find out once she met them.

She didn't sleep much the night before her trip. She had so many things on her mind to sort out she didn't know where to begin. One was that she was concerned about her future with Mel. He was her husband, but she couldn't tell him what Virgil had told her and that bothered her. What if Virgil got drunk or loose-lipped during one of his Vietnam flashbacks and told Mel everything that he had told her? Maureen shuddered just thinking about that scenario. Would Mel want to stay married to a woman with that kind of baggage?

Another reason Maureen couldn't get to sleep was because Mel felt obligated to make love to her before she left to go on her trip—even though she had tried to get out of it by claiming she had a headache. But he was horny and Loretta was on her period, so he whined until Maureen gave in.

After Mel had rolled over and gone to sleep, she got back out of bed and went into the living room. She sat on the couch in the dark for two hours. She wanted to cry some more, but for some reason the tears wouldn't come. She was sad, but she also felt somewhat like a prodigal daughter. She was going "home" . . . but to what? Her answer to that question was to get a better understanding of the biggest mess that Mama Ruby had ever initiated. *Mama Ruby, I'm so sorry. I know you didn't ever want me to know that you kidnapped me, but I'm glad I finally found out. Now I know just how much you really loved me and why you was so damn determined to keep me to yourself.* Maureen sniffed for a few seconds before she resumed her thoughts about Mama Ruby. *I hope you can hear my thoughts because I want you to know that no matter what happens when I meet Othella's folks, especially the one with the same name as me, it won't change how I feel about you and Virgil. You and him will always be my family. Nothin' in the world is ever goin' to change that.*

When Maureen returned to bed, the last thing on her mind before she fell asleep was the fact that Mel was so understanding about her going out of town without him. He had even encouraged her to stay as long as she wanted. She promised herself that she would be extra nice to him when she returned. She would cook all of his favorite meals, buy him some new camera equipment, and make love to him like she'd never made love to him before. She would even organize a romantic getaway and treat him to a weekend in South Beach. Mel would enjoy that and it would certainly lift her spirits. She knew that her relationship with Jay could go no further, so she had to make do with the man she'd married. If Mel left her someday, she could live with that, but she would never leave him.

Even though Maureen was glad that she and Virgil had occupied different rows on the plane, she held his hand in the cab from the airport to Cousin Lee's house in Thelma City, the same district in Shreveport where Ruby and Othella had grown up.

"This place looks the same as it did when Mama Ruby brought me here when I was a little girl," Maureen said, looking out the window with misty eyes.

"I wouldn't know. After Mama Ruby left home, she kind of drifted away from her family. She didn't even write to them much until after I left for the army," Virgil responded with a sad look on his face. Maureen had not seen him smile since before his confession in Ronnie's bar. "If some of Mama Ruby's family hadn't come to Florida for her funeral, I probably never would have made this trip. This will be my first time visitin' Louisiana."

Maureen gave Virgil a thoughtful look. "Virgil, one thing I don't understand about Mama Ruby is, if she was so into family, how come she didn't visit her folks more often, or write letters to them on a regular basis, or even make me and you do so? You would have thought that she would take a trip home at least once a year."

Virgil shook his head. "Mo'reen, Mama Ruby had a whole lot of demons on her back. She knew she had done wrong by takin' you. She wanted to isolate herself from the people who might figure out what she done. Besides, knowin' the way Mama Ruby's mind worked, she didn't want to be nowhere near the place your real mama came from and where you had blood relatives. It would have been too much for her to deal with emotionally. She didn't want nothin' or nobody to come between you and her."

"Tell me about it," Maureen quipped.

"She didn't ever want to let you go, not even to have a life of your own."

"Tell me about that too. I will never forget the way she carried on that day I finally moved out of the upper room. Yellow Jack was drivin' me to Miami. Mama Ruby chased that old car of his, runnin' behind us up the hill like a wild woman." Maureen paused and shook her head. "She wanted me to spend my whole life sleepin' in that lumpy bed in that damn upper room. As long as Mama Ruby was alive, I was not goin' to have a normal life."

"Well, Mo'reen, you can have a normal life now," Virgil assured her. "I don't like to get too personal, but I advise you to have some more kids. I would like to know that you will have more family in Florida, especially after I'm dead and gone. . . ."

"I wish you wouldn't talk like that!" Maureen hollered. "You ain't but forty-seven years old. You ain't goin' no place no time soon. You might outlive me! As far as me havin' more kids, well, I've been thinkin' about that myself. I'm goin' to talk to Mel about that one day before I get too old. I'm sure Lo'retta would like to have another siblin', especially a sister."

"So would I," Virgil rasped. "Another sister, too, I mean."

"Well, brother, it's too late for you to get another sister." Maureen smiled so hard her cheeks ached.

Lee Sampson, the son of Mama Ruby's deceased older sister Flodell, strolled out onto the front porch of his two-bedroom house as soon as Virgil and Maureen piled out of the cab. Maureen squinted her eyes to look at her "cousin." With his graying hair and heavily lined face, it was no wonder he thought he was so "old," Maureen thought to herself.

"Virgil? Oh Lord! Boy, it's good to finally meet you! And, Mo'reen, you done growed into a fine-lookin' woman!" Lee said, looking her up and down, amazed at how well she had filled out— and that all of her body parts were still where they were supposed to be. It was the same way he had looked at her the last time she saw him, the day he had shown her eight-year-old eyes his smelly thirteen-year-old penis and made her touch it. "My, my! It's so good of y'all to come visit me! Every time I thought about comin' out to Florida to visit y'all, I got a new ailment."

"You look mighty fine and healthy to me, cousin. As robust as a ox!" Virgil exclaimed. He set his suitcase on the ground, gave Lee a bear hug, and clapped him hard and repeatedly on the back.

"Well, I was lookin' better last year before I had my gall bladder removed. As soon as I recovered from that, I had a mean bout with hemorrhoids big as a hen's eggs. Then I had shingles for a spell. After that I had a mild stroke, as y'all can see by the way my jaw is all twisted up. It's a wonder I'm still alive!" Lee enjoyed talking about his various physical malfunctions and was sorry that he didn't have a few more to report.

"I think you look fine now, too, Cousin Lee," Maureen lied. Lee was one of the homeliest creatures she had ever laid eyes on. He was built like a toad and he had large bulging eyes and a jawline that resembled a lantern. Maureen was surprised to hear that he had been married four times. However, he must not have been the lover he thought he was because none of his wives had remained with him for more than a year or two. Now he was all alone with just an overweight hound dog to keep him company.

"I hope y'all hungry. I got a possum bakin' in the oven," Lee said, licking his lips.

"I'm glad to hear that. All they served us on the plane was some pretzels and soda pop," Maureen laughed, shifting her weight from one foot to the other, looking over Lee's shoulder wondering when he was going to invite them into the house.

"Pretzels? Now that's a damn shame! I don't know what this world is comin' to," Lee snarled. "Well, I'm goin' to feed y'all like kings. Possum today, pig ears tomorrow, and hush puppies with every meal, includin' breakfast. Virgil, you can sleep on the couch in my livin' room. Mo'reen, you can sleep in my bed. I'll sleep on a pallet in my back bedroom since I ain't got no bed in there no more."

"We won't be here but a few days. We can go to a motel. I saw quite a few on the way from the airport," Virgil said, looking to Maureen for confirmation. She nodded.

"No way," Lee insisted. "This might be the last time we see one another for a while, and I ain't goin' to let y'all out of my sight much while y'all here."

"Excuse me, cousin. I don't mean to be antsy, but do you mind if we go in the house and sit down? That plane ride, and havin' to change planes twice, was so long and uncomfortable," Virgil said, forcing out a heavy sigh and a yawn.

"Oh! Y'all come on in the house!" Lee hollered, snatching Maureen's suitcase out of her hand. "I'm so happy to see y'all I forgot my manners." He gently kicked open his front door and waved Maureen and Virgil into his living room.

Lee set Maureen's suitcase on the floor and motioned for her to sit down on his plaid couch. As soon as her butt hit the seat, Lee plopped down next to her with his arm around her shoulder. Virgil fell into a wobbly bamboo chair facing them. "Girl, you look like a film star! Diana Ross better watch her back!" Lee boomed, looking at Maureen like he wanted to eat her. "I bet you have to beat the men off with a stick. I bet you got dudes comin' in the front door and dudes goin' out the back door at the same time!"

Maureen shook her head. "Not since I got married," she said, smiling shyly. "I'm a happily married woman," she added with a proud sniff.

"That don't mean nothin' when it comes to romance. I was a happily married man to four different women, but that still didn't stop other women from chasin' after me," Lee boasted. "I'm a rare man. No matter how old or afflicted I get, women can't leave me alone."

"You said in your last letter that your wife ran off with a musician a few months ago," Virgil reminded.

"That heifer sure did! She snuck her funky tail off one day while I was on the lake fishin'. She didn't even leave me no note and she didn't even take all of her clothes. I was beside myself. For all I knew, that hussy had been kidnapped—"

"Well, I hope you didn't take her runnin' off too hard," Virgil interrupted.

Maureen shuddered. *Kidnapped* was the last word she wanted to hear right now. It had become the most frightening word in the English language to her. From the grimace on Virgil's face, he must have felt the same way about that word too. If he had not cut Lee off, Maureen would have done it herself.

CHAPTER 42

*L*EE ENJOYED SITTING SO CLOSE TO MAUREEN. IT FELT GOOD TO REST his knobby knee next to hers. Despite the fact that she was a relative, and it had been more than a quarter of a century since he'd exposed himself to her, she still excited him. But the fact that she had made it clear that she was a "happily married woman" was enough for him to restrain himself this time.

Lee crossed his legs and blinked. "I seen Othella's nephew this mornin'. He told me he got word to his cousin, the one married to my friend, that y'all was comin." Lee paused and scratched the side of his neck. "What they can't figure out, and me neither, is why y'all so set on meetin' some of Othella's folks. Especially folks y'all ain't never had no connection with before. From what I heard, Othella and Aunt Ruby had stopped bein' friends even way before Othella got herself killed. By the way, how did Othella die? All I ever heard was that she died in a freak accident out there in Florida."

"A freak accident? Uh, yeah, that's what it was," Maureen said quickly. "Miss Othella got drunk and fell out a window and broke her neck." Part of that was true. Othella had died of a broken neck, but she had not fallen out of a window on her own; Mama Ruby had given her some assistance. Even though Othella had stabbed Maureen with a switchblade during an unprovoked, crazed attack, which was why Mama Ruby had killed her, Othella was still the woman who had brought Maureen into the world. She could never forget that.

"What a mess, what a mess," Lee chanted, shaking his head. "What a mess it was for Othella to die like that." He removed a dingy white handkerchief from his shirt pocket and wiped sweat off his face. "Well, I hope y'all have a pleasant visit." He glanced at the cheap watch on his wrist. It had stopped. "Virgil, what time you got? This damn thing I got always go on the blink every time I need to keep track of the time."

"It's ten past seven," Virgil said.

"My buddy Lukas and his wife, Mo'reen, Othella's niece, said they'd be here no later than seven-thirty," Lee announced. "While y'all here we'll call the other Mo'reen *Old Mo'reen* and we'll call you *Young Mo'reen* to cut down on the confusion," Lee laughed, winking at Maureen. "It sure is a coincidence you and her havin' the same name. Now that I'm lookin' at you, Virgil, you and Old Mo'reen kind of look like one another."

"Is that right?" Virgil mused. "Well, they say all good-lookin' people got a double somewhere in the world."

"You and her got the same high-yella skin and light brown freckles. She got more freckles on her nose than you got, though, and they in the shape of a cat's paw. Just like her daddy had. By the way, he had a real bad stroke a while back and passed. We buried him on his birthday a few years ago," Lee revealed. "It was a damn shame too. Old Mo'reen was just gettin' to know him when it happened. She was raised in some asylum till she got grown and connected with her daddy's folks. He was named Isaiah just like in the Bible, but we called him Ike. He was Othella's younger brother and from what I hear, Aunt Ruby's first love." An embarrassed look crossed Lee's face. "I heard he used to pester Aunt Ruby in the cane fields, the cornfields, and even in the bushes behind Grandpa Upshaw's church!"

Virgil ignored his cousin's comments about Mama Ruby's sexual escapades, but just hearing about it made him blush. "I can't wait to meet Old Mo'reen," he said. "Why was she in some asylum if Othella had so many brothers and sisters still livin'? Couldn't they have taken her in?"

"Now, that's somethin' you'll have to ask Old Mo'reen. I don't know the woman well enough to be askin' her her business. I just see her in passin' from time to time, or at a church event every now and then, or when she come over here with Lukas," Lee answered.

"I can't wait to meet Old Mo'reen," Maureen said. "I hope she and I can be friends and keep in touch."

"Why?" Lee asked.

Maureen chuckled. "I guess because of me and her havin' the same name," she replied. She chuckled some more even though she was close to tears. It was a sad time for her. Whether or not Othella's folks wanted to have a relationship with her, meeting some of her blood relatives meant a lot to her. Now that she knew what she knew, she could not rest and go on with her life until she connected with more of her roots.

Maureen couldn't believe how many events had occurred in her life in the past few weeks. She predicted there would be more to come. Hopefully they would be pleasant. But the thought still frightened her. What if she found out that some serious physical condition ran in her family? Or some type of mental illness? This was something that was important for her to know in case she decided to have another child. If she could only tell Jay *everything*! He was the only person who could truly understand what was going through her mind.

The time dragged on. It was now 8:00 p.m. and Old Maureen and her husband still had not arrived. Finally, at a quarter past eight, Lee dialed her number.

"Woman, you and Lukas comin' to dinner or not?" Lee asked, annoyed that so much time had passed and she had not arrived or even bothered to call. "I got a mighty big possum in the oven. If I eat too late, I'll be up all night with gas." If Lee lived to be a hundred, he would never understand why black folks could never be on time. Himself included. He had been late to all four of his weddings and his own mother's funeral.

"Lukas's back just went out again. This clumsy old buzzard was tryin' to swat a fly and fell off the back porch! We won't be able to make it tonight after all," Old Maureen said. "I'm fixin' to haul him to the hospital. Like always, we'll be there for a while. You know how slow them quacks in City General is."

"Well, do you think y'all can make it later tonight for a drink? Or maybe for dinner tomorrow evenin'? Virgil and the other Mo'reen ain't goin' to be here but a few days. They got jobs and family to get back home to."

"I don't know . . . probably not. Tell Virgil and the other Mo'-reen I'll have to meet them some other time," Old Maureen said. "Maybe I can talk my late uncle O'Henry's wife into havin' a cook-out tomorrow. You remember Della Mae, don't you? She already said she would like to meet Virgil and Mo'reen from Florida."

"Is your late uncle O'Henry your aunt Othella's twin brother that stepped on a land mine in 'Nam and got blown to Kingdom Come?"

"Uh-huh. His wife is still grievin', so some out-of-town company would do her a world of good," Old Maureen decided.

Lee sucked on his teeth and groaned. "That poor man dyin' like that, and then Othella dyin' in a freak accident. Them two trag-edies must have hit your family real hard."

"Sure enough," Old Maureen managed.

Just hearing Lee mention Othella's name made Virgil's chest tighten and Maureen gasp. They wondered what Old Maureen was saying on the other end of the line. Maureen didn't look at Virgil, but if she had, she would have seen the look of despair on his face. The last thing either one of them wanted to hear was more about Othella's "freak accident."

"I think I'll take them over to my sister Monette's house if I can catch up with her. She's like a fart in a windstorm," Lee said. "I'll talk to you another time. If it ain't too late, swing by Monette's house after you leave the hospital." Lee hung up and let out a loud breath. "Well, y'all, it don't look like y'all will get to meet Old Mau-reen this time around," he said, glancing from Virgil to Maureen. "That slew-footed ox she married took a bad fall and injured his back. Every time I look up, he done injured somethin'. Last year he was laid up with a broken knee."

"He must be real clumsy," Virgil commented.

"My buddy is that and more. But his wife was the one that broke his knee when she caught him with another woman on his lap. She laid into him with a tire iron." Lee slapped his knee and guffawed.

"All I can say is, there is some real ferocious women from this state. As I'm sure y'all both know, Aunt Ruby was one of the most ferocious. I heard that even when she was a young girl, folks used to say that if they had seen her fightin' a bear, they would have helped the bear."

Virgil and Maureen nodded in agreement, but they didn't comment. Violence was another thing about Mama Ruby that they didn't like to be reminded of, or discuss.

Virgil turned to Maureen. "Well, since we might not get to meet this other Mo'reen this time, it would be nice if we could meet Othella's twin brother's wife if we have time, huh?" Virgil said to Lee, "Or any other of Othella's relatives that's still around, if you could round some of 'em up."

"I still can't figure out why y'all want to meet Othella's folks so bad when *we* got a few y'all ain't never met," Lee said, scratching his chin. "Well, Old Mo'reen just might show up here tonight, and I know my sister Monette would like to meet y'all tonight. Now, Monette's had a few mild strokes, so she might sound a little senile. She and Old Mo'reen, they been friends for a real long time, and they still pretty close. They even live next door to one another. I have to warn y'all, though, I hear that Old Mo'reen is kinda dangerous. Monette might tell y'all some stuff about her that y'all won't like. Then you'll be glad you didn't meet her after all. Y'all want to meet Monette tonight? I can see how hungry y'all look, and Monette always got a pot on the stove."

Maureen smiled at Virgil and shrugged. "It's all right with me, if it's all right with you," she told Virgil.

Lee had burned the possum he had planned to serve for dinner, so inviting his older sister to join them for dinner was out of the question. When he called up Monette, she was glad to hear that Lee wanted to bring the cousins to her house for a late dinner.

"Maybe we shouldn't have come out here," Maureen whispered to Virgil while Lee was looking for his shoes. "Maybe we should have left well enough alone. Especially since Lee thinks that Old Mo'reen is a dangerous kind of woman."

"I hear you. Like me and you agreed, Othella's people might be the kind of folks we don't need in our life. But since we came this far, let's eat dinner with Cousin Monette. If we don't meet none of Othella's folks this time, maybe we'll have better luck the next time—that is, if you still want to meet your blood relatives."

Maureen shook her head. "There won't be no next time. Like you just said, my real mama's folks might be the kind of folks we don't need. If we don't get to meet them, it's probably all for the better. I keep thinkin' they might make me feel worse than Jay's folks made him feel."

CHAPTER 43

*L*EE'S OLDER SISTER, MONETTE ULMER, OPENED HER FRONT DOOR wearing a long black duster like the ones Mama Ruby used to wear. She had on a pair of well-worn backless men's house shoes and she smelled like Bengay. She resembled Lee, except she had a lot more hair on her head, and she was much larger. She was one of the few women that Maureen or Virgil had ever seen who was almost as obese as Mama Ruby. Her neck alone must have weighed five pounds.

"Goodness gracious! Y'all come on in!" Monette greeted, ushering everybody into her neat living room. Monette was a widow and her seven children and eighteen grandchildren lived in various cities and states. She had a live-in "boyfriend," a seventy-five-year-old retired truck driver who was currently in Atlanta helping his remaining relatives look after his ninety-four-year-old mother. Monette was a lonely woman, so she was glad to have company. "Dinner will be ready in a few minutes. Y'all in for a real treat! I been cookin' up a storm all day and I hope y'all like oxtails, turnip greens, and hush puppies!"

After a lot of hugging and kissing, Maureen, Lee, and Virgil sat down on the same black leather couch facing Monette on a black velvet love seat that had duct tape holding one leg in place.

"*Two* Mo'reens in the family! A double blessin'! God sure is good. Virgil and Mo'reen, y'all don't know how bad the other Mo'reen is itchin' to meet her baby sister and her baby brother. What a blessed event this is!" Monette squealed.

Virgil whirled around and looked at Maureen, and they both shrugged. One was as puzzled as the other by the part of Monette's statement about a "baby sister and a baby brother." As far as they knew, this other Maureen was Othella's niece. They both assumed that Monette was more senile than Lee said she was.

"See what I mean," Lee whispered just loud enough for Virgil and Maureen to hear. "Monette ain't in her right mind no more." Lee paused long enough to clear his throat. Then he plastered a condescending smile on his face and looked at his sister. "No, sissy. You got it all ass-backwards. These ain't the other Mo'reen's kin-folks. Their mama, our aunt Ruby, was real close friends with the other Mo'reen's aunt Othella. They just wanted to meet some of 'em while they was visitin' me," Lee explained. He looked from Vir-gil to Maureen, shaking his head and sighing with exasperation.

Monette let out a loud breath and rolled her eyes at her brother. "I know all about Aunt Ruby and the other Mo'reen's daddy. Be-fore Othella's mama died, she told me how her son Ike got Aunt Ruby pregnant and how Aunt Ruby didn't want to raise no baby. Her bein' a teenager and so caught up in the church and whatnot, she didn't want to bring shame on her family. She gave up her baby."

"Wait a minute! Y'all slow down some," Virgil ordered, rising off the couch with his hand in the air. "Y'all confusin' me." He looked at Maureen. He could tell from her raised eyebrows that she was just as confused as he was. Was another skeleton about to fly out of the family closet? they both wondered.

"I'm in the dark here. Now what baby is this y'all talkin' about?" Virgil said, returning to his seat.

"Aunt Ruby Jean had another baby way before she had y'all two," Monette revealed with a vigorous nod.

"Do you mean to tell me that my mama was this other Mo'reen's real mama?" Virgil asked. There was an incredulous look on his face. With his mouth hanging open, he looked from Maureen to Monette and back to Maureen.

"Yeah," Monette said, puzzled and confused herself now. Her eyes got wide. "Don't tell me y'all didn't know—"

"I didn't know nothin'," Virgil rasped, wondering how he was still able to be in his right mind. The last thing he expected to hear was this bombshell that Monette had just dropped. "I thought that me and Mo'reen . . ." He paused and nodded toward Maureen. "I thought that me and *this* Mo'reen was the only kids that Mama Ruby had."

"Aunt Ruby had another baby? I declare, it's news to me!" Lee yelled. "Sissy, you must have got the story mixed up, like you do with everything else. These two youngin's here from Florida. They the only kids that Aunt Ruby had—that I know about."

"Well, Aunt Ruby had another baby when she was a youngin'. When she was just fourteen or fifteen, if I remember right. Our folks didn't like to talk about it much. See, Aunt Ruby had birthed her baby in Othella's mama's house and nobody even knew at the time that she was in the family way. And guess what? Even Othella's brother Ike didn't know Aunt Ruby had had his baby. Everybody found out about it years later when Simone, Ike and Othella's mama, went back to the asylum where Aunt Ruby had made her take the baby the night she had her. Them nuns at the asylum had named the baby Mo'reen, after the nun that looked after her the most and weaned her. What a coincidence it was that years later, Aunt Ruby gave her second baby girl the *same* name! By then Aunt Ruby's first daughter was all grown up and married." Monette stopped talking and tilted her head to the side and lowered her voice. "The first Mo'reen's first husband died in a car wreck some years later, but she got married again right away. Poor thing. She married another fool, of course. Anyway, the one thing that Simone couldn't stop talkin' about every time I ran into her was how crazy Aunt Ruby was about that baby girl she had dumped off in that asylum."

"If Mama Ruby was so crazy about her first baby girl, why didn't she keep her?" Maureen asked in a low, nervous voice. Her head was aching so badly she thought it was going to explode.

"Pfftt! Aunt Ruby Jean's mama and daddy would have skinned her alive!" Monette snapped, offering a dismissive wave with her thick hand. "Simone told me that every time she got a letter from Othella, she told her how bad Ruby wanted another baby girl to make up for the one she gave up." Turning to Maureen, Monette added, "I can see she got what she wanted. I bet Aunt Ruby worshipped the ground you walked on, didn't she? You made up for that first baby girl, didn't you?"

"Yes, ma'am. I guess I did," Maureen mumbled, barely moving her lips.

Virgil could no longer hold back his tears. He covered his face with his hands and sobbed.

"Virgil, don't you cry now. Even though you was born a boy, I know that Aunt Ruby Jean loved you just as much as she loved her two baby girls," Lee said, glancing from Virgil and then to Maureen, looking her up and down again.

Maureen wrapped her arm around Virgil's neck and pulled his head down onto her shoulder. She patted him on the back, but he continued to cry like a baby.

Virgil had cried more in the last couple of weeks than he had cried when Mama Ruby died. He wondered just how many more secrets and lies he and Maureen had to deal with. How many more tears he was going to have to shed.

Maureen was glad that she had made this peculiar trip, but she was also anxious to return to Florida. She couldn't wait to be back home with Loretta and Mel where things were normal.

Maureen decided to call home after she and the rest of her relatives had finished dinner.

"It's me," she said to Mel, speaking in a low voice on the telephone on the end table in Monette's living room.

Mel was a little drunk and disoriented, so at first he didn't even realize it was Maureen on the other end of the telephone line. Her voice sounded so unfamiliar and detached. "Excuse me?" he hollered.

"This is your wife, you knucklehead," Maureen said in a louder voice, laughing. "I couldn't wait to call and hear your voice."

Mel laughed too. "I was wondering who in the world was calling here this time of night," he said, sounding tired. And he was.

He was thoroughly exhausted. Loretta had worn him out again. He rubbed a spot on the inside of his thigh where she had bitten him during a clumsy blow job. He made a mental note to keep his shorts on or to undress in the dark when Maureen returned. He also made a mental note to advise Loretta to be more careful with her teeth in the future. That girl sometimes behaved like she was auditioning to be a vampire, he thought, almost laughing again. He even considered buying a dog. That way, if Loretta lost control of herself again, he could blame the bite marks on the dog. He did laugh this time.

"What's so funny?" Maureen wanted to know. "You sound like a hyena."

"Oh! I just recalled something I saw on TV a little while ago. Eddie Murphy was cutting up."

"Anyway, I forgot about the time difference. I meant to call you sooner, but so much has been goin' on since we got here that I didn't get to do it until now. Did you remind Lo'retta to take her vitamins before she went to bed?"

"Uh-huh. So, how are things going out there? How is your cousin Lee doing?"

"He's doing just fine and he's still country to the bone," Maureen said. "He looks a whole lot like Virgil."

Mel snickered. "So he's got a face that only a plastic surgeon could love, too, huh?"

Maureen laughed along with Mel, even though she didn't agree with his assessment. "You be nice now," she scolded. "I have a very attractive family and you know it."

Like hell, Mel thought to himself. Other than Maureen and the lovely Loretta, he imagined that a family gathering with the rest of Maureen's family would be like a live version of *The Planet of the Apes*. He decided to keep that thought to himself, but he had to press his lips together to keep from laughing again. "How was your flight to Bigfoot country, baby?"

"Too long. Honey, I wish you wouldn't call Louisiana 'Bigfoot country.' These folks out here are just as sophisticated as us." Maureen sighed.

"You're right, baby. I'm just teasing you. Well, I'm sure you and Virgil will enjoy eating some of that exotic Creole cuisine."

"I hope we will too. Especially after the oxtails, turnip greens, fried okra, and hush puppies we had for dinner this evenin'," Maureen said under her breath. "Listen, sweetheart, I have a lot to tell you when I get back home. I'm sorry I can't talk longer, but I don't want to run up my cousin's phone bill. I just wanted to check in with you and Lo'retta to let y'all know we made it here all right."

"I'm glad you did call, baby. It's so nice to hear your sweet voice. I was just lying here thinking about you and what I'm going to do to you when you get back home," Mel told Maureen. He smacked his lips and made kissing noises. Then he abruptly said, "I'll talk to you later. Bye!" He hung up.

"Who was that?" Loretta asked, returning to her mother's bedroom with two bottles of beer. She and Mel were both naked and already slightly tipsy. They had been drinking most of the evening and had only stopped making love long enough to have another drink.

"Nobody," he told her, reaching for his beer with one hand and her tittie with the other. "Somebody dialed the wrong number."

CHAPTER 44

*A*FTER MAUREEN ENDED HER CALL, SHE JOINED VIRGIL ON MONETTE'S cluttered back porch. A broken lawn mower, some auto parts that had begun to rust, and piles of newspapers dominated both sides of the porch floor. There was a glider on one side, but it was practically covered with old magazines, gardening tools, a large boom box, and what appeared to be a cat's litter box, even though there was no other evidence of a cat. The only place left to sit was on the steps. Virgil occupied the top step. Maureen sat down next to him with a hearty groan.

"Virgil, you all right?" she asked, grabbing his hand and squeezing it. She was surprised at how cold his skin felt on such a warm spring night. "You look terrible."

"I feel terrible too," Virgil replied, staring straight ahead toward a rosebush, a well-tended vegetable garden, some more useless pieces of junk scattered all over the backyard, and an assortment of fruit trees. "I'm still kind of shell-shocked, though. How about you? How you doin'? You got more of a load dumped on you than me. First all that stuff I told you, now this thing about my mama havin' a baby before she had me."

"I don't know just how I'm doin' yet," Maureen admitted. "I guess I'm shell-shocked too. A few minutes ago I was feelin' like I was havin' some kind of out-of-body experience. My body felt all right, but my mind seemed like it was floating all over the place."

"You want to talk about what Monette said about Mama Ruby's first baby?"

There was a peaceful look on Maureen's face, and she felt strangely calm. "I guess we need to talk about it some more," she answered.

"I'm still tryin' to let it all sink in. I never expected to hear what we heard this evenin'. All this time, I had a real sister anyway," Virgil said in a scratchy voice.

"Virgil, you did have a real sister all this time. Me. Now you have two."

Two hours later, Ruby's biological daughter, Maureen Clemmons, arrived at Monette's house. Her footsteps on the front porch floor were loud and moved quickly, like a racehorse galloping toward a finish line. She didn't even bother to knock or ring the doorbell. She snatched open the door and steamrolled into the living room, huffing and puffing like a wolf.

Virgil held his breath and wobbled up off the couch. He stood in the middle of the floor staring at the newcomer with his eyes burning and his lips trembling. "Oh Lord! You must be our big sister!" he managed. "Old Mo'reen."

"Well, if I ain't I'm wearin' the wrong underwear!" the other Maureen roared. "I'm here!" She punched her huge, lumpy chest with her fist and guffawed so loud and hard she choked on some air. This sister was a country woman to the bone—coarse, loud, and unapologetic. She also wore a pair of men's house shoes and a long flowered dress that looked like a tropical bedsheet. Her thick, gray-streaked hair was in a single braid, wrapped around the sides and top of her head like a crown. She had the same husky voice that Mama Ruby had had but mercifully, Virgil was happy to see, not the same girth. This Maureen was fairly tall, but she weighed only about a hundred eighty pounds. Like Virgil, she had light brown skin and attractive features. "Well, now, y'all must be Virgil and Mo'reen. My baby sister and my baby brother!"

The younger Maureen rose from her seat and stood next to Virgil. Lee remained in the wing seat by the couch. Monette, with her hands on her hips, stood in the middle of the doorway leading to the kitchen.

"I been itchin' to meet y'all for years," Old Maureen squealed. "But let's get one thing straight now. I ain't that old, so I don't want to be called *Old* Mo'reen. Since I'm the biggest, y'all call me Big Mo'reen." She paused and looked at Maureen. "We'll call you Little Mo'reen from now on." Big Maureen wrapped one arm around Virgil's waist and her other arm around Maureen's waist at the same time. "It's a cryin' shame that it took this long for us to meet." She sniffled and released a few tears of joy.

"Sister, we didn't know about you until now," Virgil said. "You bein' our sister and all."

"Aunt Othella didn't tell me everything when I met her. She told me that my mama had a baby boy after they moved to Florida. I didn't know nothin' about her havin' another baby girl too," Big Maureen crowed, smiling around the room. "Who would have thought that I had a baby sister that looks like a movie star. You can't beat this with a hammer!"

"Shoot! This ain't no real big deal if you ask me. I got quite a few half sisters and half brothers that I ain't never met. My daddy got around," Monette revealed.

"Me too, I believe," Lee said. "The rumor went around for years that my mama had a baby boy that she gave up when she was a young girl." He paused and mopped sweat off his face with the back of his hand. "Most everybody in the world got kinfolks they don't know nothin' about. Just like Little Mo'reen and Virgil."

Oddly enough, Lee's last comment made Maureen feel a little more at ease. She was glad to finally see a smile on Virgil's tortured face.

"Who would have thought that Aunt Ruby had two baby girls both named Mo'reen," Monette said.

Everybody in the room laughed.

"I . . . my grandma Simone told me that my mama didn't want no babies at the time and that's why she gave me up. When I was a kid, I prayed every day that she would want to meet me someday." Big Maureen had to stop talking and sit down on the couch. After she'd honked into a handkerchief and wiped the tears from her eyes and the snot off her nose, she continued. "When I heard about the God-fearin' woman my mama was, I figured she didn't want me in her life to scandalize her good name. I made up my mind a long time ago that I wouldn't try to find her, unless she put out the word that she wanted to be found. When I heard she died, I squalled like a panda. I wanted to go to her funeral, but I didn't want to bring no shame on my mama, not even in death. Her daddy was a man of the cloth that didn't tolerate worldly behavior. All I heard from that side of the family was what a sanctified woman my real mama was."

"I wish you could have met Mama Ruby," Maureen said, easing down on the couch next to Big Maureen. "She was one of a kind."

"That's an understatement if ever there was one," Virgil chimed in.

"Now, exactly what do you mean by that, Virgil?" Lee asked, looking puzzled.

"Um, there wasn't nobody else like her," Virgil offered.

"There never will be another woman like Mama Ruby. She was the best mama in the world to me and Virgil," Maureen added.

Around midnight, Virgil called home to tell Corrine that he had just met the sister he didn't know he had.

After boo-hooing for a few moments, Corrine told Virgil, "Now you got two sisters."

CHAPTER 45

BIG MAUREEN LEFT AROUND 2:00 A.M., BUT SHE PROMISED TO RETURN the next day after she had visited her husband in the hospital. Virgil and Maureen accompanied Lee back to his house.

Lee curled up on a pallet on his back bedroom floor and fell asleep almost as soon as his head hit the pillow.

Maureen was glad to have some time alone with Virgil in the living room. "You doin' all right now?" she asked Virgil. She eased down into a huge gray easy chair facing him on the couch.

"Somewhat. I'm just feelin' real strange . . . and sad," Virgil said mournfully, kicking off his shoes. "Everything ain't really sunk in yet." He paused and gave Maureen a pensive look. "I know you said I ain't got nothin' to be sorry about, but I want to tell you again that I am so sorry about everything."

"Do you wish Mama Ruby hadn't kidnapped me now?"

"Yeah. I mean no! Oh shit, I don't know what I mean no more. What my mama done was wrong. I can't say that enough. But havin' you in our lives was a double blessin' to her and to me."

Maureen gave Virgil a weak smile. "It's a shame that Mama Ruby couldn't keep her own baby girl, but if she had, things would have turned out a whole lot different than they did for all of us."

"You mean Mama Ruby wouldn't have stole you?"

Maureen nodded. "She wouldn't have had no reason to. You said she took me on account of she wanted a baby girl so bad."

"Yeah. That's what she told me. I think in her mind that made it all right. That and the fact that she truly thought God was in control that night. Makin' it look like you was born dead, then makin' you come back to life after she got you to our house."

Maureen looked at Virgil with a stiff look on her face. "God don't direct none of His flock to kidnap somebody's child. If He really wanted Mama Ruby to have another baby girl of her own, He would have sent her another husband and blessed them with a new baby that *they* made."

Virgil shrugged. "That's right. I guess I'm just tryin' to keep Mama Ruby from lookin' too bad."

"Virgil, we both know that Mama Ruby's heart was always in the right place. There ain't nothin' you can say about her that would make her look bad to me."

"One thing I didn't tell you . . ."

"Uh-oh," Maureen said, holding her breath, wondering if she had made her last statement too soon.

"If you hadn't started cryin' when you did that night, it would have been too late."

"What do you mean?"

"We had the shoebox ready to bury you in. I was just about to go in the backyard and dig a hole by the pigsty."

"Oh. So I could have been buried alive, huh?" The thought made Maureen's head spin.

"Uh-huh," Virgil agreed. The same thought almost made him pass out.

Maureen's flesh felt like it was trying to crawl off her bones. She rubbed one arm and then the other. "No matter what, I . . . I don't think we should *ever* tell Big Mo'reen about me and how Mama Ruby took me and killed my real mama. Not even on *our* deathbeds." Maureen narrowed her eyes and looked at Virgil long and hard. "It wouldn't do no good for Big Mo'reen to find out that her mama was a criminal, huh?"

"I'm glad you feel like that and I hope you never change your mind," Virgil said. "I guarantee you, I won't be confessin' nothin' on my deathbed."

* * *

Maureen rose with the sun the next morning and called home again. She was surprised that neither Loretta nor Mel answered the telephone. They hadn't mentioned having any jobs before she left, and it was only 7:00 a.m. in Florida. She couldn't imagine where the two of them could be this early. There was a concerned look on her face as she proceeded to leave a message on the answering machine. "I just wanted to check in and let y'all know that everything is still goin' really well. We met some cousins and a half sister we didn't even know we had. Believe it or not, her name is Mo'reen too. Mama Ruby had her when she was a teenager and couldn't keep her, so she was raised by somebody else. She's been with her daddy's family for some time now. I'll explain more about that when I get home."

When Maureen called, Loretta and Mel were in the shower together, giving each other a tongue bath. They didn't even bother to check the answering machine that day or the next. When Maureen returned home the following Monday evening, one of the first things she asked was, "Ain't that somethin' about me and Virgil havin' a half sister?"

"What half sister?" Mel and Loretta asked at the same time.

Mel was on the couch with his bare feet crossed at the ankles on top of the coffee table. Loretta was facing him in the wing chair with one leg hanging over the side of the chair arm, like she was clinging to a lifeboat. Maureen didn't approve of Loretta's position at all. It was a vulgar and suggestive way for a female to be sitting in front of a man. Especially when all Loretta wore was a bathrobe.

"Lo'retta, I hope you don't sit that unladylike in front of none of the people you model for. That's how porn stars sit," Maureen jabbed, shaking her head. "Get your lazy leg off the arm of that chair, girl!"

Loretta immediately pulled her legs together and sat up straight. "I was just tryin' to get comfortable, Mama. I got the cramps," she pouted. "I didn't even hear you come in."

"Maureen, why didn't you call me to pick you and Virgil up from the airport?" Mel asked, nervously scratching the side of his head.

"I left a message on the answerin' machine tellin' you what time to pick us up. You didn't call me back to let me know you got the message, so we took a cab home," Maureen said tiredly.

"Mama, I don't know why you didn't just drive that new car I bought you to the airport and leave it there until y'all got back home," Loretta commented.

"It don't matter. I got there and I got back home," Maureen said dryly, looking around the room. She was glad to see that everything was as neat and orderly as she had left it.

"What did you just say about a half sister?" Mel asked. He moved his feet off the coffee table and sat up straighter too.

Maureen set her suitcase down and eased down onto the couch next to Mel. "I left a message on the answerin' machine about that too," she replied, looking from Loretta's surprised face to Mel's. "Didn't y'all listen to it? I called around seven o'clock Saturday mornin'. Where did y'all go that early?"

"We had a power outage around that time," Mel lied. Lying was something he had become so good at that he could do it on cue and sound sincere. "It was the longest outage this street has had in months. We got up early that morning and went to my friend Mark's house over in Liberty City. Mel paused and groped for a few more appropriate words. "The outage didn't affect every resident on our street, or even in our building." He added the last sentence in case one of the neighbors told Maureen a different story. "We stayed with Mark until he left for Key West this morning."

"Don't worry, Mama. The power wasn't off long enough for the ham hocks you put in the freezer before you left to thaw out," Loretta threw in.

"Oh. That's good. We can have them for dinner this evenin'," Maureen said. She snatched a rolled up newspaper off the end table and started fanning her face. "Well, I'm glad to be home. It's hot here, but that Louisiana heat was stiflin'. It was as close to hell as a human bein' could get and still be alive on Earth."

"So, when do we get to meet your half sister? Is she a great big fat woman like Mama Ruby was?" Loretta asked with an amused look on her face.

Maureen chuckled and shook her head. "Not hardly. She was a little on the heavy side, but not half as fat as Mama Ruby was. I would say she weighs close to two hundred pounds."

Loretta's jaw dropped and her eyes crossed. "Two hundred

pounds? And you don't think that's that fat?" Loretta threw her head back and howled with laughter. Mel had to hold his breath to keep from snickering himself.

"Well, that is kind of heavy, I guess," Maureen chortled. "Anyway, believe it or not, her name is also Mo'reen. Everybody called her Big Mo'reen and they called me Little Mo'reen."

"How old is she?" Mel asked, looking just as amused as Loretta. "If your mama had her when she was a teenager, she must be pretty long in the tooth by now."

"Big Mo'reen is a little past fifty," Maureen replied. "She's got grown kids and grandkids. They all live in other states. She's comin' to visit us later this year, maybe for Thanksgivin' or Christmas." Maureen smiled.

Despite everything that had transpired, Maureen was in one of the best moods she'd been in since she was a child. When Mel pulled her into his arms later that night, she felt like her life was almost complete. If she could bring herself to love him, it would be.

CHAPTER 46

MAUREEN WAS GLAD TO RETURN TO HER JOB AT THE NURSING HOME, and all of her coworkers were glad to see her. Two of the people who had been on board only a few weeks before she got there had already quit. Maureen had to take over some of their duties until they could be replaced. Even that didn't bother her.

So much had been going on in the last few days, she had not had time to call up Jay and check on him. When she did, three days after she'd returned from Louisiana, she learned from the outgoing message on his answering machine that he was still out of town. She assumed he was still in St. Louis.

Catty and Fast Black took Maureen to dinner that Friday evening, and when she told them about Big Maureen, the first thing Catty asked was, "Did she take after Mama Ruby?"

Maureen laughed. "She ain't that fat," she replied.

"I don't think Catty meant that," Fast Black offered. "We hope your sister ain't the kind of woman that goes around chastisin' folks the way Mama Ruby did. Remember that one-armed man she stuck with a pitchfork that time? Killed him dead."

Maureen nodded. "I don't know if my sister chastises folks the way Mama Ruby did, but I remember that one-armed man. He shot Cousin Hattie, thinkin' she was Mama Ruby."

"Well, the reason he wanted to get back at Mama Ruby was because she was the one that ripped off his arm," Fast Black recalled.

"I remember that too. I was a little girl when that happened,"

Maureen stated. "From what I heard about the way that man as-
saulted Mama Ruby in that bar where it happened, he got just what
he deserved. Everybody was talkin' about that incident."

"There was a whole lot of stuff Mama Ruby did that even you
don't know about, but I ain't goin' to be the one to tell you. I don't
want that big woman's ghost to come haunt me. Some of the stuff
your mama done, it would curl your hair if you knew," Fast Black
said, shaking her head. "Me and my cousin Loomis and that red-
neck sheriff we called Big Red, we helped Mama Ruby cover up a
lot of shit." Fast Black gave Maureen a pitiful look. "I'm glad you
only seen the good side of your mama. Aside from all the mischief
she done, she was still a real good woman and you was real lucky to
have her for a mama."

Despite Mama Ruby's "mischief," she had been a good mother
to Maureen. "I know I was blessed to have her," Maureen acknowl-
edged, wondering what her friends would say if they knew what she
now knew about Mama Ruby. Would they still love and praise a
woman who had stolen another woman's baby?

Two days had gone by and Maureen still had not heard from Jay.
That Monday evening around seven, right after Maureen, Loretta,
and Mel had finished eating their dinner, Jay called. Maureen was
in the kitchen alone.

"I've been meaning to return your call, but I've been real busy
since I got back from St. Louis," he told her. "Then I had an interview in Key West with some TV folks. I went straight there from St.
Louis."

"I thought you didn't want to be on TV."

"I didn't and I still don't. I just turned down a show in Chicago,
one in 'Frisco, one in L.A., and two in New York. But these Florida
folks won't let up on me. I figured the sooner I do something with
them, the sooner they'd get off my back and I can return to a normal life. That's why I did that show in Key West."

"What about that lawsuit against the St. Louis cops?"

"That's my cousin's pipe dream, not mine. I don't want to have
anything to do with something like that. What happened is over and

done with, and the people who were responsible for it are dead. Even if my mother and her niece were still alive, the last thing I would want to do is send them to jail."

"I can understand that. What good would it do now? But wouldn't you want them to be held responsible for what they did to you?"

"They will be."

"I know what you mean. What they did is now between them and God."

There was an awkward moment of silence before Jay spoke again. "How did your trip to Louisiana go?"

"Oh, it was all right. We met some relatives for the first time. One was our half sister."

"You and Virgil have a half sister?"

"Uh-huh."

"You never mentioned her before."

"We didn't know about her until we went to Louisiana. My mama had her when she was a real young girl, and somebody else raised her. She's in her early fifties now and her name is Mo'reen too."

"That's interesting. Did she know that your mother was her real mother when she was growing up, or did she think that the folks who raised her were her real family?"

"She grew up in some kind of asylum. My mama had to give her up when she was born, but she knew all along who her real mama was."

"I'm happy to hear that. At least she didn't go through what I went through."

Maureen glanced toward the doorway and lowered her voice to a whisper. "Would you like to meet me for coffee or a drink or somethin' tomorrow evenin' after work?"

"I would like to, but I can't," Jay replied.

"Oh."

"Maureen, I didn't want to tell you this over the telephone, but I guess I should do it and get it over with. I don't want you to hear it from somebody else."

Maureen held her breath. Her heart rate had suddenly accelerated and she could already feel a lump forming in her throat.

"Wh-what?" she stuttered, silently praying that Jay didn't have more shocking news to reveal. She had heard enough lately to last her for the rest of her life. "Are you movin' back to St. Louis to be close to your real family?"

Jay let out a dry laugh. "Hell no!" he boomed. "I don't think I want to see any of those folks again. You wouldn't believe how many pimps and other thugs I'm related to. It seems like each time I talk to somebody on that end, I hear that there's another cousin, or uncle, or aunt in prison or involved in some other shady shit."

Maureen wanted to laugh, but she couldn't. Not until she heard what Jay had to tell her. All she could hope for was that it was something to laugh about.

She was wrong. What he told her almost reduced her to tears.

"Maureen, I know you're content just being friends with me and I appreciate that. But that's not enough for me. I'm a man and I can't continue to be around a beautiful woman like you, feeling the way I do, and not be able to do anything about it."

"I see," Maureen mumbled. She never thought he would be the one to sever their relationship. She had always thought that when and if that happened, she would be the one to do it. "I understand. Well, if you still want to call me up whenever you feel lonely or just want to talk, feel free to do so. I will always consider you a friend."

Before Jay could respond, Maureen heard a woman's voice in the background on his end. "Baby, I'm back," the woman said.

"Uh, that's Nelda. My ex. Uh, what I wanted you to hear from me is that we decided to give our relationship another shot." The silence that followed for the next few seconds was so profound Maureen thought she had gone deaf.

"Oh," she muttered. Her heart was breaking into a million little pieces and there was not a thing she could do about it.

"I would like to attend Loretta's graduation next month, if you don't mind. I'm sorry that I haven't had the chance to get to know her better by now, but I know what a big day that's going to be for her and I'd like to be there to see her walk across the stage and receive her diploma. Now, if you think that'll be too awkward, I won't come."

"No, it won't be awkward for you to be there, but you don't have to come. Especially now."

"I do want to come, so I'll be there. About this other thing, uh, well, I think I'm doing the right thing by trying to restore my marriage. You see, Nelda hasn't been with anybody since we broke up, and, well, I've been more than a little lonely myself, if you know what I mean."

"I think I do," Maureen admitted.

"Then I know you can understand why I decided to do this."

"I can," Maureen snorted. "But like I said, if you ever just want to talk, you got my number. I wish you all the best. Good-bye, Jay."

"Good-bye, Maureen. You take care of yourself."

She leaned against the wall still holding the telephone, listening to the dial tone. She twirled the cord around her finger and looked at it like she wanted to bite it.

If Mel had not strolled into the kitchen to grab a beer from the refrigerator when he did, she would have bitten the telephone cord in two.

CHAPTER 47

*B*IG MAUREEN AND HER RETIRED COOK HUSBAND, LUKAS, DIDN'T WAIT until Thanksgiving or Christmas to visit Maureen and Virgil. They had arrived unannounced on a Monday evening around five the first week in June. They took a cab to Maureen's apartment.

Lukas, a stingy, horse-faced bag of bones, tipped the cabdriver a quarter, so he had to unload their luggage himself. "If I had known these Florida cabdrivers was too lazy to haul our suitcases, I would have kept my quarter," he complained, struggling to carry the two large suitcases up onto the porch.

"I wonder how come Little Mo'reen don't answer her door?" Big Maureen said with a puzzled look on her face as she stood on the JESUS SAVES welcome mat, banging her fist on Maureen's door.

"See there. I told you we should have let somebody know that we was comin' to Florida. Now what we goin' to do?" Lukas whined, still holding the suitcases.

"I guess we'll just have to sit on this porch and wait on somebody to come home," Big Maureen decided, easing down on the porch steps. She and Lukas sat there until nosy Mr. Ben next door poked his head out of his window.

"Who y'all folks?" Mr. Ben asked, adjusting his glasses. "What y'all doin' sittin' on Mo'reen's steps?"

"Sir, do you know where my baby sister at?" Big Maureen asked, rising. "We just got here from Louisiana."

Mr. Ben opened his door and shuffled out to the porch, still adjusting his glasses. "Mo'reen gets off work around three, but she usually goes lollygaggin' at the mall or some beer garden every day. Some days she don't get home till six or seven," he stated, looking at the suitcases. "She didn't say nothin' to me about no company comin' to visit."

"She didn't know," Lukas volunteered with a sneer. One sharp look from Big Maureen silenced him.

"What about her husband and her girl? You know where they at?" Big Maureen asked.

"Oh, there is just no tellin'. They was home a little while ago because I heard 'em knockin' around in there, but them two stay on the go. I don't know why Mo'reen allows that gal to be so footloose," Mr. Ben remarked. "Y'all can wait in my place if you want to. Just wipe your feet first and come on in."

What Mr. Ben didn't know was that Loretta and Mel had piled out of Maureen's bed an hour ago and were now kicking back in a steak house gnawing on some slow-roasted prime rib. Mel had finished a shoot early, and Lo'retta had left school "sick" so she could meet up with him. They returned to the apartment an hour after Big Maureen and Lukas had arrived.

As soon as Mr. Ben heard Loretta and Mel return home, he beat a tattoo on Maureen's door. Mel snatched it open with a scowl on his face.

"Y'all got some out-of-town company," Mr. Ben announced, giving Mel a suspicious look.

"Who?" Mel asked, looking over the old man's shoulder. Mel wasn't expecting anybody from out of town, and even as dense as Maureen was sometimes, she wouldn't have forgotten to tell him they had company coming.

"Mo'reen's sister and her husband from Louisiana, that's who," Mr. Ben snapped. "I'll send 'em over here before they drink up all of my wine."

Mel and Loretta had to "entertain" Big Maureen and Lukas, and it was hellish for them. Big Maureen was a nosy, boisterous woman with a big appetite, and Lukas was a wimp who liked beer. By the time Maureen arrived home thirty minutes later with a few shopping bags from the mall, Mel and Loretta were fit to be tied.

Maureen was surprised but pleased to see Big Maureen and her husband. When she called to tell Virgil, he and Corrine came over immediately. After Virgil arrived, he insisted that Big Maureen and Lukas stay at his house, since he had more room. "You don't mind them stayin' in the upper room, do you?" he asked Maureen in a low voice when he followed her into the kitchen to get another bottle of wine. "Ain't nobody slept in that room since you moved out of it."

Maureen blinked. "Why should I care if they stay in there? The upper room don't mean nothin' to me no more," she said, giving Virgil a guarded look.

"I just thought I'd ask. I know we don't talk about that room that much no more, but it still must mean somethin' to you. I mean, for years it was like your sanctuary."

"Well, it ain't my sanctuary no more. I have a whole new life, and the upper room is one of the many things I don't want to spend too much time thinkin' or talkin' about," Maureen assured Virgil.

Maureen spent most of that Thursday entertaining her big sister and her husband. She drove them all over the Miami area to shop and sightsee, and she treated them to meals in some of the finest restaurants. She was so proud of the fact that Mel had postponed a couple of jobs just so he could accompany them to a few places. He even took several family photographs and developed them right away, with Big Maureen oohing and aahing about what a fun job he had.

Mel was very gracious, but it was all for show. He couldn't wait for these two countrified intruders to go back to Bigfoot country.

"I'm glad to see that your girl gets along so well with your husband," Big Maureen whispered to Maureen during Loretta's graduation ceremony reception that Friday afternoon on the Goons High School's spacious front lawn. They stood away from the crowd, sipping punch from plastic cups and watching Loretta and Mel as they chatted with some of Loretta's classmates near the refreshment table. "They seem like they joined at the hip bone. Ever since we got here, I ain't seen one unless I seen the other one at the same time. They must get along real good."

"They do get along real good. I thank the good Lord for that," Maureen beamed. "Especially since we hear so many ugly things about stepfathers and stepchildren. But Mel's one of a kind. I was lucky to meet him."

Big Maureen nodded. "You sure was. You luckier than most women I know. You got looks, a beautiful daughter, and a man that other women would kill for. Me, I wasn't so lucky. I had a real rough time with men after my first husband died. After him, I could have brought the pope home and my kids would have found somethin' they didn't like about him."

"I'm glad I never had that problem. I always latched on to men that my girl took a shine to," Maureen said with a proud sniff.

Big Maureen took a deep breath and gave Maureen a curious look.

"What's the matter?" Maureen asked. "You look like you got somethin' on your mind."

Big Maureen wasted no time telling Maureen what was on her mind. "I'm nosy so I got to stick my nose in your business. See, I got a feelin' there is somethin' you ain't tellin' me about you and Mel." There was an accusatory look on Big Maureen's face.

"Why do you think that?"

"The whole time I been here, I ain't seen you show not one bit of affection toward your husband. I ain't seen you hug him, kiss him, or even talk to him that much. When he took us to eat at that Cracker Barrel in Tampa last night, you didn't even sit next to him. Lo'retta did."

"Oh. It's just that me and Mel got so used to each other over the years that we don't show our feelin's in public that much any-more," Maureen explained.

"In public is one thing. A lot of women don't like to get too mushy in public. But I noticed that the first night in your apart-ment, you and him seemed more like strangers."

"What do you mean?"

"For one thing, I noticed that when he tried to kiss you on the cheek, you turned your head. Another thing I noticed, Lo'retta pays him way more attention than you do."

"Oh, she's just so happy to finally have a daddy, that's all. I wish I'd had one when I was her age."

"Uh-huh." Big Maureen gave Maureen a look that she could not interpret. "Now tell me, you in love with another man, ain't you? Don't bother lyin' to me. I ain't blind or stupid."

Maureen dropped her head and bit her bottom lip. Then she looked at Big Maureen with a wan smile on her face. "There was another man I cared about. I met him too late, though."

"Baby sister, I'm a lot older than you, and I've been around the block more than a few times. Let me tell you somethin'—when it comes to love, it ain't never too late."

"You mean I should divorce Mel and go after the other man?"

"You don't have to divorce Mel, but you don't have to turn your back on that other man neither." Big Maureen stopped talking and looked around. She smiled at Mel. He stood a few yards away near the refreshment table, munching on a sandwich. Loretta, also munching on a sandwich, stood next to him. Loretta was gazing at Mel like she wanted to munch on him next. Big Maureen searched around until she spotted Virgil. He was shaking hands with one of Loretta's teachers. Big Maureen looked back to Maureen. "Why can't you have both men?" she asked, still smiling.

"You mean like an affair?" Maureen gasped.

"You can call it whatever you want to call it. Men have been doin' it from the beginnin' of time. My first husband did it, and the nasty buzzard I'm married to now hops into bed with some floozy on Board Street every chance he gets. That's why his back is always goin' out on him. I can tell when he's been with her. I can smell her scent on his hide. That's when I make him give me some pleasure, whether he wants to or not. I straddle him and then I ride his tally whacker so long and hard, he has to soak it in Epsom salt when I'm done with it."

Maureen chuckled. "You sound so much like Mama Ruby. She said stuff like that all the time. But I don't want to cheat on my husband."

"Why not? I do it all the time."

"You cheat on your husband?"

"Honey, I done had so many affairs since I married Lukas I done lost count." Big Maureen shook her head and laughed. "It keeps my blood pressure down, and it keeps me young."

"What would you do if Lukas ever found out?"

"I wouldn't do nothin'. He wouldn't do nothin' neither. If he did, I'd skin him alive!" Maureen gave Big Maureen an amused look; this sister was definitely Mama Ruby's daughter.

"What if he got real mean, like hit you or somethin'?"

"Harrumph!" Big Maureen snorted. "The man is crazy, but he ain't crazy enough to lay a hand on me. He did one time, though. That sucker slapped my Easter bonnet clean off my head, wig and all. I lit into him like a piranha. I bit and beat the bat shit out of him. By the time I got through, his back was broke in two places." Big Maureen looked around some more until she spotted her husband. Lukas was talking to the parents of one of Loretta's classmates. "His back never did heal right. That's why a little fall or even him sleepin' the wrong way in bed makes his back go out. It was his own fault, though. He shouldn't have messed with me."

Maureen shook her head and excused herself. She decided it was time for her to mingle for a while.

Catty had come to the ceremony, but she had to leave early because she had a funeral to go to. Fast Black was visiting her son in Brooklyn, so she had not been able to attend. But Maureen saw a few of her coworkers and a few people from the church she visited occasionally. And then she saw Jay. He had told her that he would attend Loretta's graduation!

He stood next to a petite woman in her twenties. His arm was around her narrow waist. He glanced at Maureen and nodded. He didn't smile at her, but she smiled at him and nodded back. Then she quickly looked away. Just seeing Jay with another woman—a prettier, *younger* woman at that—made his departure from Maureen's life seem so final.

If only Mel were not in her life . . .

CHAPTER 48

*T*WO DAYS AFTER HER GRADUATION, LORETTA *TOLD* MAUREEN THAT SHE was going to the Bahamas with forty of the kids who had graduated with her.

"You ain't goin' no place," Maureen told her, giving her an exasperated look.

"What? Why not? Everybody else is goin'!" Loretta squawked.

"Because you didn't ask me if you could go."

"Well, can I go, Mama? They are leavin' next week."

"No," Maureen said firmly.

Even though Loretta had the money to cover her travel expenses, and there would be several chaperones, Maureen still refused to let her go to the Bahamas. In addition to the fact that Loretta waited until the last minute to even mention the trip, Maureen didn't want to let her go because she was not going herself so that she could make sure Loretta didn't get drunk and act a fool. Maureen didn't want to trust her daughter in the care of chaperones she didn't know.

Loretta cried and begged, but Maureen still didn't give in. "Like I said, you ain't goin' no place, girl."

"But I'm eighteen now! EIGHTEEN!" Loretta shouted as if she wanted the whole world to hear.

"I don't care if you are a hundred and eighteen. As long as you still livin' under my roof, you will do as I say," Maureen stated. "The only time you've even been out of the state is with me. There is no way I'm goin' to let you go out of the country without me!" Maureen was adamant, so it didn't matter how much Loretta pouted; she still didn't give in. "You don't even have a passport," Maureen pointed out.

"Yes, I do!" Loretta revealed.

"How did you get a passport without me knowin' about it?" Maureen gasped.

"Mel helped me get it. He is my daddy now, remember? I kept forgettin' to tell you about my passport."

"That was thoughtful of Mel, but that's somethin' that you or him should have let me know about by now."

"Mama, you've been so busy with that new job and gettin' acquainted with your sister and all that I didn't want to bother you with things that we can handle on our own. Mel saved the day."

Mel "saved the day" again later that evening. He suggested that he and Maureen take Loretta to the Bahamas as a graduation present at the same time the other kids were going. He had a client who had a time-share there. He had told Mel that he could use it anytime he wanted. Mel wanted to get a few shots of some exotic locations to incorporate into his portfolio and do a little socializing with some client friends who were going to be in the Bahamas that same week. Maureen thought that that was a good idea and she agreed to go, but unfortunately the only days that the time-share was available was during Maureen's workdays. Since she had already taken off the time to go to Louisiana last month, she didn't want to request more time off again so soon.

"Loretta can spend time with her friends while I'm busy shooting, but I'm sure that I will still be able to keep an eye on her," Mel insisted. "I'll make sure she stays out of trouble."

"But, Mel, honey, what if you get too busy to keep up with her? She might run off with some of those other kids and get to drinkin' and doin' all kinds of crazy shit," Maureen wailed. "Maybe even have sex again."

"Baby, Loretta is my child as far as I am concerned. I will never be too busy to keep up with her. Besides, the main reason I want to go down there is for Loretta's benefit. My friends already know that, so they won't expect me to spend much time with them."

"I don't know. The Bahamas is a foreign country and all. What if

Lo'retta gets bitten by some strange island creature or somethin' and needs a blood transfusion from me?"

"Maureen, stop talking crazy," Mel laughed.

"Well, maybe we can all go around Christmas when I have some vacation time comin'. Maybe we can invite Virgil, Corrine, and the folks from Louisiana to come with us," Maureen suggested.

Mel couldn't have looked more disgusted if Maureen had suggested they drag along his dreaded family with them. "Maureen, be serious. Do you honestly think that Loretta would enjoy a trip like that? This is a special time in her life. She wants to go at the same time that her friends are going. She may not see some of these kids again for years. The whole point of the trip is so these kids can have one final blast together. I mean, you were young once. You know how it is."

Maureen sighed. She knew when to quit fighting a losing battle. "All right, then. But don't be callin' me to complain if she cramps your style!"

Mel and Loretta started packing that same night.

Big Maureen enjoyed staying with Virgil, but she wanted to spend the last two days of her visit with Maureen in her apartment. Just getting to know each other better and trying to make up for all of the decades that they had already lost meant a lot to both of the Maureens.

Even though Maureen had known Big Maureen for only a short period of time, it seemed like she had known her for years. One reason was because Big Maureen reminded Maureen so much of Mama Ruby. If Maureen closed her eyes and just listened to Big Maureen speak, it would be like Mama Ruby was in the room with her. Big Maureen sounded that much like Mama Ruby.

"How come you didn't have no more children?" Big Maureen asked as she sat with Maureen in her living room on her next day off, which was that Thursday.

Maureen took her time responding. "I didn't want to have any more babies unless I was married. It was bad enough that I got pregnant when I was a young girl and didn't have a husband. I don't want my daughter to think havin' babies without a husband is a good thing to do."

Big Maureen looked at the side of Maureen's head. "How come you didn't marry Lo'retta's daddy?"

"He was goin' to marry me," Maureen lied. "But he passed . . ."

"Oh. Well, that's a shame. It's a shame he left you with just one child."

"I had two. Lo'retta had a twin sister. Her name was Lo'raine. She fell in a lake and got drowned."

"Great balls of fire. You poor thing you! Well, I hope you don't lose Lo'retta that way!"

"I don't think I'll ever have to worry about that happenin'. Lo'retta loves to go to the beach, but all she'll do is put on a bikini and stretch out on a towel to show off her shape. That girl won't go near the water. She won't even stick her big toe in the duck pond out at Johnson's Park," Maureen said with a heavy sigh. "I wish . . . well, my husband doesn't really want kids, but I hope he will change his mind someday. After Lo'retta leaves home, maybe I'll work on him about that."

"Someday soon, I hope. Don't put it off like I did. I wanted at least one more, but by the time I decided I was ready, Mother Nature had other plans for me. I had a lot of female problems some years ago and had to have my baby-makin' equipment removed." Big Maureen wiped a tear from her eye. "I wanted to give Lukas at least one child. He got a few scattered around the state that he never got to know because the mamas never stayed in one spot long enough."

"That's too bad. Mama Ruby was crazy about kids. She wanted a lot more than just me and Virgil and I . . ." Maureen stopped talking when she saw the unbearably sad look that suddenly appeared on Big Maureen's face. "Oh Lord. I didn't mean to remind you about Mama Ruby givin' you up. Me and my big mouth!"

"I don't hold no grudge against my mama for givin' me up. I probably would have done the same thing if I had been in her shoes. I had my first child when I was just sixteen, but I had a husband."

"Let me ask you somethin'. Do you ever think about adoptin' a child?" Maureen asked.

Big Maureen quickly responded. "Every day! Me and Lukas been tryin' to do just that for years! But we ain't that young no more. The older we get, the less chances we have of that happenin', and that's a goddamn shame! Believe it or not, black folks ain't too quick to give up babies for adoption. Me and Lukas keep prayin', though. I would give anything in this world to raise just one more child."

"I will pray for that to happen too," Maureen said, giving Big Maureen a firm hug. "I just wish that Mama Ruby was still here to see what a fine daughter you grew up to be."

"I feel her presence all the time," Big Maureen said. "She's with me in spirit. Will you or Virgil take me to where she's buried so I can put some flowers on her grave? It's the least I can do."

"I'd be happy to do that," Maureen answered.

When she drove out to Virgil's house and told him that Big Maureen wanted to visit Mama Ruby's grave, he was all for it. "It's time for us to put some flowers on Mama Ruby's grave anyhow. This is good timin'," he told her.

Maureen blinked and remained silent.

"Now I know you probably think this is goin' to be hard on me and you now that you know . . . you know what. But it's somethin' Big Mo'reen needs to do. Mama Ruby was her mama too," Virgil told Maureen, speaking in such a cautious manner he thought he was going to lose his breath.

"I know, but I was thinkin' about somethin' else." Maureen swallowed hard and blinked even harder. "There's that other thing."

One look at her eyes told Virgil what she was thinking. "Your real mama?"

Maureen nodded.

"Well, since Othella was your mama and Big Mo'reen's auntie," he said, "I'm sure she'll want to put some flowers on her grave too."

"All Big Mo'reen needs to know is that Othella was such a good friend of the family, we thought it would be nice to honor her too," Maureen said.

CHAPTER 49

*T*HE DAY BEFORE BIG MAUREEN AND LUKAS LEFT FLORIDA, THEY WENT with Maureen and Virgil to the cemetery to put some flowers on Mama Ruby's and Othella's graves.

Just being in this particular cemetery was enough to depress anybody. Some of the headstones had either been knocked over or had fallen over on their own. Dead leaves and other debris formed a carpet on the pathway that led from the road. The sky directly above seemed to be darker and gloomier than the sky beyond it on this particular day. A buzzard circled above. *Too late for a feast*, Maureen thought. Or was it? Mama Ruby had told her one time that when nobody was looking, dead people rose up out of their graves and carried on like they were still alive. Some of them didn't even know they were dead. Was Mama Ruby's spirit roaming around today? Maureen wondered. There was an empty beer can just a few feet from her grave, and everybody knew Mama Ruby had consumed at least a dozen cans of beer almost every day of her adult life. Maureen sighed and kicked the beer can off to the side.

"I would give anything in this world to have met my mama," Big Maureen sobbed as she placed a dozen red roses on top of her mother's grave. "And Aunt Othella. It's so nice of y'all to be so thoughtful to include some flowers for her grave too." Big Maureen wiped her tears with a handkerchief. "It's a shame that Lo'retta couldn't come with us, but I remember what havin' cramps was like. She need to stay off her feet. She don't want to get so sick she won't be able to go on the trip to them Bahamas in a few days."

"Uh-huh," Maureen mumbled. She didn't have the heart to tell Big Maureen that Loretta had decided years ago that it was "uncool" to put live flowers on a dead person's grave.

Mel had overheard Maureen's telephone conversation with Virgil about the cemetery visit, so when she invited him, he already had a believable bogus excuse not to go.

"It's a shame that Mel had to go do a shoot for one of his sick photographer buddies and couldn't come with us either," Big Maureen lamented.

"Uh-huh," Maureen said again. She was disappointed, too, that Mel hadn't come with them, but she never pestered him when it came to his work. Besides, he had told her a long time ago that he was superstitious about going to a cemetery before his time.

Immediately after the visit to the cemetery, they all went to Virgil's house. Corrine had roasted a duck for dinner and chilled several bottles of wine.

It had been a long and enjoyable day for everyone. Catty and Fast Black and their current lovers had even dropped in for a plate and a few drinks.

But it was a sad and bittersweet day too. Still, the two Maureens didn't want it to end. In less than twenty-four hours, Big Maureen would be gone and Maureen and would miss her.

"We still plan on comin' back for Thanksgivin' or Christmas, God willin'," Big Maureen said as Virgil drove her and her husband back to the airport with Maureen in the front seat, snapping pictures with one of the less complicated cameras Mel owned.

"When Lo'retta gets back from them Bahamas, tell her to send us some of them pictures Mel's goin' to take down there," Lukas added. "Maybe the next time we come to visit, she'll slow down so she can spend more time with us."

"I'll make sure of that. Even if I have to put a leash on her neck," Maureen promised with a wicked laugh. "Her and Mel both."

It was an emotional parting. Virgil and Maureen spent so much time hugging and kissing Big Maureen at the curb in front of the airport that Lukas had to practically drag her away so they wouldn't miss their flight.

After Virgil dropped Maureen off at her place, she drank a glass of wine and took a nap. She had to get up early to take Mel and Loretta to the airport the next morning.

When Maureen got up a little before 7:00 a.m., Mel and Loretta had already eaten breakfast and were anxious to be on their way.

"How come y'all didn't wake me up?" Maureen asked, padding into the living room where Mel and Loretta sat huddled together on the couch. "And—" Maureen gasped and stopped talking. On the floor near the door were *seven* large suitcases *and* the huge footlocker that Mel used to transport some of his camera equipment. "Why do y'all need so much luggage for just ten days? Folks will think y'all goin' to another planet."

"Uh, I wanted two or three outfits for each day. You know me," Loretta said in a nervous voice, turning to Mel. "Mel is bringin' his best camera equipment so he can get some good shots. Right, Mel?"

Mel nodded vigorously. "That's right!" he said quickly. "I had to pack a lot of outfits too. A couple of my clients from my last shoot are already down there, so there will be several parties. I didn't want to wear the same thing to each one."

"Well, I hope y'all have a good time. I sure do wish I could go too. When I do have some vacation time, we'll go again," Maureen said, glancing at her watch. "Let me get my shoes on so I can get y'all to the airport on time." She blinked at Mel. "Oh, Mel, where is your SUV? I didn't see it when I got home last night."

"Huh? Oh! I let one of my buddies borrow it until I get back," Mel responded. "His is in the shop."

"I hope your buddy takes good care of it. I know how much that SUV means to you," Maureen said.

After Maureen had dropped Mel and Loretta off in front of Miami International, giving them both long hugs and lots of kisses, she returned to the apartment and made herself some hot tea. She did some housecleaning and a few loads of laundry, and she called to chat with a few friends she had not talked to in a while.

Mel had promised to give Maureen a call as soon as he and Loretta arrived in the islands, which she felt should have happened by now. They'd been gone for almost eight hours. She was more than a little concerned. She was tempted to call the number that Mel had given her just to make sure they had made it to their destination all right. But she changed her mind right away. The last thing she wanted to do was pester them. She eventually assumed they were already having such a good time that they simply had not had the time to check in with her.

After another hour had passed and Maureen still hadn't heard from Mel and Loretta, she became extremely worried. The way she kept glaring at the telephone, you would have thought that it was responsible for them not calling.

She picked up the telephone several times, but each time she placed it back into the cradle without attempting to call Mel. After a glass of wine helped her relax, she decided that it would be better if she just waited for them to call her later that night.

But they didn't call her later that night.

They didn't call the next day either.

Maureen was frantic by now. At 6:00 P.M. on the second day, she finally dialed the number Mel had given her. There was no answer. She called four times in two hours and there was no answer. Now she was convinced that something really bad had happened. The thought of losing her only child and her husband at the same time was more than she could bear. Her life would be over because she knew she would not be able to go on.

She finally called Virgil.

"Virgil, I can't get in touch with Loretta and Mel," she hollered, clutching the telephone in her hand like she was afraid it was going to escape.

"When was the last time you talked to them?" he asked.

"When I dropped them off at the airport yesterday mornin'," Maureen replied, almost choking on her words.

"Don't go gettin' all upset yet. If you don't hear from them before you go to bed tonight, we'll figure out somethin' in the mornin'."

Virgil hung up but Maureen didn't stop with him. She called the airline reservation desk thinking that maybe they had missed their flight and were still sitting in the airport waiting on another one. She immediately realized that that didn't make any sense at all. Who would sit in an airport for a day and a half? If they had missed their flight, they would have let her know unless . . . unless something or *someone* was preventing them from doing so!

Maureen refused to believe what the woman at the airline told her. Loretta and Mel had not missed their flight to the Bahamas— *they had never been booked on it in the first place.*

CHAPTER 50

"*H*MMM. THAT'S STRANGE. MA'AM, CAN YOU CHECK ANOTHER schedule? Maybe they took a later flight," Maureen said to the representative. "Maybe I wrote down the wrong time."

"The flight you're inquiring about was the only flight to the Bahamas on that day," the woman said in a very sympathetic voice. "Maybe they gave you the wrong information."

"Uh, I don't think so. I discussed everything with them several times. I checked and rechecked with them several more times before they left. Is there somebody else I can talk to?"

"Ma'am, they'll tell you the same thing I just told you. The two individuals you are calling about did not book a flight on our airline to the Bahamas or any other destination." The woman didn't sound so sympathetic now.

"There must be somebody else I can talk to!" Maureen yelled, almost in tears. "A supervisor? Or somebody who would have been on duty durin' the time they were supposed to leave?"

"I'll transfer you," the woman said. She clicked off before Maureen could say another word.

As soon as Maureen heard a different voice, she repeated what she had said to the first representative. Before this woman said anything, she put Maureen on hold.

Maureen's heart was beating like a bongo drum. She had heard and read so many grim stories about some of the bad things that happened to Americans in foreign countries. Her hands were shaking so hard she almost dropped the telephone. She only had to wait a few minutes for the representative to get back to her, but it seemed like an eternity.

During those few minutes, every mother's nightmare had run through her mind. What if some island sex maniac had knocked Mel out and kidnapped Loretta and was going to sell her to one of those brothels that one of the cable channels had featured on a documentary last month? The world was a dangerous place for girls as beautiful as Loretta. The thought of her child being a kidnap victim, too, was more than Maureen could bear to think about! She had other thoughts that were just as unbearable. Such as, maybe some unscrupulous island cabdriver had decided to rob them on the way to the time-share! What if he had killed them and left them dead or dying in a ditch or a jungle for the jackals to eat?

"There are no reservations on any flight with this airline for those two parties," the representative told Maureen.

"Maybe they booked reservations on a different airline," Maureen said hopefully.

"Maybe they did."

"Ma'am, I'm sorry but this is my daughter and my husband. There is no reason in the world for them not to have called me by now. Don't you think that's strange?"

"Yes, it is strange, but we don't have any information to share with you."

"Is there somebody else I can talk to? Like the police?"

"Ma'am, if you feel this is a police matter, I suggest you call them." This representative sounded so abrupt and impatient that Maureen thought she was going to hang up on her.

"I don't want to call the police if I don't have to. I just . . . I just thought that maybe you could help me figure out what happened."

"Have you checked with any of the cruise lines? Or a private carrier?"

"Huh? Oh. No, I didn't think about that," Maureen mumbled.

A cruise ship or some private carrier? Wouldn't Loretta and Mel have told her if they decided to go to the Bahamas on a ship or a private plane? Maureen had dropped them off at the airport in front of American Airlines like they had told her to.

What the hell? She had to find out what was going on and she had to find out soon. But she didn't even know where to begin to look. She didn't know who else to call. Just as she was about to open the telephone book, the telephone rang.

It was Loretta. "It's me," she said. Her voice was so low Maureen could barely hear her. Maureen had never experienced an overseas telephone call before, so she didn't know until now just how odd and far away the caller's voice would sound.

"Lord have mercy, girl! I'm about to go crazy!" Maureen hollered, rubbing her aching chest. She exhaled and collected her thoughts. "You need to talk louder. I can hardly hear you. Can you hear me? Do you want to hang up and have the overseas operator connect us? Maybe we'll have better reception."

"I don't need the overseas operator, Mama," Loretta said with a sniff, speaking loud and clear this time. Now she sounded like she was calling from the next room.

There was complete silence for several seconds. The only thing Maureen could hear was Loretta's heavy, nervous breathing. It sounded like she was breathing through a tube.

"You still there?" Maureen asked, her heart thumping and a lump forming in her throat.

"I'm still here," Loretta said quickly.

"Where are y'all? I was worried sick!"

"Mama, shut up and listen." Loretta stopped talking.

"I'm listenin'," Maureen said in a tentative voice. "You goin' to tell me what's goin' on or what?"

"Mama, if you ain't sittin' down, you better do so because I need to tell you somethin' that you probably won't like. Uh, it might even shock you. . . ."

Those words alone were enough to make Maureen's legs wobble. She flopped down onto the couch and waited for Loretta to continue. "I'm listenin'." The next few moments were agonizing because Loretta was taking her time getting to what she had to say next. "Lo'retta, please talk to me. You know I don't like a lot of suspense."

"Mama, me and Mel . . . uh, we didn't go to the Bahamas."

"Well, if y'all changed your plans, I wish one of y'all had called me up and let know before now. I was on the verge of a nervous breakdown until you called me. Where is Mel? Where are y'all if you didn't go to the Bahamas? And why didn't y'all go to the Bahamas? After all the fuss you made about goin' down there!"

"Mama, please shut up and listen! We . . . we . . . are in New York," Loretta blurted.

"We who?" Maureen's thoughts suddenly got so jumbled, she couldn't think straight. First of all, when Loretta said "we," Maureen thought she meant her and some of her classmates. She knew that Mona and that Warren boy and that gay boy who had escorted Loretta to the prom were also supposed to take that trip to the Bahamas. Did they all decide at the last minute to go in a different direction? If that was the case, where was Mel?

"Me and Mel are in New York," Loretta said, almost spitting the words out.

Maureen gulped so hard her eyes watered. "New York? You and Mel went to New York?"

"Uh-huh."

"How come? Did y'all take some out-of-the-way flight or the wrong flight that rerouted y'all through New York first? Last time I checked, the Bahamas was in the opposite direction of New York, so why . . ." Maureen stopped talking and cleared her throat. Until she had all of the facts, she wasn't sure what to say next.

"We didn't get on the wrong flight." Loretta stopped speaking too.

"Lo'retta, talk to me," Maureen ordered. "What in the world is goin' on, girl?" Maureen tried not to think the worst, like her daughter being caught up in some weird kidnapping mess—her ultimate nightmare—but that seemed as reasonable as anything else. If that was the case, why would a kidnapper take Mel too? "Baby, are you or Mel in some kind of trouble?" Maybe Mel owed the wrong people some money, or maybe he had said or done something to piss off somebody. Models and photographers associated with all kinds of people. Maybe some hoochie-coochie woman's gangster husband or boyfriend got jealous of her relationship with Mel and wanted to get rid of him. If that was the case, why would they involve Loretta? "Lo'retta, I asked if you or Mel was in some kind of trouble?" Maureen was frantic. Poor Mel. He had had such a hard life. It was bad enough that he was estranged from his family and that his first wife had run off with another man. "Has . . . has some-body hurt Mel? Is he—"

"Hold on! I'll . . . I'll let you talk to him," Loretta stammered, cutting Maureen off in midsentence.

"Hello, Maureen. I hope you are sitting down and I hope you don't go off on me," Mel said in a cautious tone of voice. "Now, we don't want you to get too upset. These things happen."

"These things? *These things* don't happen to me! For your infor-mation, I'm already upset! If one of y'all don't tell me and tell me fast what the hell is goin' on, I am goin' to get even more upset!" Maureen shrieked. "GODDAMMIT!"

"Do you want to talk now, or do you want us to call back after you calm down? I am not going to try and talk to you with you hollering and screaming like a banshee."

"Look, Mel. You and Lo'retta were supposed to go to the Ba-hamas. Y'all ended up in New York—and I don't know why! How can I not be upset? I need to know what the hell you two are up to. If you changed your minds about goin' to the Bahamas, why didn't you tell me before now?" Maureen hollered. "You better have a damn good story when you get home!"

"Loretta and I are not coming back to Florida," Mel said, speak-ing so fast it sounded like one long word. A second later, he re-peated it. This time talking more slowly and pronouncing each word like he was talking to an idiot. "Loretta. And. I. Are. Not. Coming. Back. To. Florida." His voice was disturbingly hoarse.

Maureen's tongue began to flap like a flag at half-mast. She couldn't even speak again for a few moments. She held the tele-phone away from her ear and looked at it in stunned disbelief be-cause she couldn't believe what she had just heard. She wanted to hear it again just to be sure she heard right.

"Mel, did I just hear you say that you and Lo'retta won't be comin' back?" Maureen asked.

"That's what you heard!" he said defensively.

"What's that supposed to mean?"

"It means just what I said. We are not coming back."

"Why the hell not? Put my daughter back on this telephone!" Maureen heard a voice shout. A voice that sounded so strange and hollow she didn't recognize it. But it was her voice, and she sounded like an idiot. "Wh-wh-wh—" She had to stop trying to talk because gibberish was the only thing coming out of her mouth. She held her breath long enough to pull herself back together, or something close to that. "This is a nightmare and I must be losin' my mind!" It was a nightmare all right, but Maureen was not losing her mind. Just her husband.

"I'm real sorry," Mel went on, his voice cracking like he was about to cry. "I'm so sorry, Maureen."

CHAPTER 51

"WHAT THE HELL? *SORRY FOR WHAT?*" MAUREEN YELLED. "SORRY you ain't comin' back? Sorry you lied to me about where you were goin'? What? What?"

"I'm sorry that I'm . . . with Loretta now," Mel said finally. "She's my woman."

If a trunk had dropped onto Maureen's head and smashed it to pieces, it wouldn't have hurt as much as what she'd just heard. This was what real pain felt like, she realized. But she was a fighter and a survivor, so she was going to go into this battle with both guns blasting. "SORRY IS RIGHT! YOU ARE ONE SORRY-ASS BASTARD!" Maureen roared. Her breath caught in her throat and then she almost threw up. "Melvin Asshole Ross, you put my daughter back on the goddamn telephone right now!"

"I don't think she wants to talk to you right now. You need to calm down first—"

"This is about as calm as I'm goin' to get until I know what the fuck is goin' on! I said, you put my daughter back on this telephone and you put her on right now, Melvin Ross!"

Loretta let out an impatient sigh as soon as she got back on the telephone. "Mama, you better calm yourself down. You makin' this harder than it needs to be," she said condescendingly. "See, he's all mine now."

Maureen had never thought she would ever hear something so incredibly unbelievable. She got so agitated she couldn't remain seated. She stood back up, but a spasm gripped her leg and she toppled to the floor like a bowling pin, knocking the lamp off the end table. She dropped the telephone, then retrieved it and sat back down on the couch within a matter of seconds.

"Mama, what in the world was that ruckus I just heard? Aw, shoot! I hope you ain't havin' a heart attack," Loretta said, actually sounding concerned.

"Don't worry about me havin' a heart attack. You should have thought about that before. I just want to know one thing—HAVE YOU LOST YOUR DAMN MIND, GIRL?!" Maureen shrieked.

"No, I have not lost my mind—"

"You must have! Mel is my fuckin' husband—"

"Well, so what? The bottom line is, he's with me now. He just told you that—and you can't do a damn thing about it. I'm in love with Mel and he's in love with me." Loretta paused and pressed her lips together and kept them that way for a few seconds, as if she was afraid to let more words come out of her mouth.

"How . . . when . . . Lo'retta, you can't be serious," Maureen said, wondering how she was able to speak in a calmer voice now. "What I want to know is *why*?"

"What do you mean 'why'? You don't love him and you never did. You even said so! Mel needs a woman who loves him like I do. He's everything I ever wanted in a man."

"Lo'retta, let's start over. Now, you need to tell me what the fuck is really goin' on with you and Mel," Maureen ordered. "I need to—"

"Don't play dumb, Mama," Loretta interrupted. "Didn't I already tell you what's goin' on? I love him, Mama. I always have. And he loves me and wants to be with *only* me now, not you. I will love him until the day I die!"

"You just hold on a doggone minute, girl." The hair on the back of Maureen's neck stood up like quills, as if she'd just been spooked by a ghost. But this was no ghost talking to her. This was her only child, the same child who had sucked so hard and often on Maureen's right breast when she was a baby that to this day Maureen had to put a Band-Aid on the nipple of that breast at least once a month to keep it from aching. "None of this is makin' any sense at all to me!" Maureen screamed.

"Mama, the real reason Mel married you was so he and I could be together more."

"Is that what he told you?" Maureen threw her head back and laughed long and loud.

Loretta waited for her to stop laughing. "No, he didn't have to. I always knew he did and—"

Maureen laughed again.

"I'm glad you think this is funny, Mama. I didn't think you'd take it this well," Loretta snarled.

It took a lot of effort for Maureen to compose herself. She had laughed so hard, tears were streaming down the sides of her face. "So you and my husband have been fuckin' each other right up under my nose, huh?" she asked as she wiped off her face with the palm of her hand.

"The way you say it makes it sound so cheap and tacky. We've been *makin' love*, Mama," Loretta insisted.

Making love? Maureen almost laughed out loud again. If a girl *fucking* her mother's husband wasn't cheap and tacky, what was? She was glad that Loretta was not in the same room with her. She would have stomped her into the floor by now. "We didn't have sex until after I turned eighteen. Honest to God."

"I'm supposed to believe that? You just turned eighteen three months ago. Do you think I'm stupid enough to believe that you and Mel just started screwin' around *now*?"

"You can believe what you want, but it's the truth. Mel is no fool. He wasn't goin' to risk goin' to jail for sleepin' with me while I was underage," Loretta pouted. "Besides, like I just reminded you, you said from the get-go that you didn't love him. How do you think that made him feel all these years? Especially after you got all gaga over that Jay!"

"Why, Lo'retta?" Maureen asked. She was in pain all over, but the pain from her neck up was excruciating. The inside of her mouth burned with each word. Her ears rang. Her head felt like somebody had mauled it with a brick.

"Why what?"

"Why did you do this to me? How could Mel let this happen? Did he get you drunk and take advantage of you? Is that how this mess got started?"

"Mess? The only mess in this matter is you and your old-age attitude. With all that I got goin' for me, you had this wild notion that I was goin' to hang around Goons and end up like you—just a housewife sittin' on a porch! I'm surprised you don't have a cat yet to sit on the porch with you! You were wrong to think that I'd settle for so little, Mama."

"Lo'retta, I'm your mother. You got my blood and I—"

"Well, I'm nothin' like you!" Loretta cut Maureen off.

"You got that right. I would have never done somethin' like this to Mama Ruby!"

Loretta cackled like a witch. "I guess not! That's so funny. Even you wouldn't have wanted any of those baboons Mama Ruby screwed around with."

"What do you mean by sayin' you didn't want to end up like me? I have a good job, a decent home, family, and friends that love me. I've accomplished things that any mother would be proud of—and you should be too. Because everything I ever did was so I could provide a better life for you!"

"Well, you didn't do enough! For my ninth birthday, all I got was a Happy Meal at McDonald's. I never got over that!" Loretta paused and let out a long, loud, exasperated breath.

It gave Maureen time to think about all of the money she'd spent on Loretta over the years, and here she was still mad because she didn't get special treatment on her ninth birthday? What was the world coming to?

Loretta interrupted Maureen's thoughts with more ridiculous comments. "Now I got almost everything I ever wanted, and I am goin' to get even more. I will be one of the most successful models in the world, and Mel is goin' to help me get there," Loretta vowed. "There is nothin' you can say or do to make me come back home." Loretta paused again and let out another loud breath. "And another thing, Mel will be sendin' you the divorce papers as soon as we get settled."

"Tell him not to bother. I will be filin' divorce papers myself as soon as I can get to a lawyer's office!" Maureen blasted.

"I hope you are not thinkin' about cleanin' Mel out."

"You tell that son of a bitch that he won't have to worry about that. I don't want a damn thing from him!" Maureen hissed. She had to stop to catch her breath. "If you want me to pack up the rest of your shit, and his, send me the address where I can send it. Otherwise, I'm goin' to throw out everything y'all left here into the trash where it belongs!"

"We took every goddamn thing we wanted, so you can trash whatever the hell we left behind anyway," Loretta said with a smirk. "Anything else you need to say? If not, I'm goin' to get off this fuckin' phone and go take care of my man." Loretta hung up before Maureen could get another word in edgewise.

This was not Loretta talking, Maureen thought. Either it was an imposter or Loretta had been playing a role her whole life. The real Loretta had never used profanity before, at least not during her conversations with Maureen. Here she was now cussing like a sailor!

CHAPTER 52

*I*T TOOK MAUREEN SEVERAL MINUTES TO PULL HERSELF TOGETHER enough to dial Virgil's telephone number. He and Corrine were still at work, so she got their answering machine. Catty and Fast Black were also unreachable. But Maureen had to talk to *somebody* or she was going to go stark-raving mad. It had to be somebody who could understand her pain.

Without giving it much thought, she dialed Jay's number. She had not talked to him in a while, so she had no idea what he was up to these days. She almost hung up when a woman answered. Even though Jay had decided to reconcile with his ex, as far as Maureen was concerned, he was still her friend and she had every right in the world to call him. Besides, she had provided a shoulder for him to cry on when he was in pain. Now it was time for him to do the same for her.

"Uh, is Jay there? I'm an old friend of his. I used to take care of his mama," she blurted, hoping that if this woman was Jay's ex-wife, she wouldn't jump to any unnecessary conclusions. All she needed was a friend right now, not a lover.

"He's not home right now. Would you like to leave a message?" the disembodied voice on the other end said. Maureen had seen Jay's ex-wife with him at Loretta's graduation—at least that's who she assumed the woman was. Jay had not introduced her to the ex and had not revealed much information about her, so Maureen knew practically nothing about the woman. Other than the fact that she was very pretty and very young. The woman on the other end of the line sounded like a woman in her seventies or eighties.

"Uh, I'll call him later," Maureen said, about to hang up. "Wait! Are you his wife? Maybe I can leave a message with you."

"His *wife*?" The woman clucked. "Honey, I'm old enough to be Jay's grandmother. Me and his mama went to the same church. I come by to clean and cook for him every now and then. The poor thing."

"Oh. Well, what about his wife?"

"What about his wife? His *slut* would be more like it! Harrumph! That wench gets around like a chain letter. She done moved in with another man. She didn't hang around with Jay once she found out he wasn't goin' to feather her nest. She thought he was goin' to be gettin' all kinds of money from these news and book publishin' folks for lettin' them tell his story." The old woman stopped talking for a few moments and uttered a string of profanities under her breath. "Excuse me. I usually don't cuss like that, but I do when it involves that woman. Me and Jay's mama begged him not to marry her in the first place. Anyway, that boy don't want to profit off what he went through like some folks would if they had the chance. Leona didn't raise him up to be that way. Jay is just a simple man and he wants to live a simple life. He don't want no book deal or nothin' else. That boy is doin' real good workin' for the cable company. What'd you say your name was?"

"Mo'reen. I'm a friend of Jay's. It's been a while since we talked, so I thought I'd call to touch base with him," Maureen said.

"I'll tell him you called, Mo'reen."

A few minutes later, someone knocked on the door. Maureen looked through the peephole and saw a stout young white man she had never seen before. Well, since her bills had all been caught up, she knew it wasn't a bill collector. Could Mel have arranged for a process server to bring her divorce papers already? she wondered as she snatched open the door.

"Yes? What is it?" she hollered, making the man flinch.

"Oh, I'm sorry to bother you, ma'am. Did Mel leave yet?"

"What? How do you know Mel?"

"I don't really know him, ma'am. I'm the one who bought his SUV. I just wanted to let him know he left some CDs in the glove compartment," the man said, lifting a brown paper bag.

Maureen looked from the bag to the man's face and blinked. "Whatever he left in that SUV, you can keep or throw away."

"Oh! Well, thank you, ma'am. Uh, I hope he made it to New York with his fiancée all right. He seemed real anxious to be on his way. You must be the older sister he told me he lived with."

Maureen gave the stranger an eerie smile. "Somethin' like that. And, yes, he and his fiancée made it to New York all right. Now if you'll excuse me . . ." Maureen closed the door and plopped down into a chair, but she couldn't sit still. So that son of a bitch *and his fiancée* had this planned down to the last detail.

She got up and paced around in her living room for almost half an hour cussing out loud, crying, and laughing like she had lost her mind. When she got tired of doing that, she left her apartment and drove around until she almost ran out of gas.

By the time she returned home, Virgil had returned her call and left her a message. So had Jay. She didn't know which one to call up first. Before she could make up her mind, Jay called.

"Maureen, I was happy to hear that you had called," he told her. "How have you been?" he said in a cheerful voice.

She responded by bursting into tears and spewing unintelligible gibberish for a whole minute.

Jay waited until she paused before he said anything else. "Maureen, what's the matter? Please get a hold of yourself! Calm down so I can understand what you're saying. Do you want me to come over?" Jay was more than a little concerned; he immediately slipped into a panic mode. He knew that whatever Maureen was crying about had to be something major.

Maureen cried louder and harder.

He waited for her to stop crying again, and when she did, he quickly said in a soothing tone of voice, "Is this about Mel? Did he hurt you?" The last thing Jay wanted to get caught in was a domestic situation where Mel could end up hurting him, or where he wound up hurting Mel.

"Yeah, this is about Mel. He's gone," Maureen managed, choking on a sob. "He's gone for good."

"Gone? As in dead?"

"No, not dead. But he left me and he won't be comin' back. He's goin' to divorce me."

Jay wanted to clap his hands and dance a jig. He didn't do that because he didn't want Maureen to know how happy he was to hear that Mel was out of her life.

"Uh, I'm sorry to hear that. He seemed so in love with you. Is there another woman involved?"

Maureen couldn't respond right away. She was literally speechless.

"Maureen, did Mel leave you and run off with another woman?" Jay asked, hoping she'd say yes.

She coughed until she was able to form more words. "He took my daughter with him."

"Wait a minute, wait a minute. Hold on, now. I know Mel is not Loretta's real father, and I know she's crazy about him, but are you telling me that she chose to be with him over you?" Jay let out a loud, deep breath. Then he got angry. "Goddammit! I can understand you being so upset—"

"He's fuckin' her!"

Jay stumbled and fell against his kitchen wall. "What did you just say?"

"My husband is fuckin' my daughter!"

"Holy shit!"

"They've been carryin' on for years. I should have known not to trust a goddamn stepfather. I should have known better!"

"Now, don't you go condemning all stepfathers. I just might become a stepfather myself someday. I already know quite a few and none of them would even think about touching one of their stepdaughters."

"Well, this bastard did. All this time . . . all this time! I didn't see it comin'. I didn't suspect a damn thing! I encouraged Lo'retta to 'like' Mel and to 'be nice' to him so he could help her become a top model. Jay, I practically served my own daughter to that funky, low-down black dog on a silver platter! How can I live with myself now?"

Jay listened as Maureen told him how Mel and Loretta had cooked up a bogus trip to the Bahamas to throw her off until after they'd made their getaway. "I should have known somethin' wasn't right when they left here with more luggage than any normal person would take on a ten-day vacation. There is just no tellin' how long they had been plannin' this. All that time they were probably laughin' at me behind my back! The man he sold his SUV to came by a little while ago to drop off some CDs Mel left in it. Mel had told him that I was his *older sister* and . . . and that Lo'retta was his fiancée!"

"Maureen, try to calm down so we can sort things out. First of all, don't blame yourself for what happened. Things like this happen every day and in some of the best families."

"What is it about men and their goddamn dicks?! Don't they care who they hurt when they use that evil piece of meat between their legs on the wrong person?"

"Maureen, honey, with all due respect, I have to disagree with what you just said about that particular part of a man's body being evil. Sex is beautiful when it's between two consenting people, if *both* parties are old enough to handle it."

"Jay, if I wanted to hear somethin' like that, I would have called Dr. Ruth or some other sex guru. I called you for some emotional support, not a philosophical comment!"

"Maureen, I understand where you are coming from, but do you have all the facts? Like, did he rape her?"

"Did he rape her? Not hardly. He didn't have to! I would be upset if he had taken advantage of her and forced himself on her, but from what she told me out of her own mouth, *she initiated their affair*! That bein' the case, I'm even more upset than I'd be if he had raped her!" Maureen paused long enough to wail like an injured lamb for about ten seconds. "My . . . daughter set . . . me up just so she could steal my husband!" she said between sobs.

"Baby, sit tight. I'm on my way," Jay said.

CHAPTER 53

MAUREEN WAS SO NUMB THAT WHEN SHE STUBBED HER FOOT ON the doorjamb leading into the kitchen, she didn't even feel it. She didn't know that she had injured herself until she looked down and saw blood trickling from a small cut on the tip of her big toe.

After she put a Band-Aid on her wound, she walked back and forth from one room to another. It was better for her to keep moving. It was more distracting than her sitting or standing too long in the same spot. She kept glancing at her watch, wondering what was taking Jay so long. Half an hour had passed since she'd spoken to him. She even went outside and stood on the sidewalk in front of her building, hoping to see his car turn onto her street soon. For the next fifteen minutes, she walked back and forth from one end of her apartment building to the other.

When she noticed a few neighbors peeping out their windows giving her curious looks, she went back inside. Then she went into the pantry that Mel had been using as his dark room. Except for a metal desk and a trashcan, Mel had removed everything from the room. Maureen decided to check the four drawers on the desk. The first three were empty, but there was a green hanging folder toward the back in the last drawer. She parted it with her fingers and realized it contained a large manila envelope that had been folded in half and stapled shut. She bit her lip and braced herself. She suspected that this envelope contained something that was going to increase her pain. She was right.

Inside the envelope were half a dozen wallet-size photos of Loretta and Mel in various poses. In the first photo, Loretta was sitting in Mel's lap, looking directly into the camera with her tongue hanging out of her mouth in a very sexually suggestive manner. She looked like a panting dog in heat. She had on the pink and white bathrobe that Virgil had given to her for her sixteenth birthday.

The next two pictures were of Loretta alone, lounging on a bed, *Maureen's* bed, with a dreamy look on her face. She had on the same bathrobe. So far, the prints were not too alarming. But when Maureen looked at the next one, she gasped so hard she almost fainted. There it was in living color: a shot of Mel on top of Loretta. They were both naked and were in Maureen's bed. Loretta's long legs were wrapped around Mel's narrow waist.

"Right here under my own damn roof!" Maureen mouthed, slamming her fist against the top of the desk so hard it rattled. "Right up under my goddamn nose and in *my* bed!" She was too angry to cry right now, but she had to do something. She ran into the kitchen and stood in the middle of the floor, looking around for something to take her anger out on. She snatched open the cabinet above the counter and pulled out a stack of plates. She threw each one to the floor, cursing so loud old Mr. Ben next door pounded on the wall.

A few minutes later her telephone rang. It was Mr. Ben and he sounded very angry. "Mo'reen, what's all that racket over there?! I'm fixin' to call the police. I'm tryin' to get some rest and it sounds like y'all over there tearin' down the house."

"Oh, it's nothin', Mr. Ben. I'm sorry for disturbin' you. I was standin' on a chair tryin' to get somethin' out of my kitchen cabinet and a bunch of plates fell out and broke."

"I done told that gal of yours to keep the racket down in her room when I'm tryin' to take me a nap. All that moanin' and groanin' comin' out of her room, five or six times a week! I don't even want to try and guess why the headboard on her bed be bangin' against the wall so much. Especially lately!"

"I'm sorry," Maureen apologized again.

"The next time I hear all that racket, I'm goin' to call the police," Mr. Ben threatened.

"There won't be no next time," Maureen assured him before she placed the telephone back into its cradle.

This was much worse than Maureen had thought. Apparently, Mel and Loretta had no shame whatsoever. They knew how thin the walls in the apartment were. Loretta used to complain all the time about Mr. Ben's snoring keeping her awake. Didn't it ever occur to her that the old man might hear her and Mel? Apparently that was the reason they had begun to use Maureen's bed!

It was almost 10:00 p.m. when Jay finally arrived. Maureen was in the kitchen looking out the window when she saw him park in front of her building. She wiped her face for the tenth time and smoothed down the sides of her skirt.

"I got stopped for speeding on my way over here, and I must have run into the slowest cop in town. It took him ten minutes to run my license and write me a speeding ticket," Jay explained as soon as Maureen opened the door to let him in. Then he stopped talking, but his mouth was still open. "What the hell happened to you, Maureen? You look like hell! You sick or what?" Jay couldn't believe his eyes. He felt Maureen's forehead. Her eyes were red and swollen and dark circles had already formed around them. The lines on her forehead that he had never noticed before looked like trenches now. Her hair was askew, and she was shaking like a leaf in a windstorm. She had on one shoe and her blouse was soaked with her tears and snot.

Jay wrapped his arm around her shoulder and led her to the living room couch. "Now, let's talk about this thing," he said, rubbing her back. "It's going to be all right because I'll be right beside you from now on."

"Like I told you on the phone, my daughter took off with my husband," Maureen said evenly, then sniffing so hard her nose ached. She had already gone through a whole box of Kleenex. She had set a second box on the coffee table, so she opened it and fished out several tissues at the same time and wiped her eyes and blew her nose.

Jay stared at her with his mouth hanging open again. "Damn!" he boomed, anger rising in him like a tide. "This is so hard to believe!"

"They supposedly left to go to the Bahamas so Lo'retta could celebrate graduation with some of her classmates. They wanted me to go with them, but I couldn't take more time off work right now. When I didn't hear from them by the end of the second day after they left, I got worried and called up the airline. Come to find out, they never got on a plane to the Bahamas in the first place." Maureen paused. "They called me today to tell me they love each other and won't be comin' back." She paused again, shaking her head. "I even found some pictures of them together. Nasty, disgustin' pictures that would make Madonna blush. They were naked and fuckin' the hell out of each other!"

CHAPTER 54

"*D*ID THEY TELL YOU WHEN THIS ALL STARTED?" JAY ASKED, STILL RUB-bing Maureen's back. It was such a comfort to have him sitting next to her on her living room couch. She wished that she had called him sooner.

"From what Lo'retta told me today, it sounds like it started right after I agreed to let her work with Mel—when she was just *fourteen*! She tried to make me believe they didn't sleep together until after she turned eighteen, three months ago." Maureen stopped talking because Jay was shaking his head so hard. She could tell from the look on his face that he was just as disgusted as she was.

"Three months ago, my ass," he growled. "There is no way *that* could be true. The hungriest person in the world wouldn't eat that bologna!"

Maureen moaned and groaned. Not only was she in emotional pain, but also she was in so much physical pain that her head felt like it was about to melt. "I never thought somethin' like this would happen to me. I never thought that I would lose both of my kids."

"Don't look at it that way, sweetheart. Loretta is still a young girl, and girls her age do stupid shit all the time. Once reality sets in, she'll come to her senses."

"Even if she comes to her senses, how can I ever trust her again? How can I even look at her the same way again? And Mel . . ."

"Oh, fuck him! You should kick that son of a bitch right back into the hole he crawled out of!"

Maureen was stunned. She had never seen Jay so angry before. Not even after he'd had a few unpleasant encounters with some of his shady relatives.

"I shouldn't have married him in the first place. I never loved him and he knew it," Maureen sputtered, rubbing her neck. "What was I thinkin'? How could I have been so goddamn stupid to do a thing like that?"

Jay's eyes got wide. "Did I just hear you say that you didn't love Mel when you married him?"

"You heard me right. No, I didn't love that man. I told him and Lo'retta just that!"

Jay's eyes got even wider. "Then why in the world did you marry that hound from hell?"

"He kept askin' me to marry him and I was tired of bein' alone. I was gettin' older, so my chances of findin' somebody else who wanted to marry me got slimmer with each year. My brother didn't want me to grow old alone, and my friends kept buggin' me to marry Mel. And . . . and Lo'retta—she was the main one who kept buggin' me to do it!" Maureen's voice got low. She made the next statement through clenched teeth. "Lo'retta wanted a daddy."

"Well, she sure got herself one!"

Maureen closed her eyes and massaged her throbbing head. She couldn't control the images that suddenly slid into her mind like an avalanche. She pictured Mel shoving his tongue down her daughter's throat the way he used to do with her. She pictured him on top of her baby with her legs spread open and him pumping into her baby's precious young body. The visions made her so sick she thought she was going to pass out.

"Oh . . . my dear God," she swooned, laying her head on Jay's shoulder.

"Maureen, I'm here for you, and this time I'm staying," he told her as he gently rubbed her back.

Jay stayed the night, holding Maureen in his arms on the couch until she had cried herself to sleep. The following morning she opened her eyes just in time to see him walking toward the door. "I have to meet with Mother's lawyer this morning. The sooner I settle her estate the better. I'll be going into work from there, but I'll come back right after my shift ends. If you need to talk to me, call the front desk and they'll send somebody out to the field to come get me. I left my work telephone number on your coffee table."

Maureen staggered up off the couch and stumbled over to Jay. He kissed her. Not on the cheek or on the forehead like he had always done when they were just friends. This time he kissed her the way she needed to be kissed.

"Thanks for comin', Jay. I knew I could count on you," she choked, her lips still tingling from his passionate kiss.

"Try not to let this get the best of you. We'll get you through this," Jay insisted. He kissed her again.

She watched him from her kitchen window until the green Buick he drove reached the end of her block and turned the corner. Then she picked up the telephone and called Virgil. "Hi," she mumbled. "I hope I didn't wake you."

"I was already up," Virgil said. "Hey, I talked to Big Mo'reen last night. She said she'd be callin' you again later on today. I told her that she better make her flight arrangements today for them to come back for Thanksgivin' if she wants to get a good deal on airfare. Oh! Did Mel and Lo'retta call yet?" Virgil sounded so cheerful Maureen didn't want to dampen his spirits, but she had to.

"Yeah, they called yesterday."

"Good. Now you can stop worryin'," he said.

"Virgil, somethin' else has happened," Maureen croaked. "Somethin' real bad."

Virgil didn't reply right away. He sucked in some air and braced himself first. "Oh shit. What?"

"Mel and Lo'retta didn't go to the Bahamas."

"Hold on a minute now. This ain't makin' no sense to me. Didn't you take them to the airport the other mornin'?"

"Yeah," Maureen muttered.

"So did they miss the plane or somethin'?"

"Somethin' like that . . ."

"Mo'reen, I can tell from the way you sound that we got another mess on our hands. Now, I'm gettin' old and my blood pressure and heart can't stand but so much. Hurry up and tell me what's goin' on. How come they took so long to call you?"

"Lo'retta and Mel went to New York."

"Hmmm. Well, wasn't it her plan to go to New York and sign up with one of them big model agencies anyway?"

"Yeah, that's right. Lo'retta did say that she'd like to go to New York someday."

"Well, I know it ain't my business, but I don't think it was a good idea for her to go to New York this soon after graduatin'. I sure don't like the idea of her and Mel goin' up there together. Mel is always bookin' ahead, and if Lo'retta gets to be too much of a hassle for him to deal with, he might do some bookin' that don't include her."

"Virgil, shut up and let me finish." Maureen rubbed her chest and held her breath for a few seconds. Then she let out enough air to fill a balloon. "Mel and Loretta are in love."

Virgil took his time responding. A few seconds later he yelled, "In love with *who*?"

"With each other," Maureen whispered.

"Wait a minute! How and when did all this happen?"

"Instead of gettin' on a plane to go to the Bahamas, they got on one for New York. The Bahamas trip was a setup to throw me off. They knew that if they had told me the truth before they left, there ain't no way I would have let that motherfucker run off with my child. I would have beaten the bat shit out of him." Maureen cackled like a wet hen. "If only I had Mama Ruby here now."

"If Mama Ruby were still alive, by now they'd be diggin' a hole in the cemetery for whatever body parts she left of Mel. And you *know* that's the truth!" Virgil roared. "Did you call the police yet?"

"For what? Lo'retta is eighteen. Mel didn't force her to leave with him." The next few words tasted so disgusting in Maureen's mouth they oozed out like vomit. "Virgil, Lo'retta was the one that called me and did most of the talkin'."

CHAPTER 55

"*I*'LL BE DAMNED!" VIRGIL BOOMED. "I DON'T KNOW WHAT to say. Other than Mel is a dirty, rotten, horny old man and somebody ought to cut off his dick with a dull knife. If he ever brings his ass back this way, I just might be the one to do it."

"Like I said, Mel didn't force Lo'retta to go with him." Maureen looked toward the door. "I called up Jay when I couldn't reach you last night."

"What for? Ain't he got enough problems of his own? He's damn near livin' in a burnin' house. What can *he* do for you?"

"I needed to talk to somebody. You hadn't come home from work yet, and neither had Catty. I couldn't catch up with Fast Black or anybody else to talk to after I got off the phone with Lo'retta. I left Jay a message and as soon as he was able, he called me back and then he came over. If he hadn't, well, I don't even want to think about what I might have done."

"You listen to me. Don't you do nothin' stupid to yourself! I'll come over to your place as soon as I get off work today. Since this is one of your off days, why don't you come sit with Corrine until I get home? She ain't goin' to work at the cannery today, so y'all can keep one another company."

"You know, I think I'll do just that. I don't want to be by myself right now."

"One more thing I need to know." Virgil stopped talking long enough to clear his throat with a hearty cough. "You and Lo'retta had a joint bank account. . . ."

"Yeah, we did. I haven't checked it yet. Most of the money in it is hers. I put in whatever I can afford every payday so I can use it for a down payment on a house someday. A house that I thought I was goin' to share with her and Mel and my future grandkids!"

"Well, you can still buy a house someday, baby girl, and I'm goin' to help you do that. I hope that Mel and Lo'retta ain't financin' this rendezvous with none of your money!"

"Uh, I hope not. I'll call the bank's automated information number and check the balance in the account."

Maureen ended her call with Virgil and immediately dialed her bank's twenty-four-hour toll-free number. She was so nervous and angry it took her several attempts to punch in the correct account number. When she got a response, she was horrified. The only money left in the account was her portion, which was only a little over four thousand dollars. Loretta had withdrawn her entire portion, over twenty-five thousand dollars! What Maureen didn't want Virgil or anybody else to know was that she had also been *stupid* enough to open a joint account with Mel. He had deposited most of the money into that account, but at least three thousand dollars of that money belonged to her. When the recorded message informed her that there was a balance of four dollars and eleven cents in that account, she screamed. *Four goddamn dollars!* And eleven cents. Not only had she spoonfed her daughter to this monster, but she had also "paid" for it! That no-good, rotten-to-the-core, lying, cheating bastard! Maureen couldn't think of enough nasty nouns in the English language to call Mel. She knew that if she ever saw him again, she would not be responsible for her actions. She was so enraged, she wanted Mel to suffer a penalty that would fit his crimes. As far as she was concerned, that meant he needed to be dead or at least close to it.

"Ohhhhh, if only Mama Ruby were still here," she whispered.

Before Maureen left to drive to Virgil's house, she went into Loretta's room. Just looking at her neatly made bed made Maureen's head spin. She sat down in the chair at the cute little vanity table that Mel had given to Loretta last Christmas. She cried until her eyes felt like they had been set on fire.

She got up a few minutes later and looked around Loretta's room. Then she marched across the floor and flung open the closet door. Loretta had not left much behind. Just a few empty hangers and some dull-looking outfits that Maureen had given to her for birthdays and holidays over the years that Loretta had never worn. Tossing everything into the trash that Loretta had left, like Loretta herself had suggested, was not something that Maureen wanted to do. Loretta was still her baby and throwing her belongings away would be like throwing her away. Maureen was not going to give up on her too soon.

A few minutes later, she went into her bedroom and went straight to the large walk-in closet that she had shared with Mel. He had taken his best clothes and shoes with him. Most of his camera equipment was gone too. Well, everything he left behind was about to go up in smoke, literally.

Maureen sprinted across the floor to the dresser and started snatching open drawers. She used a pencil to remove some socks and boxer shorts that Mel had left in the top drawer. She didn't want to touch any piece of clothing that contained Mel's DNA—especially his underwear. Just thinking about his dick made her gag.

She stuffed everything into the same metal tub that she used when she scrubbed the inside of her toilet, shouting more obscenities than a rapper throughout this nasty chore. After she finished doing that, she took the tub and trotted out the back door to the yard. She dumped everything onto the ground next to the Dumpster and piled it into a pyramid shape. Then she struck a match. She waited until the fire had totally consumed the items and then she hawked a huge gob of spit into the ashes.

Maureen made several trips to the backyard with that metal tub and her book of matches. In less than half an hour, she had disposed of everything that Mel had left behind, even pictures from her photo album—especially the ones that included him and Loretta. She made a mental note to avoid Noble Street and the eastern part of the freeway. There were billboards in each location featuring Loretta in various ads.

After Maureen had rested on the couch for a few minutes, she got back up. No matter how tired she was, she had to keep moving. She had to keep busy to keep from losing what was left of her mind.

She stared at the telephone. Before she realized it, she had dialed Mona's telephone number. As soon as she heard Mona's answering machine, she remembered that Mona was supposed to be on that trip to the Bahamas too. Maureen wondered if that was where *she* really was. She was still Loretta's pet flunky, so there was just no telling what her role was in this mess.

Maureen looked up Mona's mother's telephone number and dialed it, praying that she wouldn't get another answering machine. One of Mona's three younger brothers answered. "Hello, Gerald. Did Mona go on the trip to the Bahamas with the other kids who graduated with her?" she asked as soon as she had identified herself.

"Yeah. Why?" fourteen-year-old Gerald said.

"Uh, I have an emergency situation and I need to talk to her as soon as possible. If you don't mind, will you give me the name of her hotel?"

"I forgot that, but I can give you the phone number she left with me if that's all right."

Maureen didn't even need to write the number down. As soon as Gerald told her what it was, she memorized it. She dialed it immediately. She was so glad Mona answered that she would have turned a few cartwheels had she not been so tired.

"Oh, thank God I caught you, Mona. This is Lo'retta's mom."

Mona let out a loud gasp, one that was based in fear.

CHAPTER 56

*M*ONA CLEARED HER THROAT AND TOOK HER TIME RESPONDING. "OH, hi, Miss Mo'reen," she said in a scared, squeaky voice. "Whassup?"

"That's what I want you to tell me," Maureen said sharply. "Will you do that?" Her words hung in the air. The fact that Mona was taking so long to respond made Maureen impatient. "Mona, can you talk to me right now?"

"Um . . . I guess," Mona muttered, coughing to clear her throat some more.

"I need to talk to you about somethin' real serious."

"Uh, I was gettin' ready to go to breakfast on the beach!" Mona's voice was trembling. That alone told Maureen all she needed to know. Mona was in cahoots with Loretta and Mel.

"I won't hold you up but a few minutes," Maureen said quickly, praying that Mona wouldn't hang up on her or that the overseas call wouldn't get abruptly dropped. "Mona, Lo'retta is supposed to be in the Bahamas with her stepdaddy. I took them to the airport myself."

"What hotel did they book?" Mona said quickly in the same scared, trembling voice.

"They didn't go to the Bahamas."

"Hmmm," Mona mumbled. "I wonder where they went?"

"They called me from New York yesterday. That's where they went."

"Dang! Now that's hella messed up, Miss Mo'reen! I knew this was goin' to happen one day. I kept tryin' to tell her how crazy that was."

"So you knew they were havin' sex?"

"Oh, yes, ma'am. I sure did. Lo'retta was my girl. She told me everything."

"Then you can tell me when this affair started?"

"Um, I don't want to get Mel in no trouble, Miss Mo'reen. He was always real nice to me. He only charged me half his regular price to do my graduation pictures. He did a lot of airbrushin' on my prints so I ended up lookin' almost like a model myself. He's a real nice man."

"Look, girl. That motherfucker was always nice to me too. Now I want to know when that 'real nice man' started screwin' my child! If you know, you'd better tell me unless you want me to pay your mama and daddy a visit and tell them that you helped Lo'retta get into this mess."

"But I didn't do nothin'! Please don't tell my mama and daddy that I was involved! They might change their minds about gettin' me a new car when I get back home like they promised."

"Mona, you need to tell me exactly when Lo'retta and Mel started havin' sex. Please. I'm her mother . . . and I need to know."

"See, Lo'retta had a crush on Mel from the get-go. She called me up the same day y'all first went to his studio. She told me that she had just met the man she had been waitin' on all her life," Mona sobbed. "She told me that she didn't care what she had to do to get in his pants—even make him hook up with you if she had to. And she sure did."

"Lo'retta was only fourteen when we met Mel," Maureen pointed out. "Do you mean to tell me that this thing started *then*?" Even though Maureen had already presumed that the affair had begun when Loretta was only fourteen, having it confirmed by Mona made it seem even worse.

"Yes, ma'am. Well, maybe not the same day she met him, but Lo'retta started workin' on Mel real quick. She thought he was the bomb. She even took the bus—usin' my bus pass—and went to his place and gave him a real good blow job before you ever called him up to see if he wanted to do her portfolio and help her get some modelin' jobs."

"So my daughter threw herself at Mel?" Even though Loretta had clearly implied that she had initiated the affair, Maureen still didn't want to believe it.

"Somethin' like that."

"Somethin' like what? Did he give her drugs or alcohol?"

"Lo'retta's goin' to be hella mad at me for blabbin' her business."

"Look, girl. You can tell me what I need to know or you can tell the police. Now what is it goin' to be? You want to talk to me now or at the police station as soon as you get back to Florida?"

"I'll tell you everything you want to know now." Mona sniffed.

"Let me ask you again. Did Mel give my child drugs or alcohol?"

"Not that I know of. I never saw Lo'retta do no drugs or drink no alcohol."

"How often did she see him?"

"Oh Lord. Almost every day. She used to make me drive her over to his apartment in my daddy's car when she wanted to see him. They'd give me some money and send me to the movies. But when she went to visit Mel for a quickie, I'd sit in a parkin' lot and wait on her. Some days she would be up in his place for a *real* long time. I had to bring my Walkman and some books to read. One time they took so long, I went to sleep in my daddy's car waitin' on them to finish."

Maureen had to sit down to keep from falling to the floor. She rubbed the back of her neck and her forehead. Pain was shooting throughout her body, from the bottom of her feet to the top of her head. The pain in her stomach was the worst. It felt like she had been gored by a raging bull. "Mona, who else knows about this? What about her other friends?"

"What other friends?"

"Like the Bronson sisters on Wallace Street. I never met them, but she used to call them up a lot and go to their house. She also started goin' to the movies with that Warren boy."

"Nuh-uh. That was part of her and Mel's plan. When you got on her case and told her she needed to spend more time with kids her own age, she and Mel made you think that she was with me or the Bronson sisters. Or with Warren. But none of that was true. Anyway, Warren got into white girls at school, as soon as we started our senior year. He wouldn't take Lo'retta or any other black girl no place no more."

"So you're tellin' me that those other kids were in on this scheme too? Those Bronson girls?"

"Oh no! They didn't know what was goin' on. On account of there ain't even no Bronson sisters. That was bogus too."

"What do you mean?"

"Lo'retta made them up to throw you off. She did go to the movies with my gay cousin a few times, but usually Mel would be waitin' for her somewhere after she left the movie theater." Mona stopped talking long enough to catch her breath. Now that she had started to spill the beans, it sounded like she didn't want to stop. "I don't know why they even bothered with all of them lies. They did a lot of their business in your apartment a lot of times. Every time Mel had a beach shoot, he checked into a room that his client paid for and that's where they hooked up a lot too. Did they already get married up there in New York?"

"SAY WHAT?" Maureen roared. "Do you mean to tell me that Lo'retta thinks Mel is goin' to marry her?"

"Yep! That's what she told me not long after they got together. She's been tellin' me that almost every day ever since. She said that Mel told her he would divorce you and marry her when she turned eighteen. Well, since she turned eighteen back in March, I guess they will get married now. Just to let you know, I don't think he felt too good about what he was doin'. I know that because a lot of times when I was around them, he couldn't even look me in the eye."

"But knowin' what you knew, you could still come over here and look me in the eye?"

"I'm real sorry about that, Miss Mo'reen. Honest to God, I am. Lo'retta kept sayin' it was all right because you didn't love Mel nohow. I didn't know they was goin' to hurt you this bad. I thought that by the time we graduated, Lo'retta would be tired of Mel. I guess I was wrong, huh?"

"I guess I was wrong, too, Mona," Maureen whimpered.

"Miss Mo'reen, I hate to say this, but I wouldn't want to be in your shoes."

"You know somethin', Mona, I don't want to be in my shoes either," Maureen replied, laughing like a madwoman.

"What they did is so messed up." Mona paused and mumbled something to someone in the background. "Sorry, Miss Mo'reen. That was Tami Barber I was talkin' to. The girl that's sharin' my hotel room. Me and her are havin' our breakfast on the beach this mornin'." Then Mona lowered her voice to a dry whisper. "I didn't tell her nothin' about this. That girl's mouth is as big as a canyon. If she ever finds out, everybody in town will be talkin' about you and how you got played by your own daughter and your own husband."

"Mona, I would appreciate it if you didn't tell anyone else about Lo'retta and Mel. Would you please do me that favor?"

"I won't say anything. Everybody will find out anyway when Mel and Lo'retta get married and she gets real famous. When that happens, if I was you, I'd move to a place where nobody knows me."

"Believe me, I'm not goin' anywhere, Mona. I don't care if they get married on national TV. This is my home and I'm not runnin' away from anything anymore."

"That's good. I like you and I hope you find another man real soon. A man that don't like young girls. Well, now that you know everything, what do you plan to do about it?"

Maureen remained silent.

"Miss Mo'reen, you all right?" Mona asked. "I'm so sorry you had to find out the way you did. I hope you get over this real soon."

A strange smile crossed Maureen's face. "I will," she said, and she knew she would.

CHAPTER 57

"CALL THE POLICE!" CATTY WAS LIVID. SHE STOMPED BACK AND forth in Maureen's living room like some man had run off with *her* teenage daughter. "If I had a daughter and some nasty-ass, dirty old man took off with her, I'd have his ass arrested!"

Catty had been rough all of her life. She had cut a few people with the straight razor she carried in her purse, bounced rocks off a lot of heads, and bitch-slapped several women who had provoked her. She had even thrown a pan of boiling hot water on one of her lovers when she discovered he had stolen money from her. She had also been groomed for violence by Mama Ruby. When Mama Ruby used to "chastise" people, Catty had been one of her most loyal co-horts.

Catty continued to pace Maureen's living room floor with the tail of her knee-length skirt flapping up and down like an eagle's wings. There was so much profanity spewing out of her mouth, it sounded like she was speaking a foreign language. She calmed down long enough to say, "You want me to take care of that horny motherfucker? By the time I get through slicin' him up, he'll have *two* assholes!"

Maureen had cooled off considerably by now, but she was still so angry that if Mel had walked back into the apartment, she probably would have beaten him to a bloody pulp with her bare hands.

"No, I don't want you to do that, Catty. For one thing, he ain't worth you goin' to jail for. Another thing is, I don't think he'll come back this way," Maureen said in a tired voice. "This was well planned. He even sold his SUV before he left, and he took some of my money."

Catty's jaw dropped. "What money?" she roared. "That cocksucker robbed you too?"

Maureen had not told Catty about the joint bank account she had opened with Mel. At the time when she opened the account, shortly after she and Mel got married, she didn't feel comfortable with it. But he had badgered her about it almost every day. After he had convinced her that their combined savings would earn more interest, she had given in.

"Yes, he stole money from me too!" Maureen admitted without hesitation.

"How much?" Catty wanted to know.

"It was some money that we had in the bank in a joint account. We had saved several thousand, but that bastard took all but four dollars and eleven cents out of that account." Maureen gritted her teeth and a scowl appeared on her face that no one in the room had ever seen before. She didn't care if everybody knew what a gullible fool she had been to open that bank account with Mel. She wanted them to know just how big of an asshole he was for stealing that money—knowing she would need it now.

"*Fo' dollars and 'leven cents?!*" Catty bellowed.

"Fo' dollars and 'leven cents," Maureen confirmed, pronouncing the words the same way Catty had.

"That motherfucker cleaned you out?" Catty shouted, stomping her foot on the floor so hard Maureen's lamps on the end tables rattled. "I still say you need to call the police. We can get him for robbery *and* statutory rape!"

"I keep tellin' everybody that Lo'retta is eighteen," Maureen whimpered. She occupied a chair facing the couch where Virgil, Corrine, and Fast Black sat, all looking like they wanted to cuss out the world.

"This didn't start when she was eighteen. I know you ain't fool enough to believe that. Mel's been dippin' his spoon in Lo'retta's honey pot for a while!" Fast Black screeched. She was just as rough and tough as Catty. Not only had she shot one of her ex-lovers in the throat, causing him to lose his voice permanently, but she had also been one of Mama Ruby's "enforcers." She knew where all of the bodies were buried—and had helped Mama Ruby bury a couple. Right now there was a sneer on Fast Black's face that could stop a clock if she stared at one long enough.

"I never did like that man! I knew there was somethin' fishy about him when I walked into the nail shop and seen him sittin' there gettin' his nails manicured!" Corrine crowed. This was the first time Maureen had ever seen her mild-mannered sister-in-law so angry. Veins stood out on her forehead and neck, and her nostrils flared.

"A manicure! Now if that ain't a sissified procedure for a man to get done, I don't know what is!" Virgil yelled, shaking his fist and glancing at his own raggedy nails. "One time Mel had the nerve to suggest that your friend Jay was a sissy! Oomph, oomph, oomph!"

"Like I said, Mel didn't just start doin' his dirt with Lo'retta!" Fast Black declared.

"I know that. Lo'retta's best friend Mona Flack told me that it started when Lo'retta was just fourteen," Maureen revealed for the first time. She believed everything that Mona had told her, but she wondered what Mona *didn't* tell her.

"Say what?!" Virgil, Catty, Corrine, and Fast Black all hollered at the same time.

"There you go! You got a witness that he started foolin' around with that child when she was still a baby," Virgil said, shaking his fist again. "Oh, if I could get my hands around that bastard's neck, he would never look at another young girl!"

"I know that Lo'retta's friend told me the truth about Mel screwin' my child when she was just fourteen, but I can't prove that everything Mona told me is the truth. Mel and Lo'retta would probably deny it all anyway," Maureen pointed out. "She claims they didn't do nothin' until she turned eighteen."

"The next time I go visit my boy up there in Brooklyn, I'm goin' to have him drive me all over New York City to see if I can track down that Mel. I'll beat the stuffin' out of him myself, and then I'll haul what's left of him to the undertaker. I won't leave till I know for sure he's straight-up dead!" Fast Black threatened.

"I wish Mama Ruby could come back to life just long enough to chastise Mel," Catty said with a mysterious look on her face. She smiled and started to look around the room, up at the ceiling, then around the room again with that mysterious look still on her face. "Mama Ruby, I hope you can hear me. We need you more than ever right now. When you get a chance, pay Mel a visit. *Amen.*"

"I second that amen," Fast Black said, waving a clenched fist in the air.

It seemed like everybody wanted to get violent with Mel, or at the very least have him arrested. Even Big Maureen. When Maureen had called her up a few hours earlier and told her what had happened, she had gone ballistic too. "I knew there was somethin' demonic about that beady-eyed dog! I even seen him eye-ballin' Lo'retta's butt a few times when he didn't know I was lookin'. I would like to cut his throat and hang him upside down till all the blood done drained out of his carcass. Just like a hog butcherin'." Maureen had no doubt in her mind that her big sister meant every word she said. Big Maureen never hesitated to use violence when she felt it was necessary. Everybody knew about the switchblade she had used to jab her husband in the butt the last time he had accused her of cheating on him. She didn't carry her weapon in her bra like Mama Ruby had; she concealed hers in a large coin purse with her loose change that she never left home without.

The whooping and hollering in Maureen's apartment went on until almost midnight. She was so exhausted by the time everybody left, she fell asleep on the couch. She'd been sleeping on the couch or a pallet on the living room floor ever since Loretta's telephone call. She had burned the sheets on her bed and sprayed the mattress with the strongest disinfectant she could find at the hardware store.

After John French had raped Maureen, she had cursed his soul, but after his death in the gas station robbery incident, she had ended up feeling sorry for him. She had even bent down on her knees and prayed with Mama Ruby for his soul. Maureen would *never* forgive Melvin Ross, but she prayed for him too; she prayed that he would burn in hell.

Even though Loretta appeared to be just as guilty as Mel, Maureen placed the bulk of the blame on him. Loretta was a child, and like most children, she did stupid, impulsive things. Mel, being a mature man and knowing the consequences of his and Loretta's actions, should have rejected her advances.

Instead of being a responsible adult, Mel had behaved worse than John French had. At least John had attempted to make up for his crime by trying to rob that gas station to get the money for Maureen to get an abortion.

Around 2:00 a.m., Maureen woke up. She looked around the apartment for things to do that would distract her and give her something else to think about. But no matter what she did—even scrubbing the inside of her toilet—Loretta and Mel's betrayal dominated her thoughts.

She went and locked the door to Loretta's room and didn't plan to go back into it again anytime soon. She knew she would probably never sleep in her own bed again, so she was going to either donate it to Goodwill or drag it to the backyard and burn it like she had done the rest of the items Mel had left behind.

A few minutes before 4:00 a.m., Maureen curled up on the couch and slipped into a comalike sleep. She didn't know that Jay had called or banged on her front door while she was having one nightmare after another until he returned that day around noon.

"You can't let this thing destroy you, Maureen," he told her when she let him in. "You've got too much to live for."

"Don't worry. I'm doin' just fine," she lied.

"Well, you don't look fine. You look like you've been through hell."

"I have," she said in a hoarse voice. "This has been one bad-ass year."

"God knows I can relate to that," Jay quipped. "Things are just now beginning to feel like normal again for me."

"Oh! I didn't mean to open up your wounds," Maureen said with a hand in the air. The look on her face was so apologetic that Jay thought she was going to burst into tears again.

"You didn't open up my wounds. The ones I got will probably never heal anyway."

Maureen let out a long, loud sigh. "I know it's early, but do you want somethin' to drink? I know I do," she said, already walking toward the kitchen cabinet where she kept the alcohol.

"Most definitely. Whatever you have is okay with me," Jay told her as he sat down hard onto the couch. He could feel Maureen's pain and anger, and he was as angry and in as much pain as she was. He was glad that Mel was out of her life, and he hoped that Mel stayed out.

When Maureen returned to the living room with two beers, she eased down on the couch next to Jay. There was a weak smile on her face. He was glad to see that the deep lines he had noticed in her forehead the other night didn't look as deep now, and her hair was in a neat ponytail. If the dark circles were still around her eyes, she had done a good job of hiding them with the makeup she had applied earlier in the day.

"Beer is all I have right now." Maureen was about to take a sip from her beer can, but Jay removed both of the cans from her hands and set them on the coffee table. Then he pulled her into his arms.

They made love on the couch.

CHAPTER 58

Monday, in the second week of July, Maureen met with a lawyer, the same man Virgil drove for. She was not going to give Mel the satisfaction of initiating the divorce. She didn't have an address for a process server to deliver the papers, but that didn't matter to her lawyer. This man had kept some of Miami's most notorious criminals out of jail, so he knew every underhanded trick and loophole in the business. "All you need to give me is that scoundrel's Social Security number, darlin'," he told her. "I'll take care of the rest."

The following Saturday was Maureen's thirty-seventh birthday. She planned to celebrate it and the fact that she would be a free woman again in a few months when her divorce was finalized. She celebrated with Virgil, Corrine, Fast Black, Catty, and Jay in Virgil's house. Corrine had barbecued some sausage links and steaks, and Jay had brought a bowl of potato salad that he had made from one of the late Mrs. Freeman's recipes.

"Thirty-seven and you don't look a day over twenty-five," Jay said as they raised their wineglasses and toasted Maureen.

"But I'm feelin' every one of my years," she laughed before she blew out the candles on the German chocolate cake that Corrine had baked. Maureen didn't even want to think about what was in store for her in the next thirty-seven years—if she lived that long. The way things had been going for her, she was surprised she had not already dropped dead.

It was a sad day for Maureen. Her birthday was the day that she'd been kidnapped and that was one thing she would have to deal with every year until the day she died.

When Jay drove her home, she invited him to spend the night. They slept on a pallet on her living room floor like they usually did. Even though Maureen had replaced the bed she had shared with Mel, she spent as little time in the new one as possible. Just being in the same room that she had shared with Mel made her sick to her stomach.

It was hard for Maureen to believe that only three months had passed since Loretta and Mel's departure.

The weather was unusually hot and humid for September this year. Even with air conditioners, large pitchers of iced lemonade, and chilled cans of beer, Maureen walked around in her bare feet with a fan in her hand. Her pain had eased up enough so that she felt comfortable again in her own apartment. She still liked to get out whenever she could. She went fishing with Jay, spent more time with Virgil and Corrine, and entertained Catty and Fast Black whenever they dropped by. She was glad that she had enough going on in her life that she didn't spend a lot of her time thinking about Loretta.

One of the things that Maureen didn't like about her job at the nursing home was that she had to wear scrubs and those ugly, thick-soled white shoes. Each day at the end of her shift, she kicked off her shoes as soon as she got into her car and drove with bare feet. Even with the unattractive attire, Maureen had begun to enjoy her job. Despite the fact that it involved a lot of unpleasant situations, and the turnover was higher than ever, doing what she did made Maureen feel important. She had gotten used to the combative patients and all of the mayhem they caused. She had learned how to duck or jump out of the way in time when one of them threw something at her, and she had learned how to wrestle them off of her when one attempted to bite, pinch, or fondle her. One man got so mean and nasty whenever he couldn't play with Maureen's titties that he soiled himself on purpose so she would have to clean his butt and the rest of his private parts. Each time she had to do that, he displayed an erection that would put a horny frat boy to shame.

Work kept Maureen's mind occupied. In fact, she enjoyed keeping her mind occupied so much that when two more aides walked off the job, she volunteered to go full-time.

She had not heard from Loretta or Mel since they had called her that one time. Because they had not given her any contact information, she had no way of getting in touch with them either—not that she was dying to do so anyway. She couldn't imagine anything they had to say about their relationship that would make her feel any better. They had told her enough.

Things gradually returned to normal, or as close to normal as it could get. People had almost stopped cursing Mel, so the subject of him and Loretta was discussed only when Maureen brought it up. She had not told her coworkers or her neighbors the whole story about why Mel and Loretta were no longer around. When one of them asked, she simply told them, "Loretta relocated to further her modelin' career, and Mel and I decided that our marriage was a mistake."

Maureen's family and friends were very important to her, and they were all very supportive. But the support and love of the man she loved was different. For thirty-seven years, Maureen had felt like half a person. Jay made her feel whole. She spent so much time with him in his house that his neighbors thought she had moved in. She loved him so much that it sometimes hurt. The sight of him, his touch, and his lovemaking made her feel that her life was worth living after all.

Maureen knew beyond a shadow of a doubt that Jay was her soul mate, the one she'd been waiting for her whole life. If she lost him, well, she didn't even want to think about that. Losing Loretta had been painful, and she knew that it always would be, but no matter what, she still wanted her child to be happy. If being with Mel was what it took for Loretta to be happy, well, so be it, Maureen told herself. Besides, there was nothing she could do about that anyway.

Even though she *knew* in her heart that she would never forgive

Mel and resume their relationship, her pending divorce would make it so final. And that hurt. She didn't like what it implied. Yes, it meant that she was no longer going to be married to Mel, but it also meant that she was "divorcing" her only child in a manner of speaking. In spite of Loretta's blatant betrayal and total disregard for her feelings, the girl was still her only child.

Big Maureen and Lukas came back for Thanksgiving. Maureen and Virgil were so happy to see them again so soon that they didn't spend much time thinking about Loretta's absence.

Jay had turned down several Thanksgiving dinner invitations from people who were still "looking after him" so that he could spend that occasion with Maureen and her family. He occupied the seat that Mel had always sat in on this occasion every year, and the high-backed chair, which didn't match any of the other chairs at the table, was occupied by Big Maureen this year, not Loretta.

Even though there was a huge Thanksgiving feast piled up on the table, a lot of hugging and kissing going around the room, and a lot to be thankful for, it was not a happy holiday. This was the first time since Loretta's birth that she had not spent the holiday with Maureen. Maureen didn't even want to think about how hard it was going to be for her to get through Christmas without falling apart.

Big Maureen had seemed distracted and preoccupied since she and Lukas arrived from the airport. After dinner, Maureen took her aside and demanded to know why she was walking around looking as gloomy as a pallbearer.

"It don't look like me and Lukas ever goin' to get us a baby," Big Maureen choked. "Them adoption folks finally told us somethin' they never told us before." Big Maureen blinked to hold back the tears that were threatening to roll out of her eyes. "There was some kind of mix-up at their main office and somebody misplaced some paperwork. We was the next couple in line to get a baby, but because of that mix-up, another couple—a couple that's been childless for the twenty years they been married—got the baby we should have got. Now we got to wait God knows how much longer."

"Well, maybe that wasn't the baby for you and Lukas. Maybe God thought that other couple who had never had a baby deserved a baby before y'all. You can't overlook the fact that you have raised some kids of your own already," Maureen said. The way Big Maureen's mouth dropped open and her eyebrows shot up frightened Maureen. She wished she hadn't added that last sentence.

"But me and Lukas ain't never had no kids together. Since my kids all so old, it don't even feel like I ever raised none," Big Maureen shot back. She immediately apologized to Maureen for her outburst. "I don't mean to be takin' out my frustration on you, Little Mo'reen. I know you got enough problems already on your plate without me addin' some of mine. I'm sorry. It just seems like I can't win for losin'." She sniffed, nervously wringing her hands.

"That's all right, Big Mo'reen. You don't have to be sorry about nothin'. I've learned to live with my problems and you will too." Maureen smiled, but it was a hollow smile. "I got a feelin' things will work out for you and Lukas, and for me," she told her big sister.

CHAPTER 59

*T*HE MONTH OF DECEMBER SLID IN LIKE A PYTHON. NEITHER MAUREEN nor Jay bothered with Christmas decorations or a tree, and neither one of them did any Christmas shopping. All Maureen did to observe the holiday was send out a few cards.

This would be the first Christmas in Jay's life that he didn't spend with Mrs. Freeman, the woman he still thought of as his mother. He invited Maureen to spend the holiday with him in Bimini.

Since Maureen's blue mood was just as dark as Jay's, she told him she would go. A change would do her a lot of good, but before she could get out of town, another monkey wrench got thrown in her direction.

Loretta called while Maureen was packing for her trip. It was Christmas Eve.

"Merry Christmas, Mama!" she chirped.

"Lo'retta? Is that you?" Maureen asked, too startled to say anything else.

"Who else calls you *Mama*, Mama?!"

"Merry Christmas to you, too, baby," Maureen said in a warm voice.

"You sure don't sound merry to me. This is the season when everybody is supposed to be jolly. You used to be!"

"I used to be a lot of things, Lo'retta." Maureen's voice went from warm to chilly within seconds. "And so did you." What she couldn't understand was how Loretta was still able to be so "jolly" under the current circumstances. She had to know that she had caused her mother an enormous amount of pain.

"Mama, get over it. What I did is old news now. You need to move forward."

"Lo'retta, I have moved forward. I hope you have too."

"Oh. Well, anyway, I've been meanin' to call you," Loretta said, sounding as petulant as a five-year-old.

"Why didn't you? And why are you callin' me now?" Maureen asked. She was in her bedroom sitting on the side of the new bed.

"I needed to talk to you about somethin'. . . ."

"Oh? Was there somethin' you forgot to say to me when you called that day back in June?" Maureen was still bitter and still very angry with her daughter, but she was glad to hear her voice, so she decided to soften her demeanor. "Is everything all right?"

"Yes, ma'am. How have *you* been? I mean, you still pissed off?"

"Yes, I am still pissed off. I probably will be for a long time to come. But like I just said, I'm movin' forward with my life, Lo'retta. Thank you for askin'."

"And like I just said, you need to get over it."

"Is that why you called?"

"Well, I was thinkin' about you. I thought that it bein' the holiday season, you'd be in a good mood."

"I am in a good mood. I still have a lot to be thankful for. I have some good friends and family who love me. I'm better off than a lot of people."

"That's the spirit, Mama. They say you can't keep a good woman down, and you've proved that that's true a hundred times over."

"I can agree with that. I feel the same way." Maureen's voice was dripping with sarcasm on purpose.

"You still workin' at that old folks' home?"

"Yes, I am."

"I hope you find somethin' better soon. You used to come home from that place smellin' like Bengay and liniment and old folks' sweat. That lobster factory you worked for all those years was bad enough."

"I hate to disappoint you, but I love my job, so I won't be lookin' for somethin' better at all. You still modelin'?"

Loretta gasped. "Eoww! What's wrong with you, Mama? Of course I'm still modelin'! What do you think I came up to New York for? Didn't I tell you I'm goin' to be a supermodel?"

"Repeatedly," Maureen hissed. "I hope you do become a super-model."

"When I do, I'll be doin' magazine interviews and TV talk shows like that black supermodel Naomi Campbell is doin'. Her mama used to be a showgirl, and I heard she is goin' to be doin' some modelin' too!" Loretta clucked. Then she began to speak in a more serious tone of voice. "I wish you was more like Naomi's mama. I don't want to go on a talk show and tell the world that my mama works in a nursin' home! I'll probably say you're just a housewife, sittin' on a porch with a cat." Loretta snickered, but she was dead serious.

Maureen rolled her eyes and sighed with exasperation. "Like I said, I enjoy my job now. I like workin' with people who need and appreciate me, but if I was just a housewife sittin' on a porch with a cat, I'm sure I'd enjoy that too."

"Oh well. Whatever, whatever. Are those old people still actin' crazy? Bitin' you and spittin' on you and stuff?"

"I'm used to it now. I told my boss to put me on full-time as soon as possible," Maureen announced, unable to keep the curtness out of her voice. Loretta's call had caught her off guard. Since she had never been betrayed on this level before, she didn't know how she was supposed to feel, think, or act by now. Loretta was still her daughter and Maureen still loved her. "I hope your life is still goin' well, Lo'retta," she offered. She meant it too. Despite what had happened, she wanted her daughter to succeed in everything she did. But she prayed that that would not include her stealing an-other woman's husband someday. "I pray for you all the time."

"That's nice." Loretta cleared her throat with a cough. "I've been gettin' a lot of work, and I've met a whole lot of important people. I'm makin' so much money, and I have a gorgeous loft in Soho! You wouldn't believe all the gorgeous new clothes I bought and all of the A-list celebrities I run into all the time. Even Al Pacino. He laughed when I told him that you've had a crush on him since 1972."

Maureen couldn't believe how giddy and upbeat Loretta sounded now. Was she so self-centered that she didn't even care about all the pain she had caused? And why had she not even asked about Virgil or Corrine or Big Maureen? Or anybody else?

"I might be goin' to Milan next year. That's in Italy," Loretta gushed, keeping the general focus of the conversation on herself.

"I know where Milan is," Maureen said. "Well, I hope you and Mel enjoy Milan, Italy."

Loretta gritted her teeth before responding. "Um, he won't be goin' with me."

"Awww, that's too bad," Maureen said with mock compassion. "I didn't think that y'all liked to spend too much time apart. Especially now. I'm surprised he's goin' to let you go halfway around the world without him. By the way, when's the weddin'?"

"Mama . . . he's with somebody else. He moved out two weeks ago," Loretta choked. "He didn't really love me after all, I guess."

"I guess he didn't." Maureen sniffed.

Mel Ross had never really loved Loretta, but she had been the best business opportunity he had ever encountered—until he met another girl who was even more gullible, more beautiful, and more ambitious than Loretta. Most importantly, the newer model was an even bigger love-struck fool. Being the astute businessman that he was, Mel had traded one fool for another. Now Loretta was devastated.

"Before we could even get settled in good, he started actin' crazy up here," she growled. "Women were callin' our place all hours of the day and night, and all the while he was tellin' me they were callin' about business! How many models or magazine people call up photographers in the middle of the night? He thought I was a fool!"

"Oh, like me, huh?"

"You don't have to rub it in. You don't have to say it because I already know how bad you want to say 'I told you so.' "

"Well, I never said that, but I'm glad you brought it up." Maureen couldn't remember the last time she felt as smug as she did now. Had she no longer cared about Loretta, she probably would have laughed and danced a jig. "I'm just sorry that you had to be the woman who did me the favor of takin' Mel off my hands. I knew how anxious you were to marry him."

Loretta didn't respond right away. Maureen thought that maybe it was because now that Loretta knew what it felt like to be betrayed, she was wondering how she was going to make up for all of those nasty words she'd hurled at Maureen the first time she'd called. Maybe she was truly sorry about what she had done and was trying to ease her way back into Maureen's life. But from what Loretta had said so far, it didn't sound like she wanted to come home.

"There's a new man in my life already. I will love him until the day I die," Loretta gushed. She had said the *exact* same thing about Mel.

Maureen couldn't resist the urge to remind Loretta of that. "Just like you were goin' to do with Mel, huh?"

"What?"

"That's the same thing you said about Mel. Word for word. Don't you remember?"

"Oh well. I was wrong! I'm not wrong this time. I've met a wonderful man. I love him and he loves me!"

Maureen closed her eyes, rubbed her eyelids, and shook her head. Her eyes were burning when she opened them again. "I hope it wasn't love at first sight this time too," she said with a profound sigh.

"It wasn't. I've known Kyle for a few weeks, and we just recently realized how much we care about each other."

"Well, I'm happy to hear that things are workin' out for you, Lo'retta. No matter what you did, I still want the best for you. I just hope that you will make better choices in the future."

"Uh, there's somethin' else. The reason I really called."

Maureen felt her entire body get tense. If Loretta was calling to ask if she could come home, would she allow her to do so? The thought of having her back under the same roof gave Maureen an instant headache. How would she deal with that? The bottom line was, if Loretta wanted to come home, Maureen *couldn't* turn her away. What else could she do?

"What did you really call me for, Lo'retta?" Maureen held her breath.

Several moments of ominous silence passed. Loretta coughed again. "Mama . . . I called to tell you that I'm goin' to have Mel's baby."

"Oh." Maureen wanted to crawl into a hole and stay there until she died. How in the world would she be able to live under the same roof with Loretta *and* Mel's baby? What would people say? Maureen knew that Catty and Fast Black would preach her funeral and talk about her so badly she'd probably have to sever her relationship with them. She had no idea how Virgil and Corrine would react to this disturbing news. But Loretta was still her daughter and she couldn't turn her back on her and her unborn baby.

"You want to come home, huh?" Maureen blew the words out as quickly as she could because as long as they stayed in her mouth, she felt nauseous.

"Oh no! Not even! The thing is, I don't want this baby. I'm goin' to get rid of it, see. I . . . well, another model I work with sometimes got herself in trouble. She died durin' her abortion."

"Please don't tell me . . ."

"That I'm gettin' an abortion? Well, I am. I just wanted you to know in case I . . . die on the operatin' table or somethin'. Uh, have me cremated and scatter my ashes on top of Mama Ruby's grave so she can look out for my spirit."

Maureen wanted to go outside and run up and down the street screaming. As if she was not already in enough pain, now here she was listening to her daughter discuss her final arrangements. Oh, if she could get her hands on that Mel!

"Then don't take that chance," Maureen pleaded. "Havin' a baby is not the worst thing in the world."

"It would be for me. The last thing I need right now is a baby. My career is just beginnin' to take off, and I can't let a baby get in my way. I'm showin' already, and I can't work again until I get my abortion and lose the weight that keeps sneakin' up on me."

"What about Mel? Did he tell you to abort his baby?"

"He suggested I throw myself down a flight of stairs to abort it so I wouldn't have to pay for it!"

That Mel. His name made Maureen want to puke. He was a dog clean to the bone. He didn't want any babies, but he had seduced a "baby" and now he wanted her to kill the baby that he'd impregnated her with.

Loretta blew out an angry breath. "As Mama Ruby would say, *that low-down, funky black dog!* If that wasn't bad enough, he thinks it's another man's baby. He's a damn liar. Mama, you know me. I wouldn't lie about somethin' this serious!"

Maureen was speechless for a few moments. Loretta's last sentence almost made her laugh. Under the circumstances, that stupid declaration was nothing to laugh about. After Maureen took a few deep breaths, she continued. "Lo'retta, don't do somethin' that you might regret for the rest of your life. Like I almost . . ."

"You almost what?"

"I was goin' to get an abortion when I was pregnant with you." Maureen heard a mild gasp, but she couldn't tell if it had come out of her mouth or Loretta's. When she heard another gasp, this time loud and clear, she knew it was coming from her. "It would have been the biggest mistake I ever made in my life."

"Why didn't you go through with it? Why didn't you get rid of me before I was born? You would have been better off."

"I don't know about that. I've enjoyed bein' your mother."

"Until now," Loretta said.

"That's beside the point. I never expected you to be the perfect child. I wasn't. That's a position that only Jesus can claim." Maureen paused and swallowed hard. "Your daddy died and I couldn't go through with the abortion."

"Are you sorry you didn't do it? I mean, look how I turned out."

"I'm glad I didn't abort you and your twin sister. Just so you know, I think you can still turn your life around."

"I'm goin' to! I'm not goin' to let Mel ruin things for me. Listen, I have to leave in a few minutes to go to my yoga class—"

"Lo'retta, if you don't mind, would you give me your telephone number?" Maureen broke in.

"For what?"

"In case I need to call you." Loretta made Maureen want to holler. She didn't, though, because she knew that if she did, she probably wouldn't stop hollering until the people in the white coats had strapped her into a straitjacket and tucked her into a padded cell. She was surprised that she was still able to speak in a civil tone of voice. After all, Loretta had said some pretty disturbing things to her.

Loretta rattled off a telephone number and then she hung up without saying another word.

Maureen shook her head and finished packing for her trip to Bimini.

CHAPTER 60

MAUREEN ENJOYED THE FEW DAYS THAT SHE SPENT IN BIMINI with Jay. For the first time in months, she was able to act like a normal person, whatever that was. They had rented a bungalow near the beach and spent Christmas night sleeping on a blanket under a cabana outside the bungalow window. They opened their eyes the next morning with a starfish and other small creatures crawling on their faces.

"You look and act like a new woman," Jay told Maureen, wiping sand off her face.

"I am a new woman." She really did feel like a new woman because she was experiencing emotions that she had never experienced before. But the pain that she had recently experienced was still lurking beneath the surface.

"A penny for your thoughts," Jay said in a cheerful voice, tickling Maureen's cheek.

"My thoughts ain't worth a plugged nickel these days. I'm goin' to enjoy my life anyway," she vowed, pulling the blanket up to her chin. They had shared a bottle of rum the night before and then they'd made love. They were both still naked.

"I'm glad to hear that," Jay said, sitting up, swatting at a swarm of gnats buzzing around his face. "I mean, you've been through a hell of a lot lately."

"So have you."

Jay groaned, but a few seconds later he snickered. "Let's try not to think about it. It'll all be at home when we get back."

Maureen didn't want to go back home. Just thinking about returning to the apartment that she had shared with the last two people in the world she expected to betray her made her sick to her stomach.

However, despite all that had happened to her lately, she was more relaxed than she'd been in years. She did things with Jay that she had never done before and had never even thought about doing. They ate snake meat at a restaurant that served only exotic dishes. They went scuba diving, horseback riding, and they danced until dawn three nights in a row.

Maureen didn't even dwell on what Virgil had told her about her kidnapping case or the fact that Loretta was now pregnant with her stepfather's baby. Those were two more pieces of her life that she was not ready to share with Jay yet—and might never be. She thought it was more important for her to focus on the things that made her feel good, like being with Jay and having Big Maureen to call up and chat with.

As soon as Maureen got back to Florida, she called up Big Maureen and told her that Loretta was pregnant and planning to get an abortion.

"An abortion?" Big Maureen shouted. *"Why?"*

"She feels that a baby would be nothin' but a big inconvenience right now," Maureen explained with a heavy sigh and a sharp pain in her chest. "It's a damn shame that the females who don't want babies always get pregnant and then get abortions."

"Oh no! Little Mo'reen, please don't let that child kill that precious baby!" Big Maureen hollered.

"Even if I tried to talk her out of it, I'm the last person in the world she'd take advice from these days."

"Sister, please, I'm beggin' you, and I'll get down on my knees and beg Lo'retta, too, if I have to!" Big Maureen bellowed. "This could be God's way of answerin' me and Lukas's prayers!"

"What?"

"Don't you see? This could be an answer to a prayer!"

An answer to a prayer? That was exactly what Virgil had said that Mama Ruby told him on the night she kidnapped Maureen.

"*You* want my daughter's baby?" Maureen asked. "Do you really mean that?"

"Oh Lord, yes, I mean it! I never meant nothin' more in my life than this. Yes, I do want that baby! I wouldn't care if it came into the world with hooves and a tail. I WANT THAT BABY!"

Maureen was glad that she was not in the same room with Big Maureen. If she sounded this desperate on the telephone, there was just no telling how desperate she would be in person.

"I can talk to her, but I don't know if it would do any good. From the way she talks, she's already got her mind made up to get rid of her baby."

"Please, please, please talk to her," Big Maureen begged. Then she burst into tears. "I need that baby," she said between sobs. "And it would be a blood relation, so that would make it an even bigger blessin'. If them adoption folks ever do come through and give me and Lukas a baby, there is no tellin' what kind of blood and background that child might have. Me and Lukas might end up with a lunatic or a born killer on our hands!"

"I don't know if it'll do any good, but I'll call Lo'retta and see what she says."

"Can you call her right now? I'll hang up and you can call me back as soon as you talk to her. Please! I won't get a moment's rest until I hear back from you."

Big Maureen hung up abruptly, but Maureen didn't dial Loretta's number right away. Big Maureen raising Loretta and Mel's baby was something that Maureen had to think about for a while. Just to keep Big Maureen from losing her mind, Maureen waited a couple of minutes and called her back.

"What did Lo'retta say?" Big Maureen yelled. "I been pacin' back and forth, jumpin' up and down and everything waitin' on you to call me back!" That explained why Big Maureen was huffing and puffing like she had just run a marathon.

"Uh, she wasn't home," Maureen lied. "I left a message for her to call me back as soon as she could. Now you go get some rest."

"Like I told you, I ain't goin' to get no rest until you talk to Lo'retta," Big Maureen vowed. "I can't!"

Maureen was not able to reach Virgil until the following morning. When she told him about Loretta's predicament, he said something that surprised her. "You tell Lo'retta she ain't got to kill her baby. Me and Corrine would be glad to raise it," he said, already sounding like a proud papa. "Corrine loves babies and you know I do. It's a pity I only had the one, and seein' him every once in a while ain't enough for me to even feel like a real daddy."

"I don't think you can have Lo'retta's baby."

"Oh. You goin' to take it? Before you do, you need to think it through real hard. Every time you look at that child, you will think about Mel and what he done. I think the best thing would be for somebody else to raise it so you won't have to."

"Big Maureen wants the baby," Maureen stated. "She wants that baby real bad."

"Hmmm. Well, if I can't have it, I'd rather see it go to a relative than to some adoption outfit or end up in some foster home. Big Mo'reen would be a good choice. I know how hard she and Lukas been tryin' to adopt. I got a feelin' that this . . . this might be an answer to a prayer."

An answer to a prayer.

There was that phrase again. Maureen had no doubt in her mind that it really was an answer to a prayer for somebody. . . .

She called Loretta immediately after her conversation with Virgil. To her surprise, Loretta actually sounded happy to hear from her.

"Hi, Mama! Whassup?" Loretta yipped.

"Hello, Loretta. I'm glad I caught you at home. Uh, I just wanted to say hello and see how you're doin'. Is everything goin' all right? Do you feel all right?"

"Yeah, why wouldn't I? I'm healthy and as strong as a mule. I can't wait to get rid of this baby. I'm gainin' weight like mad! I can't believe how bloated I look already. I did quit smokin', though. On Christmas day."

"I didn't know that you had started smokin'," Maureen said, disappointed. "I'm glad to hear you stopped. That was a smart and healthy thing for you to do." Loretta had always been a strong advocate against smoking. Maureen cringed as she wondered what other surprises she had in store.

"There's a whole lot of things you don't know about me, Mama. But it didn't take long for me to realize smokin' was bad for me, so I gave it up."

"Was it just cigarettes you smoked?" Maureen eased in with caution.

Loretta heaved out an impatient breath. "Oh, Mama! If you mean weed, I gave that up before I gave up cigarettes. I smoked my last joint last month."

"You'd better believe I'm glad to hear that. I was real worried about you, Lo'retta. I don't like you bein' pregnant in a strange city with no family to look in on you and all."

"I got a lot of new friends and they look out for me, so you can stop worryin'. I'm not your baby anymore."

You sure are not, Maureen thought to herself, tempted to say it, but glad she didn't.

"Oh, Mama! Guess what? I just came from my beautician, and I've decided to lighten my hair. Can you see me as a blonde? Everybody says that with blond hair, I would look even more beautiful and exotic with a different look than the rest of these black models up here."

"That's nice. I'm sure you will," Maureen mumbled. "Listen, I . . . do you have time to talk? About . . . your condition?"

"My *condition*?" Loretta barked, like her "condition" was something she had just realized. "You mean the baby? You want to talk to me about the baby? For reals?"

"For reals."

"I know you are probably wonderin' how it happened. I swear to God, me and Mel used protection from day one!"

"I'm glad to hear that. The last thing I wanted was for you to get pregnant and not be able to graduate with your class," Maureen said in a guarded tone of voice.

"I graduated with my class, and unlike Wanda Tucker and Melanie Bostwick, I was not pregnant when I walked across that stage to get my diploma." Loretta sucked on her teeth. "Anyway, Mel was determined not to make any babies with me, and that's why he started wearin' two condoms at the same time."

"Well, apparently wearin' two condoms didn't work," Maureen snipped. She sounded sarcastic and frustrated at the same time, and she didn't care if Loretta picked up on that.

"Believe it or not, wearin' two condoms is worse than wearin' just one. Besides sex not feelin' that good for the man, the two condoms rubbin' against each other caused too much friction and both of them broke at the same time. That's how I ended up pregnant."

The last thing Maureen wanted to discuss was her daughter's sexual encounters with Melvin Ross. "Thank you for sharin' that with me, but I called to talk to you about somethin' else."

"What?"

"Lo'retta, I don't want you to abort your baby," Maureen stated. "Please don't do that."

CHAPTER 61

Wᴴᴬᵀ ᴹᴬᵁᴿᴱᴱN ᴴᴬᴰ ᴶᵁˢᵀ ˢᴬᴵᴰ ˢᵀᴬᴿᵀᴸᴱᴰ ᴴᴱᴿ ᴬˢ ᴹᵁᶜᴴ ᴬˢ ᴵᵀ ᴰᴵᴰ
Loretta. She never thought that she would be saying such a thing to
the woman who had stolen her husband. But Maureen still wanted
what was best for her child, and now she wanted what was best for
her grandchild.

"What's wrong with you, Mama? I do not want to raise this baby!"

"You won't have to, Lo'retta."

"You want me to have it and give it up for adoption?"

"Well, yeah. Somethin' like that."

"You want me to miss out on a ton of jobs, go through all that
mornin' sickness and God knows what else, *and* lose my shape? I already told you I've gained a bunch of weight and can't work again
until after I have the abortion—and lose this weight."

"If you take care of yourself, you won't have to worry about gettin' sick every mornin' and losin' your shape. At your age, you'll
lose the weight," Maureen insisted. "Please have the baby. This is
probably the *only* thing that I will ever ask you to do for me again.
Let somebody who wants a baby raise yours."

Loretta cackled like a witch before responding to Maureen's suggestion. "Well, if you thinkin' about takin' the baby and raisin' it
yourself, no way! *If* I do decide to have it, I want it to be raised by
somebody I don't know so I wouldn't have to worry about ever
seein' him or her again."

"I see. Well, it's your life and your body—"

"And *my* baby," Loretta interrupted. "What happens to it is up to me, not you. I'll never let *you* raise a baby of mine. I don't want to come back to Florida and have a baby runnin' around callin' me 'Mama' any time soon. I don't want a child who would probably grow up hatin' me for givin' it up, to even know who I am." Loretta stopped talking long enough to catch her breath. "Shoot! They show enough movies on the Lifetime TV channel about adopted babies growin' up and trackin' down their real mother and turnin' her life upside down. I'm not about to let somethin' like that happen to me. My career would end up in the toilet so fast it would make your head spin. I don't need that kind of disruption in my life right now."

"I'm sorry you feel that way. I don't want to raise your baby, but I know somebody else that wants to raise it," Maureen said evenly. She was amazed at how well she was able to suppress her anger.

"Wait a minute. Don't tell me you've told everybody I'm pregnant!" Lo'retta shrieked.

"Only your uncle Virgil and your aunt Big Mo'reen."

"Don't tell anybody else. Not Jay or any of your friends. They don't need to know. They'd talk about me like a dog."

Maureen didn't want Jay, Catty, or Fast Black to know about Loretta's pregnancy. Jay would probably stay in a neutral position and keep most of his thoughts about it to himself. But Catty and Fast Black would have a field day. If Big Maureen ended up with the baby, nobody in Florida would ever have to know. Maybe years later, Maureen would feel comfortable enough to at least tell Jay and maybe even everybody else. For now, only she, Virgil, and Big Maureen needed to know. "I agree with you. They don't need to know. But like I said, I know somebody who would love to adopt the baby."

"Like who? And don't you even think about Uncle Virgil and Aunt Corrine raisin' my child! If I give it to them, I may as well give it to you."

"No, not them. One of my patients at the home has a niece who has been tryin' to have a baby for years and years. If you let her adopt your baby, it would be an answer to a prayer for her. The woman has been married to the same real nice man for fifteen years." Maureen couldn't believe how easily she had come up with such a bold-faced lie.

"Oh yeah? Hmmm. Well, where do this niece and her real nice husband live?"

"Huh? Oh! Uh . . . they live in Canada and they travel a lot. You would never have to worry about seein' the baby once you turn it over to them."

"Canada? A white couple?"

"Uh-uh. A black couple originally from the Dominican that moved to Canada a long time ago."

Loretta's silence gave Maureen hope, so she continued spinning her tale. "They got *beaucoup* money. He's a doctor. They live in a real big house with a huge backyard and everything. The baby would have a real good life. Better than even you or I could give it."

"What if later on down the road I wanted to take my baby back?"

"It would be real hard, probably impossible, for you to do once you sign the papers." Papers! That was another thing. But Maureen knew that between her, Virgil, and Big Maureen, they could dummy up some legal-looking papers for Loretta to sign. "You could come home to have the baby. That way me and Virgil can take care of you. Uh, the couple said they don't want to meet the baby's mother or even know her name or anything else about her. Not now, not ever . . ."

"Don't these people wonder why you don't want to raise your own grandchild? Or are they just that desperate for a baby that they don't care?"

Maureen had never been much of a liar, but she was impressed at how easily she was able to make up material as she went along. "Uh, they don't know that I'm the baby's grandmother. I thought it would be better to keep that information from them."

"I don't know. I don't want to come back to Florida and have everybody talkin' about me. I could just hear all the trash talkin' Catty and Fast Black would be doin' about me! Livin' under the same roof with you would be too uncomfortable for me, and it probably wouldn't be safe for me."

"Not safe for you? You wouldn't feel safe livin' with me? Lo'retta, I don't care what you do—I would never hurt you. I can understand you not wantin' to live with me again. It would probably be just as uncomfortable for me as it would be for you. I'll find you a real cheap motel to stay in until you have the baby. Maybe one in Tampa or Lauderdale so you won't have to worry about runnin' into anybody you know. Me and Virgil will visit you every day. I just don't want you to be alone in a strange city goin' through a pregnancy by yourself. You *know* now that you can't count on Mel."

"I already told you that I made a lot of new friends. My new boyfriend, Kyle, is in the process of movin' in with me. He already told me that he would find a full-time housekeeper to help me out."

Maureen let out a weary groan. Her broken heart was pounding like it was trying to get out of her body, one piece at a time. "A housekeeper? You mean you might decide to keep the baby?"

"Oh no! I'm not goin' to keep this baby. Why in the world would I want to do somethin' like that at a time like this, Mama? But because that other girl died durin' her abortion, Kyle even thinks I should have it and give it to some childless couple. He said he would find me a nurse so she could look after me until I have this baby, if I do—which I probably won't."

Maureen let out another weary groan. "Whatever you decide to do, I hope you make the right choice. I would hate for you to do anything you will end up regrettin'."

"Oh! I just remembered somethin'. I don't mean to rush you off the phone, Mama, but I have to go see my doctor so he can tell me why I've gained so much weight so fast. I can't stand to go around lookin' like I swallowed a watermelon. Gotta run!" Loretta hung up.

Even though all Maureen could hear now was a dial tone, she said, "Bye, Lo'retta."

As soon as Maureen placed the telephone back into its cradle, it rang. She was afraid that it might be Big Maureen and since she didn't have positive news for her, she didn't answer.

One thing Maureen didn't like to do was deliver bad news.

When she didn't have a choice, she put it off for as long as she could. As soon as the answering machine beeped for the caller to leave a message and she heard Jay's voice, she let out a massive sigh of relief. She clicked off the answering machine and took his call. "I'm here and I'm so glad it's you!" she wailed, clutching the telephone like it was the Holy Grail.

"I'm glad it's me too," Jay laughed. "How about some seafood? I just discovered this cozy little place near the beach. It's real popular with the A-list crowd. I know how you like to gawk at celebrities, and this place is a major hangout for some of your favorites."

"That sounds nice. You called just in time," Maureen replied.

"Just in time for what?"

"I need to talk to somebody about somethin'."

Jay hesitated with his response. "Oh shit," he groaned. "Not more unpleasant news, I hope."

Maureen began to speak slowly, spitting the words out like they had been dipped in poison. "Well, yes, it is unpleasant news," she said. Maureen had suddenly thought that she wanted to talk to Jay about Loretta's situation, but she caught herself in time. He probably still didn't need to know about this yet. She went in a completely unrelated direction. "Uh, I lost two patients today, both within the same hour. They were both real nice and nonviolent, so I am really goin' to miss them." Two of the patients that she cared for at the home had died earlier in the day.

"That is unpleasant news," Jay told Maureen.

"Mr. Brown and Mr. Plummer," she added. "I've been feelin' kind of down in the dumps about it."

"Uh-huh. I guess that's something you don't get used to," Jay said. "Baby, those people are on their last leg when they check into that home. But you already know that, so why do you seem so surprised and upset? Didn't you lose another one of your patients just last week?"

"Yes. Old Lady Graham passed while I was givin' her a sponge bath," Maureen recalled. "Let's stop talkin' about that before I get even more depressed. Now hurry up and come get me so we can get to that seafood place."

CHAPTER 62

*J*AY DROVE MAUREEN HOME A COUPLE OF HOURS LATER. THE first THING she did when she got inside was check her answering machine for messages. She was pleased to see that she didn't have any.

Jay didn't stay long and when he left, Maureen went from room to room looking for things to do to keep herself busy. She cleaned out and reorganized her kitchen cabinets, she did two loads of laundry, and she rearranged the living room furniture. Every time she walked past Loretta's room, her heart skipped a beat. She knew that she would have to enter the room again sooner or later, if for no other reason than to open the windows to let in some fresh air. Eventually, she would have to decide what she was going to do about the room, either use it to store things or make it into a guest room. She even thought about moving to a new apartment so she wouldn't have to deal with the room at all.

She finally crawled into bed around midnight, but she tossed and turned for two hours before she went to sleep.

The next day around 6:00 p.m., Big Maureen called, but Maureen let the answering machine take a message. She still wasn't ready to talk to her big sister again. A few minutes later, without giving it much thought, Maureen dialed Loretta's number.

A man answered and Maureen promptly hung up, thinking that it might be Mel. He was the last man in the universe she wanted to talk to. When she thought about it a little more, though, she realized that the voice had sounded too young to be Mel's. She dialed the number again.

"Hello, is this the number for Lo'retta Montgomery?" she asked when the same voice answered.

"Who's calling?"

"Uh, her mother."

Maureen heard some shuffling around in the background and then the next voice she heard belonged to Loretta. "Yeah, Mama."

"I just called to say hello."

"Hello. Well, is that all you called for?" Loretta sounded impatient, so Maureen planned to make her call very brief.

"Lo'retta, I know you have company, so I won't talk long, but I wish that you will reconsider . . ."

"Reconsider what?"

"Uh, you know . . ."

"I know what? Look, Mama, I don't have time for games. If you called to talk to me about somethin', please do it so I can go on about my business."

"Lo'retta, you don't have to be so surly. I am your mother, girl."

"Mama, what did you call me for?"

"I wanted to talk to you about your problem."

"Problem? What problem? I don't have no problems right now. Except for . . . oh that. You mean that baby."

"Yeah. I mean 'that baby.' I wanted to talk to you about what you told me you plan to do about your . . . condition."

"I am not goin' to reconsider that. Please don't bring up this subject again," Loretta snarled.

"I won't, but I do wish that you would give it a little more thought, Lo'retta. Please think about that poor, desperate, childless couple in Canada."

"Think about me waddlin' around lookin' like Humpty Dumpty—which I almost look like now. I'm thinkin' about how long it would take me to lose the weight if I went through with this pregnancy. Now please stay out of my business!"

"You will always be my business—"

"Mama, please get off my back and let me live my life the way I want to. I'm eighteen now, so I don't have to listen to anything you have to say anymore."

"Lo'retta, what is the matter with you? I can't stand it when you sass me! I'm still your mother. For that reason alone, you should have a little more respect for me. If I had even thought about sassin' Mama Ruby the way you do me, she would have laid me out like a log— Hello? Loretta? Hello?" Loretta had hung up. Maureen cursed, gritted her teeth and slammed the telephone back into its cradle.

As if on cue, Jay called a few seconds later. That was probably the only thing that kept Maureen from ripping the telephone out of the wall.

"Hello, sweetheart. You were on my mind so I thought I'd call to see if you'd like some company," Jay chirped.

"Yeah. I would like some company," Maureen decided, sounding like a wounded kitten.

"Oh-oh. Which one of your patients died this time?" Jay asked, holding his breath.

"Nobody. I just had a telephone conversation with my daughter, Jay. She was so mean and nasty to me."

"Again?"

"Again."

"Why don't you let her cool off for a day or two and then call her up and apologize."

"Apologize? I don't have anything to apologize to her for!" Maureen snarled.

"It doesn't matter if you do or not, sweetheart."

"Jay, HELLO? I'm the victim here," Maureen said firmly.

"I know that, baby—"

"She is puttin' me through hell, but I'm still tryin' to have a relationship with her. She won't even meet me halfway!" Maureen yelled.

"But you should apologize to her if you want to resume a decent relationship with her. The thing is, Maureen, Loretta needs you more than you need her. She's too immature and self-centered to realize that. She's not going to meet you halfway. She's not even going to take one step in your direction."

"So you think that I should grovel and kiss my own daughter's behind just so we can be on good terms again?"

"Baby, that's just the way it is. If you don't, you might lose her forever."

Maureen didn't want to agree or argue with Jay, but she knew he was right.

The following evening, she dialed Loretta's number again. Maureen was nervous and angry at the same time. She wasn't sure what she was going to say to Loretta. She decided that it would be better if she could leave a message on her answering machine, so she hoped to get a recorded outgoing message. And she did.

The crisp and pleasant-sounding message recorded by an anonymous telephone operator informed Maureen that the telephone number she had just dialed had been changed to an unlisted number.

CHAPTER 63

*M*AUREEN LIKED TO RECALL SOME OF THE OFF-THE-WALL REMARKS, comments, and statements that Mama Ruby had made to her when she was growing up. One that still danced around in her head from time to time was, "Mo'reen, don't kiss *nobody's* ass. If anything, bite the hell out of it and if that don't straighten 'em out, bite it again!" Maureen couldn't remember one single ass that Mama Ruby had kissed, except hers.

Loretta still had not given Maureen her mailing address. Now that she had changed her telephone number and had it unlisted, Maureen had no way to get in touch with her. Even if she wanted to kiss her spoiled rotten daughter's ass, how would she do that now?

What would Mama Ruby do? Maureen wondered. She didn't have to wonder about that for long. She *knew* what Mama Ruby would do. Mama Ruby would do whatever it took to resolve this issue. Even though Maureen had exercised her right to be independent and in control of her own life in a totally different way than Loretta, Mama Ruby had come after her with both guns blasting so to speak. Not only had she pestered and stalked Maureen after she had moved into her own apartment, but Mama Ruby had also paid a visit to the lobster factory personnel office and told just enough lies about Maureen to get her fired.

But that didn't make Maureen move back home. One night while she was asleep, Mama Ruby stormed her apartment and ripped a telephone book in two with her bare hands. She had chased away most of Maureen's potential lovers and even broke into her apartment and vandalized some of her property. She had begged, pleaded, and then ordered Maureen to move back home. She had even threatened to kill herself if Maureen didn't comply. Maureen was about to give in, but she waited too long. Mama Ruby carried out her most serious threat of all: she died.

Well, Maureen wasn't about to die if Loretta wanted to be hardheaded and mean. As much as she loved her daughter, she was not going to make a sacrifice of that magnitude.

An hour after Maureen had attempted to call Loretta, she let out a loud breath and leaped out of her seat. She scurried across the floor like a mouse and down the hall to Loretta's bedroom. She pushed open the door so fast and hard, the doorknob hit the wall, leaving a hole the size of a man's fist.

In less than an hour, Maureen had stripped Loretta's bed and stuffed all of the bedding and everything else that was left in the room into boxes. Then she called Goodwill and scheduled a pickup. The next day, she drove the car that Loretta had purchased for her to a used car dealership and eagerly traded it for the first car that a stunned but happy salesman showed to her—a four-year-old Camry. She got screwed out of a lot of money, but she didn't care. Driving a car that had been paid for with Loretta's ill-gotten wealth had begun to increase Maureen's pain.

A week after Maureen had disposed of Loretta's belongings, she called Big Maureen. "I'm sorry it took me so long to get back to you," she began. "I got real busy."

"Uh-huh. But tell me the truth—the real reason you ain't called me is because you don't have no good news for me about Lo'retta's baby, right?" Big Maureen said, her voice trembling.

Maureen sighed. "That's right. I tried. I tried real hard, but Lo'retta is determined to get rid of her baby."

"I didn't get my hopes up too high no way. If the adoption people don't come through neither, I guess it wasn't meant for me to be blessed with another child. I still got a lot to be thankful for anyway, praise the Lord."

"You and Lukas still comin' for another visit soon?"

"If God's willin'."

After a few more moments of mundane conversation, Maureen hung up. Virgil arrived a few minutes later, and Maureen was glad to see him.

"What's up with Lo'retta?" he asked, easing down onto the living room couch. "You talked to her lately?"

"Yeah. I called her up last week, but that girl sure wasn't too happy to hear from me," Maureen replied with a puppy-dog face, handing Virgil a can of beer. "She even changed her telephone number so now I can't call her at all." Maureen popped open a can of beer for herself and sat down on the other end of the couch.

"My goodness."

"I'm so glad Mama Ruby didn't live long enough to see the mess our family turned into." Maureen sniffed and blinked back a tear.

"Me too, I guess." Virgil took a long drink; then he set his beer can on the coffee table. He turned to Maureen with a frightened look on his face. "Mo'reen, how do you feel about . . . what I told you?"

"What do you mean?" she asked, wiping beer off her lips with the back of her hand.

"I mean, how do you feel about what I told you now that it's had a lot of time to sink in? You still glad I told you about what Mama Ruby done to you?"

Maureen set her beer can on the table and shrugged. "I still think that kidnappin' is a sin and a shame, but I'm still glad you told me what you told me. Just like Jay, I had a right to know the whole truth about my real mother and my background."

"Uh-huh. Now, I don't like to get in your business with Jay, but do you still think it's better not to tell him?"

Maureen gave Virgil a long, hard look. "I still don't think it would do any good for him to know about me. I still don't think we should tell anybody else. Never. So you don't need to ask me again."

"That's probably the best thing for us to do." Virgil shook his head and blinked mysteriously, looking at Maureen like she had just entered the room.

"What's wrong? You lookin' at me like I just sprouted horns," Maureen said, forcing herself to chuckle.

"Mo'reen, I hope *you* ain't keepin' no deep dark secrets from me. Somethin' you might want to get off your chest."

Without giving it much thought, Maureen nodded. "Yeah, I got a deep dark secret," she told Virgil. "Somethin' I wanted to tell somebody since I was a teenager . . ."

Virgil shifted in his seat, turning his head so he could see Maureen's face better.

Maureen glanced toward the door, then around her living room. When she looked back at Virgil, there was an anxious and puzzled look on his face. "What is it?"

"I told Mama Ruby and everybody else that that albino we called Snowball was the one that took advantage of me after he got me drunk one night and got me pregnant. I didn't tell anybody until after he died from that drug overdose so he couldn't deny it."

"You told me the same thing, remember? So was Snowball the real daddy or not?"

Maureen cocked her head and shook it. "You remember John French?"

Virgil nodded. "Old Man French's boy? The one that got hisself killed tryin' to rob that gas station? Yeah, I remember that boy. He was real cool, the blackest white boy I ever knew. You had a crush on him, and he had a crush on you when y'all was little kids. Why?"

"He was the one that got me pregnant."

"Lord have mercy." Virgil scratched the side of his neck. The puzzled look was still on his face. "Well, if he was the one that did it, why didn't you say so? He died too."

"He didn't die in time. I was runnin' out of time and I had to blame it on somebody. It had to be a man with real light skin in case my baby came out with light skin. Which she did. I mean, *they* did. Loraine and Loretta came out lookin' so white there was no way I could have blamed them on any of the tar-baby black boys I knew back then."

"Excuse me for sayin' this, but didn't you think John would have been a better choice than Snowball? John's folks had money, and Mama Ruby doted on him. That albino didn't have a pot to piss in, and he was a drug addict."

"John caught me in the blackberry patch and raped me. When I told him I was pregnant, he got real mad." Maureen shivered and swallowed hard, hoping to dislodge the lump that had suddenly formed in her throat. The bad memories left a nasty taste in her mouth, so she finished her beer before continuing. "Anyway, I asked John for five hundred dollars so I could go to that abortion doctor in Miami that all the girls in trouble went to. He slapped the daylights out of me and took off, so I assumed he wasn't goin' to help me get out of the mess he'd gotten me into. Then when I heard that he got killed tryin' to rob that gas station and that he had asked the gas station attendant for just five hundred dollars, I knew he had been tryin' to get the money for my abortion. Since he was dead, and Mama Ruby had been like a mammy to him, I didn't want to ruin his memory. That's why I told everybody that the albino was the one."

"Damn! Did you tell Catty or Fast Black?"

"Oh goodness gracious no! They would have blabbed my business all over the state by now. I ain't told nobody else until today."

Virgil dropped his head. "Not even Lo'retta?"

"I'll *never* tell her!" Maureen said quickly.

She moved closer to Virgil and rubbed his arm. He laid his head on her shoulder. "Virgil, I hope you can keep this a secret too."

Virgil let out a strange laugh. Then he looked up at Maureen and told her, "If I could keep that great big secret about you for thirty-six years, I think I can keep this one."

Maureen had finally removed a beast off her back that had been holding her hostage like a wrongly convicted prisoner. She felt better than she had felt in a long time. She felt like she was finally *free*.

And so did Virgil.

CHAPTER 64

*L*IKE MAUREEN, JAY NO LONGER FELT COMFORTABLE IN HIS OWN home. Mrs. Freeman was gone, but she was still a very strong presence in the residence. Despite the large wraparound front porch where Jay liked to sit and read his newspaper, the fruit trees in the spacious front yard, and the small statue of an angel peeking from behind a rosebush, his home for the past ten years now felt like a haunted house.

There were sad memories in each room, especially the bedroom that Mrs. Freeman had occupied. Jay had just donated her clothes and bedroom furniture to Goodwill a week ago. She had been the kind of woman who hoarded things that she had collected from yard sales, thrift stores, flea markets, and Goodwill. Over the years she had collected so many useless items, it took Jay a whole month to sort it all out before he could dispose of it. By the time he was done, the only things he had left of the criminal who had claimed to be his mother were a few pictures and the shabby Bible that she had made him study every night after dinner.

The one thing that disturbed Jay the most was her smell. It was still in the house. She had always loved the scent of roses—perfume, lotion, scented candles—and she had even used rose-scented room deodorizer. No matter how often he sprayed every room in the house with a different fragrance, he could not get rid of the smell of roses. After a while, he gave up.

Since he no longer liked to spend too much time in his house, and Maureen didn't like to spend too much time in her apartment, they spent a lot of their time in other places as much as possible. They enjoyed long, lingering dinners in their favorite restaurants. They took long drives along the coast. They even spent an occasional weekend in a beach motel. Anything to avoid his or her residence. However, in spite of all the painful memories that Maureen had to endure in her apartment, she had stopped thinking about moving. There was a lot she still liked about where she lived: the cheap rent, the convenient location, and her nice neighbors. The only thing she didn't like now was that it had been the scene of Mel and Loretta's blatant betrayal.

One day Maureen got slaphappy and scrubbed Loretta's growth chart markings off the kitchen wall. A few minutes after she had done that, she snatched some ugly drawings off the refrigerator of things that Loretta had scribbled in elementary school and ripped them to shreds. She even packed away all of the remaining photo albums that contained pictures of Loretta when she was a toddler. It was hard to believe that the same little girl grinning into the camera with her two front teeth missing and chocolate candy smeared all over her face was the same girl who had turned Maureen's life upside down.

The last thing Maureen expected that Saturday, the second weekend in January, was a marriage proposal from Jay.

After lunch at McDonald's, Jay drove to a section of town that Maureen was not too familiar with. It was the kind of neighborhood that she could only see herself living in in her dreams. The houses were large, three to four bedrooms at least. Each home had a two- or three-car garage, a large front yard, and an even bigger backyard. There were no homeless people in sight, like there was in the neighborhood that Maureen lived in now. Crime was almost nonexistent. Except for the time that a jealous doctor shot and killed his cheating wife ten years ago, the most serious "crimes" that the residents in this neighborhood had to worry about was littering, teenagers behaving badly, or somebody throwing a loud party.

"Why did you drive over here, Jay?" Maureen asked, shading her eyes to look at the large beige stucco house that he had parked in front of. "Do you know somebody out here?"

"Uh-huh. I helped install cable in almost every house on this block," Jay replied.

"Oh. Well, do you know who lives in *this* house?" Maureen nodded toward the beautiful house with a hopeful look on her face. Her dream to buy her own home someday was still just a dream, but it was one that she was determined to fulfill.

"I do." Jay paused and cleared his throat with a loud cough. "I'll be moving in as soon as the bank finalizes my paperwork," he said with a proud sniff.

Maureen gasped as she whirled around to face Jay. "Oh, baby, I am so happy for you! I know you've been wantin' to move out of Mrs. Freeman's house ever since . . . well, for a long time. A change of scenery will do you a world of good." She was about to lean over and kiss Jay until he held up his hand, which made her give him a surprised look.

"You think my wife will like it?" he asked.

Maureen's chest tightened and a grimace slid across her burning face. Now she was not only surprised, but she was also scared. She knew that Jay's ex had made one serious attempt to get him back, and it had not worked. Had that gold digger come after him again? Well, if that was the case, that heifer had picked a hell of a time! Maureen was so hopelessly in love with Jay; she knew that if he dropped her now, she would never recover. His "betrayal" would be the final nail in her coffin.

Then she would be alone again.

Suddenly, Maureen thought of every maybe that applied to her situation. Maybe it wasn't meant for her to get too close to anyone anymore. Maybe she was *supposed* to be alone. Maybe she would have been better off if her real mother had raised her. Maybe she would be frivolous and carefree like her mother had been, with men coming out of her ears. Maybe Mama Ruby had been right when she told Maureen that the only person who would never leave her was Mama Ruby herself. Maybe she should visit a pet store and pick out a cat. Maybe she was destined to spend the rest of her life just sitting on a porch with that cat. . . .

"Your wife? Oh . . . well, I hope she'll like it too," Maureen said, brushing off her jeans and sitting up straighter in her seat. She pressed her lips together and gave Jay a hard look. "I guess I know what this means, Jay."

"Do you?"

"You want to get back with your ex. Well, I hope things work out for y'all this time." Maureen snorted and wondered how she was able to look at Jay with a smile on her face. "I'll still be your friend if you want me to—and if your wife won't mind." She had to blink hard to hold back her tears. She couldn't wait to get home so she could cry like a baby and guzzle alcohol like a thirsty sailor.

Jay laughed long and loud. "Come on, Maureen. You really don't get it, do you."

"I get it, Jay," she snapped, her smile gone. Her jaw tightened and every muscle from her neck up began to ache. Why was disappointment so damn painful? She had been hurt and disappointed so many times that she was surprised she wasn't dead by now.

"I want *you* to be my wife, Maureen. I've wanted you to be my wife for a long time. Your divorce from that asshole will be finalized soon. So . . . will you marry me?"

Maureen closed her eyes and shook her head. When she opened her eyes again, she looked at Jay like she was seeing him for the first time. Now that she had finally heard the words that she had dreamed of hearing most of her life, from a man she truly loved, she didn't know what to say. "I . . . I . . . never expected you to . . ."

Jay covered her lips with his fingers. "You don't have to tell me right away. You can take all the time you need to think about it." He laughed some more.

"I didn't know you . . . cared about me like that," Maureen said, her voice so low Jay had to lean his head closer to her so he could hear her better.

"Well, I do. But after what Mel did to you, I can understand if you don't want to rush into another marriage so soon. I'll wait, but don't make me wait too long, Maureen. I'm tired . . ."

"I'm tired, too, Jay. I would love to marry you!"

He hauled off and kissed her so hard, his shoulder fell against the horn. It blared the entire time his lips were on hers.

"I know that I'm coming to you with a lot of baggage," Jay said after he released Maureen. "But that's all behind me now."

"What about my baggage?"

"What your daughter and Mel did was bad, but I think my baggage is much heavier than yours."

"Yeah, takin' on a new wife is a big step to be takin' when you still have newspeople and greedy relatives comin' at you," Maureen said, stroking Jay's arm. "Just how do you feel about what happened to you now that some time has passed?"

Jay didn't respond right away. He stared straight ahead for about half a minute before he looked back in Maureen's direction. "I haven't had any nightmares in a while, but not a day goes by that I don't think about what kind of life I might have had if . . . if Mrs. Freeman hadn't run off with me. Anyway, I think marrying a woman like you might help me accept everything a lot easier."

"Mrs. Freeman was wrong for takin' you, but she deserves credit for the man you turned out to be," Maureen reminded him. "I know exactly how you must feel. . . ."

Jay gave her a curious look and shook his head. "Thank you for saying that. I know you mean well. I was the victim of an unspeakable crime. Only somebody who has walked in my shoes could know *exactly* how I feel, Maureen. Right?"

"Right," she agreed. *If he only knew*, Maureen said to herself.

CHAPTER 65

*M*AUREEN WANTED TO GET MARRIED NEXT MONTH, IN FEBRUARY. HER divorce from Mel would be finalized by then. But the main reason she wanted to wait until then was because Big Maureen was having a cluster of polyps removed from the lining of her throat next week and wouldn't be able to travel for at least three weeks. Maureen wanted her big sister to be in attendance when Virgil gave her away to the only man she'd ever loved.

"What a damn shame Lo'retta won't be here to see you get married," Catty hissed. "That little wench is probably too busy prancin' her high-and-mighty tail around New York tryin' to be Miss Muckity Muck. Oomph! If she was my girl, I would lay her out next time I laid eyes on her."

"Maybe it's a good thing Lo'retta won't be here. That shameless hussy might cast her rovin' eye in Jay's direction," Fast Black spat.

"Lo'retta didn't like Jay that much, so I seriously doubt she would latch on to him too," Maureen chuckled. She had decided that the sooner she forgot about Lo'retta, the better. Apparently, Loretta had "forgotten" about her. But it was hard for Maureen to dismiss her only child. She prayed that someday they would at least be friends again.

So when Loretta called the last week in January, Maureen was happy to hear from her.

"How have you been, Mama?" Loretta asked as soon as Maureen picked up the telephone. "I've been prayin' for you. I hope you don't spend your time sittin' around bein' stressed."

"I'm *too* blessed to be stressed," Maureen claimed, forcing herself to sound as aloof as possible. "And you? I hope you don't sit around bein' stressed either."

"You sound real giddy," Loretta noticed, ignoring Maureen's question about how she was doing. "You drunk?"

"No, I'm not drunk," Maureen snapped. "I'm giddy because I'm gettin' married again. Probably around February or March."

"Married? *You*?" Loretta yelled. "To who?"

"Jay."

"Jay who? I don't know nobody by that name, do I?" Loretta didn't give Maureen enough time to respond. "Wait a minute! Do you mean that kidnapped man that was all over the news last year?"

"Yes. That's the man I'm goin' to marry."

"What? I thought he was gay! Why else would he wear a *white* suit to my graduation?"

"Jay Freeman is not gay, Lo'retta. He is just as straight as you are, my dear."

"Hmmm. Well, there's only one way you would know that for sure, Mama. Have you been screwin' that man?"

"Yes, I sleep with Jay and I always enjoy it." Maureen couldn't remember the last time she enjoyed smirking so much. It felt damn good and she wanted to do it some more, so she did. "So what?"

"I didn't know you still . . . *got busy*. Especially at your age."

"You mean you didn't think I would ever want to sleep with another man after Mel?

"That was different," Loretta whined. "Mel had a plan."

"I know that now. And it included sleepin' with me so he could sleep with you."

Loretta purposely ignored Maureen's last comment. "Did you do it with Jay before Mel took off?"

"No, I didn't. Jay wanted me to, but I couldn't cheat on my husband. I would never do that, even to a husband like Mel."

"Then did you sleep with Jay to get back at Mel?"

"Lo'retta, I don't give a flyin' fuck about Mel now. I'm marryin' Jay because he loves me and I love him. We've been in love with each other for a long time."

"Even before?"

"If you mean before you and Mel, the answer is yes, but I couldn't do a damn thing about it until now."

"Hmmm. Well, how come you didn't leave Mel and marry Jay? Everybody might have been happier then."

"If I knew then what I know now, I would have left Mel and married Jay a long time ago."

"What about me?"

"What about you?"

"If you had left Mel to marry Jay, what would I have done? You knew I didn't like Jay."

"You had Mel, remember? So you would have done whatever you wanted to do, Lo'retta. Like you always do." Maureen paused and rubbed her forehead, wondering why Loretta was really calling after so much time had gone by since their last conversation. "How have you been? I take it your abortion was a success."

"See, that's what I called to talk to you about."

"Well, talk to me about it." Maureen was surprised at how firm she was able to make herself sound. She hoped her daughter realized that too. She wanted this ungrateful, inconsiderate child to know that she was still moving forward with her life.

"I didn't go through with it. I'm goin' to have this baby." From the tone of Loretta's voice, it seemed as though she were revealing that she had a terminal illness.

The words hit Maureen like a ton of bricks. Her lips began to quiver. It took a few moments for her to organize her thoughts and form a response. "Oh?" was all she could manage.

"I really was goin' to abort it, though."

"Oh? Well, if you don't mind me bein' nosy, what made you change your mind?" Maureen asked, with her heart pounding against her chest like a sledgehammer. Did Loretta change her mind because Maureen's interference had had an impact on her after all?

"I didn't change my mind. See, I was scared so I kept putting it off and I put it off for too long. Dummy me! By the time I'd made up my mind to go through with the abortion, it was too late. Besides, I had miscounted anyway. I was seven weeks farther along than I thought. That's why I got big so fast! I was still havin' my period—up until July—so I had no reason to think I was pregnant."

Seven weeks farther along than she thought? So Loretta was already pregnant when she and Mel ran off back in June! The knowledge that her daughter was still living under her roof and was pregnant by her husband opened up a whole new wound for Maureen. This shocking new development was almost more than she could stand. Her chest felt like it was going to explode, and her jaw started twitching so hard it felt like she had been kicked in the face.

"Oh. Well, I still hope everything works out the way you want it to," Maureen said, her jaw still twitching.

"It will. You know I always get my way. Anyway, a lot of stuff is on my mind these days, Mama."

Maureen couldn't stop herself from injecting a dose of sarcasm into her response. "Stuff that'll do you some good, I hope."

"I think it will. I don't want you to think that I'm all bad, see. I know you probably still want to go off on Mel and give me a whuppin', but it sounds like you really have gotten over what we did to you."

"Not really, and I probably never will, but I have a good life anyway. I'm happy these days. God keeps blessin' me."

"And you should be blessed! You deserve to be happy too. I mean, you *overpaid* your dues by growin' up with a battle-ax like Mama Ruby for a mama, havin' idiot friends like Catty and Fast Black, and then to end up in that dead-end-ass job at an old folks' home! If anybody deserves to be blessed by God, it's you! You could be the poster girl for the underdogs!"

Maureen was speechless. She remained silent because she couldn't wait to hear what Loretta had to say next.

"Mama, do you still have the contact information for that couple in Canada?" Loretta asked.

CHAPTER 66

MAUREEN WAS DUMBFOUNDED. FOR THE NEXT FEW SECONDS, SHE couldn't tell if she was coming or going. She had to give a quick tune-up to her brain to try and figure out what Loretta was talking about.

"Mama, did you hear what I just asked you? Do you still know how to get in touch with that couple?"

"Couple? What couple?" Maureen had given up on the idea of Loretta letting the fictional couple in Canada have her baby. Loretta asking about them now caught her completely off guard.

"Tsk, tsk, tsk, I guess you've gone senile too," Loretta complained. "Don't you remember tellin' me about the couple who wanted to adopt my baby?"

"Oh! You mean that nice rich couple in Canada. I . . . oh . . . yeah! Of course I remember. You got it right about me bein' senile because my memory ain't what it used to be. Yes. I still have their information."

"If they still want my baby, they can have it," Loretta said quickly. "I don't want to meet them, and I don't want to talk to them, not even over the phone."

Maureen couldn't believe her ears. "Uh, are you goin' to come home and have the baby? I can take the baby up to Canada myself."

"Didn't I already tell you that I'm never comin' back to Florida? The only way I will go through with this is if *you* don't get involved."

"What do you mean?"

"I don't want to see this baby when it's born and I don't want you to see it either. One of the other girls I know changed her mind after she and her mama saw her baby, and her mama talked her into givin' it to her to raise. I know you don't want to raise Mel's baby, but you might change your mind if you saw it."

Maureen didn't want to comment on Loretta's last sentence. There were no comments that she could make without using a lot of profanity. "Uh, how do you want the couple to pick up the baby?" Maureen had not thought this far ahead. She had also not considered the possibility that Loretta might change her mind someday in the future and want to meet, or at least communicate by telephone or letter, with this bogus couple in Canada. "Uh, they want to keep this as impersonal as possible. They don't ever want to meet or talk to you either."

"I don't even want to know their names or exactly where in Canada they live. You already told me everything I want to know about these people."

"I'm glad you feel this way," Maureen said, relieved. "I think that's the best way to handle this. I'm sure I can find somebody we can trust to come get the baby right after it's born. They can take it to that couple. The husband and wife already said they would pay for any expenses involved." Maureen immediately wished she had not said anything about money. All she needed now was for Loretta to ask for some impossibly huge amount of money in exchange for her baby. She recalled a TV movie that she had seen about a greedy female who had done just that. The girl had sold her baby for some humongous amount of money to a wealthy couple. Maureen hoped that Loretta wouldn't ask for money in exchange for her baby. The thought of something like that happening almost made Maureen pass out. Poor Mama Ruby. It was a good thing she was dead. She would never put up with something like this! But if Loretta did want money for her baby, well, Maureen would scrape up whatever she could. Virgil had a nice savings and so did Big Maureen and her husband.

"I don't want anybody too close to me to pick up the baby. Not you, not Virgil."

"I understand. Like I said, I can find somebody we can trust to come to New York and get the baby and take it to that couple." Maureen was close enough to a couple of women at work. She knew she'd be able to talk one of them into posing as a representative for the couple in Canada. Who wouldn't want a free trip to New York? Maureen knew she could fabricate a believable story to tell the woman so she wouldn't have to know the truth about where the baby was actually going to end up. If she had to, she would hire some local actors to pose as the Canadian couple. Otherwise, she would have her coworker bring the baby to her, and she would take it to Big Maureen.

"What about Big Mo'reen?" Loretta asked.

"Excuse me?"

"Do you think you could talk Big Mo'reen into comin' to New York to get the baby? Maybe if that couple from Canada would get a hotel room here, too, Big Mo'reen wouldn't have to go all the way to Canada to drop off the baby."

"I don't know about the Canadian couple travelin' to New York, but I know I can get Big Mo'reen to pick up the baby and take it to that nice couple. Uh, Big Mo'reen is family, though. I thought you didn't want nobody in the family to see the baby in case they get attached to it and want to keep it, or somethin'."

"Oh, I doubt if Big Mo'reen wants to raise another baby at her age!"

Thank God Lo'retta didn't know how desperate Big Mo'reen was to raise another child! Maureen told herself.

"Since Big Mo'reen ain't had enough time to really bond with our part of the family yet, she shouldn't have trouble doin' somethin' like this. Can you call her up right away? I want to get this mess straightened out as soon as possible so I can start makin' plans for my future."

"I will call her up right away," Maureen said, speaking so fast she almost bit her tongue. "I'll make sure that couple in Canada got the papers for you to sign off on and whatnot."

"Papers? What kind of papers? I don't want to sign off on a bunch of papers!"

"Um, papers to make everything nice and legal. In case you decide later on that you want the baby back, these papers will protect the Canadian couple's interest."

"Yikes! I would never want this baby back once I get rid of it. I am goin' to be the most famous black model in the world. I can't stand that Naomi Campbell, so I want to knock her off her high-ass horse as soon as possible. Besides, when I do get married, I don't want my husband to be bothered with no *ready-made* family! That almost never works out."

Tell me about it, Maureen said to herself. "I am sure you won't want the baby back, but I am also sure that the couple would like to have some peace of mind. They wouldn't want to sit around wonderin' from one year to the next if you might come to claim your baby. You signin' the paperwork is just a formality."

"All right, then. Send me the paperwork I need to sign and I'll sign it. If things get too complicated and I have to run back and forth to some lawyer's office, I won't go through with this!"

"I'll make sure it's just some simply worded document that says you can never try to find or reclaim the baby. That's all. Virgil knows some real sharp lawyers. I'm sure he can get one to draw up some papers."

"Just make sure that Uncle Virgil gets one that'll draw up some papers that don't have a lot of confusin' mumbo jumbo and big words I have to look up. I'm not in the mood to deal with anything real complicated. Do you hear me?"

"Yes. How will I get in touch with you?"

"You know where I am, Mama. I'm in New York City."

"I don't have your address in New York City, and you changed your telephone number and didn't give it to me," Maureen said dryly.

"Is that why you didn't call me?" Loretta whined. "I wondered how come you didn't call me up and wish me a happy New Year!"

"I would have . . ." Maureen was stunned and disappointed to hear that her daughter was such a dingbat. How in the world was Loretta going to make it in the cutthroat business of modeling and become the most famous black model in the world if she was this dense?

"I guess I forgot to give you my new number, huh, Mama?"

"I guess you did."

Loretta was the last person in the world who needed to be raising a baby. Maureen was glad she didn't want to. She was also glad that Loretta had mixed up her dates, making it impossible for her to get an abortion.

After Loretta gave Maureen her new telephone number and her address, she hung up without even saying good-bye.

Maureen wasted no time calling Big Maureen. "Do you still want Lo'retta's baby?"

CHAPTER 67

"HOLD ON. LET ME GRAB A BEER." BIG MAUREEN DROPPED THE TELE-phone onto her living room coffee table and trotted into the kitchen to snatch a can of beer out of her refrigerator. She returned to the telephone in record time, huffing and puffing and slurping her beer. Flopping down onto her couch, she said, "Okay, sugar. Now what did you just ask me?"

"I asked if you still wanted to raise Lo'retta's baby?" Maureen was so excited, she felt warm all over. She felt so good that she was grinning from ear to ear, something she had not done in months, except when she was with Jay. It warmed her heart to know that at least one good thing was going to come from the mess Loretta and Mel had created after all.

Big Maureen screamed like a woman in ecstasy—and that was exactly what she was. "Lord Almighty! Do I still want to raise Lo'retta's baby? Girl, you know I do! I thought she got rid of it?"

"It's a long story, and I don't want to go into that right now. The main thing is, you can have the baby if you still want it. It'll be your and Lukas's baby, free and clear. You can name it whatever you want and raise it the way you want to, which I know will be good with you bein' so much like Mama Ruby and all. But only you, me, and Virgil will ever know who the baby's real mother is. That's one of the things that we have to agree on."

"I can agree to that! What about Lo'retta? She won't know nothin'? She won't know me and Lukas got her baby? Wouldn't she feel better knowin' her child was with family?"

"No. She thinks that some couple in Canada is gettin' the baby."

"Huh? You mean there is another couple in the mix?"

"Yes and no. Lo'retta thinks there is, but I just made them up."

"You made up a couple?"

"I had to. She didn't want anybody she knew to have the baby because she was afraid she'd eventually be around it. That's why I made up the story about a rich couple in Canada. That pleased her and that's the only way she would agree to my suggestion."

"Oh. I just don't want to get that baby and get attached to it and then find out that somebody else might pull the rug out from under me and Lukas. You sure this is the only couple you made up? You sure there ain't no real couple that might cause trouble?"

"Big Mo'reen, you don't have to worry about anybody messin' things up for you once you get that baby. You just have to go along with my plan. You have to keep all of the details a secret. That's the only way this is goin' to work."

"We can do that."

"We? We who?"

"Me and Lukas. Since he'll be the baby's daddy, shouldn't he know everything I know?"

"No! He can't ever know the truth. It's got to be just you and me and Virgil. I don't even want Virgil to tell Corrine. She might decide to leave him one day, and who knows who she will blab our business to. Lukas might do the same thing. You just tell him that some unwed young girl up in Alaska is givin' y'all her baby."

"That story sounds kinda flimsy, even to me," Big Maureen stated. "You goin' to have to do better than that, baby sister."

"Okay. How's this sound: tell Lukas and everybody else that one of the nuns from that asylum you grew up in transferred to Alaska. Somebody told her how bad you wanted a child. Say she wrote you a letter and told you that she'd help you get this Alaska girl's baby but that everything has to be kept top secret on account of the girl is kind of fickle."

"What would a black girl be doin' in a remote place like Alaska?"

"Her boyfriend got a new job up there in Alaska, and she followed him a few weeks after he left their home in . . . uh . . . Atlanta. But by the time she got there, he already had a new woman."

"And that's why she don't want to keep his baby?"

"Exactly."

"That's more like it." Big Maureen actually clapped. "Now all I want to know is when and how I'm goin' to get my new baby? Oohwee! Christmas is comin' early this year!"

"I need to talk to Virgil first. I'm goin' to get him to draw up some papers for Lo'retta to sign."

Big Maureen's mouth dropped open. "Papers? Yo Lawdy! If we involve a lawyer in this, someday Lo'retta might get a hold of him and make him tell her who got her baby!"

"Don't worry. We won't need a lawyer to get involved in this. This is just another part of the plan to keep Lo'retta in line, in case she tries to stir up some mess later on down the road," Maureen explained. Big Maureen's silence told Maureen that even more of an explanation was necessary. "We'll make Lo'retta think these papers are real, but they will be as phony as a three-dollar bill. After she signs them, you, me, and Virgil will be the only ones with copies."

"What about Lo'retta? Won't she need a copy?"

"She can have a copy if she wants one, but it won't do her a bit of good. I'm goin' to have Virgil word it so she can never try to contact her child, even after it gets grown."

"Oh." Big Maureen's silence worried Maureen. "I'm glad Mama Ruby didn't sign no papers like that when she gave me up. My daddy's mama wouldn't have been able to find me and bring me home to my real family. I'd still be the lost orphan child that I was for the first fifteen years of my life."

Maureen was tired of all the secrets and lies in her family, but she knew that for the good of everybody involved, some of the secrets had to remain. Mama Ruby had given up her own baby and then stolen one from another woman. Well, with Loretta's baby, it was time for somebody to do the right thing. But was what she had cooked up the *right* thing? Maureen wondered. She didn't know the answer to that question, and she didn't want to dwell on it. As far as she was concerned, it was the best thing for everybody involved.

After Maureen ended her call with Big Maureen, she began to

pace back and forth, almost walking a hole in her living room carpet. She had overloaded her mind with more scary thoughts. Now she had one more thing to be on pins and needles about. In addition to being nervous about getting married soon, and still trying to get used to the fact that she had been kidnapped at birth, she was scared to death that Loretta might change her mind about the baby. That night before she went to sleep, she prayed twice as long as she usually did.

Maureen dialed Loretta's telephone number several times over the next couple of days. Each time the answering machine picked up. So far, Loretta had not returned any of her calls. That made Maureen even more nervous and apprehensive. She couldn't wait for this adoption thing to be over and done with.

That Sunday, Virgil composed a very official-looking bogus contract on his computer. The next day, Maureen sent it by registered mail to Loretta. She called Loretta's residence again and left a detailed voice mail, alerting her that the "contract" was on the way. Maureen had to make sure that Loretta didn't get slaphappy and talk to one of her so-called new friends, or somebody with some legal knowledge. The message she left informed Loretta that if she involved someone else, the couple in Canada would cancel everything and she'd be stuck with a baby she didn't want.

Loretta didn't bother to return that call either. The only way Maureen knew she had received the document was when she verified its delivery with the post office.

Loretta had not only received and signed the document, but she also returned it to Maureen by overnight FedEx the next day. That was a good sign, Maureen decided. Even so, all kinds of random thoughts kept entering her mind. Like, what if five or ten years from now, Loretta had a change of heart and hired a lawyer to help her get her baby back? Or what if Loretta did something stupid and had a miscarriage? And the worst thought of all: What if Loretta and Mel got back together and he talked her into keeping the baby?

Maureen knew that she wouldn't be able to rest or sleep right again until everything was over—her marriage to Mel and the "adoption."

She waited a few more days and dialed Loretta's number again and got her answering machine once more. "Hello, baby. I hope you are takin' care of yourself. Uh, Jay and I finally set a date to get married. We are not doin' anything fancy or even in a church. Big Mo'reen recently had surgery and is taking longer to recover, so she can't make it back to Florida to see me and Jay get married anyway. We're just goin' to go to the courthouse. Virgil and Corrine will be our witnesses." Maureen knew that it would do no good to invite Loretta to come home to see her get married, so she didn't even bother with that. It broke her heart to be so cold toward her own child, but what choice did she have? Loretta knew what she wanted to do with her life, and it didn't include her countrified mother.

Three days later, Maureen received a card from Loretta congratulating her on her upcoming nuptials. It made Maureen cry. It was the plainest, cheapest (ninety-nine cent) card that she had ever received in her life. But it was still special. Maureen didn't mention the card to Jay or anybody else. She slid it back into the envelope and placed it in her Bible, paper clipped to the original copy of Mama Ruby's death certificate.

"Have you been crying again?" It was the first question out of Jay's mouth when he arrived at Maureen's apartment a couple of hours after she had read the card from Loretta.

"Somethin' got caught in my eye," she fibbed, wrapping her arms around his waist. "What's up?" She grinned.

"Look, we need to get to the furniture store by tomorrow. We have to pick out the rest of our stuff by then if we want it to be delivered before the wedding."

"Okay. Oh, by the way, Catty and Fast Black keep makin' a fuss about us not havin' a big church weddin' or even a reception," Maureen told Jay.

"That's too bad," he chortled. "I don't want to do any of that. I'm tired of bein' the center of attention."

Somehow, the news had been leaked to the press that Jay was getting married. Several photographers and a couple of reporters were already at the courthouse when he and Maureen, with Virgil and Corrine in tow, got there the following Saturday afternoon.

"I guess the world will never let me forget about what happened to me. I just hope that someday you can forget about it and we can go on with our lives and live like normal people," Jay told Maureen the day after they had exchanged vows. A picture of them running out of the courthouse was on the front page of the local newspaper that day, as were a few updated bits and pieces about Jay's kidnapping. "The way these people are carrying on, you would think that I was the only black baby in America that ever got kidnapped! It's a good thing I had the strong, loving mother I had—even though she wasn't really mine. She taught me to be strong. If I hadn't had her, I would probably be stone crazy by now. Do you know what I mean?"

A slight smile crossed Maureen's face and she nodded. "Yes, I do know what you mean."

CHAPTER 68

A WEEK BEFORE SHE WAS DUE TO DELIVER HER BABY, LORETTA CALLED home. It was Valentine's Day.

"Mama, it's me," she announced. Loretta sounded so casual you would have thought that she and Maureen had been chatting every day since her departure.

Loretta did not apologize or explain why she had not returned any of Maureen's telephone calls.

"It's so good to hear your voice," Maureen said. Her voice was shaking like she was about to throw up. "I hadn't heard from you and I was wonderin' what was goin' on with you these days."

"You know I'm a busy girl, Mama. Me and Kyle plan to get married in a few months. Oh, our weddin' is goin' to be so cute. He's real close friends with this white dude who owns a house in the Hamptons. He said we could get married on his yacht."

"A yacht? Oh my God!"

"Don't sound so surprised, Mama. You know the kind of people I like to associate with. I don't know any losers anymore."

"I'm glad to hear that." Maureen sniffed.

"Speakin' of losers, how is everybody doin' down there in Florida?"

"I don't know any losers down here in Florida, but everybody I do know is doin' just fine."

"Oh. Well, that's nice. Anyway, Kyle really loves me. Mel didn't know what real love was."

Maureen could have gotten a lot of mileage out of Loretta's last comment, but she didn't think it was worth it. What she did say was enough. "I kind of figured that out."

"Kyle's mama is a white woman. I never thought that we'd have white folks in our family!"

"Neither did I," Maureen said. She wondered what Loretta would say if she knew that a white boy had fathered her.

"And he's Jewish. I know what a Jesus freak you can be, so I hope him bein' a Jew won't upset you."

"I don't care what his religion is. I just hope this boy Kyle is good to you," Maureen managed.

"Oh, he's everything I ever wanted in a man—cute, generous, funny, ambitious, tall, and a great kisser. And he's not a *boy*, Mama! He's a mature man of twenty-two." At least he's closer to Loretta's age than Mel was, Maureen was glad to hear. "Kyle is a makeup artist, so he knows a lot of people in the modelin' industry and he's goin' to help me make it to the top."

Like Mel was supposed to, Maureen thought. The comment was on the tip of her tongue. "I hope you'll be very happy, Lo'retta. You deserve it."

"You bet I do. After all Mel put me through. And guess what, Mama?"

"What, Lo'retta?"

"Mel had the nerve to move in with some pig-faced little skank from *Detroit* of all places, the butthole of the ghetto world. Talk about scrapin' the bottom of the barrel! That hoochie-coochie woman made a lame music video with some has-been rapper—who just got out of prison—so now she thinks her butt don't stink. She had the nerve to tell me to my face that she was movin' to Miami to model. *Miami*! I told that numbskull that you don't end up in Miami, that you start off your career there. Anybody with a brain knows that South Florida is like an elephant's graveyard. That's why so many old people retire and move there to die. Anyway, Mel talked her out of it and they decided to stay in New York."

"Harrumph. I didn't know you and Mel still talked to one another," Maureen said sourly. She wanted to throw up every time Mel's name came up in a conversation.

"We don't. We just know some of the same people. That's how I get the news about him and that rag doll in blackface he dumped me for. I don't know if I told you, but you don't know how lucky you are that he's out of your life."

"Oh yes, I do," Maureen said quickly. "I wouldn't trade five Mels for one Jay."

Loretta took her time responding. "Umph! You still with *Jaaay*?"

Maureen knew that Loretta had never cared much for Jay. She obviously still didn't and probably never would. The way she spat out his name made it sound obscene.

"We got married. I left you a message on your machine. You sent me a card congratulatin' us," Maureen reminded her in a low, exasperated voice. "I hope *you* ain't gettin' senile like me."

"I just forgot, that's all," Loretta whined.

"You should be havin' the baby in about a week, right?" Maureen asked, holding her breath. She never knew what Loretta was going to say next.

"That's why I called you today. Will you get in touch with Big Mo'reen and tell her she should get up here right away? The next couple of days, if possible. I want her to be here the day I drop this load so she can take it off my hands and be on her way with it to Canada so I can put this out of my mind—and so I can start losin' this damn weight!"

"I'll call Big Mo'reen right away," Maureen said quickly.

"Good! And, Mama, please take care of yourself," Loretta advised, almost sounding like the caring, loving daughter she used to be.

"I will. You do the same, Lo'retta," Maureen croaked. "Uh, Lo'retta, no matter what happens, I'll always be just a phone call away. My number will never change and if somethin' happens and you can't get in touch with me, you can always call up your uncle Virgil. His phone number is the same one he had since he got out of the army." Maureen tried to think of other things to say to Loretta because she didn't know if Loretta was about to hang up, and she had no idea when she would speak to her again.

"Mama, I know I wasn't the best daughter in the world, but you did a real good job raisin' me. I wanted to let you know that. I know . . . I know you spoiled me on account of my twin gettin' drowned. I wonder how I would have turned out if she had lived."

"I wonder that same thing myself, Lo'retta. I spoiled you and didn't whup you enough, but I did the best I could."

"You did, Mama. I will always love you for that." Loretta actually sounded remorseful. She paused and for a moment Maureen thought she'd hear a few sobs coming from Loretta's end. But she didn't. "I wish to God that Mama Ruby hadn't died so soon," Loretta said, no longer sounding remorseful. Now she sounded angry. "She would have taken care of us! With her guidance and protection, our lives would be so different right now. She wouldn't have let Mel get close enough to even smell me or you, huh?"

"That's for damn sure," Maureen agreed. "But Mama Ruby is gone and we have to live without her guidance and protection."

"Yeah. And like I just said, I know I wasn't the best daughter in the world, but I know you loved me anyway."

"We *did* have some good times together. Before and after Mama Ruby died. You weren't the worst daughter in the world, and I still love you," Maureen assured Loretta.

"You do? You still love me?"

Maureen was surprised that Loretta sounded so surprised to hear that she still loved her. "I always will. That's what bein' a mother is all about."

"Oh. It is? Hmmm . . ."

Maureen's mind almost shut down on her. The last thing she wanted now was for Loretta to be thinking about motherhood. She was terrified at the thought that Loretta may want to keep her baby after all. Maureen didn't know what she would do if she did, but she knew that Big Maureen would never get over such a major disappointment. She immediately began to do some damage control. "Uh, but bein' a mother is very hard work. You have to be really ready for it and you have to make all kinds of sacrifices. A baby could really put a girl's career on hold, maybe even end it!"

Loretta groaned in agreement. "Tell me about it. Anyway, if you and Jay ever have kids, I hope—" She stopped. "Never mind,

Mama." Then in a very loud and impatient voice she said, "Sorry, but I gotta run! Just get in touch with Big Mo'reen and make sure she gets up here in time to pick up this baby so I won't have to deal with it that much. She can sort out things with that Canadian couple. They are probably uppity anyway, so I'm glad I don't have to deal with them. I want this baby to be out of my life forever as soon as possible. I don't even want to look at it, but I will have to do that after all. At least for the first day after it's born. I haven't told my doctor that I am not keepin' this child, and it might look funny for me not to even look at it after it's born, and then for Big Maureen to show up in the hospital and take it on the same day. I'll take it home and hang on to it just long enough for Big Maureen to situate herself and be on her way with it."

It. Maureen wondered what Mama Ruby would say if she knew that her granddaughter thought of her child as an "it." Well, *it* was going to be raised by the right—no, the *best*—mother. Just like Jay and Maureen had been.

CHAPTER 69

BIG MAUREEN ANSWERED HER TELEPHONE ON THE FIRST RING. WHEN Maureen told her she needed to get ready to head to New York as soon as possible, Big Maureen told her, "Girl, I packed my suitcase the same day you told me Lo'retta was goin' to let me have that baby!"

"Now, don't you get up there to New York and say the wrong things to Lo'retta," Maureen warned. "It could mess up our plans."

"What do you mean? What wrong things do you think I might go up there and say to Lo'retta?" Big Maureen asked in a gruff voice. "I ain't stupid."

"I know that, but we just have to make sure we keep our stories straight, that's all. Don't say nothin' that you and I and Virgil didn't discuss. If Lo'retta asks you somethin' you don't know, just play dumb, claim partial amnesia if you have to. When you get to New York, the basic story is you came to pick up the baby to take it to that childless couple in Canada. Don't add to that."

"Hmmm. What kind of story will Lo'retta be tellin' the folks at the hospital? Don't they have all kinds of rules and regulations? I can't just walk up in there and tell them to hand me over that baby. This ain't no puppy I'm goin' to collect."

"Lo'retta won't be tellin' them anything. I think she's goin' to take the baby to her place so you can pick it up there. She said you need to be in New York before or right after she gives birth so she won't have to deal with the baby any longer than she has to. And she told me she's gettin' married as soon as all of this is over."

"Married? Heaven forbid it ain't to that doggish Mel. If I could get my hands on him, I'd wring his pecker off with my bare hands like I was wringin' a chicken's neck!"

"Mel dumped Lo'retta for another girl. Lo'retta's marryin' somebody else," Maureen said glumly.

"Well, whoever he is, he has my sympathy. I'm goin' to pray for him. Lo'retta needs a whuppin' more than she needs a husband!"

"Well, it's too late for a whuppin'," Maureen whimpered, wondering if Loretta would have turned out better if she had whupped her as often as Mama Ruby had whupped Maureen when she got out of line.

"Little Mo'reen, I'm beside myself with disbelief! Only God knows what that girl will do next."

"I know. She's somethin' else," Maureen mumbled.

"Listen, I know you just got married a little while ago yourself and all, but can you meet me in New York?"

"What? Why?" Maureen gulped. "I don't think Lo'retta wants to see my face anytime soon. To be honest with you, I'm not that anxious to see hers, either."

"I just need somebody strong like you to be with me in case somethin' goes wrong after I get there."

Maureen laughed. "I don't think anything is goin' to go wrong. Lo'retta will be as anxious to get this baby off her hands as you will be to get it."

"Her words don't mean much. I love my niece to death, but I wouldn't trust that girl as far as I could spit a plum pit. I'm just glad we got her to sign them papers. And I'm glad she bought that story about the globe-trottin' couple from Canada. If she ever calls you up and asks you to get in touch with that couple, you tell her that the last you heard, they went to some remote place in Africa or Asia and can't be reached." Big Maureen snorted. "If she is still askin' questions after you tell her that, tell her you heard that couple and the baby got lost in some jungle somewhere, one of them countries in Africa where them rebels is slaughterin' folks left and right—especially foreigners. And they got a real bad hatred for foreigners. If that don't do the trick, nothin' will."

"I don't think it'll come to that. In case it does, though, I'll come up with somethin' that'll throw her so far off track she won't know what hit her." Maureen hated plotting against her own daughter, but her daughter had been plotting against her for too long. "To tell you the truth, I don't know when I'll get to a point where I want to see my daughter again anyway. She's got a *long* way to go to get back in with me."

"I couldn't have said that better myself!" Big Maureen yelled.

"Thank you."

"Now, will you meet me in New York or not? Lo'retta don't have to know you came too. You can hide out in my hotel room. You can wear dark glasses and a head scarf so she won't know you if she run into you on the street. I know you've already done a lot for me, hookin' me up with a baby and whatnot, but can you please do this for me?"

Maureen hesitated for several seconds before she responded. She could hear Big Maureen breathing through her mouth on her end. "Well, if it means that much to you, I'll meet you in New York. But no matter what, I don't want Lo'retta to know I'm there," Maureen said, letting out a long, loud sigh. "I'll bring Virgil with me. Otherwise, me and him wouldn't get to see the baby until we visit you and Lukas again."

"Bring Jay with you too. I like that young man, and I wouldn't mind seein' him again."

"No! I don't want Jay involved in this in any way. He's got enough problems without me addin' somethin' like this. Besides, he might be the one to spill the beans someday if we tell him. Lord knows if Lo'retta ever finds out you got her baby and that I lied about that couple in Canada, all hell will break loose."

"I guess you got a point there, baby sister. Then just bring Virgil with you if you can." Big Maureen snorted.

Maureen called Loretta and obtained all of the necessary information that she needed to pass on to Big Maureen. Once everything was all set, Big Maureen had to chastise Lukas with a little violent activity to make him stop asking so many nosy questions about her "going to Alaska" without him to pick up their newborn baby. By the time she got through mauling his head with her fist, he was as meek as a newborn baby himself. Everything that Big Maureen had told Lukas about the mysterious nun and the unwed pregnant young girl in Alaska seemed suspicious, but Lukas knew when to shut his mouth. He didn't even question the bogus paperwork that had already been signed by the "girl in Alaska" that Virgil had put together. With the other papers that Loretta had signed, and the fake birth certificate that Virgil was going to produce after Big Maureen picked up the baby, everything seemed to be in place.

Maureen had no trouble arranging to take the week off from work, and Jay didn't protest when she told him she had to go to Louisiana again with her brother on a private family matter. He didn't ask and she didn't tell him the real reason. "Just be careful and hurry back," was all he said.

Loretta gave birth three days later. Big Maureen had already checked into the opulent Waldorf Astoria hotel the day before. This was the first time that Big Maureen had ever stayed in such a lavish place. When she and Lukas traveled, they always checked into a Motel 6 or some other low-end establishment. This was a first-class situation. She had even purchased a first-class round-trip airline ticket for the first time in her life.

As soon as Loretta called Big Maureen's hotel room and told her to come pick up the baby, Big Maureen jumped into a cab. She carried a baby seat with her to haul the baby in and a shopping bag that contained an assortment of brand-new baby clothes.

Maureen and Virgil arrived in New York later that same evening. When they knocked on Big Maureen's hotel room door, she opened it with a smile on her face so big she looked like the Joker. "Y'all come on in and meet my precious little baby girl!" Big Maureen crooned. If she had died and gone to heaven, she couldn't have felt more blessed.

Big Maureen led Virgil and Maureen to the bedroom in her suite where the newborn baby girl lay wrapped in a pink blanket. Virgil and Maureen were in awe. This was the most beautiful baby either one of them had ever seen before.

What Maureen didn't know was that this baby, her first grandchild, looked so much like she did when she was a baby that they could almost pass for twins.

Virgil did a double take and blinked hard. He had to blink even harder to hold back his tears. He thought back to the night that Mama Ruby had brought Maureen home. It felt like he was reliving that same event over again. Even though this baby had been given up willingly, it still seemed unfair that she would go through life not ever knowing who she really was. If everybody involved kept their word, this baby would think that Big Maureen and Lukas had adopted her and that her real mother was some anonymous girl in Alaska. It had been agreed upon that if something happened to Big Maureen and Lukas, Virgil and Corrine would raise the baby. Even then, Virgil would maintain the lie about the baby's real mother being some girl in Alaska. If Loretta ever returned to Florida, Virgil wondered what believable lie he could come up with to explain why a baby he had inherited from Big Maureen, whose biological mother was some girl in Alaska, resembled her or Maureen. There were men all over the world who looked like Mel, so Virgil didn't care if the baby resembled him. The baby's appearance was the least of his worries though. For all he knew, it might not look like Loretta or anybody else they knew. But if he had to, he'd find a picture of a girl who had the same physical characteristics as Loretta and claim she was the baby's mother.

For about twenty minutes, Virgil and Maureen took turns holding and fawning over the newborn. Then Big Maureen gently placed the baby on the bed and excused herself to go use the bathroom. Then something happened that would haunt Maureen for the rest of her life. She blinked and let out a muffled gasp. She could not believe her eyes. Mama Ruby materialized out of thin air and hovered over the bed with a huge smile on her face as she stared down at the baby. Maureen thought her eyes were playing tricks on her, but when she blinked some more and rubbed her eyes, *Mama Ruby was still standing there.* And she looked as real as she had the last time Maureen had seen her. Maureen looked sharply at Virgil, who was staring toward the bed with his eyes almost bulging out of his head and his mouth hanging open.

The vision lasted almost thirty seconds. When it ended, Maureen gently nudged Virgil with her elbow. "Did you see—"

"See what?" Virgil said hoarsely, not allowing Maureen to finish her sentence.

"I think I saw Mama Ruby!" Maureen whispered.

"Oh, that's just stress. I think I see Mama Ruby all the time too," Virgil whispered back. "It's all in your mind. Mine too." He didn't sound frightened and he wasn't, but his voice was empty and weak. He was glad that Maureen just *thought* she saw what he *thought* he saw. Otherwise, he would have to sign himself into an asylum as soon as he got back to Florida.

"I don't think we should tell Big Mo'reen what we think we saw," Virgil suggested. "We don't want to stress her out too."

"I won't," Maureen agreed.

Big Maureen rushed back into the room, wiping her hands on a towel. "I held my bladder as long as— What's wrong? Y'all look like you seen a ghost! Is my baby all right, y'all?" Big Maureen dropped the towel and shot across the floor and sat down on the bed. She lifted the baby, looking from Virgil to Maureen. "The way y'all lookin', I thought somethin' had happened to my baby!" Big Maureen said, gently patting the snoozing baby's back.

"I thought I saw a mouse," Maureen lied. "That's all."

"A mouse! Eeow! I'm glad I didn't see it. I would think that Mickey Mouse is the only mouse you'd ever see in a fancy hotel like this," Big Maureen laughed. "Y'all must be seein' things."

"Yeah, that's it. We must be seein' things," Virgil said with a wan smile. There was an unbearably sad look on his face as he shook his head and sat down on the bed next to Big Maureen. She was gazing at the baby and repeatedly mumbling, "Coochy coo" as she tickled the baby's chin. "We got to give her a real special name," Virgil suggested.

"There ain't but one name that's that special." Maureen gave Virgil a pensive look. "Ruby Jean," she suggested. "But I refuse to call her Mama Ruby."

"I can live with that." Virgil grinned, taking a deep breath, hoping it would make the tightness in his chest go away. "I'm sure that

Mama Ruby—wherever she ended up—is lookin' down on us and she's real happy to hear that."

"Yeah, we'll name her Ruby Jean, then. Big Mo'reen, what do you think about that name?" Maureen said with tears in her eyes and a huge smile forming on her face.

Big Maureen nodded. "Ruby Jean is a good name," she cooed. "And it goes good with Clemmons." She paused and kissed the baby's forehead. "I don't care what I have to do, *ain't nobody never goin' to take this baby away from me.*"

Virgil looked from Big Maureen to Maureen, giving her a strange look. Maureen knew what he was thinking. He had heard those exact words before. Virgil looked back at Big Maureen to make sure she wasn't looking at him. Then he smiled at Maureen and winked.

Maureen smiled and winked back at her beloved brother.

EPILOGUE

One year later, San Francisco

SAN FRANCISCO WAS THE LAST PLACE ON THE PLANET THAT MAUREEN ever thought she would visit again. Especially at the same time that Loretta was there.

But she was not the same Loretta who had caused her mother so much pain. Loretta had morphed back into the loving daughter that Maureen had given birth to.

Loretta's modeling career ended long before she thought it would. She had gained a whopping one hundred and twenty pounds during her pregnancy. Right after the six-pound, six-ounce baby's birth, Loretta had gone on a strict diet and she'd begun to exercise for several hours a day with a trainer. But none of that had done any good. Even after all this time, she was still more than a hundred pounds overweight.

Kyle, the man she had planned to marry, had moved on and the "new friends" that Loretta had made in New York had deserted her too. The agency she had signed with offered to send her out for work with some of the magazines that specialized in "full-figured models," but that was something Loretta was much too vain to consider.

When she ran out of money, she got a job as a receptionist in an office building on Madison Avenue. While on her lunch break one afternoon, she met Thomas Bruner. He was an air force pilot who was visiting some relatives in New York. Thomas wasn't much to look at, but he was a good man. As far as Loretta was concerned, all she ever wanted was a good man. Well, she got one this time.

Before Thomas ended his month-long leave, Loretta was in love with him.

She was now married to a man who had advised her in advance that he was also "married" to the military and had fifteen more years to go before his discharge. They lived in a small, nondescript house in San Francisco, an hour's drive from the Travis Air Force Base across the San Francisco Bay. Thomas spent most of his time on the base. Loretta had no friends, but she had several pets to keep her company when Thomas was away. That didn't bother her because as far as she was concerned, this was the best she could do now.

"At least by bein' married to Thomas I'll get to travel," Loretta said when she called home to tell Maureen that she had married Thomas Bruner and had moved to San Francisco. Maureen had not heard from her since the conversation they'd had just before Loretta had her baby.

"Lo'retta, I'm sorry things didn't work out for you in New York and that you gave up modelin'. All I ever wanted was for you to be happy. So if Thomas makes you happy, that's enough for me," Maureen told her. "I wish you all of the luck in the world, baby."

"Mama, I've been wantin' to call you way before now," Loretta admitted.

"Why didn't you?"

"I didn't know what to say. I didn't know if you ever wanted to talk to me again. Anyway, I got to thinkin' about you last night, so this mornin' when I got up, I couldn't stop myself from callin' you. I'm glad you didn't hang up on me."

"I'm glad you called," Maureen replied.

An awkward moment of silence followed before Loretta continued. "Mama, I would give anything in the world if I could hug you one more time." Loretta sniffed. "I don't want to come back to Florida and face all the people I let down, but do you think that someday you can come visit me so . . . so I can hug you? And, uh, to apologize to you in person for all the ugly things I said and did to you."

Maureen was touched by Loretta's words, but she wouldn't allow herself to get too excited. She didn't care what happened from now on; she'd approach everything Loretta did with caution. She would *never* let her guard down again. Not with Loretta or anybody else. Not even Jay. But she was happy to hear that Loretta had begun to turn her life around. It wouldn't make up for all the pain she had caused, but at least it was a step in the right direction. Maureen was glad that she had not given up on her child.

"I'll come out there when it's convenient for me," Maureen said without hesitation. She was proud of herself. In the old days, meaning the days before she found out about Loretta and Mel, Maureen would have said something like "Oh! I'll be on the next plane, baby!" Well, Loretta was no longer so special that Maureen had to bend over backward and practically break her neck to please her. Now Maureen would treat Loretta the way she wished she had treated her when it mattered. Loretta was still special, but not a fraction as special as Maureen had made her believe she was during the BM—"before Mel"—days. Maureen didn't even like to speak his name now. BM made her think of "bowel movement," which was what Mel was in her book now.

"You can even bring Jay if you want to. I'm so glad that you finally found true love. I hope he comes with you because I'd like to give him a big hug too. I *owe* him one."

It was hard for Maureen to believe that this was the same Loretta who had been so arrogant, insensitive, and self-centered and who had broken her heart into so many pieces. "I'll ask him if he wants to come with me," Maureen said, hoping that Loretta would conclude the call before she broke down and cried.

"Bye, Mama. I love you and I can't wait to see you again."

Maureen hung up, but she didn't cry. She realized that she had done enough of that. This time she smiled.

Jay was apprehensive about Maureen going to visit her daughter. He declined the invitation, but he encouraged her to go anyway.

A month after Loretta had invited Maureen to visit her, Maureen hopped on a plane.

So here she was. Back in San Francisco, earthquake city.

Maureen occupied a metal folding chair in the cramped living room of the small house where Loretta and her new husband planned to live until he received his next relocation orders.

"Mama, I know I'm beginnin' to sound like a broken record, but I'll say it again. I'm so sorry about what I did to you. I just hope that someday you can find it in your heart to forgive me," Loretta told Maureen as they sat drinking iced tea and munching on Fritos. Since Maureen's arrival less than an hour ago, Loretta had apologized and hugged her several times.

"I did that a long time ago," Maureen said. "But I won't ever trust you again," she added with a laugh.

"I wouldn't trust me again either. Boy oh boy, what a fool I was." Loretta looked and behaved like she was genuinely sorry, and this time she was. "Mama, I hope that couple in Canada is treatin' my baby real good." Loretta gave Maureen a strange look.

"Oh, I wouldn't worry about that," Maureen said with conviction. Big Maureen and Lukas were treating Loretta's baby very well. In addition to the plan that was already in place, Big Maureen had eagerly agreed that if she and Lukas planned to visit Maureen and Jay at the same time that Loretta did, they would not bring the baby. Maureen and Virgil had also made Big Maureen promise that she would not even show Loretta a picture of the baby. She could show her a picture of *a* baby, but not the baby that was the center of this strange situation. Maybe years down the road things would change, but until then, they would all stick to the original plan. "Don't you worry about your baby. I know those people are takin' real good care of her. You just need to focus on the future and forget about everything that's happened."

"You're right, Mama. That poor baby is goin' to be just fine. I will focus more on my future." Loretta offered a weak smile. All of a sudden, her jaw dropped. "Oh, Mama! There is somethin' I need to show you!" She excused herself and ran into her bedroom. She returned a few minutes later waving a newspaper clipping. "Mona sent this to me. Read it."

Maureen took the newspaper clipping and read:

FORMER GOONS RESIDENT DIES UNDER MYSTERIOUS CIRCUMSTANCES IN NEW YORK

New York City police are investigating the mysterious death of a popular photographer that occurred Friday night around 11:00 p.m. Melvin Ross, 43, was in the middle of a telephone conversation with his fiancée, up-and-coming teenage model Debbie Wes, 18, when it happened. Ms. Wes told police that she heard her fiancé say to someone on his end, "Who the hell are you—" and then she heard him scream. Seconds later, she heard a loud crash. When Mr. Ross did not return to the telephone after several minutes had passed, Ms. Wes notified the building manager, who entered the sixth-floor apartment with two witnesses. Mr. Ross had either fallen or been pushed from his living room window. There were no signs of a struggle or forced entry into the apartment, and both doors were still locked on the inside. The coroner's report states that Mr. Ross sustained a gouged eye and severe trauma to his neck and head. Also, it was determined that he was deceased before his mysterious "fall" from the window. Police are still investigating this bizarre tragedy.

"Mel's dead?" Maureen asked, turning the clipping over. "When did this happen?"

"The same night I had my baby. I didn't know anything about it until Mona called me up a few days later and sent me the clipping from the Goons newspaper."

"So you stay in touch with Mona, huh?"

"Yeah, even though she blabbed to you about me. You just don't know who to trust these days. That's why I don't even want her to know I had a baby. Anyway, I'm surprised you or Uncle Virgil didn't read about Mel in the newspaper. I didn't call to talk to you about it because, well, I just didn't. I wanted that man to stay off my mind, and I knew you did too."

"Uh, I guess we both missed readin' the newspaper that day," Maureen said. "But I'm surprised Catty and Fast Black didn't see it."

"It was on page six next to a big ad about some roach repellant. Mona would have missed it herself if she hadn't been lookin' for some newspaper to clean some fish on."

"Well, I don't know what happened to Mel, but the way he lived his life, anything could have happened to him. I'm sure he had a few enemies," Maureen said. "Can I keep this clippin' so I can show it to Virgil?"

"I don't care. I had been meanin' to throw it in the trash anyway. I don't want anything in my life that'll remind me of that devil," Loretta hissed. "I just hung on to it so I could show it to you some-day." Loretta gave Maureen a pensive look. "You glad Mel died?"

Maureen didn't respond right away. "No, I'm not glad Mel's dead, but I'm not surprised. If anybody had it comin', he did." Maureen shook her head. "He was a pitiful excuse for a man."

"He sure was. Uh . . . I know I had a lot to do with him and me hookin' up, but I have to let you know that it wasn't worth it." Loretta could barely look Maureen in the eye, but she did anyway. She wanted to see what was in her mother's eyes, and she wanted Maureen to see what was in hers. Her remorse could not be mea-sured. It was the one emotion that she would feel for the rest of her life.

"Betrayin' somebody never is worth it, honey," Maureen stated. "Do you mind if I give your uncle Virgil a call?" Maureen asked, al-ready reaching for the telephone on the end table.

"I'll let you talk in private," Loretta said, rising. "I'll be on the porch."

"Virgil, Mel's dead," Maureen said as soon as he answered his telephone.

"Who killed him?" Virgil asked, not sounding the least bit sym-pathetic.

Maureen immediately read the clipping to him. "What do you think happened to him? Maybe somebody had a key and had let themselves in while Mel was out. Somebody he had pissed off. There's no telling how many women he was involved with and any one of them could have stolen his key and had a copy made. Maybe they'd heard he was marrying another girl, and snapped. They let themselves in, hid in a closet, and came out and beat him with something and pushed him out that window. They locked the door back before the manager got to the door with his key. Or, when the manager got inside, when he wasn't looking, whoever had snuck in, snuck back out the door. How else could Mel fall or be pushed from that sixth-floor window right in the middle of a telephone conversation with his fiancée?"

"Hmmm," Virgil said. "Whatever the hell happened, it sure is a strange story. You really think it could have happened that way?"

"Him jumpin' out of that window on his own or accidentally fallin' out makes no sense at all. Like I just told you, I think *somebody* got into that 'locked-on-the-inside' apartment somehow and beat the shit out of him and threw him out that window," Maureen answered with a shudder. "Somebody or . . . *somethin'*."

"I think the same thing. Somebody or somethin' . . ."

"You think it was Mama Ruby, too, huh?"

"I didn't say that!"

"But that's what you think," Maureen accused. "I know you do, Virgil!"

"I don't know! I . . . I . . . maybe his conscience finally got to him and he really did jump."

"In the middle of a telephone conversation? What about him screamin' and sayin' what he said? That man didn't commit suicide, and he didn't fall from that window. He also didn't gouge out his own eye or cause his head and neck injuries! Now you tell me, do you think the same thing that I think really happened?"

"Mo'reen, Mama Ruby is dead. She can't chastise nobody else no more," Virgil said.

Maureen let out an eerie laugh. "She won't need to now." She exhaled and pressed her lips together. She had nothing else to say.

She balled up the newspaper clipping and tossed it into the ashtray on the coffee table.

After Maureen had hung up the telephone, she walked toward the front porch where Loretta had gone. She stood in the doorway for a few moments looking at her daughter.

Loretta occupied another one of the cheap metal folding chairs that she and Thomas owned. She sat as still and mute as a sphinx, staring at San Francisco's magnificent Golden Gate Bridge. The drab gray housedress she wore looked like part of a circus tent. But at two hundred and eighty pounds, she didn't feel comfortable wearing anything but housedresses that looked like part of a circus tent.

It was hard to believe that this was the same girl who used to prance up and down the beaches in South Florida in a string bikini! And it was even harder to believe that she had once been one of the most successful black models in the business.

Maureen wondered how things would have turned out for her and Loretta if they had never met Mel. She also wondered how much of what happened was her fault. She knew of many troubled children who ultimately blamed their parents for every stupid thing they ever did. She had to blink hard to hold back her tears. She didn't know if she had succeeded as a parent or not. Because as hard as she had worked to make Loretta happy, Loretta had become her own worst nightmare anyway: a housewife sitting on a porch, with not one, but *two* cats.

LOST DAUGHTERS

Mary Monroe

ABOUT THIS GUIDE

The suggested questions that follow are included to enhance
your group's reading of this book.

Discussion Questions

1. Maureen felt that she had to do more for Loretta to make up for the child she lost. Do you think that if Maureen had not spoiled Loretta, she would have been a better daughter?

2. Despite the fact that Maureen treated Loretta like a princess, Loretta still stole her husband and enjoyed doing it—especially since Maureen admitted that she didn't love Mel. Do you think Loretta would have seduced Mel even if Maureen did love him?

3. Do you think that it's wrong to marry someone for reasons other than love? Should love be at the top of the list of requirements, or do you think that companionship and security—and in Maureen's case a father for Loretta—are more important than love?

4. Mrs. Freeman kept Jay after her niece had kidnapped him because she didn't want her niece to go to jail. Do you think that Mrs. Freeman should have notified the authorities that she had Jay after her niece committed suicide?

5. Jay's biological relatives were thugs and convicted criminals, so he had a much better life with Mrs. Freeman. Did that make up for her role in his kidnapping?

6. When Virgil realized how Maureen felt about Jay's kidnapping, and the crime of kidnapping in general, he finally decided to come clean and tell Maureen that Mama Ruby had kidnapped her at birth. Do you think that he should have taken this secret to the grave like Mama Ruby did?

7. When Virgil finally told Maureen the truth about her background, did she react the way you thought she would? Did you like the way she reacted, or did you hope she would get hysterical and sever her relationship with Virgil?

8. Do you think that Maureen would have been better off not knowing that she was the victim of a kidnapping?

9. Do you think it was a smart thing for Maureen and Virgil

not to tell anyone else about Maureen's background? Do you think she should have told Jay?

10. When Virgil and Maureen met Big Maureen, Ruby's biological daughter, was she the kind of woman you thought she would be? Were you glad they decided not to tell her that Mama Ruby had kidnapped another woman's baby?

11. Do you think it was a good idea for Maureen to cook up that scheme about a Canadian couple and persuade Loretta to give her baby to them? Do you think that Big Maureen was the best choice, or do you think Maureen really should have arranged for some other couple to adopt Loretta's baby?

12. Were you surprised when Mel dumped Loretta? Were you happy that her career ended and she had to settle for so little? Did you feel sorry for her when she ended up as her worst nightmare: just a housewife sitting on a porch with a cat (in her case, two cats)?

13. Maureen forgave Loretta and they eventually restored their relationship. However, Maureen told Loretta that she would never trust her again. If your daughter stole your husband, do you think you could ever be close to her again? Would you ever trust her again?

14. A lot people in American culture believe that "what goes around, comes around." Loretta and Mel were so arrogant, greedy, selfish, and deceitful that in the end, those things were their downfall. Do you think they both got what they deserved, or do you think that fate was a little too harsh on them?

15. Do you think that Mel accidentally fell out of his apartment window? If so, how do you think he got those injuries? Who, or *what*, do you think he was talking to when he asked, "Who the hell are you?" just before he died?

Mary Monroe weaves a stunning portrait of a family immersed in deceit . . . and the women whose happiness depends on the secrets they keep . . .

FAMILY OF LIES

Turn the page for an excerpt from *Family of Lies*...

PROLOGUE

VERA

"Thanks for inviting me to breakfast again, Vera. I thought we had already finalized the arrangements for Kenneth's surprise birthday party."

"I didn't ask you to meet me to discuss my husband's party. And you can forget about being a guest. If you come within an inch of my property, I will have you arrested for trespassing."

The look on my husband's mistress's face was priceless. I had never seen such a confused and stunned expression before in my life. Her lips quivered for about five seconds before she was able to speak again. "Huh? Wh-what did I do?" was all she could manage.

"You can stop your little innocent act right now! I know you've been sleeping with my husband!"

"Oh. Um . . . how did you find out? I didn't tell nobody."

"How I found out is not important. What's important is that I know *everything* about you now." I had to pause and hold my breath for a few seconds to keep the stomach acid from rising in my throat, spewing out of my mouth, and soiling my eight-hundred-dollar silk blouse. "I can even tell you the names of the hotels you laid up in with my husband and the dates of every single reservation—including the ones you canceled," I hissed. I had hired one of the best private investigators in the city, so I had an extensive report on my husband's latest affair. "I even know what you ordered from room service."

Lois blinked a few times. For a woman brazen enough to get involved with her much older married boss, she came across as a real wimp to me. "I hope you enjoyed having somebody spy on me," she whimpered.

"PffIt! I've had diarrhea that I enjoyed more than having somebody spy on you," I snarled.

Her hands were shaking and there was fear in her eyes. It was a true delight to watch her squirm like a worm on a fishhook. "I guess if you know everything about me, you know I'm pregnant with your husband's baby too! He doesn't even know yet!" She narrowed her eyes and looked at me with contempt.

"Yes, I know about that baby! You need a baby like you need another butthole! You are a low-down, lowlife, two-faced slut, and I hope that if you ever get married, another slut fucks your husband and has his baby so you can see what it feels like!"

"In the first place, your husband came on to me, not the other way around! Here you are all up in my face when it's him you need to be jacking! You got some damn nerve, lady!"

I gasped and shook my head in disbelief. I couldn't believe that Lois was just as angry as I was! You would have thought that *she* was the victim in this tragic mess. I gritted my teeth to keep from spitting in her face. "You ought to be ashamed of yourself, girl," I said, speaking a little more calmly now. "I heard you grew up in the church and was raised by a good woman. How girls raised like you end up being so trifling is a mystery to me. How many other married men have you fooled around with? Are you going to abort this baby like you did the other two when you were in high school?"

"Who told *you* I had those abortions? I only told my closest friends about that!"

"Why should a tramp like you even care who told me? Like I said, I know everything I need to know about you. Whose husband are you going to fuck next?"

"Who I sleep with next is none of your business, Vera!"

"Well, as long as it's not my husband, I don't really give a shit. Now, there are a few things you need to know. First, Kenneth will never divorce me to marry an ignorant, nose-ring-wearing, dollar-store-shopping tramp like you—his secretary, for God's sake!" I delivered one of my most disgusted looks across the table at my husband's latest and most threatening girl-toy. All of his other gold-digging bitches had taken all they could from him and promptly moved on. A few had been only one-night stands.

Despite the fact that my husband had spent thousands of dollars on his whores, I had not let that bother me too much. At the end of the day, I was still the Queen Bee and the *only* woman with the keys to the castle and access to his massive fortune.

I was a lot of things, but I was no fool. There was way too much money at stake for me to make a fuss about my husband dipping his silver spoon into a bowl of grits. His trysts were what I called assembly-line sex. I believed that most men were natural-born dogs. Therefore, when it came to sex, they would hump a fire hydrant. Besides, I hated having sex with Kenneth these days. It had become downright gruesome. Just the thought of him flopping up and down on top of me with his three layers of blubber and foul sweat turned my stomach. Apparently his vile body didn't bother his other women, but then the right amount of money could make just about anything tolerable.

I had never confronted Kenneth about his affairs and I never complained about him leaving me home alone so much. Because no matter which one of the fancy hotels he took his women to, he always came home to me.

But I was really worried about Lois. For one thing, he'd been with her a lot longer than any of the others. At nineteen, she was the youngest and the prettiest. And the nail in the coffin was the fact that she was carrying his baby! For the first time, I was worried that I would lose the best meal ticket I ever had. I was not about to let it go without a fight. And when it came to doing battle, I didn't fight by the rules. I did whatever I had to do to win.

"You can call me what you want. But the thing is, I'm having Kenneth's baby. I'm sure he'll leave you and marry me when I tell him he's finally going to be a daddy. He told me that he's been wanting a child for years and if I—"

"Shut up!" I had to cut the bitch off. So far, everything that had spewed out of her mouth made me feel nauseous. "Don't you think I know that, too, little girl? But . . ." I paused, leaned back in my chair, and patted the side of my head. Then I continued with the smuggest look on my face that I could manage. "At least the child I'm carrying will have his name."

Lois couldn't have looked more dazed if I had thrown a glass of blood in her face. "What . . . you're pregnant too? I didn't know that!"

"Of course you didn't know that. But you know it now. I'm two months along. You and I will probably give birth around the same time." The way Lois's face looked now, I thought it was going to melt. I enjoyed watching her reaction during the few moments of silence that followed. She looked like she wanted to cry.

"You're two months along? Kenneth told me he hasn't touched you in *six* months," she mumbled.

I froze and glared at Lois in outraged disbelief. The huge knot forming in my stomach felt like a cannonball. Kenneth and I had just made love a few hours ago! I couldn't believe that he would tell this slut such a bald-faced lie! "Sister, that brother lied to you. Married men who cheat on their wives do a lot of that, you know. By him telling you he hasn't fucked me in six months, he thought it would make you feel more special. Well, I've got news for you—he told his last three whores before you the same thing."

"The last three? He told me I was the only one . . . the only one he'd cheated with."

I threw my head back and guffawed like a hyena and clapped my hands. "And you believed him? Girl, if you knew he was lying to me when he was shacked up somewhere with you, what made you think he wasn't lying to you? You're dumber than you look!"

"I'm not as dumb as you think! You're the one that's dumb if you think Kenneth is still in love with you! He told me he's only staying married to you because he feels sorry for you."

My chest suddenly felt constricted, as if somebody had wrapped me in a straightjacket that was two sizes too small. It was one thing for Kenneth to tell his bitch that he had not made love to me in six months, if he really did tell her that. But it was another thing for him to tell her he no longer loved me and felt sorry for me. Well, I didn't believe he'd told her that. If he had, he'd lied to her about that too. One thing I was certain about was that Kenneth still loved me. I was the kind of trophy that successful black men like him— who didn't want to marry outside of the race—fought over. I was fair-skinned with keen features, slim, and intelligent. And just to sweeten the pot, I had become a blonde a few years ago.

"I'm sure he won't feel that way when I give birth to his child," I sneered. I could be just as big a liar as anybody else. And I was good at it. It was a skill that I had been honing since grade school.

"Are you sure you're pregnant?" There was a suspicious look on Lois's face. "I mean, a woman your age . . . uh, maybe it's something else."

This time I thought my face was going to melt. I gasped so hard I almost passed out. "A woman my age? What the hell— Girl, I'm only *thirty-four years old*!" I hollered. I was no longer just angry. Now I was worried too. I had spent more money on cosmetic surgery to maintain my youth than any woman I knew and here this bitch was sitting here insinuating that I was *old*. If that was true, I needed to find me some much more competent surgeons. "What the hell 'something else' could it be?"

"Maybe it's just a tumor," she answered with a sniff so aggressive it probably cleared her sinuses out for good.

"Well, you are wrong. I've been to the doctor. I'm two months along!" I said again as I rubbed my belly. I had paid a visit to my doctor but not to see if I was pregnant. Each time I found out Kenneth was involved in another affair, I got an AIDS test. Once when he was involved with a stripper I made him wear condoms when we had sex. He had balked about it, but when I told him I had a chronic yeast infection that could cause him erection problems, he stopped complaining.

Lois dropped her head and stared at the table as if she wanted to crawl under it. "I . . . I wonder why Kenneth didn't tell me you were pregnant," she said, looking back up.

"Kenneth doesn't know yet. I am going to surprise him with the news at his surprise birthday party next week. And let me make one thing perfectly clear: I will *never* give him a divorce so he can marry you. Besides, a prominent man like him is not going to leave his elegant, cultured, *slim* pregnant wife for a *plump* backstreet ghetto floozy like you! You will strut your chunkified butt out of my husband's life! And I will see to it! If I wasn't such a lady and neither of us was pregnant, I'd pimp-slap the shit out of you right now!"

I sucked in some air, which was quite stale, I noticed. I looked around the restaurant, not because I was afraid one of my friends would see me; none of them would be found dead in a low-end establishment like Denny's. I hadn't been in one since I was a broke-ass teenager still living in the hood back in Houston more than fifteen years ago. It had been my choice to meet my husband's whore in this dump because this was where she belonged, along with other members of the lowlife population. I snorted and looked around the room in disgust. A black teenage female at the table across from us wore a weave that looked like a well-used mop. She had *three* whiny, snotty-nosed toddlers in tow and was pregnant again. They were eating grits off the same plate, using the same spoon. Every other patron in the place looked as bad off as the pregnant teenage mother. A toothless, middle-aged white man occupied another nearby table, gnawing on a piece of bacon with his gums.

I shook my head and returned my attention to Lois. It was easy to see why Kenneth had been attracted to her. She was young, beautiful, and stupid. It was a damn shame to see so much dollar-store makeup on her caramel-colored, heart-shaped face. She had outlined her full lips with a dark brown eyebrow pencil and then slapped on enough bronze lipstick for three people. She looked like a goddamn clown. It hurt my eyes to look at the outrageously long weave hanging off her head like a horse's tail. It was hard to believe that there was a baby growing in her voluptuous young body. I hated the ground she walked on. And I hated Kenneth for cheating on me with her. And I was going to make him pay for it until the day he died.

"Okay, Vera. I'm busted." There was a sorry expression on Lois's face, but I knew that the only thing she was sorry about was getting busted. "Where do we go from here?" she squeaked.

"I'm going to cut to the chase because I have a very busy schedule today." I glared at Lois so hard she shuddered.

"Cut to the chase, then, so I can get up out of here. I have a busy schedule too," she threw back at me, folding her arms. I was surprised she had not touched the scrambled eggs and grits she'd ordered, especially since I was paying for it.

"I can make things very comfortable for you and your baby," I told her. "And I can assure you that my deal is a lot sweeter than one you'd get from Kenneth if you tell him about the baby."

"You mean you didn't want me to meet you just so you could get in my face for me sleeping with your husband?"

"I know you don't think I'd waste my time coming into a place like Denny's on a Saturday morning just to get in your face. Like I just said, I can make it possible for you to live like a queen."

"Why? How could you be so mad at me and then turn around and tell me you can make it possible for me to live like a queen? That don't make no sense to me." The suspicious look had returned to Lois's face.

"Marriage is hard enough without complications like you. I want you to stay away from my husband for good. I don't want him to *ever* know about the baby you're carrying."

"I work for your husband, Vera."

I shook my head. "Not anymore. I want you to resign from your job immediately."

"Lady, I need my job! You can't—What if I don't quit? What are you going to do about it?"

"If you turn down my offer and return to work on Monday, I'm going to storm that damn store and beat the dog shit out of you in front of Kenneth and all your coworkers. Us both being pregnant won't stop me! How long do you think you'd have that job then?"

"You wouldn't do something like that!"

"Try me, bitch," I said in a smooth voice. "From what I've heard, you won't be missed." According to the report I'd received from my investigator, this heifer spent more time sitting at her desk reading tabloids and filing her nails while the other clerical employees did most of the work she was getting paid to do. Ow! This shit was really hurting me. Kenneth was going to pay through the ass for this one!

Lois unfolded her arms and gave me an incredulous look. "But I can't just leave my job without giving notice. I don't want to leave Kenneth in a lurch."

I gave her a hot look. "You let me worry about Kenneth," I told her. "I'm sure the employment agency can send somebody to replace you right away. There are a lot of folks out of work these days." I would make damn sure of one thing: The next secretary the agency sent to work for my husband's electronic equipment and supplies store was either going to be a man or a fifty-year-old frump with a face like a baboon and a hump on her back. I should have known better than to allow my husband to hire a pretty young woman to be his secretary. Especially since I already knew how weak he was when it came to pretty women. But he'd felt sorry for Lois. He had told me how she had started crying halfway through the interview. As a matter of fact, by the time Kenneth had finished telling me how she had dropped out of high school in her junior year so she could get a job and help her mother pay the bills, I was almost in tears myself. According to Lois, her father had owned a janitorial service. He'd had an affair with his secretary and got her pregnant. He'd sold his business, divorced Lois's mother, and left town with the mistress. Now here was his daughter doing the same thing to me. Well this case was going to have a totally different outcome. I was going to make sure of that.

"How is your mother, Mrs. Lilly Mae Cooper, these days?" I asked, looking at Lois out of the corner of my eye. "I know everything there is to know about her too."

"My mama is doing just fine," Lois snapped. "Why? She ain't got nothing to do with this."

I shrugged. "I just thought I'd ask. Is she still waiting tables in that chicken shack where two people got shot last month?"

"Yeah, she is," she muttered, looking at the floor.

"Does she still belong to that sanctified church on Third Street?"
She nodded. "Yeah. So do I. So what?"

"Your mother is a big shot in that church and the pastor's wife's
best friend. I'm sure the congregation won't look at her the same
way when they hear her daughter's caught up in a scandal with a
married businessman. Especially after your daddy left you and her
and took off with his secretary. It must have been hard on her raising you by herself. Her having such limited skills, if she loses that
chicken shack job, a woman her age will have a hell of a time find-
ing something else."

"Don't you worry about me and my mama. I'll get on welfare if I
have to."

I rolled my eyes. She would come up with something like that.
Why young black women were still falling back on the welfare sys-
tem in this day and age was beyond me. My mother, my three sisters, and almost every other one of my female relatives had fallen
into that same trap. Before I was even old enough to have babies, I
vowed that I would not become a welfare queen. As a matter of fact,
after three abortions, I vowed that I would never have any kids anyway. To this day, nobody knew that I had my tubes tied right after
my third and last abortion fifteen years ago when I was nineteen.

"Have you told your mother you're pregnant?"

Lois gave me a sharp look. Her eyeballs looked like they wanted
to pop out of the sockets. "I didn't want her to know until I knew
what Kenneth was going to do," she bleated, sounding like she had
a sob trapped in her throat.

"Well, now that you know what Kenneth is going to do, or *not*
going to do I should say, you can tell her. But this is what you're
going to tell her." I looked around again and leaned my head
closer to hers. "You tell her that somebody slipped something into
your drink at a party that knocked you out and when you woke up,
you were naked. Do some serious whooping and hollering when
you tell her, and make sure you tell her you already asked the Lord
to forgive you."

Lois stared at me in slack-jawed amazement. "Woman, what is all this gibberish coming out of your mouth? Nobody would say some off-the-wall shit like that—especially me. Are you crazy?"

"No, I'm not crazy. But you'd be crazy to pass up the offer I'm prepared to make. Now, do you want to hear what it is or not?"

"Go ahead," Lois said with her lips trembling.

Shaking my finger in her face, I told her, "You tell your mother that somebody, uh, took advantage of you while you were passed out."

She gave me a helpless look as I glanced at my watch. "Go on. I'm listening."

"I will pay you twice your salary for this month just to give you some cushion. Then, from next month until your child turns eighteen, I will support you. I am not sure of the amount yet, but it will be more than adequate. My attorney will send you a cashier's check on the first of every month until you have your baby. After you have your baby, I will double the amount. I will cover all of your medical expenses, as well as your baby's after it's born. If you get another job or get married or if I die unexpectedly before the child turns eighteen, the payments will continue. If you ever tell anybody about this arrangement, even your mother, it's over. I won't give you another plugged nickel." I paused and sucked in some more of the stale air—which seemed to get worse by the minute. "I'll drag your name through the mud so hard nobody else in this city will hire you. San Francisco is one of the most expensive cities in the world to live in. If you have to get by with only a welfare check, you won't be happy. You and that baby will always have to live with your mother in that one-bedroom apartment in that crime-infested neighborhood. I'm sure she won't like that. And once she passes, you'll be on shit creek in a sinking boat. Girl, you'd be a damn fool if you turn down what I'm offering you."

"What all do you want me to do?"

"After you resign, you are to have no contact whatsoever with my husband. If you see him on the street, whether he's alone or with me or someone else, you will not acknowledge him. Is that clear?"

"Now you look, Vera. I don't know what you think I am—"

"No, you look." I shook my finger in her face again. "I do know

what you are. You are a scheming little whore who fucked my husband and didn't have enough sense to protect yourself."

"Kenneth didn't protect himself either. Don't you put all the
blame on me!"

"Like I said, you let me worry about Kenneth. I know him a
whole lot better than you. And for the record, you're not the first
woman he's cheated with."

"You already told me that. So?"

"So, don't you think he's told them the same lies he's told you?
We've been married for eleven years and he's had numerous affairs. And he's still with me. Does that sound like a man you can expect to have a future with? Out of the thousands of women who get
involved with married men every year, only a few end up with the
husband."

"Well, this year I just might be one of those few women!" Lois
hissed. "Kenneth is in love with me." Her words stung my ears like
a bee.

"Balls! Get real, Lois! Kenneth loves me too! And I'm his wife!
He tells me all the time that I'm a wife and a half, so compared to
you, that makes me *three* times the woman you are!"

For a man as educated as Kenneth was, he did some of the
dumbest shit a man could ever do. I glanced at my watch *again* and
started tapping my fingers on top of the table. I wanted this bitch
to know just how impatient I was. I prayed that Johnny Watson, my
twenty-two-year-old trainer and my current lover, wouldn't get impatient himself and leave before I got to his apartment across town
near Coit Tower. I really needed to see him. Not only was he a very
thorough and expensive personal trainer, but he was also a very
thorough and expensive lover and I pampered him like he was a
prince. He worked hard for his money and so did I. It had taken
me too long to land a rich husband and I wanted to keep him. And
Kenneth was the best kind of rich husband; he was twenty years
older than me and had a bad heart and a few other health issues.
He could drop dead any minute and that was what I'd been count-
ing on since the day I married him. There had been a few close

calls, but each time he had recovered. But the way things had been going lately, I knew that it was just a matter of time before I'd be a very wealthy young widow.

I was not about to let some little ghetto bitch ruin my life!

"Do we have a deal or not?" I asked, still tapping my fingers impatiently on the tabletop.

Lois took her time responding to my final question, but I already knew what her answer was going to be. "Yes, ma'am. We have a deal."